D1240365

Murder in Macon

A FRANK HAYES MYSTERY

By

CHARLES CONNOR
&
BEVERLY CONNOR

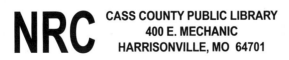

Copyright

AUTHORS' NOTE
The authors lived and worked in Macon-Bibb County, Georgia
during the period in which this novel is set. Many of the fic-
tionalized characters and events portrayed in this novel were
inspired by news reports of the day, most of which are now recorded in historical archives. Artistic license has been taken in
the portrayal of real events and in the timeline of history.

In no case are portrayals of people or events in this novel to be
taken as factual. This is a work of fiction. Names, characters,
places, and incidents either are the product of the authors'
imaginations or are used fictitiously. This novel, like all good
fiction, was designed to be read purely for purposes of enter-
tainment and personal edification.

Books by the Authors

Charles Connor

Murder In Macon

Beverly Connor

Murder in Macon

Dead Hunt: Gold Edition

One Grave Less

The Night Killer

Dust to Dust

Scattered Graves

Dead Hunt

Dead Past

Dead Secret

Dead Guilty

One Grave Too Many

Airtight Case

Skeleton Crew

Dressed to Die

Questionable Remains

A Rumor of Bones

Dedication

A special dedication in memory of Mr. Albert Glover

Table of Contents

Chapter 1

Mr. John Glover

This story began for me in Macon, Georgia on a suffocatingly hot day in the summer of 1970. I arrived at my office on the second floor of City Hall that morning to find an elderly black gentleman sitting in the visitor's chair next to my desk. He rose and turned toward me as I approached.

He was a tall man, perhaps six feet or better. He stood with a slight stoop. His short hair was white and his skin was pure black and unwrinkled except for some heavy lines around his mouth that if they had been turned in a different direction might have been laugh lines. His eyes were clear, without the cloudiness that often comes with advanced age. He had large hands with long slender fingers. With those hands he could have been a piano player.

In one hand he held in front of him a white Panama straw hat a little yellowed with age with a wide red and black band around it. With the other hand he leaned on a well-used wooden walking cane. He wore a white long-sleeve shirt with a red bow tie and a yellow vest. A couple of places on his clean clothes I could see needlework where someone had made neat repairs. He looked like a man from another time. A hard time.

I extended my hand to him and shook his. Looking at his build I'd say he had been quite a man when he was young. But there wasn't a lot of him left now. I could feel the signs of hard work on the skin of his fingers and palm. But most of the muscle was gone from his grip.

"I'm Frank Hayes," I said. "What can I do for you?" I

1

motioned for him to sit back down. I noticed on the floor next to his chair a large manila envelope bulging with papers inside it.

"They's trying to take my house, Mr. Hayes. I've lived there, me and my wife, for thirty-six years and they's trying to take my house and throw us out on the street. I built that house during World War Two, and me and my wife has lived in it for thirty-six years an' I'm not gonna' let 'em take it from us. Not if they's any way I can stop 'em. They tell me they goin' to. They showed me they papers. I can't read 'em. My wife can read but she got cataracts so bad she can't hardly see nothin' and she can't see to read they papers. But that's what they tell me they papers say—they gon' take my house. I done been to see everybody. But can't nobody tell me nothin'. I come here to ask you to help me if you can because I surely need help."

As he continued to talk he told me a rambling story I had a hard time following because it was disjointed and was completely foreign to anything I knew about. I couldn't tell who was trying to take his house or why. But he was going to tell his story in his own way.

He spoke with a strong voice rich with the dialect of a man who had lived through times and seen things most of us wanted to forget about. Eighty-nine years old. If I calculated right, this man was born in eighteen-eighty-one. Just as a burning idea crossed my mind, he echoed my thoughts.

"My father was born a slave on the Stevens Plantation in Bibb County in eighteen hundred and fifty-six. Him and all the slaves was set free after the Civil War in eighteen hundred and sixty-five."

The way he said it sounded as if he was offering his story to me as evidence that he too was a free man and entitled to all the privileges of a free man. He continued his story.

"But nobody tol' my daddy he was free. He was just a boy

and they kept him on the plantation an' worked him for thirteen more years. Then one day some gov'ment mens come to the plantation an' they showed my father some papers and tol' him he was a free man. At first he didn' know what they meant, sayin' he was a free man. They tol' him the war and Mr. Lincoln had made him a free man. What does that mean? He said he ask them. They said it meant he could go wherever he wanted to go whenever he wanted to, without having t' ask nobody. He could live wherever he wanted to live. If he wanted to get married, he could get married. He was free to go and work anywhere he wanted to and didn' have to stay on the plantation no more. They tol' him the law said he could own is own land and have his own house." John Glover took a rumpled white handkerchief from his pocket and blotted at the corner of his lips.

A couple of the idiots from the building inspector's office had stuck their heads around my door and were grinning stupid looking grins at me behind Mr. Glover's back. They were probably the ones who sent John Glover to my office. If I could believe anything he was saying, this man was a walking museum, an encyclopedia of local history, and all they could do was grin and pick their noses, too dumb to know their own ignorance.

The more of Mr. Glover's story I heard, the more I kept thinking he should be talking to the Smithsonian or somebody. But he was talking to me. He was talking ancient family history but I had the feeling that sooner or later John Glover was going to tell me something important to the present.

He asked me if he could have a drink of water. I got a large Styrofoam coffee cup and went down the hall to the water cooler. Moe and Curly were there.

"Is he telling you his stories?" One of them asked, with a shit-eating grin on his face.

I filled the cup with water.

"The old man's crazy as a loon," the other idiot said. "He's been up here a dozen times, rambling on and on. How do you like his hat? And what about that vest and bow tie? Did he show you his letter?"

"He's been up here so many times we all hide when we see him coming," the first one said. "Him and his wife live out in colored town in a rundown shack that's not fit for . . ."

He seemed to have exhausted his vocabulary and was at a loss for words. Unfortunately, he was rescued by his partner in stupidity.

"Not fit for a dog to live in," the second idiot said, emphasizing his confidence in the statement with a shake of his head and a screwed up cartoon face.

They stood waiting for a response from me. I took the cup of water to John Glover and closed the door to my office behind me. The old man drank half the water, set the cup down and thanked me. He picked right back up with his story as if he had paused only for a moment.

"My ol' father used to laugh when he tol' me the story about being set free. He said he wanted to believe 'em, so he went an' showed the papers to Mas' Stevens an' tol' him what the mens had said, and Mas' Stevens tol' my father it was true, he had been a free man nigh on thirteen years.

"When my father found that out, he felt mighty happy to be free an' he tol' Mas' Stevens he was goin' lookin' for a job at the buggy factory up at Forsyth so he could buy his own farm. But Mas' Stevens got upset, sayin' him an' his wife was gettin' old and they needed my father. So Mas' Stevens said if my father would stay on and work at the plantation on shares, like the law allowed, he could live like a free man. An' Mas' Stevens say he would put the house and land in his will to be give to my father free and clear when the time come for Mas' Stevens to pass on."

Mr. Glover paused again to take a sip of water and pat his lips with the handkerchief. He was telling his story with a lot of concentration and his energy seemed to be draining away. It was a hundred and two degrees outside. I wondered how he got from his house to City Hall. A man of his age. My God, I hoped he didn't have a heat stroke or something.

"I'm not feeling too good, Mr. Hayes. I wonder could you find somebody that might take me home where I can lie down a spell. I don't think I can make it on my own."

I was right. The old gentleman was ill. I hoped there was someone at home who could look after him.

"Do you need to see a doctor, Mr. Glover?"

He began to try to get to his feet. I steadied him until I thought maybe he wouldn't collapse.

"No. I just need to get home. I'll be all right d'rectly."

I had a couple of scares but I got him down the stairs and to the sidewalk where I sat him on a bench to wait with his envelope and his cane while I got my car.

As luck would have it my car was sitting directly in the hot sun. It must have been two hundred degrees inside when I opened the doors and rolled down the windows to let some of the hot air out. I had my 35mm camera with me and it occurred to me that the film might melt. I could only hope I didn't bake Mr. Glover to a crisp or boil him alive before I got him home. I stopped the car at the bench where I had left him, helped him into the passenger seat and got the car moving again as fast as I could to get the wind flowing on him.

He managed to tell me his address across the river in east Macon before he nodded off. I was sure he was going to die. Then what would I do with him? But in a couple of minutes he stirred in his seat and looked inside the manila envelope he held by his side. He took out a white business envelope and laid it on the car seat. I could see the city building inspector's return address on the outside of the envelope.

"I'm hoping you can help me . . . about my house," he said. "If you can spare the time, could you look at these papers and tell me what I needs to do?"

"I'll look at them. I don't know if I can do anything." Why did I have feelings of guilt about disappointing this old man I didn't even know?

"I'll do what I can," I said. I don't know why I said that. I wasn't lying. I just don't know why I said I would.

"I think you are a man who can help me," he said.

I wasn't so sure. I was making commitments I didn't know if I could possibly keep to an old man I just met who was at this moment passed out from possible heat stroke in the front seat of my car. What had I gotten myself into?

Chapter 2

Can't Get No Respect

As we headed across the Ocmulgee River bridge toward east Macon I saw green dump trucks and a bulldozer off to the left of the bridge dumping and spreading fill dirt next to the river. I made a note to myself to check the maps at the office to make sure they weren't dumping in the restricted floodplain area. I didn't have many responsibilities of any note in the county, but overseeing the protection of the scenic riverfront and floodplain was one of them.

I noticed Mr. Glover's breathing was not settling down the way I thought it should. He still appeared to be in distress.

"Mr. Glover, can I get you something cold to drink?" I asked.

"Yes, sir. That would be mighty nice of you. I ain't had nothin' to eat this morning and a drink would be mighty good."

"You didn't have any breakfast?" I asked. I looked at my watch. It was almost 11:00am.

"No, sir. We didn't have nothin' at home but a little left over from yesterday and I left that for my wife. My Social Security check ain't come yet and I didn't have no money to buy groceries."

Jesus, I thought of the scrambled eggs, bacon, grits, biscuits, jelly, fresh fruit, juice and coffee I had for breakfast and instantly fell into a pit of shame. I turned into the parking lot of the Red and White Market and went inside. I didn't know what the old man and his wife might like so I bought what I get when I grocery shop for myself. I got a pound of bologna, a loaf of bread, a dozen eggs, and a gallon of milk. I looked over the items in the basket and decided I should balance the food groups, so I picked out three tomatoes, a head of lettuce, and a jar of mayonnaise. Near the checkout lane I got us both a bottle of Coke and a Moon Pie. He and I both needed a quick fix. I put another bottle of Coke in the bag for his wife.

The Coke and Moon Pie seemed to revive Mr. Glover. I know they did me. By the time we got to Bertha Street where he lived he seemed to be better. He was awake and his eyes were alert. That was something. His breathing was more normal. His hands trembled slightly but I thought that was not unusual for a person of his age.

The streets in the neighborhood where he lived were unpaved and were pocked with some sizable potholes. He pointed me to his house off Flewellyn Drive. It was a small unpainted wooden affair of no more than three or four rooms. It had a tin roof and sat on a lot just down from the St. James A.M.E. Church. A shiny blue Dodge two door automobile with Fulton County plates was parked in the drive. A frail looking old black lady whom I took to be his wife was sitting in a wooden chair on the small stoop porch. Standing next to her was a quite attractive young nicely dressed lighter skinned black woman.

I stopped the car in front of the house and helped Mr. Glover get out. The young woman said something to Mrs. Glover and they both registered alarm on their faces. Mr. Glover picked his way slowly across the sandy yard with his cane as I got the bag of groceries from the car.

I could see concern on his wife's face as we approached the front porch. She wasn't as old as Mr. Glover but she had to be in her seventies. Her heavily streaked gray hair was medium length and pulled back against her head. She was wearing a plain house dress with a faded red floral design. She had a thin face and large dark brown eyes. She gave me a smile and a brief, courteous nod. But the focus of her attention was on Mr. Glover.

"Where you been all morning, old man? I been worried about you," she said, not in an angry way but in a familiar and warm way.

"Poppa, you don't need to be wandering off by yourself." The young woman touched the old man's sleeve gently with her long, slender fingers.

"No need to worry 'bout me," he said. "I been down to City Hall talking to Mr. Hayes here. He's gon' help us about the house. You be nice to him."

This last remark seemed to be directed pointedly at the young black woman who was eyeing me with thinly veiled contempt. Mr. Glover's wife followed him into the house. The young woman stood for a moment with her arms folded across her chest, looking down her nose at me through narrowed eyes. She turned and went into the house, leaving me standing alone in the front yard. I could hear the sounds of voices inside . . . the strident voice of the young woman and the calmer, lower tones of Mr. and Mrs. Glover. I wondered what I was doing in this man's . . . in this family's lives.

I set the bag of groceries on the wooden floor of the front porch, turned and headed back to my car. I had taken only a couple of steps when I heard the squeak of the screen door hinges as they opened and the whap as the door slammed shut. I turned around.

The young woman was standing staring at me again. I attempted a smile. She had the most beautiful green eyes I'd ever seen. Maybe it was the way the sun shone into them but I swear they seemed to shoot sparks at me.

"What?" I asked her.

She looked down at the grocery bag, picked it up and

rummaged through it briefly.

"What is this?" she asked. "Some white charity?" She sniffed derisively at the open bag. "Is this the kind of food you think colored folks eat?"

She was beating the hell out of me. I could see she hated me.

"Mr. Glover said he didn't have any food in the house. I just bought something to help out. I bought the same things I eat myself."

She looked hard and unflinching at me. I had the impression she was looking straight through my eyes into my darkest secrets to see if I was lying and if my motives were pure. I could have sworn I felt the release of her fingers from around my heart and it started beating again. I know I had stopped breathing. If she hadn't released me when she did I think my knees would have collapsed under me and I would have fallen unconscious to the ground. I thought I saw some ever-so-slight softening in her jaw line and a look almost of amusement shown for just a second on her face.

"Hmph," was all she said. She turned her back on me and disappeared into the house with the bag of groceries.

I was completely lost in my thoughts on my way back across the yard to my car. I felt some anger and some hurt but mostly I was confused. Did that young woman hate me so much because of . . . what? Because I worked at City Hall? Because I was white? Because of what somebody else white had done to the old man . . . or to her? What? I felt sick over it.

I looked up out of my contemplation to see a group of four young black men gathered at an automobile in the yard of the house across the street watching me. It was obvious I had been the object of their conversation. They stopped talking when I looked up. I did something then that in hindsight might seem foolish, but I was a city official there on official business, sort of. I walked across the street toward them feeling like a piece of white lint on a black garment.

There was an old faded '51 Chevrolet pickup truck parked outside an unpainted wooden garage next to the house. The truck had wooden sideboards around the top of its bed. On the sideboard were painted the words 'Tiny's Trading Company.' On the front porch of the house was an assortment of old and antique items, including churns, a mahogany chifforobe, wooden tables and chairs, a kitchen cabinet and a cast iron wood burning kitchen stove. The yard was decorated with several antique farm implements. One or two I recognized. The others, I had no idea what they were.

The youngest of the four men in the yard was probably sixteen or seventeen. He had short cropped hair and looked like he should be in high school. One of the others, a dude in his mid-twenties dressed in construction type work clothes, turned his back to me and put his hand somewhere inside his shirt . . . scratching an itch I hoped. Two others, both of them about nineteen or twenty, turned toward each other in whispered conversation. One of them stood with his side to me. The other stood facing me, watching me as I approached. He was going to be the point man. There was an older man who looked to be fifty or so sitting turned away from me on the front porch of the house.

The point man watched my eyes as I approached, waiting for me to speak or make a move.

"Aw'right," I said in standard man-to-man greeting.

The point man answered by a slight rise of his head and said, "Yeah, man. What you want?" He showed a look of obvious disdain for me.

"Mr. Glover tells me he's been getting a lot of grief about his house. Somebody's trying to put him and his wife out on the street. I don't think it's right for an elder to be treated that way. Do you?"

"Ain't nobody around here doin' it, man. Some white dudes from downtown. They come out here askin' a lot of questions about the old man. Stickin' they white noses into everybody's house. Say they from City Hall."

"Who was it?"

"Stupid dudes. What do you care, man?" All four of the young men turned their angry faces to me now. There was that look of hate again. "You after some of that black honey?" He flicked his head in the direction I had just come.

Jesus, this conversation was taking the wrong direction. Out of the corner of my eye I could see the blue steel of a gun barrel on the floorboard of their car. I thought of the old shotgun I carried wrapped up in the trunk of my car for rattlesnakes when I was working on the pipeline. I wasn't sure the damn thing still worked. Surely we weren't to the point of a gun battle in the street, unless they had been watching too much TV news. Maybe I had been watching too much TV news.

I didn't want to start any trouble but it looked like I might have walked into it. My only choice was whether to stand my ground or turn and run. The point man waited.

"Mr. Glover came to see me," I said. "He got sick from being out in the heat and not having anything to eat. I brought him home. He told me somebody is trying to take his house. I might can help him if I can find out the truth of what's going on."

"The truth?" he said. "The truth is, they tryin' to take all the property in the neighborhood and run everybody out. They want to put in they country club so the rich Chucks can drink martini's and poke them white bitches. And the neighborhood's in the way."

"Is that what it's all about?" I said. "Who's doing it?"

"Shit, man, I don't know. All you white folks look alike to me." He ended his challenge with a sneer.

I reached as non-threateningly as I could into my pocket, took out my business cards and handed one to point man. He took it and looked at it.

"Office of Urban Beautification?" he said, wrinkling up his face. "I ain't never heard of no office of urban beautification. You plannin' on beautifyin' this neighborhood? Somethin' ugly here you don't like?"

I thought they were all four going to jump me. I was desperate. "No, man. It's just a job. Building parks and things. I work for the mayor."

"The mayor?" Point man said. "You work for that honkie bastard?"

An appeal to my political connections was apparently the wrong move. As my thoughts were returning to a consideration of just how much shame there really would be in running, my eyes flashed on St. James A.M.E. Church and then I lied a little about the reach of my authority. "Part of my job is to save important historic landmarks. If I say that church is a historic landmark and can't be torn down, then there won't be any country club here."

Point man and his crew appeared dubious and unconvinced. There was a moment of uneasy calm. The older man on the porch turned and held out his hand to the young man holding my business card.

"Let me see that, Skeeter," he said in a deep bass voice that put my baritone to shame.

He was big and muscular. He could have been a bouncer once . . . a little past his prime now maybe, but still a hell of a man. He was dark and mean looking. I had been inside the state pen a couple of times . . . as a visitor only, you understand . . . and he had a look I had seen there. He had the look of prison.

"You dudes go on along and let me talk with Mr. Hayes," he said. He was obviously some kind of local patriarch or strong man because the four young men got into their car and drove away without so much as a word of protest. One of them did spit out the window in my direction as the car backed into the dirt street, but I don't think that really counts.

I held out my hand to the big man. "I'm Frank Hayes," I said.

He offered me his big meaty hand and shook mine more gently than I had expected.

"I'm Tiny," he said. "Tiny Glover."

"You related to Mr. John Glover, I guess?" I said, motioning with my thumb.

"Yeh," he said, without further explanation.

"Can you tell me any more about what's been going on with Mr. Glover's house?"

"Just what Skeeter already said. Some white dudes who said they from the buildin' inspection office come out here. Give the old man a bad time. Tell him he might have t' move out o' his house. Got him all upset. Ain't up to no good. They's somethin' else goin' on, too. Lot's of crews out here surveyin' and measurin'. Maybe you can find out what they up to."

"I ought to be able to find out something from city records," I said. "You give me a call if you see anything happening to Mr. Glover or his house."

I was about to turn to leave when Tiny said to me, "You watch out for them boys. They ain't got good judgment sometimes. They ain't bad, they just full of piss and vinegar and ain't got no patience. They think they tough as gorilla shit. They ain't scared of nothin' or nobody. I been trying to keep 'em alive and out of trouble. But I can't watch 'em all the time, an' I can't always trust 'em to do the right thing. You understand what I'm sayin'?"

"I do, and I'm grateful," I said.

I got back to my car without further threat to my health or my good looks and took out my camera. The door to the house opened and the green eyed woman came out onto the porch. I snapped a couple of shots of the St. James A.M.E. Church and a couple of Mr. Glover's house. As I got into my car she walked across the yard and stopped beside my door. Her posture was less hostile and her voice was softer but still no nonsense.

"You don't promise that old man something you can't deliver and give him false hope," she said, looking at me with those beautiful green eyes.

"I was hoping I could give him any kind of hope at all," I said. I took another of my business cards and gave it to her. She looked at it and smiled but didn't say it. A little bead of sweat formed at the base of her neck, ran down the smooth skin of her chest, took a detour across the curve of her right breast and disappeared into the cleavage of her dress where my eyes couldn't follow. I wasn't breathing again. Her eyes looked up and caught mine briefly. She turned and walked back across the yard to the house.

I was the wrong man for this job. I had no influence in City Hall and I was hated by every black person who saw me even before they knew my name or heard me open my mouth. No, that's not true. I don't think Mr. Glover or his wife hated me. I don't think they cared who I was if I could help them. I don't think Tiny hated me. I think Tiny was probably struggling hard not to hate. Or maybe he had just accepted it like you accept that there is evil in the world. I looked down at the envelope Mr. Glover had left on the front seat of my car.

Chapter 3

Revenge of the Studebaker

I took it as a good omen when I got back to City Hall and found a parking space on the shady side of the street. I hoped it was payment to me for a good deed. Of course I would have to feed nickels into the meter but that was a small price to pay not to be roasted alive. I've been working on this idea about how to turn a hot car into a Turkish bath but I don't have the details worked out yet. I think the demand for it would be huge. You know, you leave work, you get a free sauna on the way home to supper. You just leave the lava rocks in a little bucket right in the sun. You get in, you pour sun-made hot water over the rocks. I was thinking about calling it the Sun Sauna, or Sauna on Wheels. Maybe not.

I went back to my office and checked my desk. No new business had arrived that I couldn't avoid until the afternoon. I walked down the hall to the building inspector's office. Moe and Curly were just on their way out the door to lunch. I propped myself in the doorway to get their attention.

"What's the deal out on Bertha Street in old man Glover's neighborhood?" I asked Moe. He looked up at me and back down at the floor. He shot a quick glance at Curly, thought for a minute in mock concentration and rolled eyes of dumb innocence at me.

"I don't know. Nothin' that I know about," he said. He turned to his sidekick. "You know about anything?"

"I haven't heard about anything," Curly said.

They were lying.

"What about old man Glover's house?" I asked.

Moe's eyes darted. "Got a complaint," he said.

"A complaint from who?" I asked.

His eyes darted again. "Don't know. Anonymous. Said this old man and his wife was living in an unsafe structure. Gave us the address."

"You inspect his house?" I asked.

"Had to. That's the law. We get a complaint, we have to follow up."

"So I call up and tell you the mayor is living in an unsafe structure and you have to go inspect his house?" I asked.

Moe smirked and Curly giggled.

"Not hardly," he said, "unless I want to lose my job."

"So you went to the Glover house. What did you find?"

"What the complaint said. It was an unsafe structure . . . rotted wood, dangerous wiring, leaky roof. The whole place was a violation of code. We had to issue him a citation."

"So what happens now?"

"The citation requires that he bring the house up to code or it will be condemned and demolished."

"How long does he have?"

"Six months from the date of the citation."

I didn't think it possible but it sounded as if the idiot had memorized the building inspector's code book.

"When was the citation issued?"

Moe let out a sigh of exasperation, mumbled something to himself on the way to his desk where he sorted through a pile of forms until he found the Glover citation.

"Five months ago."

"That means he has to have all repairs made within thirty more days?"

"He has to have repairs completed or show significant progress and apply for an extension of time. Otherwise, at the end of the six-month period the house will be condemned, the sheriff will vacate and secure the building, and it will be turned over to a contractor for demolition at the owner's expense."

Moe recited the manual like a robot but I felt pretty sure he was repeating what the city code said. The door to the inner office opened and Craig Linder, the building inspector, stuck his head out.

"You fellows still here?" he asked. "I want those inspection reports back in here before five o'clock."

Moe looked up at me accusingly. "Just on the way out, boss," he said over his shoulder.

Linder smiled and motioned to me.

"Frankie, I thought I heard your big rumbling voice out here. Come on in."

I went into his office and sat down in one of those wooden office chairs with the curved arms and the bottom that hurts your butt after five minutes. He opened a refrigerator in the corner, took out two bottles of Coca Cola, popped their tops with a silver bottle opener shaped like a frog and handed me one. It had little slivers of ice floating in it. The cold felt good all the way down.

"What you up to, Frankie?"

"Making the city beautiful."

He laughed. "You taking pictures?" he said, pointing to the camera hanging from my shoulder.

"Oh, yeah. Flowers and pretty stuff," I said. "I was just over in east Macon with a survey crew. What's the latest on the country club anyway?"

He looked at me and paused hardly long enough to be noticeable. He must have decided it was safe to talk with me about it.

"I don't know if they'll ever get it put in. From what I

hear, the investors can't agree. I think some of them are overextended. It takes a big chunk of change to put in eighteen holes of golf course. Even after you get the land . . . which can be one hell of a problem itself . . . you got the construction, the landscaping, irrigation, lighting, fencing. The clubhouse alone is going to cost five hundred grand. The only way they'll ever make it pay is through collateral real estate development."

Collateral real estate development. That sounded suspiciously like what the neighborhood bad boys had told me.

"You thinking of investing?" Linder asked.

"I'm already seriously overextended. Or maybe I'm undercapitalized. I was thinking more along the lines of the hotdog concession."

"Don't laugh," he said. "That may be the place to make the real money, particularly if they can get the golf course put on a tour. If you're serious about it you might want to get in a bid early. Food services is a tough business to make a buck."

"No, I was joking. I've been looking at some cheap real estate in the area."

"No kidding?" Linder's eyes lit up. "You've found something? I thought all that had been claimed a long time ago. But listen, you better be careful there. You're messing with the big boys. They'll eat you alive. I'm serious. You better get out of that and stick to hot dogs unless you've got a partner on the inside."

There was a knock at Linder's door and I looked up to see a lime green blazer.

"Hey, Jeff. Come on in. Frank and I were just finishing up."

The green blazer was occupied by a thirty-something man with black hair and a lime green tie. He must have been color blind or he had a sick sense of humor. Craig made the introduction.

"Jeff, this is Frank Hayes, our city beautification coordinator. Frank, shake hands with Jeffrey Green of the law firm of Green and Green and as you probably know, a member of the planning and zoning board."

"I like your blazer." What else could I say?

"I wear it for the recognition," Green said. "You know, green blazer, green tie. Green and Green. People always remember who I am."

"Great idea." I can be a shameless liar. "Kind of like the alligator."

Green looked at me with a puzzled expression.

"On the shirts," I said, pointing above my shirt pocket. "The alligator on Alligator shirts."

"Oh yeah, sure." Green nodded. "The same thing."

"Listen, Frankie," Linder interrupted. "Jeff and I need to discuss some business. Talk to you later, OK? Let me know how that deal comes along. If it turns into something, I might be interested in investing."

I closed Linder's door behind me on my way out. I stopped at Moe's desk just long enough to locate the Glover citation and put it in my pocket. I never knew espionage could be so easy.

It wasn't completely surprising to me that the building inspector was so closely involved with local land developers, since I wasn't born last week. But it did nothing for my innocence. If I kept going at this rate, I could get cynical.

I couldn't do anything about the building inspector's moral turpitude or the stupidity of his gofers but it looked as if there might be a solution to Mr. Glover's housing crisis. If he could have even part of the required repairs made he could avoid the condemnation. I felt better.

I dropped by my office and picked up the land-use plan

for the riverfront. I needed it to make sure those dump trucks and bulldozers weren't violating my responsibilities. I checked the number of unused pictures in my camera and saw that I had another twenty shots left on the roll. On my way out of City Hall I met Mayor Tommy Lee Tyler and his bodyguard coming up the long winding marble stairway toward me. Tommy Lee wore a big smile showing lots of white teeth. His black hair was slicked back with something oily and he was in happy politician mode.

Tommy Lee was a good looking guy by the standards of country music and the gospel circuit. He believed himself to be quite good looking and quite a talented singer. Macon was the home of a long string of big-time musicians. You could often see their limousines or their motorcycles coming and going from a major recording studio located directly across the narrow side street from City Hall. When they were really cranked up and hot in a jam session with all their woofers booming and their tweeters screaming, the windows in City Hall would buzz kind of like hornets stirred up in their nest. Tommy Lee thought if he recorded in a famous recording studio, some of their success might rub off on him. He cut a couple of records there. I heard one. He had a great voice.

Tommy Lee was a local rising star Republican, much to the disappointment of the Republican Party who had a love-hate relationship with him. They loved him because he seemed unbeatable in local elections. The first Republican elected mayor of Macon since the Civil War. They hated him because he was an unpredictable and uncontrollable renegade who kept sticking his finger in the eye of the Republican establishment. He was a total embarrassment to those with a sense of propriety. He was a politician.

"Hello, Frankie," he said. "Hearing lots of good things about you."

"Well, thank you, Mr. Mayor."

For some reason the mayor was smiling on me today. I noticed the bodyguard looking me over like I might be a suspicious character. I was suspicious and growing more suspicious by the day of the whole bunch at City Hall.

"I spoke with some members of the Historic Preservation Society yesterday and they were telling me how impressed they are with the plans for our city beautification program. Some good folks, Frankie. Keep them happy if you can."

Ah yes, the Historic Preservation Society. They came to my rescue only this morning.

While the mayor was talking, his left hand went into his coat pocket and came out with a shiny piece of gold jewelry between his fingers. It was a tie tack in the shape of a Thompson submachine gun formed from the letters of his last name. Cute.

"I thought you might like to have one of these, Frankie. A show of my appreciation in these embattled times."

I thanked the mayor again and he gave me a quick pat on the arm, a wink and a smile as he turned and was off again on whatever mission he was on. I looked at the Tommy Gun shaped tiepin. Tommy Lee had become known as Tommy Gun Tyler following a recent episode of urban near-warfare. A number of businesses had been burned out over a period of several nights in one of Macon's low rent commercial districts. Young black men were seen looting and some of them were chased by the police into a public housing development. A couple of city policemen got themselves corned by a black mob. They were roughed up and their patrol car was burned.

When it came to lawlessness, rioters and looters, Tommy Lee often brought up his service as a combat soldier in the Korean War to bolster his image as a hardline law-and-order man. At the height of the trouble he personally took charge of the city response and sent platoons of police carrying automatic weapons into the trouble areas. He was recorded over the police radio that night firing a machine gun and telling the police squads, "I want to hear those Tommy Guns talking." No one was injured.

That got him national publicity. He adopted the Tommy Gun tie tack as his symbol and sold them to finance his upcoming campaign. He had graced me with a free one. Once again I wondered if I knew what I was doing.

As I walked to my car I heard the roar of big engines and loud clanking noises totally out of character to the usual street sounds. I turned to see the mayor and a small crowd of onlookers watching activities at a tractor-trailer rig parked in front of City Hall. It had dropped its loading ramp and a large green WWII Sherman tank was rattling and clanking onto the street. What the hell now? Tommy Lee was beaming. I resisted the urge to ask the obvious questions.

I picked up two barbecue sandwiches, a large iced tea, and a bag of chips at the Pig and Whistle, drove to a spot next to the river and parked in the shade where I could see the green dump trucks and bulldozer working on the other side.

There's something serene about the greenway along the river. You can almost see the river boats from a hundred years ago on the water. Today there was only the occasional swirl of a fish or the wake from a swimming turtle on the calm surface. My contemplation was interrupted by movement in the underbrush. It was a college-age boy and girl making out au naturel on a blanket in the bushes near the river bank. Judging from the stickers on the car parked next to me they were probably Mercer University students. I watched them for a minute until I became ashamed of myself. I envied them. I hoped they had put on insect repellent or they would end up with chiggers in some delicate places.

I studied the maps of the greenway land-use plan as I ate

my lunch, trying to ignore the yellow jacket wasps attracted to my barbecue sandwich and iced tea. One of the nuisances of picnicking. They're pesky . . . buzzing around and lighting on your food. When I was working on the pipeline job I had them swarm around me so bad they would cover my hands and my food, get into my drink and crawl across my lips. They're generally harmless and hardly ever sting unless you happen to eat one.

According to the maps, the operation across the river was definitely dumping into the restricted area of the greenway flood plain. I got out of the car and took a couple of pictures of the dump-and-fill operation from this side of the river. You couldn't see much from here but you could see where it was. I didn't take a picture of the couple who were still at it, or at it again. The photo shop probably wouldn't have given the prints back anyway.

I drove across the river bridge and turned left into the road where the dump trucks were entering and leaving. I pulled down to one side of the roadway and got out of my car. I snapped several pictures of the bulldozer in operation, landmarks identifying the spot, the trucks . . . taking care to get their tag numbers in the photos . . . and of a couple of men in hardhats supervising the operation. I got good shots of them because they were watching me. I put my camera back in my car and walked down the road to the hardhat who appeared to be the foreman.

"How are you?" I said. I extended my hand to him. He squinted at me.

He was a roughneck looking kind of guy, around fifty, six feet, big muscled but overweight, dressed in construction khakis with the name Scott stenciled over his shirt pocket.

"What do you want?"

The words he threw at me sounded as much like a threat

as a question. I took one of my business cards and handed it to him.

"I work for the city," I said. "Do you know you're dumping in a restricted area?"

He looked at the card and at me with obvious irritation. He put the card in his pocket.

"No, you're in a restricted area," he said, thumping his yellow plastic hardhat with his middle finger. "I filed my permits at City Hall. Why don't you get the hell out of here before you get hurt?"

He turned his back on me. I walked back to my car and took out my camera again. I snapped pictures until my roll of film was used up. There was some conversation going on between the two men while I was making the photos. The one named Scott stopped the bulldozer operator who looked back in my direction. Before I realized what was happening the dozer was backing full speed toward my car. I stepped across the road behind the red pickup truck and watched in disbelief. I heard the scrape of metal and saw my car sway as the big yellow Cat pulled to a stop in the road in front of me in a cloud of dust, roared its big engine and clattered back off toward the piles of concrete rubble and dirt fill it had been spreading. The bulldozer operator never looked up. When the dust cleared, my car sat with its left front fender torn loose and hanging at a wide angle to the left from a single ragged piece of sheet metal. It was dancing up and down like one of those little dolls that goes in the back window of your car.

The foreman walked up the road to me and handed me one of his business cards.

"Damn, it messed that up, didn't it?" he said. "File a claim with my insurance company." And he turned and walked away. I could see some of the workmen laughing.

I was about to get mad. It wasn't that my old Studebaker

Silverhawk was worth that much. It was basically a junker but it was all I had. Besides, it was the principle of the thing. I looked at the damage for a minute. I couldn't drive it like it was. The fender would be hanging right out into oncoming traffic.

I had a little score to settle. I got in the car and started it up. I pulled onto the dirt road, up close and just ahead of the new red super duty pickup truck. I put the old heap in reverse and pushed the accelerator to the floor. My tires spun on the loose dirt and the car roared backward. The dangling front fender banged into the front of the truck and knocked out its right headlight. I continued to accelerate backwards and turned my steering wheel hard to the right, pushing my left front fender into the side of the truck and scraping a nasty gash down the entire length of the pickup. The sound of metal scraping against metal would make your fingernails curl. As I passed the rear of the truck the remainder of the crumpled metal of my front fender punctured the pickup's rear tire and blew it out, caught on the rear bumper of the truck, ripped off, and hung there like something dead. I looked in the direction of the foreman. Most of the men were standing and staring, a couple were moving in my direction. I waved to them and drove onto the street, across the bridge, and toward the body shop of a friend of mine. I felt good.

I had met Ron the first day I arrived in town. A car mechanic is always the first person I meet when I move to a new place. Sometimes they even meet me halfway. My car usually arranges the introduction.

"Geez, Frank. What happened?" Ron asked as he leaned over the bruised and battered corner of the car where the left front fender was supposed to be.

"I hit a deer," I said.

"Yeah, I see. It was painted red."

I told him what happened.

"I would loved to of seen that."

"Do you think it's worth fixing?" I asked.

He looked at me and took the stub of a cigar out of his mouth.

"Sure. We can fix it up for a couple hundred. You can't replace the car for that. Of course if you want a complete paint job, that'll be at least two-fifty more."

"Hold off on the paint," I said. "Do you have anything I can drive while you're working on it?"

He thought for a minute, looked at me and considered. "You can borrow that motorcycle over there." He pointed to a black Harley Sportster. "If you promise not to wreck it. It's like brand new."

I felt a tingle of adrenaline. "Sure, that'll be great. I used to ride one just like it."

Three kicks of the crank starter and I was sitting astride the deep-throated Harley feeling my testosterone pumping as the big bike throbbed between my legs like a horse ready to run. Ron didn't have a helmet my size so I put on my sunglasses and let my hair blow in the breeze. The first time I opened up the throttle on the street I thought the acceleration was going to jerk me off the seat and leave me sitting on my ass in the middle of the pavement.

I could feel myself grinning as I pulled to a stop at a red light in front of the movie theater and looked at my reflection in the plate glass windows. I looked a lot like Peter Fonda in *Easy Rider*, only better. The deep rhythmic sound of the Harley echoing off the buildings on either side of the street gave me chills. I wanted to head out on the highway and not go back to the office. I went back to the office. On the way I dropped the roll of film off at Rapid Foto. They said I could pick up the prints after lunch the next day.

Parking is easy for a motorcycle. I found a shady spot between the sidewalk and the back steps to City Hall and chained the Harley to the handrail. I had to control myself. I was beginning to strut. My hands and legs were still tingling from the vibration of the bike when I walked into my office and found my boss waiting for me.

George Dolly was one of the mainstays of the city bureaucracy. In my experience with him he had been competent, easygoing, and so far had left me alone to do my job while he went about his. But like all longterm bureaucratic managers he had to smooth the waters from time to time and prevent disruptions in normal operations. He had to keep his bosses and the political structure happy. Sometimes that meant reining in a wild hare. That was me in this case.

George was so mild and inconspicuous I could not tell you a single outfit of clothes he wore to work. He always wore a white shirt and a necktie and some color of gray or charcoal pants. But I couldn't tell you if he wore the same outfit every day or if he wore a different combination each day of the week. I couldn't tell you if he had two neckties or twenty. His gray hair was always neatly trimmed and combed in place and he usually spoke with a soft, even voice. Today his voice sounded a little strained and his complexion was a bit mottled.

"Frank," he said. "What the hell do you think you're doing?"

"Beautifying the city and protecting the greenway. That's what the city pays me to do."

George was not amused. "I got a call from the mayor. He said he received a complaint that a city employee named Frank Hayes assaulted a contractor named Scott Taylor about an hour ago in the presence of half a dozen witnesses."

I told George the truth of what had happened.

"So you see, George," I said, "in my haste to escape an

assault on myself I accidentally sideswiped Mr. Taylor's pickup."

George looked at me with more than a skeptical eye. "Did you report the situation to the police?"

"I didn't stop to file an accident report because of the highly volatile situation. Those fellows were in no mood to be reasoned with. The only witnesses to the assault, other than myself, were Taylor and his employees. It's their word against mine and they're all in it together. I will have hard evidence of the violation when the photographs come back from processing. I was just coming here to ask for a cease and desist order against the operation until the matter can be brought before the commissioners."

The answer I gave was not exactly the whole truth but in my opinion it served justice. George was clearly in a dilemma.

"All right," he said, "I'll inform the mayor of what you told me. I'll make a personal inspection of the site. But those photographs better back up your story."

"Take a camera with you, George. Be sure and photograph everything. I think it's best if I keep my distance from them."

I managed to make it through the rest of the day without offending anyone. I got home after work that evening to find my air conditioner on the blink. You don't want to be in Macon, Georgia in the dead of summer with no air conditioning. It was too hot to eat. I had a quart of ice cream and three cold beers for supper.

Beer in the evening usually fades me right out but I lay awake in my bed that evening unable to go to sleep. All I could do was lie in the dark and sweat. I tried to open a window but it was stuck shut from twelve or fifteen coats of paint and wouldn't budge. A big old fashioned ceiling fan hung over my bed but I hardly ever used it because it made a tick, tick, tick,

tick sound that drove me crazy. But I found that when I turned the fan on high and lay on top of the sheet the warm breeze evaporated the sweat from my skin and left me almost comfortable, so long as I turned over from time to time to keep the wet side up.

It wasn't just the heat. I had something on my mind. It was the green eyed woman. Images of her were running in my mind over and over again. I could see those flashing green eyes shooting warnings at me. The soft smooth skin. The brown hair with a cast of cherry red and sunshine pulled back into a ponytail of soft, light curls. Sharp, full lips that I knew I could nibble and kiss all night and not get enough of. She was standing next to my car now and I could smell her fragrance. It was like vanilla and almonds with a little honeysuckle mixed in. I watched that bead of sweat slide over her skin down between her breasts. I wanted to be that bead of sweat. It was hopeless. She hated me.

Chapter 4

A Warm Heart

I got up the next morning not knowing if I had slept any the night before. I must have, because the alarm woke me, but I know the last time I looked at the clock before the alarm went off, it had been four-thirty. A cold shower helped some. The motorcycle ride in was a little help too.

Breakfast that morning was with the League of Women Voters to discuss the design of two mini parks to be built by the beautification program on Mulberry Street downtown. The median strips of several of Macon's downtown streets are twenty feet or more wide. You put in a crosswalk, some antique brick paving, a couple of park benches, a gas light, some azaleas and daffodils, a cherry tree, a couple of dogwoods, and a small fountain, and you have a median mini park for shoppers and other pedestrians to sit in the shade for a rest and conversation. This was in the days before the appearance of hordes of street people when winos came in ones rather than in multitudes. It was also in the days before the wards of mental hospitals had been emptied onto the streets. The only oddities you had to worry about were the town characters like the blind guy who yelled a constant stream of abuse at his guide dog, or the umbrella man, or someone selling fresh eggs on the street.

The umbrella man? He was this old fellow dressed in a black coat and tails who walked from his home to downtown and back each day carrying fifteen or twenty umbrellas. He usually had only two or three open at a time . . . perhaps a big black one and a multicolored golf umbrella . . . but he carried another in his other hand like a cane. Across his back hung a golf bag and in it, tied onto it, and hanging from it were more umbrellas in a wild assortment of sizes and colors. Nobody seemed to know why.

One of my chief responsibilities as beautification czar was to be responsive to the sensitivities of the citizenry, particularly the more influential elements of the citizenry, regarding the aesthetic appeal of our beautification efforts. To seek their advice, their goodwill, and their donations of time and money. I once asked the umbrella man what he thought of a sidewalk park on Mulberry Street. He said, "I think it's a mighty fine idea. Yes, I do." It gave me a sense of job satisfaction to know that my efforts were meeting the approval of at least one of our citizens. In addition to my informal sidewalk surveys I attended innumerable luncheons, teas, coffees, breakfasts, dinners, and banquets, as well as a thousand meetings of civic and service organizations.

Before you write off this breakfast meeting with the League of Women Voters as an ineffectual coffee klatch, let me point out that most of the women of the League were either professionals themselves or were married to the movers and shakers in town. If you can't persuade the banker directly, you can try some persuasion on his wife if you can get yourself invited to speak at the League of Women Voters. It is a big help if the point upon which you wish to persuade just happens to be one of passionate interest to the wife or if you yourself just happen to be of passionate interest to the wife.

This all occurred to me as I sat next to Shirley Willingham and told her the story of John Glover. Shirley was assistant director of the Department of Family and Children's Services for Bibb County. She was also wife of one of the largest real estate developers in town. By the time I finished telling Shirley the story of John Glover's origins as the son of a slave and his present sad situation she had tears streaming down her cheeks. She also had her hand wedged firmly between my legs. I could see that I had gotten lucky. I could get her help with John Glover and I could find out about the east Macon country club development. She removed her hand long enough to dry her eyes and blow her nose.

"Why don't you bring Mr. Glover by my office?" she said. "It sounds as if he may surely be eligible for food stamps or emergency assistance. I'll see that his situation is reviewed for all the appropriate services."

"Would today be convenient?" I asked. "His situation seems very critical to me. Of course I'm not a professional in the matter, such as yourself."

"Oh, Frank," she said, "you have such a warm and generous heart." There was the hand again. "The poor man. You've also got me worried about that little church. I'll bring that before the Historic Preservation Society board on Thursday evening."

Did I mention that Shirley was also a member of the board of the Macon Historic Preservation Society? I could see how Shirley and I might be working closely on several fronts.

Of course it's mostly a game. The flirtation, I mean. Usually more a fantasy rather than the real thing. You use words, gestures, soft caresses, and unspoken language to raise the passions and give the promise of excitement, adventure, wild abandon, love, whatever. But you have to be very wary when you're dipping your fingers in the honey pot of the rich and powerful because poppa bear can make life a living hell if you mess up his bed. And mamma bear can be a bitch too if things go sour. Shirley didn't strike me as the type to want the real thing. Well, not too much of the real thing. She mainly wanted the illusion, the feeling she used to have when she was free and men were after her. That was OK with me if the illusion would serve to generate some aid for John Glover and his wife. I'm a slut. I have no pride.

I'm not complaining, you understand. Shirley was quite an eyeful and quite a handful. She had been Miss Bulldog, or Miss Sorority Sister, or Miss something in college and she hadn't lost a bit of it during her ten years of marriage to Stafford Willingham. She had blue eyes, blonde hair, red lips and smooth creamy skin, all in the most exquisite combination. If I had to describe her in one word, the word would be 'voluptuous.'

Shirley was twenty years younger than old Staff. He should be a happy man. She wasn't just good looks. She had an MBA and brains enough to stay out of trouble. She might have liked my looks but as I sat there using my charm on her I knew I probably came way down on her list below her Lincoln, her clothes, her house in the best neighborhood in town, her wealthy friends, her vacations to Aruba, her standing in the community, or her career.

I have no hard feelings toward Shirley or any of her class, so long as they're giving and not taking. But somebody was trying to take from John Glover and he didn't have anything left to give.

Transportation was going to be a problem. I couldn't throw the old man on the back of my bike and go roaring over to the county DFACS. I was hoping the shiny blue Dodge with the Fulton County plates was still in town. Maybe the green eyed beauty of my daydreams could bring him. I looked forward to the chance to refresh my own fantasies. I wondered if I wanted the illusion or the real thing. It's kind of scary to ask yourself such personal questions. Particularly when you don't know the answer you'll get.

My dilemma was solved for me. John Glover was waiting for me when I arrived at my office. No, the blue Dodge didn't bring him. I found out later she had gone back to Atlanta, leaving me to dream. Mr. Glover had been dropped off by the neighborhood bad boys.

I looked at him and wondered how he had made it through the hot night in that little house of his. I wondered how he had found the strength to get up and get himself back downtown to my office.

"How are you feeling this morning, Mr. Glover?" I asked.

"I feel all right today. Thank you, Mr. Hayes. I'm mighty beholdin' to you for helping me home yesterday."

"Glad to be of help. Listen, I checked with the building inspector's office. They tell me you have some problems with your house that's putting it in violation of city safety codes. Did they talk with you about exactly what needs to be fixed?"

"They come out to the house and looked all over it. They said some things but I couldn't understand the words they was usin'. They left me a paper but I couldn't read that neither. So I come down here to City Hall and talk to they boss, but he wasn't no help neither. They tell me I need to bring it up to standard but I don't rightly know what that means. And even if I did, I don't know how I could do it. Mr. Hayes, I've lived in that house for thirty-six years with just about no problems at all and now they tell me I have to pay for repairs I can't afford to do, because they say it ain't safe to live in. I wonder, could you take a look at my house and explain to me what it is they say is wrong with it and what I need to do? Whatever it is, if I am able to do it I surely will try to do it."

I could see the old man was upset. I somehow had thought that pointing him in the direction of having repairs made would solve the problem. But it was going to be more complicated than that.

"Mr. Glover, I don't want to insult you in any way but I talked with a lady I know, a friend of mine who works for Family Services." I shortened the name so it didn't sound like the welfare department. "She didn't make me any promises but she seemed to think that if you would come and talk with her she might be able to find a way to help you with your problem. If you'll talk with her I'll go out to your house and see if I can make some sense out of the building inspector's report."

He didn't seem insulted at all. He seemed to gain a calmness from the fact that someone was finally trying to help him. I could see a relaxation in his posture.

"Why, yes sir, Mr. Hayes, I'll talk with your friend if she thinks she might can help. I would be most grateful."

So here I was again feeling guilty about the old fellow's circumstances and getting more involved rather than less. I borrowed George Dolly's city vehicle and drove Mr. Glover the five blocks to the county DFACS office. We got in to see Shirley after a wait of only ten minutes or so. Some kind of new speed record. It took only minor prompting for Mr. Glover to tell enough of his story to Shirley to verify all I had told her at breakfast. She called in her personal assistant to escort Mr. Glover to the various departments for evaluation. On his way out the door Mr. Glover stopped and thanked us both again.

"If you want to inspect my house, Mr. Hayes, I keep a key in a tin can underneath the corner of the front porch. Won't be nobody home 'till after dinner time but you're sure welcome to go right on in."

As soon as we were alone I turned to thank Shirley. She was standing with her face in her hands crying quietly. I went over to her, unsure exactly what I should do. She looked up at me. I looked back sympathetically and she pressed herself against my chest. I put my arms around her and patted her back as she sobbed gently. I hoped no one came in and misinterpreted what was going on. After several seconds of uneasiness on my part she stepped away and dried her eyes.

"I'm sorry, Frank. Sometimes I just can't bear the sad stories. I hear them all day long, one after another. I try to keep an emotional distance but it just gets to me sometimes. That poor old man."

I was redrawing my picture of Shirley. She wasn't just skin deep after all. "Nothing to be sorry for," I said. "It's only natural. I feel for him myself. What do you think might be his chances of getting help?"

"We'll do the best we can. It all depends on his income and resources and the nature of the problems he's having. We have to go by regulations that can be very rigid. Did I hear Mr. Glover say you're to inspect his house this morning?"

"Yep. That's part of my bargain with him. Though I don't know what good I'll be." I pulled the building inspector's report from my jacket pocket. "I don't know much about building standards."

"Let me see that." She took the inspection report from me and looked it over quickly, front and back. "I'll go with you," she said. "I got my start in real estate development. That's where I met my husband. I've dealt with building specs quite a lot."

Shirley told her secretary not to expect her back before lunch and we drove toward east Macon in Shirley's black Lincoln. I sank into the soft leather seat behind the dark tinted windows and enjoyed the cool air conditioned breeze filling the car. I wondered how much Ron would charge me to tint and air condition my old heap.

Chapter 5

Shirley Willingham

This was something I hadn't expected. It was hard for me to visualize Shirley Willingham in the middle of a low rent black neighborhood inspecting substandard housing in her designer pumps. I try to keep an open mind but even as we drove around the potholes in Bertha Street and pulled to a stop in John Glover's drive I still wasn't sure I believed it.

The first thing that caught Shirley's eye was St. James A.M.E. Church next door. She wanted some pictures for her presentation to the historic preservation society. I shot them until she was satisfied she had enough. I noticed Tiny watching us from his front porch across the street.

"Shirley," I said, "excuse me just a moment. I need to check in with the neighborhood watch."

She headed toward the Glover house, inspection report in hand. I walked across the dusty street to where Tiny sat.

"Hey, Frank," he said. "What's going on? You got a new woman?"

I smiled and shook my head. "Damned if I know what's going on, Tiny. That's Stafford Willingham's wife over there inspecting Mr. Glover's house. I think she's on our side."

"Good lookin' bitch. Nice car." He grunted and laughed. "I heard about you and the bulldozer."

"How did you hear about that? It only happened yesterday."

"Marcel, one of the neighborhood boys you met over here yesterday, he does shit work for Scott Taylor. He saw it all.

Marcel say you the man that whupped up on Taylor's pickup truck." He laughed again. "He say Taylor was mighty pissed off. You watch yourself, Frank. Taylor an' his men is a dangerous bunch."

He looked back across the street at Shirley coming around the outside of the house. "Looks like you got yo' hands full, Frank. Wish it was me."

Every time I talked with Tiny he left me wanting to know more . . . more about him and more about what he knows.

Shirley met me at the front of John Glover's house. She was irritated.

"This is piddle shit, Frank. There's a little dry rot around the eave on the side of the house. Insulation on some of the outside wiring is cracked and peeled. But it's no immediate danger to anyone. It's natural for a house this old. There's a little sag at one spot on the floor of the back porch but that's nothing either. I need to see inside."

She was talking with her hands and waving the inspection report about. It was fascinating to watch her build up so much enthusiasm. She didn't seem to notice my amusement. I knocked on the front door just to be sure no one was home.

The outside of the house looked just like any one of a thousand other small old houses that could be found anywhere in the South. They varied in design but they were variations on a theme. I had seen them in small towns, rural communities and large cities. I had seen them in the country, sometimes standing alone and sometimes in clusters or in rows. Sometimes they were the only remaining evidence that a farm or a community had once existed around them. You couldn't tell by their appearance how old the houses were. Once the wood siding weathered to a uniform faded brown color, they seemed to quit aging until dry rot, baking from the sun, the inevitable effects of weather or the weight of years of human traffic took their toll.

Sometimes they were raised high off the ground on the side of a hill and you could imagine children playing under them or hound dogs sleeping in their shade. Sometimes they were low to the ground for warmth. Mr. and Mrs. Glover's house sat on a flat sandy lot and was low to the ground. The outside was Spartan with little accumulation of the clutter you might expect after thirty-six years of habitation. It was weathered but neat. The yard was mostly sand with sparsely scattered sprigs of pale green grass.

I located the key in the can under the porch, unlocked the door and we went inside. The basic, almost primitive four room house was clean and well cared for. Shiny linoleum, the kind that comes in a roll in different colors and designs and is cool to the feet but keeps the winter cold out, covered the tight-fitted wooden planks of the floors. The walls were of smooth pine paneling grown dark with time. Some walls were covered in very old wallpaper. There was a clean, almost medicinal smell to the place but if you closed your eyes and breathed deeply it seemed as though you could smell a lingering fragrance that had merged itself with the wood from decades of heating with kerosene heaters.

The accumulated furniture and other items from Mr. Glover's lifetime of almost ninety years and Mrs. Glover's seventy-five years made the house seem older than it was. Small items spanning over a century sat on table tops and shelves. There were pictures of black men and women in couples, large and small family groups and solitary portraits, many of them on paper yellowed from age. There was an old wooden butter churn in one corner, crocheted doilies on the arms and backs of chairs and on tables. Mr. and Mrs. Glover's spirit seemed to be there even when they weren't.

We went from room to room with the inspection report. Shirley checked the wiring, the plumbing . . . everything that I knew nothing about. She seemed to know what she was doing. The bedroom was the last place we looked. It was comfortable and quiet. The iron bed was covered in a white chenille spread with a large floral design in the middle. There were at least two dozen photographs of family members in all sizes and types of frames. Some of the photos looked ancient. On top of a dresser was a series of the green eyed girl from childhood to almost the way I had seen her the day before.

Shirley looked at the pictures for several minutes, finally turning and heading for the door. "I've seen enough," she said.

We locked the door behind us and I put the key back in the can under the porch. I looked across the street as we left the house. Tiny was no longer there. The dark tinted windows of the Lincoln hadn't prevented the car from heating up in the baking sun. Shirley turned the air conditioner on high and I leaned back in the seat and let the air blow on my face. Shirley didn't talk at first. She seemed to be going over something in her mind.

"So, what do you think?" I asked her as we turned onto Shurling Drive.

"The inspection report is bogus," she said. "The wiring distribution box is antiquated but it's not dangerous. The inspection report says it's substandard but it's not. The report says the kitchen circuits are overloaded but the only real power draws are the refrigerator and the stove, and the circuits are adequate to handle those. The report cites the plumbing and sewage systems as being out of compliance but they are not. They're old and would not meet standards if they were installed new today but for an existing structure of that age the plumbing is within allowances."

"So, what's going on?" I asked.

"My opinion is that either the inspector is incompetent or the deficiencies were purposefully exaggerated and falsified."

"Incompetence is a possibility but the guy who did the inspection is a kind of idiot savant. His brain is about the size of a Mexican jumping bean but he knows the housing code by heart. What would be the point of falsification?"

"Someone at City Hall may be trying to have Mr. Glover's house condemned."

"For what purpose? Is it connected with the country club development, do you think?"

Shirley just looked at me, smiled, and shrugged. "Why are you doing this, Frank?"

"What?"

"Going to all this trouble to help a man you didn't even know two days ago."

"The poor old guy asked me for help. How could I not help him? He and his wife need protection from whoever is trying to take their house away from them. I couldn't sleep at night if I didn't do something."

"Does he not have any family?" she asked.

I thought of Tiny and the green eyed woman and wondered what their relationship was to the old man. "Apparently not any who can help him."

"What about you? Do you have any family close by?"

"No. None here. I have an aunt and uncle who raised me over in Birmingham."

"What about your parents?" she asked.

"They're both dead," I said, "since I was five years old."

"I'm sorry. Maybe that's the reason then." She reached and squeezed my hand.

I hadn't thought about it. Maybe she was right. I just knew I was haunted by the old man and his wife. We were quiet for several moments. I could see she was working up to something.

"Could you have lunch with me, Frank? I need you to do something for me."

"Sure," I said. "Anything."

I didn't know where she had planned to go for lunch. It really didn't matter. It was good to be away from things and with a beautiful woman who smelled as good as she did.

"What is that fragrance you're wearing?" I asked.

"You like it?"

"I certainly do," I said, raising her hand to my nose. "It smells kind of like lime and rum and coconuts."

"That's funny," she said, "It's called Caribbean Breeze."

"Yeah, that's what it smells like."

We had left the bypass and were headed north out of Macon toward Lizella.

"Where we going?" I asked.

"Lake Dunwoody. There are some things in storage in the attic at the lake house and I need your help getting to them. It's only twenty minutes from downtown. We can have lunch there. It's pretty and quiet. You'll like it."

She was right. I did like it. Lake Dunwoody was the weekend home for many of Macon's well-to-do. It was all waterfront wooded lots, upscale cottages, peace, quiet, and solitude. The Willingham cottage was a bit more than a cottage but not extravagant. It was cedar, glass, decks, soft carpet and comfort. The living room was probably thirty feet across with a wall of tinted glass looking out over an unspoiled lake view. Shirley got us a couple of cold beers from the refrigerator.

"Nice view," I said. "I wouldn't mind living out here."

"You might talk with your boss. He's thinking of selling his place and building something new."

"Craig?" I asked. "He lives out here?"

"He has a cottage just across the lake. You can almost see it from here. George Dolly has a little cottage out here too, a mile or so further around the shore."

"Too rich for my blood. It must be nice."

"Gives you something to work toward," she said, smiling at me as if to say there might be other advantages to living on the lake with her. She led me down a hallway to where we stopped under a pulldown door in the high ceiling.

"Uh, huh," I said. "You needed a tall guy. I thought it was my brains that attracted you."

"We had planned to put an office in the attic but we got only as far as putting boxes of storage up there. We were supposed to have stairs here but . . ."

"You got a pole with a hook or something?" I asked. She shrugged and smiled.

After several harebrained efforts I finally managed to stand on a barstool and use a coat hanger to fish the end of a rope out of the door. I pulled the stairway down, unfolding it amid a cloud of dust and paint chips. I followed Shirley up the steps to the attic, admiring the shape of her butt all the way and trying unsuccessfully not to look up her dress. Her panties were the color of champagne.

It was your typical attic storage. Dust, cobwebs and old stuff. Shirley opened the drawers of a couple of old file cabinets, thumbed through the folders and looked into some cardboard boxes but apparently didn't find what she wanted.

"I'll just have to come back when I'm wearing old clothes and have time to look," she said. "I'm sorry. I thought I would be able to find what I'm looking for."

"No problem," I said. "I'm always open to adventure. You never know what you'll find in an old attic."

We went back down the stairs and I closed the trap door after tying a length of string to its rope so Shirley could reach it next time. She looked at me and laughed.

"What is it?" I said.

"Come here." She led me down the hallway into a large bathroom. She pointed to the mirror. I had a smudge of gray dust on my forehead and a rather creepy looking cobweb in my hair. She took a couple of tissues and said, "Bend down so I can reach it."

I leaned over and she pulled at the cobweb. It clung to my hair and tickled my ear. My face was about six inches from her chest and I could smell the warm fragrance from her skin.

"I'm sorry," she said.

"No problem," I said. No problem at all. I wanted to smell some more of that fragrance.

She wet a washcloth with a little soap and water and wiped my forehead. I finished the job and was about to hand the washcloth back to her when I noticed a gray smudge on her white dress jacket right on the tip of her left breast.

"Do you want me to get that for you?" I asked, indicating the smudge.

She looked down at the soiled spot and said, "Oh, darned," took off her jacket and turned to the sink to clean the spot. She was wearing a plain champagne silk blouse that wasn't exactly see-through but there wasn't much I couldn't see. She wasn't wearing a real bra. It was kind of a silk halter.

There wasn't anything suggestive or inappropriate about what she did. It must have been the closeness or the atmosphere. She looked up in the mirror and saw me watching her. She looked at me for a moment. I saw her breath catch and a change in her eyes. She turned around toward me. In the light I couldn't stop my eyes from looking at her breasts. She was definitely breathing. And her eyes had a look that I love to see.

She took a step toward me and said, "Frank, I . . ."

The next thing I knew, her arms were around my neck and I was standing with my back against the door with Shirley climbing me like a tree, her lips holding me so tight we couldn't have been closer if we had been turned inside out. I did a quick mental adjustment and flipped her from column A to column B in my illusion vs. reality model.

I don't remember how we got to the bedroom. I don't even remember her taking my clothes off or hers either. I do remember being amazed at just about everything else, including the quality of her underwear. Shirley was more than good looking and smart. She had talents I would never have thought or believed. If Stafford Willingham wasn't a happy man there was a serious problem somewhere. Two hours later I was limp as a bowl of warm jello, too weak to run, and my eyes were glazed over.

Shirley stood next to me as I sat on the side of the bed leaning against her. She looked down at me with an expression that can only be described as a lover's smile.

"Well, that was good," she said.

"It gives a whole new meaning to the word," I said, nibbling my way across her bare tummy. She took my head in her hands and rubbed my lips gently across her breasts. I pulled her down to me, kissed those wonderful lips and was just thinking about asking for a rematch when she said, "I have to get back."

"I didn't plan this," she said as we drove back to town. "I really don't do this kind of thing. It was just something I needed and you seem so kind and trustworthy. I can't really explain."

"You didn't just find me irresistible?" I smiled at her.

"That, too." She took my hand in hers and put it to her lips. "Don't call me at home, OK? I have to be very careful." Her eyes seemed to be searching my face looking for something. I didn't know what she was telling me. I didn't even know what I wanted her to be saying. Did that mean I could call her at work? I guessed I would find out later.

"Sure," I said. "I don't want to cause either of us a problem." That seemed to be what she wanted to hear.

Fifteen minutes later she pulled into her parking place at the DFACS office and took a quick look at her face in the rearview mirror.

"Call the office later, Frank, and I'll let you know the progress with Mr. Glover."

I tried to look as normal as possible as I walked on still-shaky legs back to George Dolly's car. I had a lot to think about.

Chapter 6

Finance 101

Lunch had been very satisfying but not very nourishing. I dropped by Ron's body shop on my way to find something else to eat. He looked up with a peculiar grin when he saw me coming and he nodded his head to one side like he had something funny to show me. In a repair bay on the opposite side of his shop from my heap was a new red super duty pickup with a nasty gash the full length of its right side.

"Is that funny or what?" Ron cackled.

I had to admit, it was funny.

"I feel like the hospital emergency ward on Saturday night," he said. "You guys beat each other up and I get the business from both of you." He laughed again.

"Hilarious," I said without enthusiasm.

"Say, Frank." He watched himself roll his cigar stub between his fingers. I wondered if it was the same cigar he was smoking the last time I saw him. It looked the same. "I wonder," he continued, "if you would mind riding the bike for a while longer. I'm having trouble finding parts for your car."

I noticed that it hadn't been touched. "Jesus, Ron. I don't suppose he paid you extra not to fix mine, did he? How much are you getting for his repair job?"

"Don't know for certain until all the charges are in. Maybe three thousand . . . thirty-five hundred."

"Oh, man."

"Nothing personal, Frank. You understand. I have to do the big job first. I need the inflow of cash."

"I like riding the bike, Ron, but sooner or later it's going to rain and I'll need my car back."

"OK," he said, "here's another deal. You like the bike?"

"Yeah, I like the bike."

"OK, what say I sell you the bike for like two thousand . . ."

"Two thousand?" I shouted. "Don't be crazy."

"OK, OK, that was just a hypothetical figure. We agree on an amount, you pay me the money for the bike, that solves my cash flow problem. I get your car repaired and back to you within a week. How does that sound?"

"How much for the bike?"

"Fifteen hundred."

"Twelve hundred."

"All right, the bike is yours for twelve hundred. And two hundred for repair of the car."

"Twelve hundred for the bike and the car repair and I'll pay you cash. Half now and half when the car is done."

"A thousand now for the bike and two hundred next week when the car is ready."

"All right," I said and we shook hands on the deal. "But you have to promise to have my car ready by next week," I said before I let his hand go.

"Yeah, sure. You have my word."

My checkbook showed a balance of $497. I had maybe another $500 in savings. I wrote Ron a check for $1000.

"You can't deposit that until tomorrow, OK? I have to switch some money around."

"OK, no problem. Oh, by the way," he said, pointing to his neck, "you got lipstick and a hell of a hickey on your neck. What is that, Strawberry Red? You smell good too. What kind of work do you do anyhow?"

I wiped at my neck with my pocket handkerchief and made a note to clean myself up before I went back to the office. He wrote me out a bill of sale for the Harley dated the next day. We shook hands on it again and I walked out of his repair shop suddenly wondering what in the hell I had done. Ten minutes ago I was happy and debt free and ten minutes later I am in debt over my head and kiting checks. It just shows you the corrupting influence of motorcycles. Next thing you know I'll be wearing really ugly clothes, acting loud and obnoxious, getting tattoos, and running with a gang of B-movie misfits. Oh yeah, and riding a really tough looking woman on the back of my bike. Of course some people already think I wear really ugly clothes.

Before any of that could come to pass I determined to secure a personal loan to put my accounts back in balance. I dropped in at the bank where I do my checking and savings. I was somewhat distressed to discover I had forgotten about a previous dip into my savings account which showed a current balance of only $350. I also failed to consider outstanding service charges and an automatic withdrawal for my auto insurance from my checking account. My total net cash worth stood at $804.27 and it was almost a week until payday. I was in deep doo-doo.

Should I slink back into Ron's body shop and admit my poverty, the lack of forethought and judgment in my impulsive decision to buy the bike and ask him to give my check back? A real man doesn't admit that kind of mistake. You make a mistake, you stand up like a man, take the consequences and go on to your next stupid move.

The financial officer at my bank found it hard to believe I was asking him to lend me $1,200, and the only collateral I had to offer was a five-year-old motorcycle and a thirteen-year-old wrecked Studebaker. According to his books the total worth of my assets was about $150 and on his risk tables I fell into the column headed 'Do Not Lend to This Applicant Under Any Circumstances.' He didn't throw me out of the bank but he did escort me to the door and suggested I consult a different type of financial institution for a loan. He gave me a business card for such an establishment.

I drove across town to the American Home Guardian Finance Corporation. It was on a street with a long line of finance companies, used furniture stores, pawn shops, and a gun emporium. Some of the storefronts had been burned out or scorched during the recent nighttime disturbances. At American Home Guardian which had somehow remained intact I was introduced to my very own personal financial manager. His name was Bob Felton. I was impressed by Bob's professional tone.

"Those dickheads down at First Citizens sent you, huh? Geez, they're stupid," he said. "They turned away a fine reliable low risk client like you? Sure, AHG can help you."

Twenty minutes later I walked out of American Home Guardian with a check for $1,500 in my pocket. I figured what the hell, get a little extra for some clothes to go with the new bike. Of course the interest rate for an AHG loan was a little different from the bank. When I asked Bob what the interest rate was, he said, ".068% adjusted daily periodic rate." I asked what that meant in real annual interest rate and he said 24.9%. The interest rate was outrageous. However, I was in no position to be outraged. I was grateful to have the check in my pocket and as Bob pointed out, if I payed the loan off within thirty days I would pay a fee of only $130.

I discovered later in the fine print that if I failed to pay off the loan or if I was more than twenty days late with any payment, American Home Guardian was authorized to seize my bike, my car, my bank accounts, my stamp collection, any personal property or real estate I owned anywhere in the free world, all the assets of all my family and friends, and garnish my wages until the end of the century. That seemed a little unfair, but as I said, I was in no position to complain. Besides, if I paid it off in installments over three years it was only $65 per month. I could live with that. I never was all that good with math anyhow. I deposited my new fortune in my checking account, keeping out three hundred for my new wardrobe.

As I drove George's car back to City Hall I vacillated in my mind between flaunting my lipstick smudge or hiding all possible evidence of my sexual adventure. It's hard for a guy not to want to strut after he just had his brains screwed out by Miss Bulldog. It must be some kind of primitive animal thing. I felt like grunting and beating my chest to let the other gorillas know who the stud was in the neighborhood, drive away the competition and attract the females. Or maybe it's just that the higher intellectual functions temporarily shut down and hadn't started back up again. All the energies channeled away from the brain to the pecker. Nature's way of making sure that maximum effort is focused on planting those seeds in fertile ground. That was a scary thought.

I decided the aggressive social image I was having of myself was a byproduct of the motorcycle as I drove home on it for a quick shower and change of clothes. I did have one last moment of personal crisis before I stepped into the shower. The smell of Shirley was still on my skin and I wanted to retain that memory for as long as it would last. The fragrance of her perfume was on my shirt. That would have to do.

Chapter 7

A Little White Lie

It looked like it was up to me to find out who was behind the false inspection report on John Glover's house and what their motive was if I was to help the old man. But I had to be careful not to get myself tagged as being on the wrong side of whatever dirty deal was going on, because I didn't have anyone to help me if I got in trouble. I wasn't afraid of trouble. After just one day on the Harley I wasn't afraid of anything. But if I got knocked out of the game the old man and his wife were helpless.

The cool shower and the breeze through my hair on the motorcycle ride back to the office revived my little gray cells and a plan formed in my mind. The plan grew out of remembering what I saw and heard that morning at breakfast. Pictures of Tommy Lee's tank in front of City Hall were all over the front pages of the newspapers and on TV. People were talking, wondering what it all meant. There was an undercurrent of tension and worry about all the trouble. Also some smirks, laughter and shaking of heads.

Craig Linder was alone in his office when I arrived back at the planning and zoning office. I slipped the Glover inspection report back under the stack on Moe's desk. I tapped on Craig's open door and assumed my most serious and responsible posture as he looked up.

"Come in, Frankie," he said. He looked at me quizzically. "Something different about you? You weren't wearing that shirt this morning, were you?" The old gorillas were watching me.

"No. I dropped my bike and messed up my clothes. I had to change."

"Oh, yeah," he said, "I see the Band Aid on your neck. You're not hurt, are you?"

"Only my pride," I said. "Nothing serious. A woman pulled out in front of me."

"Isn't that just like a woman? You better be careful on that motorcycle. They can kill you. You heard about the guitar player next door, the Allman boy, didn't you?" Craig waved his thumb in the general direction of the recording studio down the street. "Hit a truckload of peaches they tell me. Killed him on the spot. Bad business. Drivers got no respect for a motorcycle."

"Yeah, I'm always watching," I said.

"What can I do for you?"

"I just stumbled across something I thought you should know about. It's none of my business, but I just wanted to pass it along to you."

"Shoot. What is it?"

"I think your office has had some dealings with an old fellow named John Glover?"

"Oh, Jesus. The old colored guy. My inspectors tell me he's been driving them crazy. I must have seen him in the office a dozen times. I thought for a while he must be moving in here. Is it about him?"

"Him . . . and the NAACP."

Craig's attention focused. "The NAACP? The last thing we need. What's going on?"

"The old fellow almost passed out in my office yesterday. I was afraid he was going to have a stroke or something so I loaded him up in my car and took him home to his wife and a young woman who has been looking after him. Apparently he had wandered off from home and they didn't know where he was."

"It's a wonder he didn't drop dead in the street in this heat," Craig said.

"My thoughts, exactly. Anyhow, I come in this morning and Mr. Glover is sitting in my office, looking worse than ever. The old man is practically delusional. So I borrow George's car and take him home again. When I pull into his place I notice this crowd of black guys around a big new shiny Lincoln sitting just across the way. I put the old man out. But before I can get out of the drive these guys have me hemmed in, wanting to know who I am and what I'm doing in their neighborhood."

"Jesus, Frankie. It's a wonder you didn't get hurt."

"That's what I was thinking the whole time. I show them my business card and tell them I'm just bringing the old fellow home. It looks like they're ready to crawl all over me but one of the older guys who seems to be in charge comes up. He starts asking me all kinds of questions about the building inspector's office and why you're harassing folks in their neighborhood."

"My office harassing them? We treat them just like anyone else. What harassment?"

"I know that, Craig. But these guys had a serious attitude problem. I'm telling you, they were looking at me like I was barbecue."

"Jesus."

"The guys in the Lincoln make me get in and they tell me they're from the Atlanta NAACP and one of the guys has come down from national NAACP headquarters in Washington, D.C."

"What did they want?"

"They said people are telling them about a campaign of harassment from City Hall against black homeowners in

Macon and Bibb County, particularly coming out of the building inspector's office."

"There's not any harassment."

"I know that, Craig. But they start asking me about Mr. Glover and what I know about a falsified inspection report on his house. I tell them I don't know anything about it. It turns out finally after a lot of talk, the NAACP guys have seen reports on TV about Tommy Lee's Sherman tank and him firing a machine gun into the black housing project."

"Jesus, Jesus. I told Tommy Lee he was going too far, but you know him. He's his own man. He runs his own show. He thinks he has his finger on the pulse of his voters. He won't listen to me or anyone else. He has this idea about running on a national ticket."

"So these guys say they're looking for a test case, an example of gross injustice by the mayor and city hall against black citizens. They seem to think Mr. Glover is an ideal case."

"What's the deal with Glover that makes his case so special?"

"Well, look at it from an outsider's point of view, Craig. Someone with an axe to grind. Here's this eighty-nine year old colored man who can't read or write. He's living in retirement, barely struggling by on a little Social Security check in a house he and his sickly wife have owned free and clear for thirty-six years. Along comes the building inspector after an anonymous complaint and tells Mr. Glover his house is unsafe. Mr. Glover can't read and he doesn't understand what the building inspector is trying to tell him. After many trips to City Hall and after talking to anyone who will listen to him, Mr. Glover catches the ear of someone who knows someone who knows the NAACP is looking for a vulnerable spot in Macon."

"I can see where this is going," Craig said.

"It gets worse. The NAACP guys bring in some hotshot

building engineer who takes Mr. Glover's copy of the inspection report and goes over the house item by item. The engineer says the inspection report is phony baloney, done by an incompetent inspector."

"I'm going to kill those guys. I've told them to be double sure of every deficiency they record on those reports."

"The engineer is even saying the inspection looks falsified to him, so the NAACP guys put Glover at the top of their harassment victim list and go on down the street talking to other colored folks who are having problems with City Hall."

Craig was getting a wild panicky look in his eyes. He ran his fingers through his hair. "What are they doing now?"

"Last I saw of them, the NAACP guys were talking to their lawyers and their nonviolent action planners. I got out of there as soon as I could. I took Mr. Glover with me and I dropped him off at the county DFACS office. The old fellow and his wife are completely out of money, with no food in the house and no way to pay their bills. He's looking for some emergency food and some financial assistance to get him through the month. It's a sad case really. I mean, the way he's being used."

"They want to hold him up as an example of injustice from City Hall while they drive around in their big cars and fly all over the country but they can't find a few dollars to help him out," Craig said. He reached for the phone. I got up to leave. "Stay right there. We need to talk to the mayor."

Well, shit. My clever lies to trick Craig into getting off the old man's back were pulling me deeper into a place I didn't want to be. After a minute on the phone with the mayor, Craig stood up and motioned for me to follow him. We walked down the winding marble stairway to the floor below. Tommy Lee's secretary nodded to us and we were let right into his office.

Craig repeated the gist of my lies to the mayor, adding enough disclaimers to absolve himself of culpability in connection with any possible wrongdoing. In response to the mayor's questions I confirmed the story as I had made it up. The mayor sat and listened, his elbows resting on his big mahogany desk, looking at us over the steeple of his fingertips pressed against the bridge of his nose. Craig finished his report and there was a silence. The mayor looked at me, then he looked at Craig, then he looked at me again for a long ten seconds. I was sure he didn't believe a word of truth in it. Craig cleared his throat nervously. I could see Tommy Lee's jaw muscles working and his eyes wrinkle and close and then focus on me again. I tried to remain calm. He sprang up from his chair and grabbed his suit coat as he headed for the door.

"Let's take a look," he said. "Get that inspection report."

Within fifteen minutes the three of us were turning onto Bertha Street in the mayor's car. A block ahead of us we could see the rear of a black Lincoln with dark tinted windows just rounding the corner heading toward Shurling Drive. Jesus, I knew it was probably Shirley Willingham leaving from a visit to the Glovers or to look over the church.

"There they are now, Tommy Lee," Craig said. "You want to try to catch them?"

"No," the mayor said. "I'll wait until they want to see me, but I want to be ready for them when they come."

Thank you, God. "This is the house, Mayor," I said, indicating Mr. Glover's place.

Tommy Lee stopped his car in Mr. Glover's drive and the three of us got out looking, if possible, even more out of place than I had the day before. Tommy Lee stood and looked in a full circle. He wore a tailored suit with a western cut and black polished square-toed western boots. He struck a pose the way actors do that made him look as if he were an important person on an important mission. Or he might have been trying out in his mind how he would look in a photo shoot in those surroundings. Apparently satisfied with what he saw or didn't see, he marched right up onto Mr. Glover's front porch and tapped on the screen door.

The old gentleman came to the door and stood for a moment looking through the screen at the three of us. I thought I saw in his eyes for a moment a recognition or perhaps a remembrance of some past time. Then his eyes cleared as Tommy Lee spoke to him.

"Mr. Glover?" he asked.

"Yes, sir," the old man said to the mayor who was less than half his age.

"Mr. Glover, they tell me you've been having some problems with your house."

"Yes, sir, they tell me I have."

"Well, I've come here to see if there is any way I can be of help in solving the problems you're having. Would you mind if I come in and have a look for myself?"

"No, sir, I don't reckon I mind."

Tommy Lee opened the door and shook the old man's hand as he introduced himself. I spoke to Mr. Glover and introduced Craig as the three of us filed into the small house. Mrs. Glover had come from the kitchen and stood listening, wringing her hands in her apron. Tommy Lee put on his best smile, took her hand in his and spoke to her. She nodded and smiled nervously.

"I apologize for barging into your home, Mrs. Glover," he said.

"You go right ahead, Mr. Mayor," she said. "We are grateful that you are here to see for yourself."

"We'll be out of your way just as fast as we can be."

"Well, you just take your time. We ain't in no hurry," she said.

He turned to Craig with the unspoken directive to show him the items indicated on the inspection report. Craig consulted the report and fumbled about the house, seeming to only half know what he was looking for. He managed to give the mayor an unconvincing description of each of the infractions which were not apparent even after careful inspection. Ten minutes and the mayor had said his apologies again to the Glovers and we were back in his car headed out on Bertha Street. I saw Tiny and several residents of the neighborhood watching us.

"Craig," the mayor said, "we're on shaky ground here. You get 60 Minutes in there and they'll rip us a new asshole."

"Tommy Lee, these are all technical violations."

"You know me, Craig. I'll fight when I'm right. But I can't see it here. If 60 Minutes or the NAACP starts ripping assholes, it's not going to be mine. This looks suspicious. Whether it is or it's not, you have to admit it looks suspicious."

"I guess it could." Craig read the signs. He was bowing to the mayor.

"You're damn right it could. Who actually does these inspections? I mean, who actually goes in and looks and files the reports?"

Craig told him. I knew it was bad news for Moe and Curly.

"We have to sacrifice them," Tommy Lee said.

"What do you want me to do?" Craig said.

"I want those two out of the inspector's office. I'll find something for them to do. I want new clean faces in there and I want them to know what they're doing. No screw ups. Find somebody respectable. And I want one of them to be black."

"Jesus, Tommy Lee."

"No shit now, Craig. You do what I say and this will be good for us."

Craig shook his head and grimaced but he accepted it.

"I want you to drop inspection complaints against all homeowners with property values of less than $25,000. Get me a list of their names and addresses and I'll personally send them a letter informing them we are discontinuing complaints against them."

"Jesus, Tommy Lee." Craig seemed to have his needle stuck in the same groove.

"And I want that same exemption to extend to all our homeowners who are dependent on their Social Security Retirement income for their livelihood. And to those who are living on disability income."

"That's a bigger order, Tommy Lee. We don't have that information," Craig said.

"Then put a notice in the newspaper. I'll hold a news conference."

Tommy Lee was thinking now. I could see it in his posture and hear it in his voice. He was on a roll.

"What's your estimate of the cost of correcting the problems with Mr. Glover's house?" Tommy Lee said.

Craig scratched a few figures on his notepad. "Probably $500," he said.

"Five hundred dollars?" Tommy Lee was incredulous. "All this trouble over five hundred dollars?" He thought for a minute. In the reflection in the rearview mirror I could see his eyes darting. "Frank, I want you to have Mr. Glover down at my office tomorrow morning at ten o'clock."

"Yes, sir," I said.

"Dress him up just a little bit to have his picture made with me. Have his wife come too. She's very sweet looking."

That was the first time I had seen leadership power being wielded so blatantly, deliberately and ruthlessly. I was happy the machine seemed to be backing off Mr. Glover's doorstep and I felt damn clever about what I had done. But I also felt cynical. My cynicism moved up a notch when we arrived back at City Hall and I heard Tommy Lee giving instructions to his secretary to arrange a press briefing and photo shoot for tomorrow morning at ten o'clock and to be sure that all network affiliates were there.

As soon as I knew it was safe to talk I called Shirley at her office to let her know what was going on and to tell her about our near miss on Bertha Street.

"The mayor?" she said. "How did the mayor get into it?"

"Don't ask," I said. "All I can tell you is he's planning some kind of news event tomorrow morning."

"What is he up to?"

"I don't know. I'm just hoping it won't be as bad as the tank or the machine gun."

"What an idiot," she said. I didn't know if she was talking about the mayor or about me.

"What about Mr. Glover?" I asked. "Were you able to help him?"

"We can provide him with one-time emergency financial assistance but that's all. The income from his and his wife's Social Security is enough to disqualify him for regular assistance."

"They seem to be barely getting by," I said.

"I know. But he doesn't have a housing payment or any dependents of minor age to care for or even any unusual medical expenses. His biggest financial problem seems to be that he owes significant debts to three different finance companies and those payments are eating up his income."

"What are the debts for?"

"I don't know. All I know for sure is that his only hope for relief is to get rid of those debts. I have to go now," she said. "I'll try to call you this evening."

I went to Bertha Street that afternoon to break the news to the Glovers and prepare them for whatever was to happen the following morning. All I could tell them was that I thought it might be good news. Mrs. Glover insisted I call their granddaughter and ask her to be there. Who was their granddaughter, I asked.

"Why, Mr. Hayes," Mrs. Glover said, "you met her right here yesterday. Our granddaughter, Johnny Mae Glover."

Now I knew the green eyed girl's name. She was Johnny Mae Glover, named after her grandfather John Glover, and her grandmother Sara Mae Glover. I also now had her phone number. I called her that evening as Mrs. Glover had requested.

"The mayor wants to make a presentation to your grandparents," I told her. "I know he's going to cancel the inspection complaint and I think he wants to present something to them . . . maybe some money but I don't know. TV and newspaper reporters will be there. Your grandmother wants you to come."

It was quiet on the other end of the phone line.

"What have you gotten them into?" Johnny Mae said.

"The publicity was not my idea. That's the mayor. I think he wants to make a gesture."

"A gesture? You're using my grandparents."

"No, I'm not. It's . . ."

"Isn't it bad enough what's already been done to them? Poppa was never even taught how to read and write. That's why he's in the trouble he's in. How many times does he have to be a victim of you white people? You mistreat him, neglect him, and take advantage of him, and his father and mother, and their parents, and theirs back four hundred years. Poppa's father was a slave of white people, for God's sake! Now you want to give Poppa a little money to ease your conscience? Put him up in front of TV cameras and give him a few pieces of silver so the mayor can look good and you can feel better? You ought to be ashamed. You make me sick."

"Wait just a damn minute."

"Don't you curse me."

"Wait just a minute, please."

How in the hell did this happen? Jesus, did I step into the middle of something. I took a long breath to try and slow my heart from pounding. She waited.

"I'm sorry for what's happened to your grandparents. It wasn't my doing. The things that happened to them happened a long time before I was on the scene."

"Don't give me that. That's the same old story all you people tell. It's never your fault. It was always somebody else. But somebody is still doing it to them and millions of other colored people right now. Whose responsibility is it now? Somebody's got to take responsibility sometime and put an end to it."

"I'm trying to do my part. You can't blame me personally for the misdeeds of some other person . . . regardless of their race. I'm doing my best to do the right thing."

"By being that white bigot mayor's errand boy?"

"Listen to me. I've lied to the mayor. I've lied to my boss. I've stolen city records. For no other reason than to help your grandfather and grandmother keep the house that belongs to them."

"You got a guilty conscience for some reason?"

"I'm not doing it out of guilt. I'm doing it because it's the decent thing to do. I would do it for my grandparents and I'll do it for yours. I can't stand by and watch innocent people get hurt. I'm putting my job and my income on the line."

"Well, pat yourself on the back."

"You have to ask yourself if you would do the same thing for an old helpless white couple."

"If my grandparents are helpless, it's because of what's been done to them."

"I'm not arguing with you about that. But I didn't do it. You need to think about something. You hated me from the minute you saw me."

"No, I didn't."

"You know you did. You looked off that front porch and saw me with your grandfather and you despised me. You knew from the minute you saw me that I was up to no good. And you knew it on the basis of nothing whatsoever except that I'm white."

She was quiet on the other end of the phone.

"I'm taking responsibility to see that the right thing is done by your grandparents," I said. "You need to give me a chance."

It was quiet again for several seconds.

"I'll be there to take them," was all she said.

I hadn't seen that coming but I guess I should have. I would be pissed off if someone were trying to take my grandparents' house. I would be just as angry as she was I guess. But it hurt me that I was trying to help and she despised me anyway.

I had stopped by Rapid Foto and picked up the prints from the pictures I made the day before. In one of the photos of the Glover house there was Johnny Mae standing on the front porch. I sat in a dark little bar downtown that evening drinking a frozen margarita and looking at the photograph of her, those green eyes looking back at me. Damn, she was beautiful. And she was mad at me. It didn't matter. There was something about her that had taken hold of me. I couldn't let it go and I didn't know what to do with it. Some women are like that. You get close to them and they exert an invisible force on you. They control the way you feel about things. They control what you want. It must have been the same kind of force Ingrid Bergman had over Humphrey Bogart in *Casablanca*. Or maybe I was just tired and the margarita was exerting its force.

I started for home around 9:00. It was still hot and steamy, too hot to go home to my stifling hot apartment. The night air felt good blowing through my shirt as I rode the Harley up Riverside Drive. I didn't have any particular place to go, just riding down the highway hoping something would come my way. The big white sign of the Dew Drop Inn stood out in the night, its red letters announcing the appearance in their lounge of Del Shannon, a blast from the past. I'm a fan of rock and roll so I pulled in to see what was going on.

It was crowded inside, maybe three hundred people. The cigarette smoke was thick. Lots of local night crowd, traveling businessmen staying the night and college kids from Mercer, Wesleyan, and Middle Georgia College. Del Shannon was just coming on stage, backed up by a local band. The atmosphere of the place cheered me some.

I found a seat at a table to one side and ordered a frosted mug of draft beer. A couple of local college girls sat down across from me. They were cute. One of them, the blonde, had a California accent. The reason I knew it was a California accent was that she kept talking about how great California was and, like, how people kept asking her about her accent and things, and how she didn't really have an accent, you know, but all the people in Georgia had really bad accents for sure, and there was this one guy. Well, you get the idea. She was almost cute enough to overlook her silliness.

Her name was Jennifer and she told her friend Sheila how she was in really big trouble, I mean, like, really big trouble, because she had spent, like, all her allowance on some really neat clothes and stuff, you know, those really tight black shorts, and that really gorgeous green bikini, and some shoes and things, and she hadn't made her car payment, and her dad was, like, going to be, I mean, really mad if he found out, and she was desperate and would do just about anything to get her hands on $200, I mean anything, because she had to, like, have the money, because if her father found out, he would, like, take her out of school, and well, she just couldn't deal with that.

I heard all this as background to the band. For the first thirty minutes they played rock and roll standards from the fifties and sixties. Del did his big hits from the 60s. They weren't half bad. During the first intermission I looked up to see the mayor and Craig Linder coming into the lounge. The mayor was all smiles, winks, and handshakes. He was dressed for nighttime in one of his white western suits with black trim and shiny black leather boots and was wearing one of those black string ties with a turquoise stone set in silver. One thing about him, you always knew when he was in the room. The mayor spotted me from midway across the room and made his way in my direction. It would probably be more correct to say he spotted me sitting with two really cute girls and made his way in our direction.

He was all smiles and twinkly eyes when he spoke but the twinkles in his eyes were for the girls, not me. He nodded and smiled to them, looking them over, looking for a certain response from them. He apparently saw what he wanted.

"Frank, won't you introduce me to these beautiful young ladies?"

He was taking a lot for granted but I managed not to disappoint him.

"Sheila, Jennifer," I said, "this is Mayor Tyler and Craig Linder."

"Tommy Lee," the mayor corrected me. "Are you girls college students?"

That was a no-brainer.

"You like the music?" he said.

They smiled and nodded. Either they were impressed with the mayor or they were good actresses.

"I'd like a drink. How about you Craig? Frank? Let me buy you girls a drink. What would you like?"

I had one more cold mug of draft. Sheila and Jennifer had something with paper umbrellas in them. The mayor had two fingers of Wild Turkey on ice, and Craig had a glass of ice water. By the time I finished my draft and was getting up to leave, the mayor had ordered another round of drinks. The band was playing again and he was telling Sheila stories of high intrigue. Craig and Jennifer were laughing about something. The mayor looked up at me with a big smile, winked, and took a shot at me with an imaginary pistol.

"See you in the morning, Frank. Ten o'clock."

It was a relief to get out of the lounge and back on my bike. The night started out good with the music and all, but I just wasn't one of the mayor's groupies. I felt uncomfortable in that social situation with the mayor and with those girls. Heaven knows I'm no prude but I felt out of place. I tried to clear my head of the thoughts. The beer helped. I had just enough in me to put me to sleep when I got home.

Chapter 8

It Gets Complicated

I guess I should feel good about what I accomplished. At ten o'clock the next morning the mayor, showing no effects from the night before, presented Mr. Glover with a check for $1,000 to make needed repairs to his house, telling the assembled reporters the story of how Mr. Glover had come to City Hall looking for help. Tommy Lee's version was that he had looked into the matter and discovered a large number of the city's citizens . . . good, responsible homeowners . . . in need of and deserving assistance. Mr. Glover was a special case, he said, because of what he represented, he being the son of a former slave and having worked hard all his life to own a little piece of America. Now in his advanced years Mr. Glover was entitled to respect and a little return for his tax dollars. And Tommy Lee was going to see that Mr. Glover and other citizens like him, regardless of color, would be served by their government.

In that spirit he was directing that a moratorium be placed on inspections and condemnation proceedings against the homes of the city's proud but economically stressed homeowners. During the past twenty-four hours, he said, he had talked with business and community leaders and he had assembled a special task force to plan a project he was calling Operation Breakthrough. He was directing the task force to work with local leaders, community groups, and the federal office of Housing and Urban Development to find a way, if possible, to make decent, affordable housing available to every citizen of Macon and Bibb County. The task force was to be co-chaired by Craig Linder representing the mayor and City Hall, and by the head of the Planning Commission, Stafford Willingham.

As I said, I should have felt good about the outcome. I didn't. I felt dirty and used. Beyond the presentation of the $1,000 check I didn't believe there was a word of sincerity in the mayor's announcement. But I would have to hide my doubts. I started something that had snagged me into it and it was dragging me along with it. I was appointed special assistant to the task force to aid Linder and Willingham in relations with the community. I could feel my butt slipping into a very deep crack.

I will have to say the event seemed to offer encouragement to Mr. Glover and his wife. The old man was practically overwhelmed with the confusion of the ceremony and the attention focused on him. But even in his unease he was reserved and dignified. He held his hat in his hand and prefaced each of his answers to news reporters' questions with his thanks for the generosity he and his wife were receiving. The two of them were the only sincere ones present among the host of politicians, business people, news reporters, and city officials. I looked at the two of them and was ashamed of myself.

Johnny Mae was there in the background. I worked my way around the onlookers and stood beside her. I know she was aware of me but she didn't acknowledge it. She looked straight ahead, no expression I could read on her face. When the ceremony was over and reporters were still crowded around her grandparents, Johnny Mae and I were alone at the back of the room. She finally turned to me and I saw the hardness was gone from her eyes. I could see a tear stain on her cheek.

"I could have been wrong about you, Frank," she said.

"Considering all that's happened to them," I said, nodding in the direction of her grandparents, "you had a right to be suspicious. Let's call a truce and start over, OK?"

There was an uncomfortable pause while we waited for the activities to end.

"Are you in town for the rest of the day?" I asked.

"No, I have to go back to Atlanta. I have to work this evening."

"Where do you work?" I asked without stopping to think that it might be too personal, too fast.

"I'm a nurse," was all she said.

Whatever tack I might have tried from that point was interrupted by the approach of Craig Linder and a distinguished looking man of about fifty-five years. He had well-groomed hair that had once been red but now was about two-thirds gray, and was wearing a very nice dark pinstriped suit. Everything about the man said he was someone important.

"Frankie," Craig said, "I want to introduce you to the man you'll be working for on this project along with me." He made an introductory gesture. "This is Stafford Willingham. Stafford, this is Frank Hayes."

If Stafford Willingham had ever heard of me he didn't reveal it in his face. He shook my hand in a perfunctory way and said, "Glad to meet you, Frank. Looking forward to some exciting times ahead."

He couldn't have known how right he was. But Stafford Willingham's attention wasn't on me. From the time he had walked up, his eyes could hardly stay off of Johnny Mae. I don't know why but it made me angry. He extended his hand to her.

"I'm Stafford Willingham," he said with a smile I thought was conveying something more than a how-do-you-do.

Johnny Mae took his hand and smiled noncommittally. I was envious. She had never taken my hand. In fact I had never touched her.

"I'm Johnny Mae Glover," she said, "Mr. and Mrs. Glover's granddaughter."

Stafford Willingham continued to hold her hand in his as he studied her face.

"I thought you must be," he said. "I think I may have known your mother many years ago. I think she may have worked as a housekeeper for my parents. Was your mother's name Esther?"

Johnny Mae's face and mood changed abruptly. She was suddenly hard again and the bitterness was back in her eyes. Damn him. Whatever he had said, damn him.

"Yes," she said.

"It's been a very long time," Willingham said, "but you look just like her."

Johnny Mae said, "Excuse me, I have to see about my grandparents," and with only a quick sharp look at my eyes, she walked away from us.

The three of us, all for our own reasons, watched her walk away.

"Nice looking girl," Craig said. "You knew her mother?"

"Yes," Willingham said. "Much longer ago than I care to remember." He recovered himself quickly with a smile but there was something left in his eyes when he looked at me. "You know my wife Shirley, I believe," he said to me.

Gee, that was an understatement.

"Yes, of course, Shirley Willingham." I smiled back at him, trying like hell to look completely innocent. "I met her when I spoke at the League of Women Voters this week, and just yesterday when I took Mr. Glover in search of help at the DFACS office. She was very helpful."

"You be careful with Shirley," he said. "She'll recruit you into every one of her pet projects and work you to death."

"She does seem very enthusiastic," I said. "The League has been helping with the median parks we're doing on Mulberry Street."

"Ah, yes. Very nice, and quite a good idea," he said. "I hope Craig can find someone to take that over from you because I think for the foreseeable future the three of us are going to have our hands full with Operation Breakthrough. Craig tells me you may have some contacts with the NAACP?"

"Not directly," I said truthfully. "I had a chance encounter with some of them. I know some of the black leadership who may have direct contact with them."

"Well, I think Tommy Lee has outmaneuvered them," Craig said.

"Now, Craig," Willingham responded, still smiling, "we want to bring the NAACP into this whole mix. I've already been in touch with Senator Talmadge's office and he agrees that we need the local and national black leadership on board if we are to get federal approval of the kind of large funding from the Department of Housing and Urban Development we're looking for. I think we should ask Frank here to serve as a liaison with the black community since he already has contact with them."

Now wait a minute, I was thinking to myself. I only made up this lie yesterday. How in the hell did Senator Talmadge, HUD, and large federal funding arrive on the scene so quickly? And what's this liaison shit? I didn't know any black community leadership except Tiny and I don't think that's what Willingham had in mind.

I was convinced at this point that Stafford Willingham, by whatever means, had found out about his wife and me and he was going to humiliate me all over town by showing me up to be the liar and corrupt public official that I was.

"Oh, you're just imagining the worst," Shirley said when I finally got a chance to talk with her on the phone. "Stafford doesn't know anything. That's just his way. He comes in, takes charge and tries to intimidate. Just ignore him, that's what I do."

Yeah, well maybe if you hadn't, I thought to myself, we wouldn't be in this situation now. But I knew truthfully I had been her more-than-willing accomplice.

Chapter 9

Angel of Mercy

The good news was that rain had moved in to cool off the hundred-degree temperatures. The bad news was that my only transportation was still the motorcycle. Fortunately, Macon had a pretty decent bus system, so I found myself commuting to work by not-so-rapid public transit. If you have an ear tuned to it, a public bus can be like a little public opinion sampling booth. I decided I would see what the transit-riding segment of the Macon-Bibb County population thought about the goings on at City Hall.

On the first leg of my trip the white riders thought the mayor and City Hall were catering to black troublemakers and that the circumstances of poor hard working white people were slipping to new lows. On my transfer bus the black riders thought the mayor and City Hall were plotting yet another disingenuous scheme that would leave the poor black citizens even worse off than they had been before. I'll have to say I was shocked when I realized I fell into the category of asshole sons of bitch bureaucrats and politicians that both blacks and whites found untrustworthy. I kept my occupation carefully hidden. I decided not to publish the results of my personal opinion poll.

One thing I had to do before I began serious work in pursuit of my community liaison responsibilities was to follow up on the greenway dump and fill operation. I dropped into George Dolly's office to give him the photos I had taken.

"Here they are, George," I said. "The photos tell the story. If you look at the maps of the protected greenway you'll see that this operation is clearly in violation."

"I agree," George said. "It was obvious to me when I went out there to have a look for myself. Our biggest problem may be in placing responsibility."

"Here's Scott Taylor and his men in the photographs," I said. "Here are the vehicles, showing their tag numbers. If we start with them and charge them they should start squealing and lead us to whoever hired them."

"Maybe," George said, "but these are pretty tough guys. Scott Taylor may be willing to keep his mouth shut and pay the fines with money given to him by whoever is behind the scenes."

"Who owns the property? Aren't they automatically liable when a violation like this occurs?"

"Not necessarily." George tugged at his shirt collar. "The owner may have signed a long term lease with a second party or a corporation that allows for development. It may be the lessee who is committing the violation."

"Well it doesn't appear to me that it matters," I said. "If we issue a cease and desist order, any lessee will lose value from the use of the land and the land owner will lose the lease income. Either way, whoever is being hurt should squeal."

"It doesn't always work that way, Frank. I've been trying to track down some of these cases for years. By the time you finally identify the guilty corporation it's no longer in business."

"It can't be that hopeless," I said. "We can find some way to ferret out the culprits."

George just looked at me the way a wizened old hand looks at a green-behind-the-ears rookie.

"Don't you think they're trying just as hard to figure out a way to do what they want to do and not let themselves be caught?" he said.

"Then it's just a case of who is the most experienced and the smartest," I said, slapping him on the back. "I say get the vehicle ownership information from the tag numbers and seize the equipment as collateral against the cost of cleanup of the dump and fill. That dozer is worth fifty thousand. That'll get someone's attention."

George thought for a minute. "That might produce some results," he said, taking the packet of photos from me. "I'll see what I can do."

My next stop was Craig Linder's office. I had to convince him I needed a city vehicle to drive until I could get my car out of repair. He was ahead of me. In recognition of the elevated status of my new responsibilities I had been assigned a car from the motor pool. I went to pick it up.

Like something sticky you can't seem to get off your shoe, who should turn up working in the motor pool but Moe and Curly. If you've ever walked into a room where you knew that everyone there would like nothing better than to smell the aroma of your roasted private parts on a skewer over an open fire, then you have a pretty good idea of the atmosphere at the motor pool when I showed up. I told Curly I was there to pick up a car. He went back inside the office where there was some hushed discussion between him and Moe. Moe came out carrying a key with a numbered tag attached. He filled in the line on the log book and handed me the pen to sign for the car.

"It's in the lot," he said.

I looked at the key and the not-so-subtle smirk on his face and said, "This car is for the mayor's secretary. If there's anything the least bit wrong with it you'll be hanging off the back end of a city garbage truck tomorrow."

The smirk dropped from his face. He took the key back from my fingers.

"Oh," he said, "I just noticed the number on the tag. It

says 49. That's the wrong car. It's supposed to be 94. Wait a minute. I'll get it."

Moe walked straight back into the office and out again. He handed me the key to car 94, without the least bit of good humor. I signed the log book.

My lies had paid off again. Car 94 was a brand new air conditioned Chevy sedan with tinted glass. My only misgiving was that the mayor's secretary might somehow end up with car 49. Not to worry, Tommy Lee would take care of that if it happened.

I headed to Bertha Street. I had some fast sleight of hand to arrange. Tiny Glover truly was my closest contact to the black community. I could only hope for his help. It didn't seem right to come that close and not drop in on John Glover so I parked the car and tapped on his door. He met me with a big smile and a handshake and Mrs. Glover hugged my neck. The story with their pictures was in all the morning papers and was on every TV news program in the area. The Glovers had become celebrities of the moment. Mr. Glover couldn't read the newspaper articles but he could see the pictures of him and his wife. Even though Mrs. Glover and some of the members of his church had read him the newspaper stories already, he asked me to read the front page article to him again. He handed me the paper.

"They didn't put your name in the paper, Mr. Hayes," he said. "Here you are right here in the picture and you're the one what brought all this about. It don't seem right that they left your name out."

I looked at the front page picture. It surprised me, and you probably wouldn't recognize either of us unless you were looking for us but sure enough, there I was standing in the background next to Johnny Mae. I assured Mr. Glover I was very happy to remain in the background behind the scenes.

My reward I told him was in seeing things work out well for him.

"Well, God bless you, Mr. Hayes," he kept saying and I truly hoped that He did. Otherwise I might be riding my motorcycle out of town for good.

Mrs. Glover showed me the pastries that neighbors and friends had brought them in celebration. I had a piece of coconut cake and a cup of coffee with them before I went over to talk with Tiny.

"Mr. Glover," I said, "Tiny Glover across the street tells me he's related to you. Is that right?"

I guess I couldn't have said a worse thing. Mr. Glover got a very dark look in his eyes and he set his jaw. He said, "I don't know nobody named Tiny Glover."

I knew that couldn't be true but all I could say was, "I'm sorry, I must have misunderstood what he said." I tried to smile and return the atmosphere to its previous high spirits but it was no use. I said my goodbyes to Mr. and Mrs. Glover and walked out on the porch. Mrs. Glover stopped me at the steps.

She said softly to me, "We don't talk about Tiny. It happened a long time ago."

"I'm sorry," I said, "I didn't know."

"Of course you didn't, darling," she said. "Don't think no more about it." She looked at me with a coy smile. "I talked with Johnny Mae last night after she got back to Atlanta, Mr. Hayes. Could be she's got the sweets on you."

"Mrs. Glover," I said, "You're going to make me blush." But I hoped she was right.

I couldn't stop thinking about what John Glover had said as I walked up on Tiny's porch and sat down in a wooden chair facing him.

"Frank, my man," he said, "folks around here are sayin'

you got the power to change the heart of a sinner. Some say you might be able to walk on water."

"That's all bullshit, Tiny. I just gave the mayor a new wagon to pull and I don't even know what the wagon is carrying or where he's going with it. Right now I need your help."

Tiny got serious. "What you need from me, Frank?"

I told Tiny the whole story of how I had gotten the mayor involved, where we were now, and the direction the whole thing seemed to be heading. He started laughing before I got started good and he was still laughing after I finished. He got up and went into his house and came back with a corked bottle of clear liquid.

"Here, Frank." He handed me the bottle. "Have a drink of this and relax. We'll figure this whole thing out."

I sniffed at the bottle delicately. It was moonshine whiskey. White lightning.

"It won't hurt you," he said. "Go on. Take a big snort. We gon' both need a drink."

Not wanting to appear to be afraid of the bargain I seemed to be entering, I turned up the bottle and took a big swallow. As the gulp went down I at first didn't think I would be able to breathe. But then I decided no, I could breathe but I would probably breathe flames. The burn moved from my throat, down my chest and settled in my stomach.

"Give it a minute," he said. "It'll be worth it."

After about two minutes, all of a sudden it seemed as if my mind cleared of worry. I was now confident and happy to be . . . just happy to be.

"That's pretty good," I said.

"Now take another sip," he said, "just a sip."

I wanted to take another slug but I did what Tiny said and took a sip that just slid over my tongue, around the back of my mouth and down my throat.

"The trick is," Tiny said, "to take just the right amount real slow. Just keep that good feeling so that you thinkin' clear. Don't guzzle it down and get yo' self all drunk an' out o' control. It's the difference between them that knows how to drink an' them that don't. It's somethin' I learned in prison."

Tiny took a little sip and was quiet for several moments.

"Now you tell me," he said, "how you need me to help you."

"I need a black leader who knows what's going on in the community to serve on the mayor's task force on housing. On this project he calls Operation Breakthrough. Somebody the black community respects."

"Somebody who can deal with white businessmen an' politicians." Tiny said.

"That's right. I don't know what the mayor really wants to happen but there might be some good that can come out of it."

"The mayor wants to look like a good an' wise man," Tiny said.

"He could have fooled me," I said.

"But he don't know how to look good an' wise because he ain't."

I laughed. "So how do we make him look good and wise?"

"You already know that, Frank. That's how you got the ol' man his house back. You got to tell Tommy Lee what to do, but you gotta make 'im think it's all his idea, an' that it's good for him. You got to drop a little trail of crumbs for him to follow."

"I don't know if I can keep making up stories. It's getting too complicated. I've got to have some of it be true."

"You exactly right," Tiny said. "A lie ain't no good if it looks like a lie. Put just enough truth in it that it all looks true."

He took a small sip from the bottle and sat quietly for about thirty seconds. "The man you want to speak for the black community is Reverend Jerome Brown."

"Where do I find him?"

"Right across the street. He's the preacher at the St. James A.M.E. Church."

"You think he's the one?" I said looking at the unimposing little church.

"He's the one. You tell him the truth like you told me. You can trust him to work with you. He's a humble man. He speaks the truth an' he knows how to say it without insultin' nobody."

"OK," I said. "What about the NAACP?"

"After you talk with 'Rome you get the Atlanta telephone book an' find the number for the NAACP." He chuckled to himself.

"There's got to be more to it than that."

"You tell 'em you work for Tommy Gun Tyler an' he wants you to make a deal. You tell 'em to come to the St. James A.M.E. Church on Flewellyn Drive an' meet with you an' The Reverend Jerome Brown. 'Rome will vouch for you."

Tiny handed me the bottle. "Take just a little sip now. Just a little at a time."

I took another sip and sat quietly until I felt my brain respond.

"Don't you tell them NAACP folks everthing, like you told me," Tiny said. "They got they own reasons for coming down here, an' we want 'em to work for us, not for theyselves. You tell 'em the same kind of lie you told the mayor, only make it sound right for them. They won't trust you, so you use that too. You work it out with 'Rome befo' they get here."

"You say he's a preacher?"

"He carries th' word of God with 'im."

"All right," I said. Somehow it all seemed so reasonable. If I could just keep my head this clear. "Why are you helping me like this?" I asked.

"I got a debt to pay," Tiny said. "I set here every day trying to figure some way to pay it. Then you come along like some kind of white angel."

I had to laugh. Tiny laughed too.

"A lyin' white angel," he said laughing. "But you know, in the Bible angels comes in many forms."

"I'm not any angel," I said. "In fact I'm often ashamed of how bad I am."

Tiny looked at me and smiled. "You not bad, Frank. You might know bad when you see it but you not bad. You lookin' at bad right now."

"I can't see it, Tiny. You're doing the right thing. You're helping me. You're helping your neighbors."

"I'm gon' tell you somethin', Frank. Because I truly believe you was sent here by God to help me."

"Tiny, you've had too much to drink." I wasn't kidding.

"No, Frank. I'm tellin' you the truth. You don't see the whole picture that's here. I'm gon' show you some things you don't see right now. I'm not drunk and I'm not crazy. I'm gon' tell you the truth an' you got to be able to deal with it."

"If I'm the angel you say I am, then I should be able to handle it."

"That old man over there." He nodded his head toward John Glover's house. "That old man over there is my father. He ain't spoke to me in twenty-five years."

"But, why?" I asked.

"Because twenty-five years ago, right there in his front yard I shot and killed my wife, a woman that him and my mamma had knowed all her life, a woman he loved like his own daughter and that was the mother of their grandbaby."

"How did it happen?"

"I was a young fool. More wild and more fool than them boys you met here the other day. Just like them I wasn't afraid of nothin'. I was strong and worked hard an' I loved that woman. She got with child an' I was happy as a man could be. But when that child was born I knowed it couldn't be mine. It had skin about as white as yours. An' look at me. I'm black as midnight. It changed me. I was all full of hate. I tried to make her tell me whose child it was. She said it wasn't true. That it was my baby, mine and hers. But I knowed it couldn't be."

"Oh Jesus, Tiny." I wasn't sure I could hear this but I couldn't make him stop. He wanted me to know. I reached for the bottle to take a bigger drink but he put his hand on mine and set the bottle aside.

"My wife Esther worked 'til she was along with child. In them days there wasn't but one kind of work a colored girl could do, an' that was to be a cook or a maid or a nurse or a housekeeper for white folks. The white folks my wife worked for was rich an' they had some boys, some young men about her age that still lived at home. I thought in my mind it had to be one of them. She was makin' good money an' I figured out that I knowed the reason she was makin' good money . . . money that was too good. I got to drinkin' an' I got my hands on a gun, a pistol. I told her I was gon' kill all them white boys unless she told me which one it was, an' then I would just kill him. The old man tried to talk sense into me, and my mamma too. But I was too full of hate to listen. He tried to take the pistol away from me. I hit him on the head and knocked him out. Then Esther tried to pull it away from me an' the gun went off. It shot her through the heart an' killed her dead, right over there in the front yard of that house. She was dead even befo' I could tell her I was sorry.

"Every day for twenty-five years I've wanted to take back that one day in my life so I could undo what I did. I went to prison for it an' served eighteen years. I come out an' I been livin' here for the past seven years tryin' every day to find a way to pay my debt to my father an' my mamma an' my daughter. My father won't speak to me. My mamma has to talk to me behind his back so he won't know. An' my daughter don't know I'm her daddy. I don't guess I am her daddy any more. I guess I done give up the right to that because of what I done."

I'm not a crying kind of person but I have to tell you, as Tiny told me his story I was holding back the tears.

"An' then you come along, Frank. Seven years to the day from when I got out of prison an' come back here. I ain't never told that story to nobody befo'. But it was clear to me that I was suppose to tell it to you. Here," he said, handing me the bottle.

I shook my head and refused the drink.

"So you see, Frank, you not bad. You been sent here to help a bad man, an' a innocent girl that ain't got no daddy."

"Your daughter?" I asked. "What can I do for your daughter? She must be a grown woman now."

"She's all full of hate, Frank, because of me. She growed up without her mamma or her daddy, not knowin' who she is. She's mad at ever'thing and ever'body. I think you can take that hate away from her."

"Tiny, I'm not some messenger from God."

"No, Frank, you just a man."

"You're talking in riddles, Tiny."

"It's Johnny Mae, Frank. It's Johnny Mae that needs you. I can't help her but maybe you can."

My head was spinning and I didn't think it was from the liquor. I shook it trying to clear my thoughts. Johnny Mae was

Tiny's daughter?

"Tiny, Johnny Mae's skin is not that light. She's as brown as maple syrup."

"I told you I was a fool. I didn' really know nothin' about newborn babies. Mamma tried to tell me that colored children is oftentimes light skinned when they born. But I was too full of hate an' anger to listen. I thought she was just tryin' to cover up. Johnny Mae was light skinned right at first. As time went on she got darker and darker. But by then it was too late. I had done killed her mother and Johnny Mae was lost to me."

I had other thoughts I couldn't say to Tiny. I thought of Johnny Mae's green eyes and the blonde and cherry red highlights in her soft hair. I didn't know if her family had come directly from Africa or if they had been Jamaican or Cuban or what. There was European blood there somewhere but it might have been fifty or a hundred years back. It might have been her father's but it didn't have to be.

"Tell me, Frank. What was you doin' seven years ago?"

I was embarrassed to say. "I was a freshman in college."

"Uh, huh. An' what you been doin' since then?"

"After college I just floated from one place to another looking for the place I wanted to be, hoping I didn't get drafted. I worked on a job putting in a water pipeline in Alabama. I operated a bulldozer for a while. The last job I had before coming to Macon was working the night shift at the state mental hospital in Milledgeville. Just jobs. Nothing worth talking about. I saw an ad in the paper for an urban beautification planner in Macon. I thought, what the hell, I like flowers and pretty things and I've had a lot of experience with manure. It sounded like the kind of job I wanted after Milledgeville . . . a nice clean, quiet office job. So I used some creative writing on the job application and to my surprise I got the job. Just an accident of fate."

"You think about that, Frank. For seven years I been here in this spot waitin', an' for seven years you been growin' an' floatin' about like a dandelion seed blowed by the wind, lookin' for a place to light. If God wanted you in that war, you would be there. You gon' try to tell me it was just a accident you ended up on my front porch?"

Our rambling speculations into the science of chance and probability and the will of God were interrupted by the arrival of the same group of bad boys I had escaped from the first time I came to Tiny's house. It was raining again and they ran from their car to the front porch laughing and horsing around. Their attitudes had changed. They were no longer hostile toward me. Good deeds have their reward. The one called Skeeter picked up the newspaper that lay on the floor next to Tiny.

"Hey, look at this, man. Here's a picture of old man Glover at City Hall with the mayor."

He looked more closely at the photograph and pointed at the picture.

"Look here, here's Frankie boy too. And look who he's standing next to. It's Johnny Mae."

They all made oooing sounds and started a round of taunts at my expense.

"I think Frank's got a hard on for Johnny Mae."

"Ooo Ooo."

"There's nothing between me and Johnny Mae," I said. But it was hopeless.

"No, they ain't nothin' between you but it ain't from lack of tryin', I'll bet."

Then another of them. "You ain't gon' get nothin' from Johnny Mae. That woman is too much woman for you, Frankie."

"If you ever got close to her, Frankie, she'd whup you."

"She'd grind you up, spit you out, and stomp all over yo' heart."

"Then ol' Frankie could get hisself some dark sunglasses, a slouch hat, and an old guitar and he could come down here and sit on Tiny's front porch and sing the blues because he would know what the blues is."

"Yeh, he be singin' *Frankie and Johnny*."

The laughter lasted longer than the joke.

"Hey, Frankie," Skeeter asked. "You need some body work on yo' car?"

Laughter again.

"It's in the body shop," I said.

"Ron say he ain't gon' paint it."

"Are there no secrets in this town?" I said.

"No, man, I work for Ron sometimes. Me and Tyrone will paint it for you," he said, indicating the other young man of his age. "You pay for the paint and stuff and we'll paint it for a hundred dollars."

As bad as my car looked, I had reservations about handing it over to Skeeter and Tyrone for a paint job. I looked at Tiny. He barely opened his eyes and gave me a just-perceptible nod.

"All right," I said.

"Aw'right," he said. "What color you want it?"

"The color it was, I guess."

"What? You want it faded dirty gray? How about we paint it red?"

"No red. How about British racing green? You know what that looks like?"

"'Course I know what British racing green is. You want some stripes on it?"

"No stripes."

"How 'bout some flames? We can paint you some nice flames."

"No flames. I just want a nice, even, shiny coat of British racing green."

"Aw'right man, whatever you say. I was just trying to make you look good. Maybe we throw in some new seat covers."

Chapter 10

Truth To Power

I was saved from further humiliation at the hands of the bad boys by the arrival of Rev. Jerome Brown at the St. James A.M.E. Church across the street. The rain had slacked for a few minutes and Tiny and I walked the fifty yards to the side office door of the church. We were invited in by a tall man with white hair and dark brown smooth skin. Tiny introduced me to Rev. Brown and we shook hands. He studied my eyes and face as he held gently onto my hand. I had the same feeling I had when I first met Johnny Mae, as if he were looking right into my soul. I hoped what he saw there was favorable.

I laid out the whole story to Rev. Brown as Tiny had said I should. I didn't hold any punches but I did clean up my language. Rev. Brown watched my face the entire time I talked. He gave me the feeling I was in the presence of an oracle or one of the Old Testament prophets. His voice resonated like musical notes and was soothing and hypnotic when he spoke.

"The Lord works in mysterious ways, does he not, Mr. Hayes? I look at Tiny and think sometimes that the Lord's ways are almost too mysterious to contemplate. Now here you come along. And Tiny says you're an angel of mercy. If you're an angel of mercy, then Tiny has to be a prophet because he has anticipated your arrival. If all this is correct, then I find myself in the presence of a miracle and the movement of the hand of the Lord upon the earth."

"Frank thinks it all come about by chance," Tiny said.

Rev. Brown looked back into my eyes and shook his head slowly. "No, it's something other than chance. I'm naturally inclined to trust the gifts the Lord sends us, and I think we should make the most of those gifts so that we may show our thanks to Him. So, Mr. Hayes, what plan of campaign do you propose to lead the forces of righteousness in victory over the dark forces that are oppressing my people?"

I described my plan to Rev. Brown as well as I had formulated it at that point. Basically, the mayor and the task force had to believe that powerful outside forces were watching and poised to strike inside the city should the reforms and initiatives he had begun not be carried through. A visit from the NAACP would represent such a threat.

"'And ye shall compass the city, all ye men of war, and go round about the city once.' I can hear the trumpets now as Joshua's forces circle the walls of Jericho," Rev. Brown said.

"That's the idea," I said. "Only, we want to avoid the part about the city being destroyed."

Rev. Brown agreed to serve on the task force and to recommend other black representatives to serve, so long as all members served and voted equally. That seemed fair enough to me. I left Rev. Jerome Brown who preferred that I call him 'Rome, with the task of getting the NAACP representatives to meet with us.

I drove my brand new air conditioned Chevy back to City Hall. The rain had stopped and the sun was out. The humidity stood at about 99 percent and the temperature, according to the bank sign next door, was 98 degrees. I was wet with sweat before I got inside to my office. I called my landlord to complain again about my broken air conditioner and learned to my surprise that it had been repaired. A clear pattern had emerged. Every time I went to Bertha Street to do a good deed I was rewarded by something good happening to me.

I walked down the hall to Craig Linder's office and reported to him that I had approached the Rev. Jerome Brown about serving on the mayor's task force and he had indicated he would be willing.

"Yeah, I know 'Rome," Craig said. "He's a good choice. I think we can recommend him to the mayor. Let me run it by Willingham first."

I didn't exactly like the sound of that. I thought it was my responsibility to recruit community representatives. But it occurred to me that I probably had been naive about the amount of independence I might have. Later that day I was called to a meeting with Linder, Willingham and the mayor to discuss progress so far. When I arrived, the three of them were standing over a conference table with maps and papers spread out over it. They looked up briefly as I came into the room.

"Come on in, Frankie," Craig said.

"So, basically, what you're proposing is a land swap," Tommy Lee was saying.

"Technically we can't use that terminology," Willingham said. "Technically, the purchase of parcels in the recreational development area will be accompanied by a guaranteed first choice on housing in the Hanover Hills development."

I wasn't used to reading subdivision maps and it took me a few minutes to get an orientation on the objects of their discussion. When I did, my stomach turned over.

"This is the proposed golf course development in east Macon, right?" I asked, waving my fingers over one of the maps. Willingham looked up at me like I was an annoyance, an irritating yellow jacket buzzing the food at his picnic. Craig pulled me aside and spoke quietly to me as the mayor and Willingham continued their conversation.

"What the Operation Breakthrough task force is proposing," Craig said, "is that we put resources into east

Macon to give that area an economic boost. We would do that by designating the area as a major recreational development."

"You mean a golf course," I said.

"A golf course would be part of it. A Lake Arrowhead recreational area would also be part of it. The development would allow the cleanup of a lot of substandard housing that's blighting the area. In return, property owners in the development area would be given the opportunity to purchase brand new HUD financed moderate income housing in the Hanover Hills subdivision that will be built off Eisenhower Parkway." Craig pointed to the other map on the table.

"So this will be a forced relocation?" I asked.

Craig looked at me with disappointment showing on his face. "There's only so much land available in the city. If we're going to offer new, decent housing, it has to go somewhere. Both these areas are currently underdeveloped. They have inadequate water and sewer and the streets are substandard. These two developments together will increase the single family dwellings in the city by nine hundred units. That's a lot of new affordable housing. And that's just phase one."

"What will be the price of a typical house?" I asked.

"$35,000 to $50,000," Craig said. "It's low interest rate and low down payment, government guaranteed thirty-year loans."

"What's that a month?" I said. "$350? How is someone like Mr. Glover going to make a $350 house payment out of a Social Security check of $188? He's eighty-nine years old. How is he going to be approved for a thirty-year loan? You're talking about destroying his neighborhood and his life. How long has this been planned?" I indicated the maps. "All this wasn't worked up since yesterday. What? We take Willingham's master real estate development plan and call it Operation Breakthrough?"

I noticed too late that I was the only one in the room talking.

"That's very irresponsible talk," Craig said.

"Maybe you're not the right man for this job," Willingham said.

"We're all men here, right?" I said. "Is this what you want, Tommy Lee?"

"There's no way we can make every single case fit, Frank," Tommy Lee said. "We have to do the best we can for the most people."

"Then, this is not it. This is the same old game we see all the time. Condemn the property, seize the property, sell the property at ten cents on the dollar. Guess who buys it? The developers. Develop the property, sell the property at ten times . . . a thousand times . . . its purchase price. The government finances it and guarantees it. The bankers and developers get rich. The poor property owners get screwed. What do you get out of it, Tommy Lee?"

"Get him out of here, Craig." The mayor was pissed at me.

"How many realtors, bankers and developers are on the planning and zoning commission?" I said. "You are, aren't you, Willingham? You ought to be thinking real hard about Mr. and Mrs. Glover. I think there's still a debt unpaid there. They live in this east Macon development area."

Willingham had blanched white. I think he would have killed me right there if there hadn't been witnesses.

"Damn it! Get him out of here, Craig, or I'll call the guard." The mayor was headed my way, fists clenched.

Craig was pulling me with one hand and opening the door with the other. "Come on, Frankie. You've made your point."

I handed the key to city car 94 to the mayor's secretary as I passed her desk on the way out. I knew I wouldn't be needing it any longer. "It's parked right outside," I said, and smiled at her. "It's a great car. You'll enjoy it."

Craig didn't say a word until we were upstairs and in his office behind closed doors. But I knew what he was thinking.

"Frank, you stupid son of a bitch, do you know what you just did?"

"Gave my opinion. Isn't that my right as a member of the project team?"

"Those weren't opinions. Those were insults and accusations. That was the most unprofessional behavior I've ever seen. You embarrassed me. You embarrassed and insulted the mayor and one of the most important businessmen in the city, who also just happens to be on the Planning Commission that signs your paycheck. What did you think you were doing?"

"Who's fooling whom here, Craig? You're talking about using the power of the city to seize property from the hands of poor residents so you can put in a golf course for the amusement of rich white folks. How many of the poor residents of east Macon do you think will end up in the new houses in Hanover Hills? Not one in a hundred. What happens to the other ninety-nine? They'll end up in some poor neighborhood paying rent to a landlord instead of living in the home they already owned. It's the same old dirty game."

"That's a very one-sided point of view. Who are you, Robin Hood?"

"How many sides are there? Who are you, the government lackey for the real estate developers? Where is your professional integrity, your duty to the citizens?"

"I'm very aware of my duty. Who made you the moral conscience of the city, Frank? You were hired to administer the beautification program, to meet with the garden club, and design parks, not to stir up trouble. What makes you think your judgment is better than everyone else's?"

"I use my brain and keep my eyes open, Craig. I think I'm performing my duty as a public employee to uphold the laws that govern us, particularly the right to equal protection of the law for everyone. I don't think the law gives Stafford Willingham the right to take John Glover's property just because Stafford and his friends think a golf course would be a swell idea. I don't know anywhere in the code of ethics where it tells me to turn a blind eye."

"You're impossible," he said, turning his back on me and leaning against the windowsill. He turned back around to face me. "Look, I think you had better get out of here for a while. Take the rest of today and tomorrow off to give yourself some time to think about this and let everything cool off. Take next week off. I'll see what I can do to smooth things over but I'm afraid you may have gone too far. If I were you, Frank, I'd be looking for another job. But I'm not giving up on it. I'll see what I can do."

I didn't know whether to tell him to forget about trying to patch things up or to beg him to keep my job for me. I thought about my car repair, my new motorcycle and my new loan, and wondered if I had lost my mind. But that was only a passing reaction. I knew I had told the truth and we would all have to live with it. I could find another job. At least Mr. and Mrs. Glover had their house back along with their dignity and a happy memory.

This was one of those cases where I did have to take it like a man. I took the bus home and got my motorcycle. Thank God the rain had stopped. I drove to Bertha Street to break the news to Tiny and 'Rome. We sat on Tiny's front porch and I told them the whole story, except the part about Willingham's unpaid debt.

Tiny laughed and slapped me on the leg. "You got no idea how many folks would like to have heard that."

"Any of them want to hire me?" I said.

"Somethin' will come along," Tiny said. "No need to worry about that. You just be true to yo' self. Take a good long ride on yo' motorcycle. You done the right thing."

"I think perhaps Tiny was wrong about you," 'Rome said. "You're not an angel of mercy. You're an angel of vengeance. *'The righteous shall rejoice when he seeth the vengeance: he shall wash his feet in the blood of the wicked.'"*

"I'm going to be no help to you now at City Hall," I told 'Rome.

We talked and laughed for a while longer until 'Rome had to leave. Then it was just Tiny and me on his porch again.

"You like barbecue, Frank?"

"I could eat it every day if it's good barbecue."

"I used to cook barbecue for a thousand men when I was in prison. It was so good the prison used to sell it to folks on the outside that wanted it. Some weekends we'd sell $2,000 or more of my barbecue. Cookin' barbecue's kind of like drinkin' whiskey. For it to be good, you got to know what you doin', an' you got to be patient."

"You ever thought about opening a barbecue place?" I asked.

"Lots of times. But a fifty-year-old black ex-con can't get no line of credit. I need a partner. He need to be smart, an' honest. Be best if he be some kind of angel."

We both laughed.

"You think about it," he said.

Chapter 11

Deep In Love

I got out of bed that Friday morning with a new perspective. Being unemployed can have an exhilarating effect. Technically I wasn't unemployed. I was taking a day of leave time. But there was no doubt in my mind that technicality soon would be replaced by a pink slip. I knew that Linder and Willingham and the mayor would never trust me again and would never again see me as anything but a troublemaker and an inferior being. I also knew I could never reconcile my personal views of right and wrong with what the people I had been working for viewed as normal everyday business. Actually I didn't give a damn that I was about to be fired. In fact, not only did I not give a damn, I was feeling positively happy. I was a free man. Free to go anywhere and do anything I wanted. A free man with a new motorcycle and money. I realized that for the first time since I came to work for the city I no longer felt dirty. It helped that I had about a thousand dollars in the bank and next week was payday. It may have also helped that the weekend was coming up and the reality of my altered status would not really sink in until Monday when I didn't go back to work. But that was not on my mind that Friday morning.

I had a whole lot of things to think about and sort out. At the very top of the list was the fact that last week I had no woman in my life and now all of a sudden I was mixed up with a married woman. Mixed up was the right word for me. I was having sex with Shirley Willingham but my thoughts kept returning to Johnny Mae Glover. What was there about

Johnny Mae that was so appealing to me? Why couldn't I get her off my mind? She was a beautiful woman for sure, but I saw beautiful women every day. And what did Tiny mean when he said I could take the anger and hate out of her? I'm not some kind of white angel, regardless of what Tiny thought.

About lunchtime I picked up a couple of bottles of beer and a sandwich and rode my bike down to the riverfront to the spot I had seen the two students making love in the woods. It was quiet. Nothing was going on at the dump-and-fill operation across the river. I sat in the shade of a tree and looked out across the water. A pair of ducks were swimming in the calm backwater of the river. An old man and a young girl were fishing from the far bank. She looked up at one point and waved to me. I waved back.

I don't know what I thought would happen if I sat there thinking. Perhaps I would come to see things more clearly. But the only thing that came to me clearly was Johnny Mae's face. I could see it angry, her eyes sparkling, and I could see her softer, considering me. I took out the photo and looked at it. I had never been involved with a black girl. Maybe that was her attraction. No, there were lots of beautiful black women who didn't have this kind of hold on me. Maybe it wasn't Johnny Mae. Maybe I was feeling sorry for her, sorry for her grandparents, sorry for Tiny, sorry for the things that were done to them, for the things that happened to them.

But what I was feeling was not sorrow or pity. I could recognize it clearly enough to know I was being drawn to Johnny Mae by something strong. When I thought of her I didn't think sorrow. I thought happy. I thought . . . I was in love with her. I didn't know why. I didn't really care why. I don't even know if there is a why. The why is because of something indefinable. The only thing I knew for certain was that I had to find out if it was true and if it was possible she could love me too or could come to love me if she had the chance.

I didn't know where in Atlanta Johnny Mae lived but I had a phone number. When I got back to my apartment I threw a change of clothes and a toothbrush into a bed roll and tied it on the bike. I didn't have a plan. I didn't have any reason to think Johnny Mae would want to see me or would even talk to me, but it didn't matter. If there was a way, I would see her, or at the least I would give it a damn good try. If I tried and she could honestly tell me she wasn't interested in me, then I would just go somewhere, feel sorry for myself and try to get over her. But I knew I had seen something in her eyes, something softer, something forgiving in the little bit of a smile she had shown me. Even the way she stared hard and unflinching at me told me she was considering for herself just what I was. I had to believe she really could see into me. That was my only real hope.

I had been to Atlanta enough times to know the major streets and landmarks. I rode in on I-75 and arrived in downtown Atlanta mid-afternoon. The ride up from Macon was soothing and exhilarating. The farther I got away from there, the better I felt. I sat in the traffic on Peachtree Street and looked at myself in the office windows. I was cool. As men in neat, clean suits walked by me on the sidewalk, the low rumble of my idling engine, almost like some tribal drum, awoke something in them, some mixture of envy and fear. Some of them would smile openly. Some would wave or nod. Others would look down their noses at my tan, windblown look, but I knew that either from fear or envy they were feeling goose bumps inside those suits. The women were pretty much the same. Some turned their noses up in disgust, but others threw me meaningful looks and smiles and body language that needed no translation.

I stopped at a pay phone and called Johnny Mae's number. There was no answer. It was early. She was probably at work. Or did she say she worked nights? I couldn't remember if she said. I stopped in a diner on Peachtree and had a cup of coffee and a slice of pie. I wasn't doing anything but I was having fun. I rode past the Fox Theater. I thought about all the famous movies and celebrities who had appeared there. I would liked to have seen Elizabeth Taylor's violet eyes on the big screen. I wondered where violet eyes come from. Where do green eyes come from? I didn't know, but I knew some green eyes I desperately wanted to look into.

It was after five o'clock. I stopped at Lenox Square and called Johnny Mae's number again. I let it ring too many times and was about to hang up when the phone picked up.

"Hey, honey," a breathy female voice said. "I'm here. I just got home. What time is it?"

"Is Johnny Mae in?" I asked somewhat uncertainly.

"Johnny Mae? Oh, I'm sorry. I thought you were someone else. This is her roommate, Reggie. Who is this? This Anthony?"

Anthony? Jesus. I should have expected she would have men in her life. I suddenly felt as if I might be making a big mistake.

"This is Frank. What time do you expect Johnny Mae home?"

"She ought to be here about anytime now. Is she expecting you to call?"

"No. I just dropped in from out of town. She doesn't know I'm coming."

"Oh. Well, that'll be a nice surprise. You can come on over. She ought to be here in a little bit."

"I don't have her address. I've just got her phone number. I'm at Lenox Square now. Am I anywhere close?"

"Oh, yeah, honey. You're not more than ten minutes in light traffic, but it might take you half an hour in the five o'clock rush hour. Get off Peachtree and come by the side streets."

Reggie gave me directions and I pulled to a stop in front of their apartment building within twenty minutes. I hadn't even looked at myself. I must be a mess after being on the bike for the better part of three hours. I ran my fingers through my hair as I walked up the sidewalk. I knocked lightly on the door. Nothing. I knocked again. I could hear a voice on the other side of the door. It sounded like the voice I had talked with on the phone. Still nothing happened. I waited until I thought no one was going to answer. The door swung open.

I was greeted by a knockout of a beautiful black woman who looked dressed for a night out. The expression that met me looked ready to be angry with me but it slid into something much friendlier.

"So, you're the man who's got my roommate all upset?"

"Reggie, cut it out." It was Johnny Mae's voice from somewhere behind Reggie.

"I ought to be mad at you, Frank Hayes," Reggie said. "You had me invite you over here without telling me everything I needed to know." She looked me over in an undisguised appraisal. "Johnny Mae, honey, you didn't tell me he's so good looking. No wonder he's got you so upset." She stepped back from the door. "Well, come on in here and get it over with. You can't stand out on the doorstep all night. You two either fight it out or kiss and make up."

I stepped inside. Johnny Mae was on the other side of the living room looking out the window, half-turned away from me. She was wearing a white nurse's uniform. I couldn't tell if she was going to work or just getting off. She wouldn't look at me. It didn't look good.

Reggie looked at me again and out the door. "How did you get here, honey? Are you on that motorcycle? I love motorcycles. Johnny Mae, he's on a big old motorcycle. Johnny Mae, why don't you let me have this one? I'll trade you Lionel for him."

"Take him," Johnny Mae said.

Reggie looked at my eyes and smiled a knowing smile. "Don't you pay any attention to Johnny Mae. There is no way she could not be glad to see a good-looking man like you." She moved to pick up a suitcase and overnight case sitting near the door. "I'm going to be leaving, so you two can do whatever it is you're going to do. You got a place to stay, Frank?"

"No, I just got in town."

"Well, honey, you can have my room if she won't let you stay with her. And if you do sleep in my room, don't change the sheets, OK?" She reached up and kissed my cheek. "I like the smell of a man in my bed, especially one as long and tall and good looking as you are. Johnny Mae, honey, is he long all over?" She looked at me and winked. She looked at Johnny Mae, but Johnny Mae didn't say anything or acknowledge her. "Why, I don't believe she knows," Reggie said, coyly. "I'll just leave you two to figure it all out. Johnny Mae, honey, I'll call before I come back. I can stay away past Monday if everything works out OK between you and Frank. Oh," she said with a sudden recognition, "it's Frankie and Johnny all over again. You wouldn't do her no wrong, would you Frankie?"

I shook my head. "No, I wouldn't."

She squeezed my hand. "No, I don't think you would. But if you do, I'll whup your ass." She smiled. "You sure you don't want to go with me, Frank? I'm going to a Jethro Tull concert in Birmingham. We could have a really good time on your motorcycle."

I shook my head and smiled. "Sorry."

"Mmm, hmm. If you can resist me, I guess you really can be true to Johnny Mae. You be good to her."

The door closed behind her and we were left alone together. Johnny Mae still hadn't moved, looked at me, or said anything to me. After thinking about her constantly for most of the day, I couldn't think of what to say to her. It seemed like a very long time before either one of us said anything. She hadn't moved and I hadn't moved. I took that as a good sign. She hadn't kicked me out.

"What are you doing here?"

The hardness was still in her voice. I had to get through that some way.

"I came to Atlanta to buy myself some clothes."

She looked at me with those angry eyes. I smiled and shrugged. She ran her eyes over me.

"Well, you need some." She looked away again. "You got no business coming here."

I tried to be calm. I felt like begging. "I thought maybe if I tried I could make you fall in love with me."

She flinched.

"Is that what you thought? Did you think I would be that easy? You just come in here, sweet-talk me, tell me what you think I want to hear, and I would just fall for you?"

"I never thought it would be easy. Maybe not even possible. But I would never lie to you."

"I don't know if I can believe you. I don't know if I even want to talk to you. I'm still very angry about my grand-parents."

"I only tried to help them."

"I could have helped them. I would have. He never told me how much trouble he was in."

"He's a proud man. He wanted to solve the problem himself, on his own. It's part of being a man."

"And what do you want from me now? Do you want me to

pay you for what you did? Is that part of being a man?"

"It has nothing to do with what I did for them. That's just the way I met you."

"Well, what do you want from me?"

"Just the chance to be near you. I want you to know me. I haven't been able to stop thinking about you since that first day."

"What would I want with a white boy like you?"

"That's what you'll have to decide. Just give me a chance. I'm not a white boy. I'm just a man who can't stop thinking about you. I wouldn't ever do you any harm."

She flinched again and I thought she was going to yell at me or throw something.

"I have to go to work." She picked up her purse and her nurse's cap from a side table. "You need to be gone from here when I get back."

The door closed behind her and I was alone in her apartment. She still hadn't thrown me out. She hadn't smiled or looked me in the eye or spoken a kind word, but she hadn't actually told me to get out. I was afraid to leave. I was afraid the door would lock and I couldn't get back in.

I looked at myself in her bathroom mirror. I was a handsome devil but I needed to wash the road grime off me and out of my hair. I propped the front door open long enough to get my bedroll from the bike and to chain the bike to a lamp post.

Their bathroom looked like a girl's bathroom. It had girl things in it, some of which I couldn't even identify. I had a shower and shampoo and ran my dirty clothes through their washer and dryer. I found some things I recognized in the refrigerator and made myself a couple of sandwiches. They had plenty of wine but no beer. I forced myself to have a couple of glasses of something pink and sweet which was pretty good.

The first three hours went fast, but after that I was getting tired. I figured it would probably be an eight hour shift but was only guessing. I remembered what Tiny had said about drinking and decided it should work with wine too. I lay down on Reggie's bed and sipped the wine slowly. A sip didn't seem to work so I tried a whole glass. Then I sipped the next two glasses. After a while I seemed to rise up from my body. I was having wonderful visions of Johnny Mae and me. I could see her green eyes and I could feel her touch as if it were real. In my dreams I talked with her and told her all the things I wanted her to hear but was afraid she would never let me tell her.

Sometime in the darkness I heard the front door open and close. I could hear movement and see lights and shadows. I knew she would be tired. And I didn't want to argue in the middle of the night. I didn't get up. I heard the shower in the bathroom. After a while it was dark and quiet again. I went back to sleep and dreamed again. Sometime later in my dreams I felt my hand being taken and I was being led somewhere through the dark. Then I was awake and wasn't dreaming. I was in Johnny Mae's bed in her arms and she was crying and making love to me. I wanted to ask why she was crying, to try to mend it, but I just held her in my arms and let her cry.

I couldn't do justice to the rest of that night by trying to describe the physical sensations and the emotions I experienced. I can only tell you it was like no other experience I have ever had. It was more intense and more personal, more exciting, more intimate and sweeter than I had ever had with a woman. It wasn't just the sexual part, though that was breathtaking. There was a union, a grasping and holding on, a melding that was more than sexual. There was a total giving over of emotion, a total immersion that neither of us wanted to part from.

When I awoke, sunlight was coming through the window and I was alone in bed. I knew she had been there. I could still feel her. I could smell the fragrance of her. I closed my eyes and smelled the pillow where she had lain. I opened my eyes and she was standing beside me wearing a clingy nylon something-dainty and holding a tray with fruit and orange juice.

"Here," she said, smiling at me with those beautiful green eyes on me, "you're going to need your strength."

She set the tray on a chair next to the bed. I wrapped an arm between her legs and pulled her onto the bed with me. We made love again. She smiled at me and said sweet things about what a man I was, the kind of things you want to hear whether they're true or not. I lay next to her and told her what a woman she was. All the things I said were true. We drank coffee and orange juice and ate ripe, sweet sliced peaches. If there was any way I could have managed it I don't think I would ever have gotten out of her bed.

I told her everything I had been wanting to say to her, everything about me, everything I had thought about her from the first time I had seen her. She listened and watched my eyes and my lips. Sometimes she kissed my fingers or my lips or my chest. I told her about the dirty dealings in City Hall, about the foolish things I had said to the mayor about his housing plan, and I told her about getting fired. She laughed out loud and I laughed too. I couldn't believe I was with her and I was making her happy.

I didn't mention the name of Stafford Willingham. I wanted to keep the conversation away from any mention of him. I didn't tell her of my suspicions about Willingham and her mother. I didn't tell her about Tiny and her mother. I knew that someday I would have to tell her those things, but this was not the day. I didn't tell her about Shirley Willingham. I would never tell her about that.

We went out to a restaurant for lunch, one of those trendy places where young successful people go. I didn't want to take my eyes from her or let go of her hand. She had smiles on her lips and happiness in her eyes when she looked at me.

"Frank," she said, smiling self-consciously, "behave yourself. People are looking at us."

People were looking at us. Most were looking the way people look at lovers, with that kind of dreamy faraway look in their eyes, wishing they were in love the way we were. Others were seeing us with irritation or disgust, their natural inclinations distorted through a pane of bigotry kept dirty by the demagoguery and buffoonery of people like Tommy Gun Tyler. But I had seen *Hair*. There was a new time coming. I could feel it in the air. I had seen its sunrise in Johnny Mae's eyes.

I smiled at her and kissed her hand. "They're just jealous," I said. "They all want to be in love."

"Are you in love with me?" she said.

"Yes, I am."

She held my hand and her eyes glistened with moisture.

She took me to three different stores to help me pick out clothes. I bought an Italian jacket of soft brown leather, matching boots and belt. With my blue jeans and leather I looked very European and damn handsome. I bought her a matching outfit. We stopped in one of those little photograph booths at Lenox Square and had our picture made. Riding my motorcycle on the way back we were too beautiful to be true. We would have looked good together anywhere—anywhere except where we ended up.

Johnny Mae had to work again that evening so we picked up some pasta and salads, some more fruit and wine, and went back to her apartment to spend time together before her shift at Emory Hospital. We made love again. I knew I would never get enough of her. Afterwards I held her in my arms, her head against my chest, and she talked to me. It didn't come as easy for her as it did for me. She wasn't used to baring her soul to anyone, man or woman. But bit by bit she told me about her life.

"Mamma and Poppa love me, and I love them. They did everything they could for me in their own way. But somehow there's always been something missing. They were always so much older than me. When I was in grade school and high school all the other kids had younger parents they did things with, you know? I feel like I missed that."

I knew that feeling.

"I've felt like an outsider most of my life." She held up a leg and ran her hand over it. "My color is too light for some people and too dark for others. And my eyes." She looked into mine. "You don't know how mean people can be."

I took her face in my hand. "I wish my skin were the color or yours. And no one has eyes like yours. They're the most beautiful eyes I've ever seen. I've never seen green eyes before."

She kissed my fingers. "Not everyone sees them that way. They look at my green eyes and they see white blood and they don't like it."

"You mustn't be mad at all white people for the way some white people are. It makes no difference to me."

"Frank, honey, you are so naive. It's not just white people. Colored people can be just as prejudiced as white people. Don't you know that?"

"No, I never thought about it. I thought all black people were . . ."

"Alike?" she said.

"No, not alike. I thought black people shared an identity, a sense of community or having something in common. A common sense of discrimination if nothing else."

"Discrimination can come from both directions. One time when I was in college I had this friend named Doreen. Doreen was really light skinned. She could pass for white just about anywhere. Well, Doreen and I decided to bleach our hair blonde just for fun. We wanted to look like Hollywood movie stars, you know? We both went home with Reggie to Chicago for spring break and the two of us, Doreen and I, were standing on a street corner with Reggie's brother. He's dark and has black kinky hair. So we were standing on the corner in this big northern city, further north than I had ever been, me with my brown skin and bleached blonde hair, and Doreen looking like a white girl sure enough, and Reggie's brother looking like himself. This car full of white boys comes by and one of them yells out, 'Get your black ass away from that white girl!' At first I thought they were yelling at me, and then I realized they were yelling at Reggie's brother. I was so embarrassed for him and for Doreen too, I just wanted to cry. I didn't know that kind of thing would happen in Chicago. In Macon maybe, but Chicago?

"Then we were supposed to pick up Reggie's cousin to go shopping. Only, they wouldn't let Doreen or me go to the cousin's apartment because she lived in a neighborhood where all the black people are really black. I mean, no white blood whatsoever is allowed to even walk the streets of that neighborhood. Those folks are as black as soot and they want to keep it that way. If I had showed up there with my blonde hair and Doreen looking like a white girl, anything could have happened to us."

I was pretty much in culture shock listening to Johnny Mae's story. All I could do was stare vacantly and shake my head. "I had no idea."

"There's more skin shades among colored people than you've got names for. And they can be just as mean as white people. I decided right then to dye my hair back dark and never be blonde again." She chuckled. "I can laugh about it now, but it scared me then. I never will forget going to Chicago."

"Your hair is beautiful. I wish mine were the color of yours, then we would match even more when we wear the same clothes."

"You're sweet, Frank. I've never known anyone just like you."

She cried some and I talked to her some.

"I grew up without parents too. They were murdered when I was six, and my aunt and uncle raised me. They're my only living relatives."

"Murdered? Why?" She asked. "Was the murderer caught?"

"No. The police never found out who did it or why."

"That is so strange," Johnny Mae said. "My mother was killed when I was a baby. She was shot accidentally by a drunken man in the neighborhood. That's why my grandparents raised me. I never knew my father. You and I are so much alike."

I felt almost overwhelming guilt for what I knew and was withholding from her. "Your grandparents must be very proud of you," I said.

"I always tried to make them proud. I was valedictorian of my senior class in public school in Macon and I won a scholarship to Fisk University in Nashville. Fisk is like the Harvard of black universities. I can remember how proud they were."

"Do you like nursing?"

"Yes, I do."

"Where did you go to nursing school? Was that at Fisk?"

"It was at Mahary Medical School just next door to Fisk. Very prestigious."

"You like your job?"

"Love it. I get treated like a professional."

She looked at her watch. She had to get ready to leave for work. I wanted her to stay with me but I couldn't ask her to do that.

"I'll be here when you get home," I told her.

"I'll be back as soon as I can get back," she said.

When she started out the door she stopped and looked at me.

"I think I'm in love with you, Frank."

It was hard for me to let go of her hand.

I cleaned up her place, mostly from the mess I had made. I changed her bed clothes and washed and dried her sheets and washed the dishes. I finally ran out of things to do, took a shower and lay down with a glass of wine to wait for her. I was intoxicated but it wasn't from the wine. It was from her. I awoke sometime after midnight to the sound of the front door opening. I was happy to hear her coming in.

But it wasn't Johnny Mae. There were male voices in whispered tones.

Suddenly there was a flashlight shining in my eyes blinding me. I held up my hand to block the light and tried to get up. I was wrestled to my face on the bed and I felt the cold metal of handcuffs being clipped around my wrists.

"Wait a minute," I said, trying not to panic. "Who are you? Who are you looking for?"

"Are you Frank Hayes?" a very gruff voice said.

"Yes, I'm Frank Hayes. What is this all about? How did you find me?"

"Mr. Hayes, just come along quietly and there won't be any trouble."

I was pulled to my feet. I didn't have on any pants or a shirt or any shoes. I was shoved toward the door.

"How about my clothes?" I said, trying to stop. "Can't I have some clothes? Look, at least tell me what this is all about."

"Get his pants, Arthur," the gruff voice in charge said. "There's his shirt and shoes."

"Where are you taking me?" I asked, but it was pretty obvious. "If you're police officers, you need to identify yourselves."

"You're being taken to the Bibb County jail, Mr. Hayes. You're under arrest on suspicion for the murder of Mr. Stafford Willingham."

"I haven't been anywhere near Willingham. I've been here since Friday afternoon. When was he killed?"

"Can anyone vouch for your whereabouts during the time since you left your office on Thursday morning?"

The other policeman was ransacking the apartment, looking for something.

"I rode up from Macon early yesterday afternoon. My friend here can tell you. She'll be home from work later. She's on the night shift. Please don't tear up her apartment. There's nothing here. She doesn't know anything."

"Anything about what, Mr. Hayes?"

"Anything about any murder."

"Was your friend on the night shift last night?"

"Yes."

"What time did she get home?"

"I don't know exactly. I was asleep. Three-thirty in the morning, I guess."

"You were alone until that time?"

"Yes, I was. I was here in the apartment."

"Any witnesses?"

"Not after six o'clock yesterday evening until Johnny Mae got off from work."

"This your girlfriend?"He picked up a picture of Johnny Mae from the top of a bookcase.

"Yes, that's her," I said.

"You staying with a colored girl?"

"He's staying with two colored girls," the other officer said, looking into Reggie's room. "You must be quite a man, Mr. Hayes. These your whores?"

"No, they are not. Look, I don't know anything about the murder of Stafford Willingham, and neither do these girls. I just came up for a visit."

"You can tell us all about it on the way to the Bibb County jail. Let's go. I've got to get back to Macon before morning. I've got a girlfriend there that can just hardly wait to see me."

He shoved me through the front door and into the night. People were watching. I tried to talk to someone, to tell them to tell Johnny Mae what had happened to me, but the two policemen pushed me into their car and wouldn't let me speak with anyone.

"Can I leave a note or something? She'll be worried if she comes home and I'm not here."

One of them laughed. "She'll get over it."

I didn't think she would.

Chapter 12

Good Cop / Bad Cop

Detective Melvin Miller was short for a cop but he was muscular and he carried a real gun. He had fair skin and receding sandy hair that left a round shiny head showing. Detective Miller tried to be my friend. According to him, he actually had only my best interests at heart.

"You don't look like the kind of boy who would be mixed up in a murder." Miller watched me in his rearview mirror as we pulled onto Interstate 75 and headed south. "You know you don't have to talk to us, but if you can tell us the truth about your involvement with Stafford Willingham we might be able to clear you of suspicion."

Detective Arthur Stevens was a big man. Over six feet. He had a rough complexion and dark hair. He was the one doing all the manhandling. Detective Stevens did not want to be my friend. He despised me, hated everything about me and thought I should go to the electric chair.

"Come on, Miller. Have you gone soft? He's guilty as hell. He's got those black whores working for him. You know what kind of person that is. There's no telling what he's mixed up in . . . drugs, extortion, gambling. I'll be willing to bet I can tie him to at least two other unsolved murders."

"Is that right, Frank?" Miller asked. "Are you involved in those things? Is he going to be able to connect you to other nasty business?"

"No, I'm not doing any of those things. I'm not connected with anything illegal." I adjusted my weight in the back seat of the car, trying to stop the handcuffs from cutting my wrists.

"No, I don't think you are either," Miller said. "From everything I know about you, you're a different class of person than what Detective Stevens thinks you are. He's been dealing with low life too long. He mistrusts everyone. They tell me you're a very decent fellow. You knew Willingham, didn't you?"

"I never met him outside of City Hall."

Miller's eyes shot a quick glance at me in the mirror. "That's good. That'll make it easier to clear you from this whole mess. You haven't ever been to his house or anything, have you? To a social gathering or anything?" He was looking at me again.

If they knew I had, then they knew. I had to lie and hope they didn't know.

"No," I said.

"You see?" Stevens almost jumped up from the car seat. "You see? He's a lying son of a bitch." From behind, Stevens looked a lot like a toad. And when he moved and gestured, it was a lot like a toad.

Miller shook his head. "We found your fingerprints all over his house at the lake, Frank."

Oh, Jesus.

"Can you tell us how they got there?"

"Why do you think they're my fingerprints? I've never been fingerprinted. I don't even have a fingerprint record."

"You see?" Stevens snorted. "He thinks he's a smart guy."

"We got them from your house," Miller said.

"You've been in my house?"

"Sure." Stevens grinned a mean grin at me over the back of his seat. "We've seen everything you've got. Looked at everything. Taken prints off of everything. We saw your pictures of Mrs. Willingham too, and of your colored

116

girlfriend."

The pictures. I gave the pictures to George Dolly. That means they talked with George and with Craig and probably with the mayor. They must have talked with Mr. and Mrs. Glover too and asked them troubling questions about me. Shit. What a mess. I didn't know what to do. I was worried about what Johnny Mae was going to think when she came home from work and found me gone. I needed to get word to her.

"What about the lake house, Frank?" Miller asked.

"I was at the lake house on Tuesday at the request of Mrs. Willingham. It's the only time I've ever been there. I was working with her on the parks project with the beautification commission."

Stevens laughed. "Beautification commission, my ass. You were screwing Willingham's wife."

I didn't say anything.

"Is that right, Frank? Because, if it is, it could put you in very serious conflict with Mr. Willingham. You see that, don't you?" Miller said.

I didn't say anything.

"I need you to help me, Frank," Miller said. "I'm not supposed to tell you about the evidence we have, but . . ."

"Jesus Christ, Miller," Stevens shouted, "don't tell him what we know!"

"I'm not supposed to tell you, Frank, but I know there's an explanation and I think you'll be able to tell me and we can stop spending our time investigating a dead end. We found your fingerprints on the bedposts and the headboard, the night stand, and in their bathroom. We also found pubic hair in the bedroom that we're going to have to match, and a man's hair just about the color and length of yours."

"Damn, Miller." Stevens seemed exasperated. "Why don't you just give him our whole case? Why don't you just tell him everything? Then he can lie his way out of all of it."

"He's going to find out sooner or later if he goes to trial," Miller said. "I can understand if you screwed his wife. She is one beautiful woman. But that's nothing for a reasonable boy like you to commit murder over, is it?"

I didn't say anything.

"You're going to have to talk to us if I'm going to keep you out of jail," Miller said. "I can understand about the woman. You were having sexual relations with Mrs. Willingham, weren't you? Because we have the physical evidence."

"I was at her place one time," I said. "It wasn't planned. It just happened."

"When was that?" he asked.

"Tuesday morning," I said, "from about ten until about noon."

"I can understand how something like that could happen," Miller said. "I'll have to admit to some indiscretions in my own life. It happens to a man sometimes. That doesn't make you guilty of anything but being a man." He paused. "Is there any way, when you were at the lake house with Mrs. Willingham, that she might have gotten her hands on your shotgun?"

"My shotgun?" I said. My mind was racing like mad. If they were trying to scare me, they were doing a hell of a job.

"Yeah," Miller said, "Mr. Willingham was killed with your shotgun. We know it was yours because it has your fingerprints all over it, and no one else's. Did you take your shotgun into Willingham's lake house or did you give the shotgun to anyone who could have used it to kill Mr. Willingham?"

"No. That doesn't make any sense," I said. "That shotgun's been wrapped up in the trunk of my car since I worked on a pipeline job almost a year ago. I haven't touched it since then. My car's been in the garage since Monday morning."

I saw a quick glance between Miller and Stevens. I wondered if I had told them something they didn't know or if I had confirmed what they already knew.

"Quit talking to him," Stevens said. "He's lying through his teeth. He was screwing Willingham's wife. They killed Willingham to get him out of their way so the wife could get the money and they could live happily ever after."

"That's not true, is it, Frank?"

"No."

"What did happen?" Miller said.

I didn't say anything.

Miller said, "You're going to have to talk to us, Frank, or we'll have to regard you as a serious suspect."

We rode in silence. I didn't know what to do. I knew I hadn't killed Willingham. But how did my shotgun get there? The last time I saw it, it was in the trunk of my car. I left the car with Ron at the body shop. Ron couldn't be involved in this, could he? Someone else at the body shop? Taylor. Scott Taylor's truck was at Ron's garage. Taylor or one of his men saw my car at Ron's body shop and . . . and what? Looked in my trunk? Besides, what connection did Scott Taylor have with Stafford Willingham, other than being in the general construction business?

Oh, shit. The neighborhood bad boys. Skeeter works at Ron's garage. He might have opened the trunk during the body repair, and . . . what? See the gun and take it? Then what? Would Skeeter tell someone else he had a stolen shotgun? Would Tiny know about it? Tiny and Johnny Mae. Willingham and Johnny Mae. Tiny found out that Willingham is Johnny Mae's father. Is he? Didn't Tiny already know who Johnny Mae's mother worked for? Yes, of course he did.

Nothing was holding together but the possibilities were disturbing.

Shirley. The trip to Shirley's lake house wasn't spontaneous after all. She had lured me there so when Willingham was killed my fingerprints would be in all the wrong places. That didn't feel right. I've been fooled before but that would be a world class job. On the other hand, Shirley did do a world class job. But how would Shirley know about my shotgun and get her hands on it? Shirley and Scott Taylor? Shirley and Ron? Shirley and Tiny? Nothing made any sense.

Miller slowed down to pull off the interstate at Forsyth, halfway to Macon.

"You going to stop?" Stevens asked. "Come on, Mel, let's get back to Macon. I've got something sweet to take care of and it's getting late."

"It's too late already, Arthur. I need to piss and I'm getting tired. Let's get a cup of coffee and something to eat. You need to go to the bathroom, Frank?"

"I need my arms moved," I said. "These handcuffs are killing me."

"Quit whining," Stevens said. "You can blow a man in two with a shotgun but you can't stand handcuffs on your wrists? You make me sick."

"Show a little mercy," Miller said. "The kid's scared."

I was scared. I was scared and I was confused. Someone had set me up for murder . . . either intentionally or because they got their hands on my shotgun. I didn't know which and I didn't know why. All I knew was that my life was being wrecked. This really wasn't fair, just when something good was happening between Johnny Mae and me.

Miller pulled up to the front of the Waffle House, got out and opened my door. He took my arm and pulled me out of the car.

"Turn around," he said, "and face the car."

I did as he said. Late night customers inside the Waffle House were watching us through the windows. The kind of clientele that frequents the Waffle House at two in the morning . . . I'm sure they had seen it all many times before. They had probably been standing in my shoes before. But I didn't see any sympathy. I felt the pain ease up as Detective Miller released the handcuff from one wrist.

"Turn around," he said. He put the cuff back on my wrist but moved my arms in front of me this time and not so tight as before.

"Thank you," I said and I meant it. He gave me just the smallest smile with a brief twitch of his mouth and a nod of his head and led me inside.

We sat down in a booth at one end of the long narrow Waffle House as far away from the other customers as we could get. Detective Stevens sat next to me and boxed me in. Miller sat across the table from me. The waitress came with a pot of coffee and three cups. She set the cups in front of us and filled each of them with the steaming black coffee. Her name tag said Doris.

Doris was somewhere in her middle or late thirties, but it had been a hard thirty. She had blonde hair that had been bleached too many times with an inch of darker roots showing. She was a sexy looking woman in a crude sort of way with large breasts that stood up amazingly well and were held firmly by the uniform that was just a little too tight on the top and the bottom. She had full red lips and smiled easily. She just missed being pretty but she had a scar on her face and a look in her eyes that said she had been through some bad times and some mistreatment. She popped chewing gum between her teeth. Her eyes kept looking me over. Doris set the pot down on the counter, took her pad from her waist pocket and her pencil from her fluffed-up hair.

"What you fellows gon' have?" she asked.

Miller ordered a bowl of chili, Stevens had a hamburger, and I had a grilled cheese.

"Is that all you want, honey?" Doris asked me. I nodded my head and she took the order to the cook.

Detective Miller went to the bathroom, leaving me alone with Detective Stevens.

"Why did you do it?" Stevens asked.

"I didn't do it," I said.

"Shit, you didn't. We got enough evidence on you right now. A jury wouldn't take ten minutes to convict you."

He put two spoons of sugar in his coffee, stirred it and tasted it. He reached for the cream pitcher and poured enough to fill his cup to the rim.

"What happened? Did Willingham catch you balling his wife? Threaten to have you fired? Whose idea was it to kill him? Yours or hers? What did she do, did she tell you about the big insurance policy? What was it, get fired or get rich?"

He took a couple of sips from the cup, set it down and stirred in another spoon of sugar.

"You're a college boy aren't you? I guess you thought you were pretty smart didn't you? You thought you could kill the man and get away with his wife and his money? Well I got news for you." Stevens turned on me with his big face. "You've been had, sucker. Shirley Willingham turned you over. She's going to let you take the whole fall."

What was he talking about? I didn't look at him. He flexed the fingers on his big hand resting on the table.

"That colored whore of yours is from Macon too, isn't she?

"Watch your mouth," I said.

He looked at me hard and mean. I didn't know if he was going to hit me or spit on me.

"Damn, man, don't you have any standards?" he said. "Why don't you stay with your own kind? Do you think she's some kind of queen or something?"

I didn't say anything. I didn't know if he meant what he was saying or if he was just trying to rattle me. He had me rattled. And if he was trying to confuse me, he was doing a great job. I didn't know if he had accidentally told me things I didn't know about Shirley Willingham's involvement or if he was just trying to get me to talk, to say anything. Whatever his scheme, I didn't want him treating Johnny Mae the way he was treating me right now.

Detective Miller came back to the booth. He looked back and forth between me and Stevens. He could see I was upset and that Stevens was a little hot under the collar. Stevens cursed under his breath, got up and went to the bathroom.

"Detective Stevens is basically a good cop," Miller said, "but he's not a patient man. And to tell you the truth, he has some prejudices that get in the way of his reasoning sometimes. I can keep him under control most of the time, but not always. He didn't used to be that way. About two years ago a young white boy very much like yourself got involved with some colored prostitutes. He got in way over his head. The first thing you know, he was into drugs and blackmail. The boy ended up getting killed. It was Detective Stevens' cousin's boy. Arthur can't seem to get over it. That's why he's being so hard on you. He sees that boy in you. He really wants to help you out of this situation and I do too. I don't think you did it. I think somebody set you up. But you're going to have to talk to me if I'm going to be able to help you."

Detective Stevens came back to the booth. The waitress brought our order and put it on the table. She was making eyes at me. She looked at my handcuffs.

"Who did he kill?" she said as a joke to Detective Miller.

"Do you read the papers?" Stevens said.

She went down the counter and picked up a newspaper lying next to the cash register. She looked at the front page and turned to the short order cook, pointing to the paper and looking over her shoulder at me. The cook looked over at me and I could see the other customers asking what was going on. They were all stealing glances back at me.

"The evidence looks all one way right now," Miller said. "The evidence says you were screwing Willingham's wife at the lake house. He was killed at the lake house with your gun which had no one's fingerprints on it but yours. You and Willingham had words shortly before his death that resulted in you being fired. And you've got nobody who can supply you with an alibi. If you can tell us something different, you need to tell us. Otherwise, it looks like you did it."

I knew I was going to have to tell the truth from here on out, as much of it as I could. I couldn't afford to be caught in another lie.

"I was at the Willingham lake house one time only, this past Tuesday morning. I never had sex with Mrs. Willingham before that time or since that time. I've never even been alone with Mrs. Willingham except for that one day."

"Did you go anywhere else with Mrs. Willingham, besides to her lake house?"

"She went with me to inspect the house of an old gentleman who was applying for services from her agency."

"What is his name?"

"John Glover. Mr. John Glover." Why did I feel that I had just betrayed John Glover?

"Glover?" Miller said. "Isn't that your girlfriend's name? Isn't she a Glover?"

Jesus, no . . . don't bring Johnny Mae into this. Not because of me.

"Yes," I said. "Johnny Mae is Mr. Glover's granddaughter. Johnny Mae has no connection with the Willinghams."

"Now, I don't know if that's true, Frank." Detective Miller said. "It seems to me that she does. How long have you and Johnny Mae been involved with each other?"

"I just met her on Monday morning."

"How did you meet her?"

"She was at her grandparents' house the first time I went there with Mr. Glover."

"Johnny Mae was at her grandparents' house in Macon four days ago?"

"Yes."

"And that's the first time you ever saw her?"

"Yes."

"When did you see her again?"

"She came down to the ceremony the mayor had for Mr. Glover at City Hall on Wednesday."

"Can you describe your contact with her on Wednesday?"

"She picked up her grandparents and brought them to City Hall. I talked to her for maybe a minute or two after the ceremony. She took her grandparents home and she went back to Atlanta. That's all."

"What did you talk about?"

"She thanked me for helping her grandparents with the problem they were having with the building inspector."

"What else?"

"Nothing else. I asked her if she was going to be in town for the day and she said no, she had to go back to Atlanta to work that night. She told me she's a nurse. That's all. That's all we said to each other."

"Did she talk to anyone else at the ceremony?"

"Craig Linder, the building inspector, came up. He and Stafford Willingham. Craig introduced me and Johnny Mae to Stafford Willingham. That's the first time I ever spoke to Willingham."

"But you knew who he was?"

"I had never met him. I knew who Stafford Willingham was because he was on the Planning Commission. That's who I work for, the Planning Commission. The mayor had just appointed me to assist Craig Linder and Stafford Willingham on the mayor's new housing project."

"So, Willingham was your boss?"

"Not technically. I was just going to be assisting him on this special project. Craig Linder is my boss."

"That must have been hard for you, having to work for Willingham when you were having sex with his wife."

"I was not having sex with his wife. Only one time."

"The day before you were introduced to him?"

"Yes."

"Did Willingham know about it?"

"Not that I could tell. Shirley said he didn't."

"You discussed the possibility with his wife?"

"Yes."

"When was that?"

"I called her Wednesday afternoon to tell her I thought he might know."

"Why did you think he might know?"

"He acted peculiar toward me I thought. Nothing specific. He just implied that I should stop working on the park project with his wife and devote myself to the mayor's project."

"He told you to stop working with his wife?"

"No, not like that. It was more of a power thing with him.

He thought his project was more important than the other things I was working on."

"So he was throwing his weight around?"

"That's the way he operated. He tried to intimidate."

"He tried to intimidate you?"

"Not me in particular. It was apparently his style of interaction."

"So what did his wife say when you asked her if he knew?"

"She said no, there was no way he could know. It was just his manner of dealing with people. She told me to ignore it."

"Tell me again about the introduction. You said Linder introduced you and Miss Glover to Willingham?"

"Yes."

"How did Miss Glover react to Willingham?"

"Not at all. Willingham told her that he thought he knew her mother years ago."

"Willingham knew John Mae Glover's mother?"

"He asked her, he said, 'Was your mother's name Esther?' Johnny Mae said yes. Willingham said Johnny Mae looked just like her mother."

"Does she?"

"Does she what?"

"Does Johnny Mae look like her mother?"

"Her mother died when Johnny Mae was a baby. I never saw her."

"So, Willingham knew Johnny Mae's mother, what? Twenty-something years ago?"

"Johnny Mae is twenty-five."

"So Willingham had connections with the Glover family going back at least twenty-five years?"

"Willingham said Johnny Mae's mother worked for his family when he was a young man, that he remembered her, and that Johnny Mae looked just like her mother. That's it."

"So, what you told me before is not true?"

"What?"

"You said Miss Glover had no connection to Mr. Willingham."

"No connection that she knew about."

"Did she tell you that?"

"No."

"So finish telling me about you and Miss Glover. You first met her five days ago at her grandparents' home. How long did you talk with her there?"

"Maybe five minutes."

"You talk with her five minutes on Monday, two minutes on Wednesday, and you're sleeping at her place and screwing her on Friday night? I don't understand that."

"I don't understand it either," I said, "but it happened."

"So are you paying this girl money or anything?" Miller said.

"No, of course not. I'm in love with her."

"Jesus, what a crock of shit," Stevens said. He had been quiet as long as he could manage. "Either you're paying her or she's paying you because she's your whore."

"That's not the way it is."

"You want to drag this girl into this?" Miller said.

"It's the very last thing in the world I want to do," I said.

"Then you need to help us clear it up as quickly as we can so we can keep her out of it."

"I'm telling you everything I know. She has nothing to do with Willingham's death."

"Do you know that for a fact?"

"She couldn't have. When was Willingham killed?"

"Between 10:00 p.m. and midnight on Friday night."

"Johnny Mae was working at her job at Emory during that time. She's a nurse there."

"Do you know that for a fact? Or is that what she told you? Or are you just making it up, hoping I'll believe it?"

"She told me. She has no reason to lie to me."

Detectives Miller and Stevens looked at each other. Stevens moved his head with a short jerking motion. They got up and walked to the other end of the diner, leaving me alone at the booth but within their sight. The waitress glanced over at them, picked up the coffee pot and sauntered over to my booth. She filled my coffee cup and smiled a sincere, friendly smile at me.

"You don't look like a killer to me," she said, watching my face.

"I didn't do it. Somebody wants it to look like I did, but I didn't."

Doris was looking me over, considering it.

"Listen," I said, "my girlfriend works the night shift at Emory Hospital. She's going to be scared and worried when she comes home and finds me gone. She doesn't know anything about me being arrested and there's no one to tell her. They won't let me make a call."

I could see something in Doris's face. Sympathy maybe. But she wasn't ready to trust me.

"So, what are you going to do?" she asked, glancing in the direction of Miller and Stevens who were in whispered conversation.

"I've got about fifty dollars in my billfold in my back pocket and there's a slip of paper in it with her phone number on it. Would you take my billfold and call her, please? You can have all the money I've got. Just let her know what's happened to me."

She backed away half a step giving herself some distance from me.

"Please. Tell her Frank asked you to call her. Tell her I've been arrested for the murder of Stafford Willingham and they're taking me to the Bibb County jail. Tell her I didn't do it and I don't know anything about it."

I could see the indecision in her face. Miller and Stevens were headed back our way.

"Please," I said. "Her name is Johnny Mae. Tell her Frank said he loves her. Tell her not to worry. Tell her I'm sorry."

Doris leaned across the booth and filled Miller and Stevens' coffee cups. She straightened up, looked toward the two detectives and smiled. She was nervous. She reached across to pick up the dirty dishes and knocked a glass of water onto the table in front of me. She grabbed a cloth from the counter and rushed to catch the spill.

"Geez, I'm sorry," she said to them as they walked up to the booth. "Did that get on you, honey?" she asked me. The water was on the seat beside me. "Don't move. Let me get that before it gets you wet," she said.

She was all over the seat beside me before any of us could say anything, wiping with her towel and pushing things back on the table top. I leaned forward to let her get around me and she had my billfold out of my pocket and into her towel as slick as any pickpocket.

"I'm sorry, sugar," she said. "I don't think you'll melt, will you?"

I smiled and said, "I'm fine. Thank you."

"It may be the last bath he gets for awhile," Detective Stevens said, taking my arm and pulling me from the booth. "Come on, we're leaving."

As we pulled out of the Waffle House parking lot onto the

street I saw Doris lifting the receiver from the pay phone. I would have paid her a thousand dollars to make that call. I hoped she got through.

Chapter 13

A Welcome Extortion

The Bibb County jail was a violation of the Geneva Convention. Despite Detective Miller's assertion that he didn't believe a nice boy like me could be mixed up in murder, and the implied promise that he would keep me out of jail if I came clean, I was booked, fingerprinted and thrown into the Bibb County lockup with worse Saturday night low-life scum than I had ever imagined possible. There were guys moaning, talking to themselves, fighting, and sleeping on the floor. There were guys with bruises, cuts, black eyes, and swollen lips. Guys urinating in their pants and vomiting anywhere and everywhere. I was rubbing elbows with bodies that hadn't been bathed during this century. I thought I was going to gag on the smell.

Except for the small amount of sleep I'd had at Johnny Mae's, I had been almost without rest for the better part of two days and nights. But there was no place to lie down. I ached all over. I had a headache that was killing me. My mouth tasted like the bottom of a dirty cat box. My eyes were dry and scratchy. My scalp itched. My skin was crawling and I desperately needed the privacy of a bathroom. I just couldn't bring myself to take care of personal business in a cell with a dozen men watching.

There were no good prospects ahead. Even if they were to grant me bail, I had no money. I had no friends, no family, nobody to get me out. If this was what jail was to be like, I knew I couldn't do it. I tried not to talk to anyone despite the fact that there was a parade of men hitting me up for first one thing and then another. Someone wanted cigarettes. Someone wanted money. Someone wanted me to arrange bail for them. That was a laugh. Someone wanted sex. That was not a laugh. I could see the time coming when I couldn't just say no and would have to stand and fight. All these guys looked too tough for me. Except for one old man.

His name was Pop, or that's what they called him. I found a corner next to the bars and sat on the floor with my back to the wall. After a while the old man came over and stood quietly, looking down at me with uncertain eyes. Considering the amount of worry I had about my own prospects, I wouldn't venture a guess how long this feeble, vulnerable and defenseless old man could survive in this brutal hell hole.

"Would you mind if I sit down here?" he asked. He pointed cautiously to a spot on the floor next to me.

I nodded to him and said, "Sure," and laid my head back against the wall with my eyes closed. I don't know why he chose that spot next to me. Because I was younger and bigger and didn't look threatening I guess. If he thought he was gaining a measure of protection by sitting in my shadow, I didn't want to deprive him of that small comfort and I didn't have the heart to tell him how worthless I was as a protector.

He sat down and drew his knees up in front of him. He was very quiet. He watched everything from his little spot. He made me think of a mouse. Maybe he would be my protection. A watch mouse to warn me if danger came our way.

The lights were never turned off. There was continuous noise. Men's angry voices barked and shouted. Other men's distressed voices whined and begged. The cell door clanged open and shut with the passage of men in and out. There was no rest. I was numb with fatigue.

Sometime after midnight Sunday night, after almost twenty-four hours of this relentless torture, I had laid my head across my knees and was finally managing to nod off to sleep when Pop nudged me. I was suddenly aware of a huge pair of work boots standing directly in front of my toes.

I looked up and realized I was about to die. Standing before me was the biggest, ugliest, meanest looking black man I had ever had the misfortune of being in the same cell with. He looked down at me with a hard stare. His big voice growled out, laying over and squashing the other voices in the cell.

"You Frank Hayes? The man that killed Mr. Willingham?"

I didn't know whether to pee in my pants or beg for forgiveness. "I'm Frank Hayes."

"Get up off the floor," he ordered.

So he wanted to kill me standing up. I guessed that he had been sent by friends of Stafford Willingham. I held onto the cell bars and pulled myself to my feet. He was about my height and about half again as heavy as me.

"I'm Leroy Jackson," he said. "Tiny sent me to look after you."

He must have seen me trembling.

"This man is Frank Hayes," Leroy announced. "He been locked up for murder. Of course he innocent. We all innocent. He be Tiny Glover's boy. Anything happen to him, you answer to Tiny . . . and me."

He looked around toward one of two cots in the cell. The cot was occupied by a gentleman who, judging from his appearance and manner was of very low repute and high hostility rating.

"How about you get up and let Mr. Hayes lie down a bit," Leroy said to the man. "He go before the judge in a little while and he got to rest."

There was no protest. Normally I wouldn't have been caught dead sleeping on a cot in that cell but considering the alternatives, I lay down on the cot. I was too tired and too scared to sleep but I closed my eyes. Leroy squatted down beside me.

"Tiny say to tell you he's sorry, ain't no way he can make yo' bail, so he sent me."

"I'm grateful to you and to Tiny," I said. "I won't forget this."

"No bother," he said. "I owe Tiny. Ain't nothin' to me to be in here."

"How did you get in?" I asked.

"I stole my brother-in-law's car. He'll drop the charges when we ready."

There was a lot to life I didn't understand.

"Tiny say you been thinkin' about the barbecue business."

I laughed to myself. Extortion. He keeps me alive and I become his partner.

"You tell Tiny when you see him he's got a deal. Tell him we'll call it Tiny's Bighouse Barbecue. You've got a job there if you want it. You can be the bouncer." I laughed and must have fallen asleep immediately.

I awoke to my name being called out by the jailer. Or I tried to wake up. I had my eyes open but they didn't want to focus and I couldn't seem to stand on my feet. I was exhausted.

"You all right, son?" the jailer asked.

I wanted to tell him hell no I wasn't all right. My eyes began to focus. I nodded my head and took a couple of steps. My legs were working again.

"Time to go before the judge," he said.

My fear index shot off the top of the scale. All of a sudden my sight cleared. He led me through some tunnels into a slow elevator that took us up two floors. Then down a hallway to a waiting room where I sat with four other prisoners. I was the third one called. I couldn't have waited more than thirty minutes but it seemed like half the morning. I was led into the courtroom and taken to stand before the judge.

Everyone else in the room seemed to be dressed in suits and ties, except the judge who had on the black robe representing a level of authority which until that moment I had not fully appreciated. Everyone in the room stood before him. I was at his mercy. I looked and smelled like a vagrant. I felt like a vagrant. I felt like I looked guilty and I probably looked like I felt guilty. I didn't know what I was supposed to do or what was supposed to happen next. The thing that caught my eye was the court reporter. She sat at one of those little recording machines with the keys and the roll of paper coming out of it. I never understood how they could copy all the words onto that little strip of paper.

The bailiff read from the docket. "The people vs. Mr. Frank Hayes on charges of murder in the first degree."

That couldn't be correct. They must have the name wrong. Someone had made a big mistake.

"Samuel Washington of the District Attorney's office representing the people, Your Honor," a man in a pinstriped suit standing across from me said.

"What have you got, Mr. Washington?"

"Here is a summary of the defendant's statement to the police following his arrest, your honor." Washington handed the judge a typed document of many pages. "We request that Mr. Hayes be held without possibility of bail, pending trial, Your Honor."

"Mr. Hayes?" the judge looked at me.

"Yes, sir," I managed to say. But what I wanted to say was that everything was all wrong. They had the wrong guy.

"Mr. Hayes, are you aware of the charges that have been

filed against you in this court?"

"No, sir."

The judge looked sharply at me, apparently unwilling to believe me. This was not getting off to a good start.

"Prior to appearing in this courtroom you were not informed of the charges against you?"

"No, sir."

"Do you have an attorney present to represent you?"

"No, sir, I don't."

"Were you informed of your right to have an attorney present at this hearing? And were you given the opportunity to contact an attorney?

"No, sir, I was not."

"You were not what? Informed of your right to an attorney, or given the opportunity to contact one?"

"Neither one, your honor."

I could see the judge's level of aggravation rising along with his voice. He flipped through the pages of the document. "Mr. Washington, I don't find a Miranda waiver attached to the defendant's statement."

"Your honor . . ." Washington said.

The judged motioned for him to be quiet. He looked back at me. He looked impatient and angry.

"Mr. Hayes, prior to answering any questions by the arresting officers or making any incriminating statements to them were you informed of the right to have your attorney present during questioning?"

"No, sir, I was not."

"Your Honor," Washington said, "Mr Hayes waived his right to an attorney at the time of arrest and gave the voluntary statement you have before you."

"Mr. Hayes," the judge said, shooting an agitated look at

the prosecutor, "I ask you again, at the time of your arrest did the arresting officer inform you of your right to have an attorney present to represent you and did you waive your right to an attorney?"

"Your Honor, I don't recall the word 'attorney' being used in my presence at the time I was arrested or at any time since. I have no idea what the legal procedures of this court are. I never told anyone I didn't want an attorney. I definitely feel that I need to have an attorney."

"Is the arresting officer . . ." the judge flipped the pages of the documents in his hand, "Is Detective Melvin Miller or Detective Arthur Stevens present in the courtroom?"

He looked over the courtroom for a response. There was no response.

"On a charge of murder, the arresting officer is not present at the probable cause hearing?" His eyes were beginning to glaze over.

There was no response.

"Your Honor," Washington said, "Mr. Hayes gave a voluntary statement."

"Mr. Washington, I don't care if the arresting officer found him standing over the body with a bloody knife in one hand and the victim's still-beating heart in the other. The law requires that the arresting officer must inform the accused of his Miranda rights at the time of arrest and prior to taking any statements from the accused if those statements or any evidence uncovered as a result of those statements is to be used in a subsequent prosecution. Do you know what that means?"

"Yes, Your Honor," Washington said with his head bowed.

"Mr. Washington, I'll see you in my chambers."

"All rise," the bailiff yelled. I was already standing.

Washington shot me a look that said he thought this whole mess was my fault and he was taking it as a personal affront. He and the judge disappeared behind a closed door next to the judge's bench.

Court proceedings were delayed for less than ten minutes. Washington reappeared first. He was not happy. The judge followed and took his position behind the bench.

"Mr. Hayes," he said, "the laws of this country require that every arrest of one of its citizens and the prosecution of every case be conducted by rigid standards designed to insure that justice is done, that the guilty are convicted, and that the innocent are protected from the improper exercise of the power of the state. The officers who conducted your arrest did not adhere to that rigid standard and by doing so they corrupted due process. Because any case brought against you arising from that arrest would be resting on a rotten foundation, the case ultimately would not stand. I am therefore, over the protest of the District Attorney's office, dismissing all charges against you."

My knees went weak. I couldn't believe what he was saying. I was prepared to rot in jail, to be attacked and molested, and now . . . What had happened?

"You need to understand, sir, this does not mean you have been found innocent. Nor does it mean you are guilty but free on some technicality of the law. What it means is that this charge is dismissed without prejudice. The District Attorney's office is free to file new charges against you and have you arrested according to proper procedure should they feel justified. But it is fair to tell you as I have told Mr. Washington, nothing you told them while you were in their custody the first time may be used to support charges against you unless the District Attorney's office can demonstrate how they arrived at the new charges through evidence entirely free and independent of any information learned from your prior statements to them. You are free to go, with the apologies of this court."

I was in shock. I didn't even know which way the door was. I turned around and there were a hundred pair of eyes watching me. I felt a hand on my arm. The bailiff opened the gate of the bar and led me through it. I could see the aisle in front of me and the door beyond. I walked toward the door, trying to figure out what had happened to me during the past thirty-six hours. It didn't make any sense.

I don't know why but I expected Johnny Mae might be waiting for me when I walked out the front doors of the courthouse. She wasn't. No one was there except a lot of people who looked at me like I was a criminal. I wanted to run because I expected the police to put me under arrest again and take me back to that hell hole of a jail. I couldn't run. I could barely walk.

Walk where? I didn't have my car. I didn't have my motorcycle. I didn't have my billfold or a penny in my pocket. I didn't have my checkbook. I didn't know what to do.

I started walking just to put some distance between me and the courthouse. I kept looking for a police car, expecting to be stopped and handcuffed. I walked a couple of blocks and suddenly became aware that a car had pulled up beside me. It was a black Lincoln with tinted windows. It was Shirley Willingham. I didn't know whether she was going to shoot me or run over me. The electric passenger window rolled down. I looked across at her. She was dressed in a navy blue suit. She didn't look as good as the last time I saw her or as bad as I thought she might, considering that her husband had just been murdered.

"Get in, Frank," she said.

Chapter 14

A Sweet Dream

If I had an attorney he would tell me the last person I needed to be seen with was Shirley Willingham. I could feel Detective Arthur Stevens' big hand reaching for me even as I stood looking into her car.

"Get in," she said again.

I didn't know what to say to her. "I don't think I should," I managed to mumble.

"Where are you going?" she asked.

"I don't know." I didn't. "Home, I guess." I couldn't make my words come out clear.

"How are you going to get there?"

"I don't know."

"You look exhausted." She was smiling and shaking her head at me. "Get in before you fall on your face."

I looked around me trying to think what I could do. I expected to see a pair of handcuffs coming my way but I didn't. How was I going to get home? I tried to think. It was no use. I opened the car door and slid slowly onto the soft, inviting, leather seat. I closed the door. It seemed safe inside. Shirley took my hand in hers. I didn't look at her. I was afraid to. I had this fear that if I looked into her eyes she would take control of me.

"I'll take you home," she said. "What's your address?"

I couldn't remember my house number. I was confused. "Go out Pio Nono. Turn left on Clarendon." I closed my eyes.

Everything was in confusion. It's funny what your mind

does when you're exhausted, frightened and traumatized. It locked on the name of the street, Pio Nono. It was Portuguese for . . . something, I couldn't remember what. The pronunciation among the genteel white class was Pia Nóna. The colloquial pronunciation, black and white, was Pie Nóhner. I used the genteel pronunciation but no matter how hard I tried, my tongue caught on it every time I said it. My mind was drifting away on thoughts of pio nono, pia nona, pie nohner.

"You can sleep when I get you home, Frank. Stay awake right now. I need you to give me directions. Talk to me."

It was Shirley's voice. I was in her car. Oh, shit.

"When's the last time you had anything to eat?" she said.

"Yesterday . . . last night . . . I don't know. Doris . . ." I said.

"You want something to eat?"

"I want to go home."

"Jesus, you need to get those clothes off and get cleaned up. You stink."

I rolled my head to one side and looked at her. "Jail stinks," I said. "It gets on you. You don't ever want to go there."

There was a break in her voice. "I'm sorry, Frank . . . for what you've been through."

"Oh, think nothing of it. I met some nice people. We'll be lifelong friends."

I remembered my address as soon as I saw it on the entrance to the driveway. We managed to get me out of the car and to my front door. That's when I realized it.

"My keys are in Atlanta," I said.

"Do you have a spare somewhere?" she said.

"A spare?" I said. "Maybe . . . somewhere. I don't know."

She looked under a flower pot and turned over a couple of rocks. Nothing. She walked over to the door, reached up and felt around the black wrought-iron light fixture that was supposed to look like a lantern. When she turned back she was smiling and holding a key between her fingers.

Shirley helped me into my apartment. It was hot. I turned the air conditioner on high.

"Go get cleaned up," she said. "A shower will make you feel better. Do you have any food in the house?"

I shook my head. "I don't think so. There may be some beer in the refrigerator."

"You don't need beer," she said. "I'll go pick up a couple of things while you're in the shower."

"You shouldn't be here," I said. She shouldn't be there, because of the police, and because of Johnny Mae.

"I can't leave you in this condition. I'll fix you a BLT or something. You need to eat before you go to sleep. You'll feel better tomorrow. Go on." She pushed me toward my bedroom. "I'll be right back."

"How about a couple of them?" I said sleepily.

She smiled at me. "Sure. I'll get you some milk, too. It'll do you good."

I heard the door close behind her as I stepped into the bathroom. After not having seen the inside of a clean bathroom for about thirty-six hours, I found a whole new appreciation for the simple pleasures of life and offered my thanks to the inventor of the water closet.

I took off my jail clothes and dropped them into a pile on the bathroom floor. I couldn't decide whether I should wash them or throw them out. I put them into a plastic bag. Take them to the laundry, then decide. I might want to frame them.

The air was still warm. It was going to take a while for the apartment to cool off. I thought about the cold beer in the refrigerator. I knew that what I needed most in the world was a cold beer. The six pack in the fridge had only one gone. I took one of the cold bottles and held it against my neck. That felt good. I opened it and took a long guzzle. Oh, that was good.

I liked salt with my beer. I shook about a teaspoon of salt into my palm from the shaker. I pressed my tongue onto the little pile of white grains and poured a long drink of beer over my tongue. Very satisfying. I stood naked in the kitchen and finished off the remainder of the bottle. The beer and the salt didn't come out even. I opened another beer. The apartment was cooling some. I felt better but dizzy. I stood in front of the air conditioner and let the cool air blow directly on my chest and face. Yes, I felt better.

The next thing I had to do was brush my teeth. I brushed and gargled until I thought all the jail germs and all their relatives were dead and cleansed from my mouth. It made the beer taste better.

Johnny Mae. I had to get in touch with Johnny Mae. My billfold. Her number was in my billfold. I didn't have it. What was it? 369 . . . something. No, it was 639. I couldn't remember. I dialed information. Johnny Mae Glover, 3810 Lindsay Lane, apartment 107. Got it.

No answer. Where was she? Looking for me? At her grandparents? They didn't have a phone.

I wrote Johnny Mae's number on the corner of a page in my phone book, tore it off and put it under the edge of the phone. Maybe she was working. Maybe she and Reggie went somewhere together. Maybe . . .

I took a long, long, cool shower, washing everything, including my hair, three or four times. I had reached about the shriveling point when I stepped out and dried off. I could smell bacon frying. Regardless of what I had said earlier, I was ravenous. I slipped on some clean jeans and a t-shirt and dialed Johnny Mae's number again. Still no answer. I stumbled my way to the kitchen. Shirley was just setting a plate of food on the table for me.

"You look better," she said.

"Yeah, I'm better," I dropped into a chair. The truth was, I could hardly sit up and hold my eyes open.

"You poor baby," she said.

She shouldn't be in my apartment. I knew it but it didn't seem to matter right then. The only thing that mattered was food and rest. Those two BLTs were about the best two sandwiches I had ever eaten. I passed on the milk, against Shirley's protest, and had another cold beer. By this time I was about to fall asleep on the kitchen table. Shirley pulled me up from the chair and half carried me to the bedroom. She lay me on the bed and I passed out. I had some bizarre fitful dreams and awoke several times thinking I was still in jail and that Detectives Miller and Stevens were interrogating me. I was looking for Johnny Mae and couldn't find her.

The last time I awoke, the apartment was dark. It was nighttime. I fell into a deeper sleep and I dreamed of Johnny Mae again. She was with me in my bed. I held her close and told her I loved her and we made the sweetest, most wonderful love. It must have been the exhaustion and the hallucinations I had been experiencing in my dreams, but they seemed realer than real, like she was really there in my arms. I didn't want it to end.

When I opened my eyes it was daylight again. I felt like I had been drugged and beaten, but better than yesterday. I smelled something pleasant . . . but it didn't seem right somehow. Oh, damn. It was Caribbean Breeze, Shirley's perfume. She was still in my apartment. The fragrance still on the other pillowcase told me she didn't sleep on the couch. I had to get her out of my apartment.

I stood in the shower and thought about my dreams. I had to find my way back to Atlanta. I pulled on some clothes and checked the clock. It was nine in the morning. I called Johnny Mae's number again. Still no answer. It didn't feel good. I found Shirley in the kitchen looking very much at home. She was wearing one of my long shirts and I wasn't sure what else. She had made coffee and there was a bowl of cereal and milk on the table for me. She really was being a sweet woman. I had a hard time thinking of her as a murderess.

"Who is Johnny Mae?" she said, smiling and watching me eat my cereal.

"Did I talk in my sleep?"

"More than just talk. You absolutely took my breath away. I mean, I've had good sex but that was something else."

"Sex?" I said. "You mean . . . last night?"

Her smile left no doubt. My dreams had been more than real. They had been surreal. I was in real trouble now.

"I hope you don't mind," she said. "I didn't think you would mind. I know you were asleep in the beginning, but you seemed so eager. I mean, you were wonderful. I thought you were awake."

It had been wonderful for me too but it wasn't her I was making love to.

"It was Johnny Mae, wasn't it?" she said.

"Yes, I'm sorry. I'm in love with her. I was exhausted. I thought you were her."

"Don't be sorry. Lucky girl. I'm the one who's sorry. Who is she?"

How was I going to explain this? She's your late husband's illegitimate daughter? Your stepdaughter? She's a black girl I've known for less than a week? You're OK, Shirley, but you're no Johnny Mae? There was no way to tell her.

"She's someone I met. She lives in Atlanta. I was with her when I was arrested."

"The poor thing. I'm sorry, Frank. I would like to say I was just trying to help yesterday, but to tell you the truth I needed someone I could trust near me last night. And you were the only one. I didn't mean to cause you any more problems than I already have. I'll get my things and get out of here."

"It was great, Shirley. You have been great. I would do anything to help you. If things were different, if I weren't in love with Johnny Mae . . ."

There was a gentle knock at my front door. Shirley and I looked at each other. I don't know what she thought but I thought of two detectives I did not want knocking at my door. I motioned for her to stay where she was. I went into the living room and opened the front door. It was Johnny Mae. She had a suitcase sitting beside her. She had the most beautiful smile on her face and tears in her eyes.

I was in torment. I was the happiest man in the world at that moment and the most distressed. I held my arms open to her.

"Johnny Mae," I said.

She fell into my arms and kissed my lips. I couldn't believe she had come to me. And the suitcase. She cried against my chest and kissed me again. She took my hands in hers and pulled me into my living room.

"I've been so worried about you," she said. "The police questioned me for hours. I got away just as soon as I could."

She wrapped her arms around my neck and kissed me in a way I didn't want her to stop, but I knew something horrible was about to happen. If I could hold onto her long enough, until Shirley could get away. . . get out of my life. I felt Johnny Mae tense. She pulled away from me just an inch.

"What is it?" she said. "What's the matter?"

I'm sure she saw the desperation in my eyes. She looked around me into the apartment.

"Are you alone? Is someone here with you?"

Shirley was in the kitchen wearing nothing but my shirt. Her clothes were somewhere in my bedroom. There was no way out of what was going to happen and I was sick beyond endurance.

There was movement behind me and Shirley appeared in the kitchen doorway. I don't know which of them was shocked the most . . . Johnny Mae, seeing a half-dressed woman in my apartment, or Shirley, seeing a black woman in my arms.

Shirley recovered first. "You must be Johnny Mae," she said, trying to be cheerful. Johnny Mae's face said it wasn't working.

"This is not what it looks like," Shirley said, but it was obvious to an idiot that she had spent the night in my apartment.

I couldn't have hurt Johnny Mae more if I had hit her in the face. For a minute I thought she was going into shock. She was staring at Shirley but her eyes were vacant. I reached for her to try to explain what couldn't be explained at that moment. But she pulled away from me. I could hear her breath catching in her throat. She looked at me like an innocent child might look at the devil, fearing the evil but not understanding the nature of it.

"Johnny Mae, please," I said, "sit down and let me explain. I love you, Johnny Mae. I love you and no one else."

"Did she stay with you last night?" she said, looking at Shirley. I couldn't answer.

She looked at me and I saw a shiver go over her. I thought she would slap me or curse me. I wanted her to. But she didn't say anything. She backed out through my front door.

"I brought your things to you," she said. Without looking at the suitcase she turned and walked away.

"Johnny Mae, wait for me." I went after her but she wouldn't stop and she wouldn't listen. "Please, Johnny Mae, don't go like this. You have to stop and let me tell you what's happened. I've been trying to get hold of you. Please, don't go."

But she wouldn't listen. She glared at me with a hardness worse than I had ever seen in her eyes.

"You lying white bastard!" was all she would say to me.

I wanted to hold her and not let her leave but I knew it was impossible. She slammed the door to her car and drove away. She was gone and I felt as if I had been stabbed in the chest.

Chapter 15

A Time For Truth

I hated Shirley Willingham. If she hadn't been there Johnny Mae would be in my arms instead of being hurt and angry at me. Angry wasn't strong enough. Unless I could find some way to fix it, Johnny Mae would never look at me or speak to me again. It seemed as though every move I made was more stupid than the last and this time I really didn't know what to do. I was ready to throw Shirley out of my apartment onto the street. I was almost too angry to look at her.

"I need to borrow your car," I said.

Shirley hesitated. "Where are you going? What are you going to do?"

"I have to go after Johnny Mae," I said, looking for her car keys.

"Frank, hold on just a minute. Calm down just a minute and think about it. She's very angry right now. She's not listening. Give her a little time for her anger to calm. She'll listen later."

"I'm afraid I'll let her get away."

"Frank, I would never have been here if I had known."

"You shouldn't have come here. I don't know why your husband died but it has nothing to do with me. I've just hurt the only woman I've ever loved because of you."

Shirley stumbled backwards into the kitchen door. She put both her hands over her mouth and her eyes showed her shock. I saw the effect my words were having and I was ashamed. I was blaming Shirley for something I myself had done, or let happen. Shirley had her own problems. I looked at her and she was almost as lost as I was. She had been putting a good front on it but she had to be in bad emotional condition. Her husband had been murdered three days ago and here she was with me looking for comfort . . . looking for something. I couldn't really figure her out. Either she was a very kind, unselfish, and warm woman, or she was the most devious, calculating bitch I had ever met. I wasn't sure I was equipped to discover which. I walked over to her and wrapped my arms around her.

"I didn't mean that," I said. "I didn't mean to hurt you because of what I've done to Johnny Mae."

She put her arms around my waist and laid her head against my chest.

"I'm sorry, Frank. I never wanted anything bad to happen to you."

I moved gently away from her to arm's length and held her there, my hands on her shoulders.

"I have to find some way to get her back," I said. "I'm fond of you, Shirley, but the way I feel about Johnny Mae is something else."

"I had no idea, Frank. Maybe if I talked to her . . . told her there's nothing between us."

"I don't think that would work and it wouldn't exactly be the truth either, would it?" I said.

"I don't know what the truth is, Frank. I do know that I don't want to cause you any hurt. You've given me something I needed at a very bad time for me. I love you for that and I'll always be grateful but I don't want to own you or separate you from someone you love."

"I'm a grown man. I take responsibility for my part. I don't know how I'll do it but I'll get her back."

"It looks to me like we're both in very serious trouble," she said.

I found a couple of cold bottles of Coke in the refrigerator and we sat down across the kitchen table from each other. She wasn't looking like the bouncy, boobsy Miss Bulldog right now. She was looking like a real honest to goodness woman, the kind of woman you want to be kind and loving to.

"I'll do whatever you want," she said. "What do you want from me?"

"I want the truth."

"About what?"

"About everything. I want to know first of all what a woman like you is doing here with me instead of with your friends and family at a time like this in your life."

She didn't answer at first. She just stared at her hands. "I get to ask you questions too, don't I?" she said.

"Yes, you do. But I want you to start by telling me about you and Stafford."

She hesitated a minute, her eyes downcast. I thought she was going to ask, "What about me and Stafford?" but she looked up at me and began to talk.

"When I met Stafford I was out of college just long enough to know that life wasn't going to give me everything I wanted from it. I had been pumped up to expect that my good looks and my intellect would bring the world to my feet begging to give me position and opportunity. I was a college beauty queen and I had an MBA. My parents, my college professors, my friends, everyone expected me to be a star and be happy. They told me I would be successful at whatever I did."

She paused, then her voice quivered.

"The world came to my feet all right. Every sleazy, lecherous man, married or single, with a little money in his pocket came to me wanting to buy me just enough trinkets to get into my pants. I got so I almost hated my looks. I started out working in real estate here in town. It seemed like every deal I made carried with it the expectation that I would end up in somebody's bed or the back seat of their car. Then I met Stafford.

"He was a realtor. He and I cooperated on a few deals. Stafford had real money. He was twenty-five years older than me. He was married and had children almost my age. I wasn't interested in taking him away from his family. He wanted me and he came after me.

"He was a good looking man for his age, and in good condition. I know now that he was in a midlife crisis but I didn't see it then. I saw a rich, respected, established, good-looking man who was desperate for me, and I was disillusioned with my prospects as a single woman. I let him seduce me.

"He was wonderful to me. Never any concern about petty things. He treated me the way I wanted to be treated. Of course it got serious for us, especially for him. He left his wife . . . an awful, nasty divorce. His children were grown and he left her a fortune to live on so she never had to worry about money, but I can see now what she must have gone through.

"I knew deep inside that he couldn't keep up the hectic pace he had begun with me. It lasted for five or six years but then it tapered off until finally, for the past couple of years, there was nothing physical. It was mostly his age, I think, a decline in strength and endurance. He began to see himself as too old for me. He was aging rapidly but I wasn't. He just seemed to be losing interest in life.

"To tell you the truth, I didn't miss the physical part all that much. But something happened to Stafford during the past year or so. He was much more withdrawn and contemplative. I got the idea he was filled with misgivings and regrets but I didn't know about what. I suspected it involved me and the breakup of his first family but I wasn't sure that was it. I tried to talk with him several times but he wouldn't admit to anything out of the ordinary. I knew he wasn't telling me the truth but all I could do was keep on going, hoping he would work it out or eventually confide in me."

I listened to Shirley's story and believed she was telling me the truth. I wondered if her husband's regrets had more to do with a much earlier family obligation that he had left unfilled. Shirley wasn't sobbing but she was wiping tears from her eyes.

"Do you think his problems were with his business or with something else?" I asked.

Shirley looked directly into my eyes.

"I thought for a long time it might be business but last week I saw something that made it all come together. It was something you showed me."

"Me?" I said. "What?"

"When we went to Mr. Glover's house there were photographs there. Photographs I had seen before. Photographs Stafford had stored away in the attic at the lake house. That's why I asked you to go there with me. I needed to find those pictures."

"Pictures of what?" I asked.

"Pictures of Johnny Mae. When I saw the pictures in the Glovers' bedroom I knew I had seen pictures of that same little green eyed girl in Stafford's things. She's hard to forget. I asked him about the pictures years ago . . . who she was and why he kept the pictures. He just put them away and said she was the child of a friend he used to know. I knew there was more to it than that but there were many things about Stafford's past we never talked about. There were things I knew he wanted to forget had ever happened. I just didn't know what. I never got the opportunity to find out from him about the photographs."

What Shirley told me confirmed my own conclusions, though my conclusions had been based on deduction and speculation, not fact.

"I think Stafford was Johnny Mae's father," I said.

She reached her hand across the table toward me.

"I think he probably was. You have to understand, Frank, I never saw Johnny Mae before she walked through that door a few minutes ago. I didn't know her name. I never guessed that you even knew her and certainly not that you were in love with her. I would never have done with you what I did if I had known."

"Why did you get involved with me?" I asked.

"You don't know yourself very well, do you?"

"I used to think I did. Now I'm not sure I know anything."

"You're so kind and so sweet," she said. "You never came on to me. Oh, I flirted with you. That's all the fun I've had in the past couple of years. But you never came back at me. You never hit on me, even when we were alone at the lake house."

"I was thinking it," I said.

"Of course you were. We all think it, but you didn't impose your thoughts on me. And that old man and his wife. You helped them because of a basic goodness in you. You didn't want anything from them. I don't know another man in this town who would have done that. When I asked you to help me, you helped me, and you didn't ask for anything in return. I told you before but you thought I was only kidding. I told you I was attracted to you because you're kind and trustworthy."

I smiled and shook my head at her. "Who would ever have thought that being good would pay off like that?"

"If you knew very much about women you would have

155

known it. Of course you're also very good looking. But the bottom line is, you were just the right man at the time I needed you. OK, I've told you. Now you tell me what's been going on with you."

I told her the whole story of meeting Johnny Mae, finding out who she was, falling head over heels in love with her, about getting fired, and about tracking her down in Atlanta and begging her to love me.

"That's the most beautiful story I've ever heard," she said.

"It was beautiful until the arrest. Now it's turned into a tragedy for all of us. I don't have any confidence in the police investigation. It just seems to keep sucking us further into it. I've got to get this thing off my back. You need to tell me what you know about your husband's murder."

"I don't know anything. I honestly don't."

"You had no indication from him, any of his friends or business associates, that anything was seriously wrong?"

"Nothing but a growing unrest in him. . . until last Wednesday. There was definitely something unusual going on last Wednesday. He didn't come home until almost midnight, which is late for him. He was upset but he wouldn't say about what."

"The day of the ceremony at City Hall?"

"Yes."

I hesitated.

"What?" she asked.

"Johnny Mae was at the ceremony. He was introduced to her. He recognized who she was."

"How do you know?"

"He couldn't keep his eyes off her. He said he knew her mother many years ago and that Johnny Mae looked just like her."

"So he knew who she was," Shirley said.

"Yes, I think he knew he was meeting his own daughter."

"Who else knows about his connection to Johnny Mae?"

I wasn't prepared to tell her about Tiny. "I don't know who else may know. I pieced it together from things I've learned, things that someone close to Johnny Mae told me."

"It has to be connected to his mood change and his agitation." she said.

"What happened the rest of the week?"

"He came home early in the day on Thursday after the run-in he had with you in the mayor's office about the development project. He was totally absorbed with something. He paced about and worried to himself. He made some phone calls and he went out again."

"What about Friday?" I asked.

"More of the same on Friday. In the morning he was up early and distracted but he seemed happy somehow. I don't know. I thought perhaps he had solved whatever problem had been worrying him. He went to work as usual. He called me later in the day to say he would be out late and not to expect him for dinner. He never made it back home."

"Who found him?" I asked.

"He had arranged a late evening business meeting at the lake house. Some of his business partners found him when they arrived."

"What was the meeting about?"

"I don't know."

"What happens to his business interests now that he's dead?"

"I honestly don't know. I'm sure he has a will but I've never seen it. And he has a trust set up to hold most of his estate in case of his death. He has hundreds of thousands of dollars, perhaps millions in his businesses and I don't know anything about them. He wanted me out of the real estate development business after we got married. That's why I got involved with the DFACS office. Stafford arranged that through some of his contacts."

She stopped talking and was staring down at her lap, breathing heavily.

"I'm not a bad person, Frank. It's not that I didn't care for Stafford. I did. Everything I have I owe to him. He was good to me and I tried to be good for him. I never would have wished any harm to him. But now that he's gone I have no one to turn to. Stafford's family won't talk to me. My family doesn't have the foggiest notion of what's been happening and if they did, it would be beyond them. Stafford and I have no friends my age that I can turn to. All our friends are his business friends and are no comfort to me. There's no one at our home. It feels big and empty there. I can't go to the lake house where . . . it happened. I don't know what to do."

Chapter 16

Victim Or Accomplice?

I was in a hell of a quandary. Life was throwing me more curve balls than I could swing at. The one woman I would be willing to die for just walked out the door hating me. The widow of the man I stood accused of murdering was sitting across from me in my kitchen wearing nothing but the smell of me and one of my old shirts. I was on my first official day of forced retirement at an untimely age. My personal financial manager at Home Guardian Finance was probably waiting with anticipation for me to miss my first loan payment so he could seize my assets. I now had an arrest record for murder that would follow me for the rest of my life every time I filled out an application for anything worthwhile. That might have a bright side to it—maybe it would keep me from being drafted. The one thing I could imagine worse than my current condition would be to spend a couple of years in Vietnam. But that was a distant shadow. Right now I had more urgent things to worry about. I had to take care of some serious problems. The first one was Shirley.

"Do you have any family or friends you can call to be with you?" I didn't want it to sound like the bum's rush. I took her hand in mine and gave it a light kiss. "I know you need someone, but being here is going to cause us both some problems."

She smiled, nodded, and kissed my hand back. "I have a sister who may be able to come for a while."

"Is she as pretty as you?"

"Just as pretty and younger. You'd like her. Her husband

is a Marine."

"Ouch. Good choice. She should be perfectly safe."

"Can I ask you something, Frank, without offending you?"

"Sure. I think you're entitled."

"Are you sure you know what you're doing getting involved with a black girl? She's a beautiful girl, I know, but have you thought about what kind of life the two of you can possibly have together? Who would your friends be? Where would you live? What about your two families?"

"All I can tell you for sure, Shirley, is I can't see myself without her. I don't know the answers to your questions, except I know I would be willing to go anywhere or do anything to be with her. Our friends will be those who can accept us. Our families will love us, just as we love them."

She kissed my hand again. "I hope I haven't made you angry by asking. I just want to be sure you know what you're in for."

I wasn't angry at Shirley for expressing her concerns. She wasn't asking anything I hadn't asked myself during the past week. I knew there were many people who wouldn't accept a mixed couple but they didn't matter to me.

Shirley looked at the kitchen clock. "I have to go," she said. "I have to be at my attorney's office. . . and there are arrangements to be taken care of."

I felt for Shirley. I knew she needed comfort. I had needs of my own that had to be tended to. As she passed behind my chair she squeezed my shoulders.

"We'll find some way out of this mess," she said. I hoped she was right.

Shirley Willingham might be an unwilling victim or she might be an accomplice. I didn't know which. She had never done anything to deliberately hurt me, as far as I knew. I would give her the benefit of the doubt as long as I could. Whatever else she had done, Shirley had been good to me. I hoped it wasn't just a ploy.

One thing was for sure. Someone had killed Stafford Willingham. I knew it wasn't me or Johnny Mae but the aftermath of his death was destroying our lives. I didn't know if I was still a serious suspect but I knew for damn sure I wasn't going back to jail for it, even for a day. Like it or not, Johnny Mae and I had somehow gotten pulled into the middle of whatever was going. If she and I were to find happiness, the thing running over us and ripping us apart had to be stopped or we had to get out of its path.

I couldn't do anything sitting at home. I slipped on a shirt and a pair of shoes and was contemplating my next move when Shirley came out of my bedroom. She looked just as good in the navy blue suit today as she had yesterday. Not a wrinkle in it. I guess she hadn't worn it all that much.

"Can I drop you someplace?" she said.

"Yeah. Ron's garage. I've got to do something about transportation."

She stopped me just as we were about to go out the door of my apartment, turned to me and put her arms around my neck.

"Even with everything that's happened," she said, "if I had it to do all over again I would still want to be your lover. You're the one thing during this past week that's been good for me."

Looking into those blue eyes and seeing those soft lips up close again, feeling that gorgeous body leaning against me I had to admit she was just as beautiful and desirable a woman as ever. She just wasn't the woman for me.

"I said before," I told her, "and I meant it, you've been great. I hope you can understand there is only one woman for me now."

"I do understand. Johnny Mae is a lucky woman."

Understand or not, she laid a hell of a parting kiss on me. I guess she wanted both of us to remember what might have been. I was glad we were going out the door. Glad, that is, until I opened the door. Standing just outside my apartment was my second worst nightmare. Shirley and I stood face to face with Detectives Miller and Stevens. It was not a social call.

Detective Arthur Stevens couldn't resist the opportunity. He handed me his handkerchief. "Wipe the lipstick off your mouth," he said.

I used my own handkerchief. "You guys come for another lesson in due process?" I asked, being a smart ass. They were unaffected by my wit.

"We need to ask both of you to come down to the police station for questioning," Miller said. He didn't look as if he were enjoying himself. I was beginning not to enjoy him either.

"Come on." I said, "You guys know I didn't kill Shirley's husband."

"I can't believe you people," Shirley said. "If you want to talk to me you'll have to do it through my attorney." She turned to walk past the detectives but Miller held out an arm to block her way.

"You'll have to go to police headquarters with us, ma'am. You can call your attorney from there. Detective Stevens will drive you in your car. Frank, you ride with me."

"Are we under arrest?" I asked.

"We can arrest you," Miller said. "But if we arrest you, you'll have to be booked and held in jail. I don't want that and I don't think you want that either. We can avoid that if you'll come along voluntarily. Now, do we have your cooperation or do I read you your rights?"

Well, put that way, yes, I was willing to cooperate. Detective Stevens and Shirley headed out ahead of us in Shirley's car. Miller and I followed in the same police car they had brought me in from Atlanta.

"What's this all about, Detective Miller?" I said. "I was hoping you had concluded that I am innocent."

"To tell you the honest truth, Frank, I was beginning to think you could be innocent. That someone . . . we didn't know who . . . had set you up for Willingham's murder. But now we have a new problem we have to deal with and you don't look so innocent after all."

"What new problem?"

"I think you may need an attorney, Frank. Have you got the money to pay for a good lawyer?"

I laughed. "When I get paid this week I'll have just about enough money in the bank to pay off the loan I just took out to buy my motorcycle, pay for my car repair, and buy one tank of gasoline to get the hell out of Macon. I've got no job and I've got no savings. How much lawyer can I buy with that?"

"But you see, Frank, that's the little problem we have to work out."

"What?"

"You understand that because you are a prime suspect in a murder investigation we got authorization to look at your finances."

"Then you know I'm telling you the truth."

"No. What we found was, you have recently received a very large amount of money."

"What, $1,500?" I told you, I took out a loan to pay for my motorcycle."

"Not $1500, Frank. $25,000."

"You've been looking at the wrong account. As of last Thursday, not counting the $1,500 I borrowed from Home Guardian Finance, I had approximately $804 total cash worth."

"No, Frank. As of midnight last night you had a checking account balance of $27,000."

"You're crazy. I've never had $27,000 in my life."

"You're account records show that you received $25,000 directly into your account on Friday afternoon."

"$25,000? From where?"

"From the bank account of Mr. and Mrs. Stafford Willingham."

"There's got to be some mistake. That doesn't make any sense. I haven't received any money that I know about from anyone."

"You know what this looks like, Frank. It looks like Shirley Willingham gave you $25,000 on Friday afternoon and you killed her husband on Friday night. Then just three days later, here she is spending the night in your apartment with you. How does that look to you?"

"It looks to me like whoever tried to frame me for Willingham's murder is not giving up."

I spent the rest of that day at the Macon-Bibb County police headquarters being asked a lot of embarrassing and intimidating questions by Melvin Miller and Arthur Stevens. They were still doing the good cop, bad cop routine. I couldn't tell if they were just acting out their parts or if they really believed the things they were saying to me. They seemed to be trying to get me to say something that would support their murder-for-hire scenario but it just wouldn't fly.

"Listen," I said, "if Shirley Willingham wanted to pay me for a hit on her husband, why would she be so dumb as to transfer the payment directly from her account to mine, knowing the transaction could be traced? Shirley is not dumb. She knows business and she knows money. It looks to me more like someone is trying to frame Shirley and me."

"Maybe she's trying to frame you," Detective Stevens said.

"What?" I said. "And implicate herself at the same time? It just doesn't hold water."

"Who do you think would be able to do that?" Miller said. "I mean, who could have $25,000 taken out of her account and put into yours without her knowing about it?"

"That should be the kind of problem they teach you to solve in detective school," I said. "Off the top of my head I'd say either someone forged the transaction using her signature or someone did it from the inside."

"Inside where?" Miller asked.

"Inside the bank maybe?" I shrugged. "Who can cause money to move from one account to another? Is the Willingham account at the same bank as my checking account or is it at a different bank?"

"You don't know?" Miller asked.

"Shit no, I don't know anything about Shirley Willingham's finances."

"What about Miss Glover?" Miller said.

"What about her?" I was afraid he was going to tell me $25,000 had been deposited in her account too.

"I thought you were in love with the girl and here we find you sleeping with the widow Willingham before her late husband is even in the ground."

"That's not the way it was."

"That's what you say about everything," Detective Stevens snapped at me. "Everything with you is different from what it looks like it is. Well I say if it looks like a duck, it walks like a duck, and it quacks like a duck, then you're a lying bastard."

"A lying white bastard," I corrected him. "But if someone just a little smarter than you is trying to pin this murder on me, that's just what it would look like to you, isn't it?" I thought Detective Stevens was going to come across the interrogation table and strangle me. I wouldn't have blamed him, if I had been on his side of the table. But I wasn't.

"Tell me your version of this menage à trois between you, Mrs. Willingham, and Miss Glover," Detective Miller said. "If you love the Glover girl the way you say you do, then what was Mrs. Willingham doing spending the night with you last night?"

"Shirley scraped me up off the sidewalk after I got out of jail yesterday and took me home. I was completely exhausted, had no money and had no transportation. She stayed there partly to take care of me and partly because she didn't have anyone to look after her. She needed my company as much as I needed her help. She fixed me sandwiches yesterday and cereal this morning and slept in my apartment. That's all there is to it."

"Just a couple of Good Samaritans, eh?" Stevens smirked.

"Just two injured people," I said.

"Why wasn't Miss Glover with you?" Miller asked.

"You probably know that as well as I do," I said. "She said you questioned her for hours."

"When did you last talk with Miss Glover?"

"This morning, a little while before you showed up at my apartment."

"What's her part in this whole thing?" Miller asked.

"Just an innocent victim," I said.

"What if I were to tell you Miss Glover and Mr. Willingham met here in Macon on Wednesday afternoon?" Detective Miller said, his eyes fixed on my face.

I couldn't hide my shock. "That would depend on whether

you're telling me the truth." I put my hands in my lap to hide their shaking.

"What if I told you Mr. Willingham contacted his personal attorney on Friday morning to initiate changes in his will, leaving a very large piece of his wealth to Miss Glover upon the event of his death?"

My heart was pounding. This was not what I expected or wanted to hear. If Johnny Mae had met with Willingham, wouldn't she have told me?

"How did she meet with him?" I said. "Where did she meet with him?"

"So you didn't know?" Miller said.

Chapter 17

Booby Trap

Detectives Miller and Stevens were trying to keep me off balance so I would slip up and tell them something incriminating. It wasn't going to work because I didn't know anything incriminating. I was determined not to let their allegations and insinuations spoil my feelings for Johnny Mae. I didn't know what meeting, if any, had taken place between her and Stafford Willingham. When the time came I would let Johnny Mae herself tell me about it.

"I just want you to tell me the whole truth about everything you know, Frank," Detective Miller said. "I don't want to see you or Miss Glover in any deeper trouble. You tell me the truth and if it checks out, the two of you walk away from this free and clear."

"You're the same detective who told me on Saturday night you needed my cooperation in order to keep me out of jail, aren't you?"

"You're not in jail are you?" He paused, I assumed to let me think about that. "I think you do love the girl. There's nothing I would like better than to find that the killer is somebody else and the two of you had nothing to do with it."

"I'm telling you the truth," I said. "I know absolutely nothing about any money being deposited to my bank account. I didn't kill anyone and I didn't receive any money for that purpose or for any other purpose. I have no personal knowledge of any meeting between Stafford Willingham and Johnny Mae except at the City Hall ceremony I told you about."

The interrogation went on a lot longer but it was rehashing the same questions over and over again. The only inconsistency they got from my answers was due to fatigue and frustration. In the end they let me walk. So here I was twenty-four hours after getting out of jail the first time, back in the same spot, standing on the street in front of the police station wondering what was going on, who was so determined to pin the Willingham murder on me, and what I could do about it. But this time Shirley wasn't there to pick me up.

I thought perhaps I should call Shirley to be sure she was OK. But she had an attorney and I was sure he was earning his money. I decided instead to walk the four blocks to Ron's garage to check on my car. I needed transportation.

"Hey, dude!" Ron said when he saw me standing next to the car he was lying under. "Been reading about you in the papers. You out on bail?"

"Charges dismissed," I said. "I'm an innocent man. I was the wrong person in the wrong place at the wrong time."

Ron rolled out from under the car on his creeper, got to his feet and wiped the grease off his hands with a shop cloth.

"Man, did you pick a bad time to jump in the sack with the Willingham woman. Can't blame you though. I've seen her. She's a knockout. You're not charged?"

"No charges. Somebody laid a trap and I walked into it but I didn't do it."

"You walked into it?" Ron said. "I thought old man Willingham walked into it."

"What do you mean?"

"The way he was killed. He walked into a booby trap."

"A booby trap?"

"Yeah. Didn't you know? Somebody left a loaded shotgun rigged to go off when he went into his bathroom."

"No, I didn't know that. So he wasn't actually killed by

somebody holding the shotgun?"

"That's what my buddies down at the police station tell me. They say he went to the lake house alone, went to the bathroom to take a piss or whatever, and whamo . . . a load of buckshot right in the chest."

"So the trap could have been set at any time," I said. My mind was reeling.

"Sure. That's one reason it's going to be damn hard to pin the murder on anyone."

"Speaking of the shotgun. He was killed with the shotgun that was in the trunk of my car when I left the car here with you last week."

"No shit. The two Dragnet detectives asked me a hundred questions about it. I told them and I'll tell you, I don't know a damn thing about any shotgun. You see that sign?"

He pointed to an old dirty printed sign taped to the wall of his garage. The sign read, *Management not responsible for articles left in vehicles. Please remove any valuables.*

"That means just what it says." Ron punctuated his statement with his cigar. "Too many people come in and out of a garage. We can't watch everything all the time to make sure nobody walks off with anything."

"So you never saw it?"

"Never saw it."

I looked around the garage. Scott Taylor's red pickup was still there. It was taped and primed, waiting for a paint job. I noticed that some of the vehicles in the garage had their doors or their trunk lids open.

"Where do you keep the keys when a car is being worked on?"

"In my office hanging on a hook, along with the work order."

"Is it possible someone could have taken the gun from the trunk of my car sometime last week?"

Ron was beginning to look a little bit aggravated. "Sure, Frank, anything is possible. I'm not here all the time. I go to get parts, I tow cars in, I go to the bathroom, I eat lunch, I eat supper. Somebody could've come in here and took the shotgun out of your trunk without me knowing anything about it."

"Where's my car now?"

"Done and gone." Ron stuck the stub of a cigar back between his teeth. "Skeeter Jackson said you told him to pick it up when it was ready. He was telling the truth, wasn't he?"

"Yes, that's right. I just didn't know he had gotten it already." A thought occurred to me. "Is Skeeter Jackson related to a big, ugly, tough looking guy named Leroy Jackson?"

"Yeah, Leroy. He's a cousin or something. He came in here with Skeeter Saturday afternoon to get your car. Skeeter said you would pay me. You owe me two hundred dollars for the repair. But if this murder business has got you short of cash, you can pay me later."

"I'll send you payments from the bighouse."

"Don't laugh. I've seen innocent men go to prison."

"It was only a joke. My billfold, checkbook, everything got left between here and Atlanta when I was arrested. I'll pay you in the next day or two."

"No problem. I've got a lien on your car. You don't pay in thirty days, I take your car." Ron looked at me with a friendly if somewhat unsettling smile. "It's just routine business. No hard feelings. How's the bike doing? Running like a top, I hope?"

"The last time I saw it," I said. "I've got to get a ride to Atlanta to pick it up."

"I'm going up that way tomorrow. You still need a ride,

call me before noon. You can ride up with me."

I couldn't do anything without money. I left Ron's garage and walked toward my bank. Finding out Stafford Willingham was killed by walking into a booby trap had sent my mind to spinning. To a passerby I must have looked like one of the Macon street characters walking along lost in thought, stopping to think, mumbling to myself. All I needed was a bundle of umbrellas and I could have been the umbrella man. I was thinking all along the person who killed Willingham had to be there when he was killed. But if he was killed by a trap set for him, that wasn't true. Whoever set the trap could have done it hours or even a day or more before the murder.

I remembered now, Detective Miller didn't ask me where I was between ten and midnight the night Willingham was murdered. He asked me where I had been after I left work on Thursday . . . a day and a half before Willingham died. I didn't pick up on that. I had to stop thinking about where people were at the time of the murder. That was no longer critical. What was critical was the shotgun. How did the shotgun get from the trunk of my car to the murder scene?

Assuming Ron was telling the truth, he never saw the gun. So I didn't know whether it was there and he didn't see it or if it was missing. The car went into his shop on Monday morning. The murder was on Friday night. Skeeter and Leroy picked up the car on Saturday afternoon. Between Monday and Friday there might have been a hundred different people in and out of the garage, any one of whom could have taken the shotgun. That included Scott Taylor or any of his men. Or Skeeter, for that matter. The next time I had occasion to talk with Detective Miller I had to remember to tell them about my unpleasant connection with Scott Taylor.

Another disturbing thought occurred to me. Everyone was assuming the trap was set for Stafford Willingham. But what if it was set for someone else? What if it was set for

Shirley Willingham and Stafford just happened to walk into it? I didn't even know where to begin with that line of thought. Or maybe it was set for me. Did Stafford find out about Shirley and me and set a trap for us at the lake house? How would he have gotten hold of my shotgun?

My contemplations and deductions had led me nowhere except to the bank. As if I didn't have any really important things to worry about, I hit a bit of a snag trying to get my money out of the bank. I didn't have my checkbook so I needed to use a counter check. In order to cash a counter check I needed a picture ID. I didn't have my billfold so I didn't have a picture ID. The bank teller and I went three or four rounds on this before she finally called the assistant manager. He was the same guy who had refused my request for a loan the previous week.

"Mr. Hayes," he said, "what seems to be the problem?"

The assistant manager's name tag said Jack Russell. I thought a Jack Russell was a dog but I refrained for the moment from mentioning that association.

"Well, Jack, I've been temporarily separated from my checkbook and my driver's license. I need to withdraw some money from my checking account."

"How much do you want?"

I couldn't miss the opportunity. I had never before had $25,000 in my checking account. "Can you tell me my balance?" I asked.

The manager and the bank teller both consulted the computer terminal. He turned and went into an office with lettering on the door that said Henry Wallis, Vice President. I couldn't hear their conversation but I could see their serious expressions through the glass wall of the manager's office. Mr. Wallis came out to give me personal service. He did not offer his hand. Perhaps he thought mine had blood on it.

"Am I to understand that you wish to withdraw from your checking account, Mr. Hayes?"

"Yes, that's right."

"It will take a few minutes to confirm the status of the account," he said. "There have been some irregularities with it, as you probably know."

I sat in Mr. Jack Russell's office while the vice president talked on the phone in his office. After several minutes Mr. Wallis came out. I noticed a bank guard had stepped to within a few feet of me to my right. I took that as a bad sign.

"Your checking account has been frozen under court order, Mr. Hayes. No funds may be placed into the account or taken from it until the order is lifted."

That was not what I had expected. I was expecting a warm and fuzzy feeling at seeing my hugely swollen bank balance. Instead, I was suddenly without any money whatsoever.

"I can't get any money from it?" I asked, just to make sure.

"No."

The vice president, the assistant manager, the teller, and the guard all stood silent, looking at me. To say that I felt awkward would be one of the great understatements of my life. I was about to turn and leave in total humiliation. The teller whispered something to Wallis and Wallis nodded his head.

"You do have a balance in your savings account that is accessible, Mr. Hayes," the teller said somewhat shyly.

Temporary salvation. "Give me whatever is in it."

"Do you want to close it out?" she asked.

Somehow the question seemed completely irrelevant at the moment but she was being sincere.

"How much do I need to leave in the account to keep it active?" I asked.

She looked quizzically in the direction first of the vice president, then the assistant manager. They were unresponsive.

"Oh, any amount at all," she said.

"Leave one dollar in," I said.

She punched some numbers into her computer terminal and looked up at me with a sweet smile, trying like hell to act normal. "How would you like your money? Cash or check?"

"Cash," I said.

She opened the cash drawer and counted out a stack of bills and some change.

"Here you are. Three hundred, forty-nine dollars and thirty-seven cents."

I thanked her but made it a point to ignore the vice president and assistant manager who were showing me no sympathy. I said to the guard, "No need to escort me out, I think I'll be safe." He wasn't amused. The last I saw of the four of them they were still standing watching me when I turned the corner outside the bank.

It hadn't occurred to me that my account would be sealed. I guess I thought if I wasn't under arrest or charged then I was free and clear. I was wrong. If the $25,000 came from Shirley's account, then it belonged to her and I would have given it back to her anyway. But it pissed me off that I couldn't get to my own money. I didn't have a clue as to what would happen to my checking account, when or how I would be able to get what little money was rightfully mine. I didn't know how the $25,000 had gotten into my account. I needed to find out if Shirley knew anything about it. I found the nearest pay phone and called Shirley's number. There was no answer.

I had a funny thought. The bank would send me a statement month after month showing a balance of one dollar. I wondered how much the statement would cost to prepare and mail. If I left the dollar in the account to draw compound interest, how much would I have in fifty years? As I said, I never was really good with numbers.

I needed some advice and some help. I caught the bus to east Macon and walked the half-dozen blocks from the bus stop to Tiny Glover's house.

Chapter 18

Low Down Business

Tiny could just as well have been sitting in the same spot on his front porch since the last time I saw him. He looked as if his eyes were closed but I knew he was watching me as I walked up because he started to grin.

"My boy Leroy find you?" he said.

"He did." I nodded. "He watched over me through one of the worst nights of my life. I'm indebted to you."

"It'll all even out. Leroy told me they dropped the charge against you. You think they still want you?"

"They want something." I told Tiny about being arrested and released, about my bank account being seized, and everything I had learned about the murder. I didn't tell him about Johnny Mae and me. I wasn't ready to do that, not just yet. "Tiny, there's a real problem with my shotgun."

"Umm hmm, sho' is."

"As nearly as I can figure, somebody took it out of the trunk of my car when it was at Ron's garage."

"That's the way it looks."

"Ron swears to me he didn't know the gun was in the car. I think I believe him."

I had to be careful how I said the next thing.

"Did Skeeter work at Ron's garage last week?"

"Some," he said.

"Do you think he could have seen anything?"

"I'll find out," Tiny said. "You let me handle that."

I didn't argue with that. If I started asking Skeeter or

Skeeter's friends any questions about the shotgun, it could very quickly start sounding like a suspicion or an accusation. I didn't want to be in that position.

"I need to know how the gun got from the trunk of my car into the hands of whoever set the trap for Willingham."

"May be best if you stay away from it," Tiny said. "You could still get burned."

"If somebody has got it in for me, I think I should find out who it is. Otherwise I'll never know who I can trust."

"What if you never find out? Then who you gon' trust?" Tiny shifted around and looked up at me. "Maybe somebody needed a gun, they found yours, and that's all."

"Too much coincidence. They just happened to be planning to kill Stafford Willingham, the man I worked for and just had a run-in with and . . ." I couldn't bring myself to say the rest.

"I read about it in the newspaper. Look to me like his wife set you up."

"Jesus, I should never have gotten involved with her."

"Don't beat yo' self up, Frank. It'd be easy for a man to want to get involved with that woman. It got its price. You payin' it. You young. You'll get over it."

"I need to get to the bottom of whatever is going on. I don't think the police have any suspects but me and Shirley Willingham."

"I tell you what. You set us up in the barbecue business and I'll be yo' own personal private eye. I think you might need one." He laughed.

"How much do you think it would cost? The barbecue business, I mean. I don't know anything about the business except on the consumer end."

"I can do the buyin', the cookin', and the sellin'. But I might need you to do the financin' up front and the

178

bookkeepin' in the back. I been doin' some figurin' since the last time we talked."

He took a notepad from under the newspaper lying on the floor beside him and flipped through its pages. I guessed that ever since he sent Leroy to look after me in jail he had been planning a barbecue venture.

"How much you got?"

I laughed. "Just barely enough to eat with until I get paid."

"I figure we can get started in business for $2,000 and be makin' money the first week."

"I'll tell you what. If I can get my hands on $2,000, we'll talk about it."

"Think hard about it, Frank. I'm serious. You and me could do all right together."

"Right now I've got a problem with transportation. My motorcycle's been in Atlanta since I was arrested and I'm trying to find my car. Ron over at the garage said Skeeter and Leroy picked it up from him on Saturday. You know where they took it?"

"Yeah, they got an old building where they do they paintin'. Skeeter gon' be by here d'rectly. You hang around, you can see him."

A series of loud bangs, scrapes, and clattering from across the street at Mr. Glover's place interrupted our conversation. A pair of white workmen were unloading lumber and building materials from a flatbed truck in the front yard of the house. I had been so immersed in my own problems I hadn't stopped to ask about Mr. Glover. I was hoping the money from the mayor would take care of his problems.

"Mr. Glover having repairs made to his house?"

Tiny nodded his head, but with a look of disgust. "He's messin' with them white trash contractors. He ought not be.

They ain't no good. But they ain't nuthin' I can do about it."

"Who are they?"

"They somebody he found out about from the finance company."

"What finance company is that?"

"Home Guardian."

American Home Guardian Finance, the home of my personal financial manager, Bob Felton. "Is that who he owes money too? DFACS said he's paying a big chunk of his monthly income to loan payments."

"He is. He borrowed so many times he don't even know what he's payin' for no more. The old man won't ever get clear of 'em."

"How much do you think he owes?" I asked.

Tiny didn't look up at me. He continued to stare at the two workmen coming and going from his parents' house.

"I don't know for sure. My mamma might tell me but the old man won't tell her nuthin' about the finances. He did say when he went this time to borrow the money for a used 'frigerator, the man at Home Guardian paid off all his old debts an' set him up a new loan."

"A debt consolidation loan." I cringed at the thought of Mr. Glover paying the same high interest rate I was paying on my motorcycle.

"Yeh. They make him think they doin' him a favor but they just diggin' they fingers in deeper. They gon' choke the life out of that old man. He never would listen to me or Mamma. I'm 'fraid he's gon' fool aroun' 'till some loan shark gets they hands on his house."

"How would they get his house?"

"Collateral. They make the old man put his house up for collateral. Tha's the only way they lend him money. Him or my mamma get sick or somethin' an' can't make the payments on time, the loan company takes the house. They happy to loan money to anybody that got a house or a car or somethin' to put up. The old man don't know what's happenin' so he signs his mark on the papers. As soon as he does that, they got him three different ways.

"First off, the furniture store charges him way too much for the stuff they sellin'. Maybe $300 for some old used piece of junk I could find in the want ads for $50 or $75. He can't pay cash so they finance it for 'im and give 'im four or five years to pay for it. They say, 'you just pay us $15 a month for this fine refrigerator.' If he does make all the payments, they done charged him so much interest that by the time it's paid for, he done paid $900. An' we talkin' about somethin' that never was worth more than $100.

"They just keep on sellin' to somebody like the old man until he got so much debt ain't no way he can pay it off. Then when the old man don't make his payments, they got a lawyer who takes the papers to court and the judge tell the sheriff to auction off the house to pay the debts."

"Somehow that doesn't sound legal."

"That's what they do. It happens every day. 'Cause when he puts his mark on that finance contract he don't know it but the contract say he puttin' his house and all his property up for collateral. Here," Tiny said, handing me the paper lying beside him. "Look at the legal notices in the want ads."

I opened the paper to the want ad section. There were pages and pages of notices of foreclosures and public auctions. Most of them were just what Tiny had described . . . public auction of property seized as a result of failure to pay debts.

"You ever been to a' auction on the courthouse steps?" Tiny said.

Of course I had not.

"They pay a dime on the dollar for what the property ought to cost. The old man's house might sell for $1,000 or $500. Sometimes it might go as low as $200."

"It's hard to believe," I said. "I never heard of such a thing."

"You see all the low rent houses in the neighborhood that's got signs on 'em from Riverside, Willingham and all them other real estate companies? Where you think they got them houses? You know they didn't build them shacks. They bought 'em on the courthouse steps. Then they turn around and rent 'em back to the same folks they took 'em from. Why you think black folks are burnin' they own neighborhoods on TV? They done had enough. They burnin' down the property that's been stole from 'em."

I followed Tiny's gaze across the street to Mr. Glover's house.

"Tiny," I said, "did you know Stafford Willingham if you saw him? Do you know what he looked like?"

"Yeh, I seen him."

"Was he here last week?"

Tiny's expression grew dark and brooding.

"Yeh, he come over to the old man's house the middle of last week. Come drivin' up in that big black Lincoln in the afternoon the day of the big to-do down at City Hall."

"Did he talk with Johnny Mae?"

"Umm hmm. Johnny Mae was there. He went into the old man's house and stayed a while. Then he come outside an' him an' Johnny Mae set an' talked in his car for a long time. How'd you know about that?"

"Something one of the police detectives said to me. You got any idea what Willingham might have been doing here?"

"I might got some ideas but I don't know."

"What do you think?"

"You don't know?" Tiny didn't look at me. I didn't say anything. "He down here in the neighborhood slummin'."

"What would he have to talk to Johnny Mae about?"

His voice fell into a low guttural sound, almost a growl. "The Willinghams has always kept colored women aroun'. He was prob'ly offerin' her a job to come to work for 'im. You seen Johnny Mae. What man wouldn't want her aroun'?"

It made me hurt inside to know that Tiny was carrying those ideas about Willingham and Johnny Mae. And if my own suspicions were right, Tiny was so wrong. I wanted to tell him but I couldn't bring myself to do it.

"Whatever it was, he's gone now," I said.

"I think somebody done us all a favor," Tiny said.

Across the street Mr. Glover was on his front porch holding the screen door open for the workmen to carry a sheet of plywood inside. I walked over toward him. He nodded and spoke to me as I stepped up to his porch.

"I'm getting some work done on my house, Mr. Hayes. They gon' bring it up to meet the rules of the building inspection."

I shook his hand.

"I'm glad to see it, Mr. Glover. I'm happy for you."

The door opened and one of the two workmen came out. He looked at me with a particularly surly expression as he went past me on the way to his truck. The lettering on the side of his truck said 'Taylor Contracting and Home Repair.' Taylor? Scott Taylor? How did he get involved in this I wondered. But my immediate concern was with something else.

"Mr. Glover," I said, "did you see Mr. Stafford Willingham when he was out here last week?"

"Yes, sir, I did. It was a terrible thing that happened to Mr. Willingham."

"Yes, it was. How did he happen to come to see you?"

"It was because of you, Mr. Hayes."

"Me?"

"Because of what you done for us. Mr. Willingham heard all about it. He was down at City Hall for the big ceremony. He saw me there and he spoke to me and shook my hand. Sho' enough." The old man shook his head as if a wonderful thing had happened. "He come by the house here later to talk with me. His family and my family go way back. He remembered me from all them years ago. I used to do work for his daddy. Odd jobs, you know. I helped to build the house he grew up in. He wanted to know all about how I been doin' and what done happened to everybody. He stayed quite some spell."

We moved to the end of the porch to get out of the way of the two workmen coming and going.

"I guess he talked with Johnny Mae?"

"Oh, Lawd, yes. He just made over Johnny Mae. He talked with her for a good long while. He seemed real proud for what she done made of herself. He remembered Johnny Mae's mamma when she was alive."

The old man grew silent in remembrance and his face darkened with grief. Then he brightened some as he spoke again.

"I told him all the trouble I been havin' and how grateful I am for the help that's been give to me and my wife. I told him all about how you helped us, Mr. Hayes. It brought tears to his eyes. Mr. Willingham was a goodhearted man."

I couldn't say that I shared Mr. Glover's view of the late Stafford Willingham. I said my goodbye to him and walked past the workman, who had grown no less surly. He was marking measurements on a board to be sawn.

"How's it going?" I asked.

The look on his face showed a very bad temper. "I'm trying to finish this job as fast as I can and get the hell out of here," he growled at me.

"Why did you take the job if you don't want it?" I asked.

He gave me a quick once-over nasty look. "It ain't my idea. I just do what I'm told to do."

"Who do you work for, Scott Taylor?"

"What about it?" he asked, as if I had thrown him a challenge.

"I know Scott. But I didn't know he's in the home repair business."

"He's into everything . . . home, business, big, little, white, black . . . anywhere there's a dollar to be made he's in it."

"Hard man to work for?"

He looked at me like a dog sizing up a fire hydrant. "Sometimes. He don't bother me." Further conversation was cut off by the noise of his electric saw.

I noticed Skeeter's car had pulled up in Tiny's driveway and Skeeter was on the front porch talking. I walked back across the street to where they were. Something was wrong.

Chapter 19

Don't Mess With Me

Skeeter was obviously upset. He walked back and forth, shaking his head and gesturing animatedly. Tiny looked up when I got there.

"Hey, Skeeter," I said. "What's going on?"

He didn't answer. He was sitting now, holding his head in his hands.

"The boy's birthday come up in the draft lottery," Tiny said.

Jesus, the fear that had been hanging in the back of my own mind.

"What number are you?" I asked.

"Number eight, man. They gon' call me in."

He was right. Based on the number of men who were needed for the draft, the Selective Service boards had been calling up at least the first hundred and twenty-five birth dates chosen in the annual lottery. Number eight was a sure bet to be drafted.

"I'm sorry, man," I said. "Maybe it'll be over before they can even process you."

"Man, I ain't goin' to die in no white man's war. They not killin' me. Nobody gon' napalm me. I'm stayin' right here. I ain't about to get my legs and arms blowed off in no jungle because some white general made a big mistake. Let 'em take you," he said, stabbing his finger in the air at me. "Let 'em eat white meat."

There was nothing I could say to comfort him. I looked at

Tiny, indicating my helplessness. Tiny just shook his head.

"You got to look at the advantages," Tiny said.

"What advantages?" Skeeter said. "Being dead ain't got no advantages."

"Shit, man. You get all muscled up, get in yo' uniform, you'll have more ass than you can take care of. Don't believe what you see on TV. Women loves a man in a uniform."

"Shit," Skeeter said. But I could tell from his voice he wanted to believe it.

"I tell you, man, you go to California, you'll have California girls. You go to Germany, you'll have German girls. You go to the North Pole, you'll have Eskimo girls. And you go to Vietnam, you'll have cute little Chinese girls that know how to do things you never even heard of. They'll screw you 'till you so weak you can't even stand up."

"Can't nobody do that," Skeeter said.

"I'm tellin' you, man. You gon' have to eat raw eggs and oysters to keep yo' pecker up."

Skeeter laughed. He really wanted to believe it. "I'm not dyin', man," he said.

"Course not," Tiny said. "Your old man went through Korea. He didn't die. I went through prison for eighteen years an' I didn't die. If I can live through eighteen years of prison, I know damn well a strong boy like you can live through two years in the Army gettin' his pecker screwed off. They prob'ly send you to Hawaii. You'll be screwed to death by pretty little Hawaiian girls in grass skirts an' no underpants. You know the girls in Hawaii don't wear nuthin' on they top. They run around on the beach with they bare tits stickin' out, wearing nothin' but a grass skirt an' flowers layin' across their tits."

"No, they don't." Skeeter laughed.

"You ask Frank. I know Frank's seen pictures of 'em. Ain't I right, Frank?"

"I've seen the pictures," I said.

"No shit?" Skeeter said.

"I swear."

"Damn."

"Frank wants to know about his car," Tiny said. "He ain't got no wheels."

Skeeter seemed to come back from somewhere. "It's half done. It'll be a couple more days."

Tiny looked at me and gave me a little nod.

"How about I pay you the hundred dollars for the paint job?" I said. "I'm sure you've got some expenses." That seemed to brighten him. I counted the hundred dollars out of the roll in my pocket.

"Thanks," he said. "I got to go. You need a ride somewhere?"

"I could use a ride back to my apartment."

As we drove across town I told Skeeter about the G.I. Bill and how the government would pay his way through college or trade school if he joined the service. I told him Tiny was right about all the places he could go. I was trying to pump myself up as much as him in case my number came up.

When he stopped to let me out in front of my apartment, a shiny blue Dodge sat outside my door. Skeeter knew cars. If he hadn't been distracted by his own thoughts he would have recognized it as Johnny Mae's. I didn't say anything.

I tried to stay calm as he drove off and I turned and opened my apartment door. The situation inside was too surreal. The air was filled with the aroma of bread baking and the smell of food cooking. Johnny Mae was stirring sliced potatoes in a pan on the stove and green beans were simmering in a pot. She turned and looked at me at the sound of my approach. Looking at her, it might have been just another day at the office for me and a hot meal when I got home. I wished it were so. I couldn't figure out why she had come back. I had been afraid I might never see her again.

"You want something to eat, Frank?" Her face and voice didn't tell me what she was thinking. But her eyes were showing me a warning to tread carefully.

"Yes, thank you."

"Wash your hands and sit down," she said.

I wanted to ask her what was going on, what had happened to bring her back, but I didn't. I wanted to put my arms around her and tell her I was the happiest man in the world that she was there. I didn't do that either. I was afraid to say or do anything. I washed my hands and sat down at the table.

"I had to buy some groceries. I couldn't find anything in your kitchen. I don't know what you've been eating."

I shrugged. "Not a balanced diet, I guess. I'm very happy you did this." I indicated the food she was putting on the table. "But, I mean, you didn't have to . . ."

The look she gave me renewed my caution.

"I had to eat." She sat down opposite me.

"I really am grateful. I mean . . . having you here."

"Shut up and eat your dinner, Frank."

It was easily the best meal I had eaten in days. She had made cornbread, panfried potatoes, pork chops, green beans, sliced tomatoes, and iced tea. It would have been a perfect meal except for the tension I sensed was coiled within her and the uncertainty and fear I was feeling, mixed with an almost irresistible desire to hold her in my arms. We ate in silence.

After twenty minutes of not meeting my eyes she sat sipping her glass of iced tea and looked across the table at me. I reached my hand out to her. She just shook her head and continued to look at me.

"Where do you think we would eat if I hadn't cooked for us?" she said.

"I could take you to a restaurant maybe?"

"Where? What restaurant?"

Her eyes still hadn't left me. They weren't warm and loving eyes. They were hard eyes. Not steel hard, just no nonsense. I felt like some defective part on an assembly line somewhere and she was the quality control inspector.

"Anywhere you wanted," I said, but was at a loss to come up with a name. I knew why, all too painfully well.

"You see how it is, Frank? We go to a white restaurant, they don't want me. We go to a black restaurant, they don't want you. I could never be happy waiting for somebody who didn't like one of us or both of us to say something or do something. It's not just restaurants. It's everything."

"We can go someplace else," I said. "Atlanta. Anywhere we have to."

"I live in Atlanta and I've lived in other big cities. You've got more freedom there but you can go just so far and then it's the same thing. I've got white friends and I've got black friends but they lead separate lives."

"I think if we love each other we can make a world we can live in and be happy."

She shook her head. "I wish I could believe that, Frank. I started my life in east Macon and I've spent the past twenty-five years trying get away from it. I studied my way out of poverty. The only way I knew how. I'm the only person in my family . . . the only person in the whole neighborhood . . . ever to have gone to college. I've got a college degree and a graduate degree in nursing. I work as a professional. I speak proper English. I wear the right kind of clothes. But I can never get away from prejudice. It follows me everywhere I go. I've been walking a narrow line trying to strike just the right balance between black and white, trying to be happy and comfortable. Then you come along and pull me right back into east Macon. I've been forced to deal with people and issues that humiliated and disgraced me."

"I never wanted you involved in any of this," I said. "I'm very sad for any hurt you've felt because of me."

"Why did you have to mess with me? I was happy."

"I wasn't messing with you. I was following my heart. I want you to be happy again. I want us to be happy together." I reached my hand to her again. But she wouldn't take it.

"Do you? Then you need to help me understand about your involvement with the Willingham murder. And you better start with the woman I found here this morning."

I wanted to tell her everything. But I didn't want to tell her anything else she would have to forget or forgive.

"I had one brief sexual encounter with Shirley Willingham before I was involved with you. Someone found out about it and tried to use it to frame me for the murder of Stafford Willingham. He and I had a run-in at the mayor's office over his bogus housing project and I was fired because of it. He was killed with an old shotgun I had in the trunk of my car and hadn't touched in a year. My fingerprints were found at the lake house where he was murdered because I was there that one time with Shirley Willingham. And someone arranged to have money transferred from the Willinghams' bank account to mine, making it look like Shirley paid me to kill her husband."

"What was she doing here this morning?"

"After I was arrested at your place Saturday night I was held in jail without food or sleep for over twenty-four hours. When I was released I was weak and exhausted. I had nobody to call, no money, no transportation, no food, and no way to get home. Shirley Willingham found me on the street outside the courthouse and drove me here. I'd slept no more than four hours in over forty-eight hours. I ate a sandwich and went straight to bed and slept until nine o'clock this morning."

Johnny Mae's face still showed disapproval. "Why did she stay here last night?"

"Her husband was killed only three days ago and she had no family member, no friend, no one to be with her at home. She stayed here in my apartment last night just to have a place to stay where she wouldn't be alone. Her husband was dead, she was scared. Nothing happened between us. I told her I'm in love with you and that you will be the only woman in my life from now on. I tried to call you on the phone from the time I got out of jail until just before you walked through my door this morning."

Her eyes still had not left me. "You better be telling me the truth, Frank. You've had me upset enough to kill you and her too."

"Every word I've told you is the truth. I had nothing to do with the murder of Stafford Willingham and there is nothing going on between Shirley Willingham and me. I wish I had never heard her name. I swear to you, you are the only woman I have ever loved and I love you now. Won't you please believe me and love me?"

I know she softened. I could see her breathing had changed and the tension was gone from the muscles in her neck and jaw.

"There's a man who wants to marry me, Frank. His name is Anthony Boudreau."

Oh, Jesus. I thought I was going to come apart right in front of her.

"I was at Fisk and Mahary with him and Reggie and now we all work together at Emory. He's an intern now. He'll be a doctor soon."

I could feel my whole body trying to reject what she was saying. I was holding my breath so I wouldn't cry out. My heart was beating so fast I thought it might explode into pieces.

"His family has money and respect. He drives a new Mercedes and takes me on vacations to the Caribbean. Tell me why I should be messing with an out-of-work white boy who doesn't have but two dollars to his name, who tells me stories only a naive girl would believe, and who is likely any day to be picked up by the police for murder."

It took me a moment to be able to speak.

"I just hope you'll listen to your heart for the answers to those questions because I think your heart knows the truth."

"So you think it's my heart that's been talking to me?" she said. "I thought maybe it was another part of my anatomy."

"That has to be there too."

"If I find you lying to me I'll kill you, Frank."

"I'll die before I tell you a lie," I said and I meant it, from that moment on.

"I catch you with another woman, I'll kill you."

"Then I'll live to be a happy old man."

She got up from the table and stood beside me.

I was still afraid to move. I reached out my hand to her.

"Come with me," she said, and took my hand.

Chapter 20

In The Name Of Love

At eight o'clock the next morning we were still in bed when my phone rang. It was a voice I didn't want to hear.

"Frank?"

"Yeah."

"This is Shirley. Have you heard the news?"

"No, what?"

"Three black men were arrested last night for Stafford's murder."

I sat up straight and tried to clear my head of sleep.

"Who are they? Do you know?"

"According to my attorney, one's an older man named Walter Glover. He goes by the nickname 'Tiny'. I wonder if he's any relation to John Glover? The other two are younger men. They're brothers named Andrew and Leroy Jackson."

Tiny, Skeeter, and Leroy. What reason could the police have for arresting them? The shotgun maybe?

"I just thought you would like to know, in case you haven't heard."

"No, I hadn't. I guess the police questioned you about the $25,000 that showed up in my checking account?"

"Yes, they did and I know nothing whatsoever about it. I certainly didn't put it there if that's what you're asking."

"I'm not accusing, just asking," I said.

"I don't know anything about it. The district attorney says the bank records show the money came from my and Stafford's account but I have no knowledge of it."

"You think it's a setup?"

"What else could it be?" she said.

"I don't know. Thanks for the call. I'll call Detective Miller and see if this puts me in the clear."

Johnny Mae turned over and was waiting for me to tell her what was going on. This was not the way I had planned to begin the morning.

"Uncle Tiny?" She said when I told her the news. "What has Uncle Tiny got to do with Stafford Willingham?"

How was I going to answer this one?

"What do you know about Tiny?" I asked.

Johnny Mae slid off the side of the bed and headed for the bathroom. "I never knew him growing up. He was away in prison. Poppa and Mamma never would say much about him."

I went to the kitchen and put on a pot of coffee. Johnny Mae came in wearing my bathrobe and nothing else. She was about the sexiest looking thing I had ever seen. I still couldn't take my eyes off her whenever she was in the room.

"What is it?" she asked.

"You're the most beautiful thing I've ever seen."

"I could get to like having you around. Keep saying those sweet things." She came over and ran her fingers through my hair. "You're cute in the morning with your hair tousled."

Between the kisses, hugs, and playing nurse and patient, we managed to cook up a pretty good breakfast. She did the bacon and eggs and I did the toast and jelly. Afterwards we sat across the table from each other sipping coffee and smiling a lot. Her feet were caressing mine. Damn, I loved her.

"Tell me about your Uncle Tiny," I said.

"He was the white sheep of the family." She smiled. "A little black humor. I never knew him. I guess you know, Poppa won't even talk to him—something that happened between them before I was born."

"What kind of man is he?"

"Could he commit murder, do you mean? I think he probably could but it would probably have to be something personal. I don't think he operates at a very high level."

"You're being very hard on him. I've talked with him some. He strikes me as being a very bighearted man."

"This is my Uncle Tiny we're talking about? The junk man? The ex-con who does practically nothing but sit on his front porch all day? Big hearted? About what?"

"He's very worried about your grandparents and I think he's upset that he can't do anything to help them. Do you know what he was in prison for?"

She shook her head. "Mamma and Poppa never talked about it. Some deep, dark family secret. He went to prison when I was just a baby and was still in prison when I left Macon to go to college. I didn't even know I had an uncle until he got out of prison and moved back to the neighborhood."

"What about Skeeter and Leroy? Do you know them?"

"I went to school with Leroy. He's about my age. I know he's been in jail several times and he's been in trouble a lot more times than that. Andrew was a lot younger than me. I just remember him as being a little kid."

"Do you think any of them could be involved in Willingham's murder?"

She shrugged. "I really don't know. It's hard for me to think of them involved in something like that but I guess you always feel that way about people you knew as a child. You have to realize too that Mamma and Poppa kept me away from the neighborhood boys. I didn't know any of them that well."

"What do you know about Stafford Willingham?"

"I don't guess I ever heard of him before last week. Poppa told me he worked for Mr. Willingham many years ago. Oh, I knew about Willingham Realty. It's been around Macon for as long as I can remember, but I didn't know Mr. Willingham."

"Your grandfather told me Willingham came out to his house last week after the ceremony at City Hall. Why do you think he did that?"

"As I said, Poppa worked for him many years ago. Mr. Willingham said when he found out Poppa was still alive and in Macon he wanted to come by and see him. He seemed like a nice enough man." She shrugged again.

"Your grandfather said Willingham talked with you for a long time. What did the two of you talk about?"

"Why are you asking me all these questions?"

"There's a good chance Willingham's death is connected to real estate development in east Macon," I said, warming up to my new theory. "I thought maybe he said something that might tell me why he came to east Macon that day. Please, tell me what you can remember that he talked about."

"A lot of reminiscing, talking about the way things were when he was a young man, and knowing my grandparents and my mother. He seemed kind of lonely and unhappy to me–the kind of thing you see in a lot of middle-aged people who are unhappy with their lives. I got the feeling he wanted to be young again. He didn't seem to like who he was."

I imagined that Willingham's thoughts were a lot more than just reminiscing.

"He asked me about myself. He said he remembered seeing me as a little girl. He wanted to know what I do for a living, if I'm married, do I have children, that sort of thing. He told me several times how much I look like my mother. If he was up to anything, I don't know what it was. He never made a move on me or anything like that. I thought at first that's what he was up to, but he wasn't. He just seemed like a sentimental old man to me."

"You know about the new golf course and country club?"

"I've heard about it. Why?"

"From what I saw of the long range development plans for east Macon, I suspect real estate developers are trying to acquire land in the east Macon neighborhoods by whatever means they can. I think someone is trying to get their hands on your grandparents' property."

"They're trying to get Mamma and Poppa's house?" Her brow creased into a deep worry.

"Theirs and every other piece of property surrounding the proposed golf course. It's going to be a prime real estate development area."

"So the police think Uncle Tiny killed Mr. Willingham because he was trying to get Mamma and Poppa's house and property?"

"That's one possibility."

"Do you think the police are right?"

"I think there's a good chance Willingham's death was connected in some way to the real estate development but I don't know that it had anything in particular to do with your grandparents' house."

"Why do you think they arrested Uncle Tiny?"

"I don't know."

I motioned for her to come to me. She came around and sat in my lap, her arms around my neck.

"I'm going to have to try to help Tiny," I said.

"Why would you do that?" she said, searching my face.

"He believed in me and helped me when I was in jail and had no one I could turn to."

"Maybe he believed in you because he knew who did it," she said. "How did he help you?"

"He sent an angel to look over me."

"An angel?" She looked at me skeptically. "What are you talking about?"

"A big, black, ugly angel named Leroy Jackson. Leroy had himself arrested so he could be inside and protect me from harm while I was in jail."

"Leroy Jackson is no angel. Why would he do that?"

"Because Tiny asked him to. Tiny believes I'm some kind of angel too, a messenger from God sent to look after your grandparents."

Johnny Mae was looking at me as if I were suddenly babbling nonsense.

"Frank, you are crazy. All this talk about angels and messengers from God is freaking me out. Do you believe what you're saying?"

I laughed. "No, I don't believe it but I think Tiny does. But whether he does or not, he sent Leroy to protect me. And believe me, I felt in need of protection. So now that he needs someone, I've got to help him."

"What can you do to help Tiny Glover?"

"Find out the truth. Maybe arrange for a lawyer or bail if I can, but try above all else to find out the truth. It's the only way any of us are going to be free of this threat that keeps hanging over us. Someone is trying to protect themselves from discovery and they don't seem to care how many of us they hurt in the process."

"You're a good man, Frank."

I kissed her and held her against me.

"Remember that. No matter what may happen or what I may get involved in, remember and believe that I'm working to help and protect you and your grandparents, Tiny, Skeeter, and any other innocent person who gets caught up in this thing."

"Does that include Shirley Willingham?" she said.

I gave her a slap on the butt. "I think Shirley Willingham has enough money and lawyers to take care of herself."

"Are you sure she's not the one behind everything that's been happening?"

"No," I said, "I'm not sure of that."

"Before you go out to save the world would you like to go back to bed for a little while?" she said, nibbling my ear.

I put my hand inside her bathrobe. "I can't think of anything I'd rather do."

We stood up and started across the living room toward the bedroom. There was a loud knock at the door. We looked at each other. I shrugged and shook my head, indicating that I had no idea who it might be. I didn't really want to see anybody right now. I walked to the door and looked through the peep hole. I motioned for Johnny Mae to go into the bedroom. When she had closed the door behind her I opened the front door.

"Detective Miller," I said.

Detective Miller was not happy. He was almost apologetic. He was accompanied by a police woman. She looked tougher than he did. Her gun was just as big as his.

"I'm looking for Miss Glover," he said. He turned and looked at her car. "Is she here with you?"

I stood back and asked them to come inside.

"Would you ask her to come out, please?" he said.

"Is she under arrest?" I was afraid I had learned all too well to read Detective Miller's mood and there was little else the presence of the police woman could mean.

"Please, just ask her to come out."

I went into the bedroom and closed the door behind me. Johnny Mae had overheard Miller. She was slipping her clothes on. She nodded to me. Her hands were shaking. I went back to the living room.

"She'll be right out," I said. "Can you tell me what's going on?"

He didn't respond.

"With the new arrests, does that mean you're no longer investigating me?"

He still didn't respond.

It was only a couple of minutes before Johnny Mae came out. She looked scared. She stopped beside me and I put an arm around her.

"Miss Glover," Miller said, "Mr. Hayes, I'm placing the two of you under arrest on charges of conspiracy to commit murder in the death of Mr. Stafford Willingham. You have the right to remain silent . . ."

He didn't finish reading us our Miranda because Johnny Mae had fainted. I caught her in my arms and laid her on my sofa. I wanted to smash Detective Miller's face in. He seemed to be aware of my feelings.

"I'm sorry, Frank. I didn't want to do it but the D.A. left me no choice. It was me or someone else. I thought maybe you would prefer that it was me."

The police woman was bending over Johnny Mae checking her eyes and her pulse.

"I would prefer that you arrest whoever is behind Willingham's murder and leave innocent people alone. Do you know you're ruining our lives? You've given me an arrest record, now you're giving Johnny Mae one. She's struggled to become the respected professional that she is. This arrest will be on her record forever. Do you realize the consequences of that?"

"A man's been murdered, Frank. We're following the evidence. The evidence led us to you two. I'm sorry for you and I'm sorry for her but unless some new evidence can be found that points in another direction, we're left with no choice. If you're innocent it will come out."

"You really believe that? Someone is after us, Miller. I haven't seen any justice lately. Do you believe that Tiny and Johnny Mae's innocence will be magically triumphant in the face of the power of the D.A.'s office? Who can they get to represent them that will balance against the white legal establishment? And what about poor little Skeeter? That kid will be scared to death. He couldn't kill his own shadow."

Maybe I had answered my own question. Someone had to be brought in who could balance the scales. I knew what I had to do and I was dying inside.

"Do I get to make a phone call?" I asked.

Detective Miller nodded.

The call I had to make was the last call in the world I wanted to make.

"Will you come with me so I can use the phone in the bedroom?" I said in a near whisper, "I don't want Johnny Mae to hear me if she comes around." I turned to the policewoman, "If she wakes up, tell her I'm in the bedroom, please."

Miller and I went into the bedroom. I picked up the receiver and dialed Johnny Mae's number in Atlanta, hoping Reggie would be there. She got it on the first ring.

"Reggie?" I said. "This is Frank Hayes."

"Frank, is Johnny Mae with you?"

"She's here in Macon with me, yes. Listen, Reggie, Johnny Mae is in serious trouble. You have to stay calm and do exactly what I say. I can make just this one call. Do you understand?"

"Sure, Frank. You been arrested again? What in the world is going on?"

"Reggie, Johnny Mae's been arrested for the murder of Stafford Willingham."

"Oh, no. Not Johnny Mae. They can't do that to Johnny Mae. Frank, you got to get her out of there."

"Listen, Reggie. I'm also under arrest. I don't have a lawyer, I don't have any money, there's nothing I can do to help Johnny Mae. You have to call Anthony. Anthony can help her. Do you understand me?"

"Yes." Her voice was almost too calm.

"I don't want my name mentioned. Only you and I and Johnny Mae know I exist. Do you hear me?"

"Yes, Frank, I do. I'm sorry for what's happened to you."

"I don't matter, Reggie. You call Anthony and tell him Johnny Mae is in need of his help as soon as he can get here. Tell him to get the best lawyer he can afford and get her out of jail. And I mean today. Johnny Mae can't be allowed to sit in jail in Bibb County. She would never be the same. Do you think you can make him understand the urgency?"

"Yes. I'll call him right now. He'll know what to do."

"I don't want my name mentioned in the same breath with Johnny Mae's. Tell Anthony the police called you. Do you understand?"

"Yes, Frank. I know what you're saying. She loves you, Frank."

"And I love her. Call Anthony right now. I can't help her. He can. You make him take care of her."

"Goodbye, Frank."

"I'll catch you next time around, Reggie."

"I hope so."

Chapter 21

Homecoming Dance

They put me in the back of the police car next to Johnny Mae. Both of us were in handcuffs. She looked at me from behind frightened eyes. I held her hand to try and reassure her but the two pair of handcuffs side by side seemed to make it twice as bad. It seemed to me it would have been more appropriate if they had handcuffed us together.

She was withdrawing away from me, deeper and deeper inside herself. I tried to tell myself it was a natural psychological defense and the best thing for her right then, but it was killing me to watch her. I tried to keep a calm voice.

"It's going to be OK, sugar. Try not to be scared. Help is coming. It's on the way." Her eyes were looking about, not seeing anything, and she was shivering. "Listen to me. You're going to be all right. Hold on just a few hours. Don't tell the police anything except your name and address until your attorney gets there. You haven't done anything wrong. You're protected by the Constitution."

I only half believed it but she had to hear it. I kissed the back of her hand.

"Just think of me," I said. "Don't think of anything else until help comes. I won't stop thinking about you."

At the station they pulled us out on opposite sides of the police car. Johnny Mae looked at me and tried to reach out to me but Miller had me by the arm and the policewoman had Johnny Mae.

"I love you, Johnny Mae," I said as we were pulled in different directions.

I caught glimpses of her inside the police station during booking but then I was taken into an interrogation room and I didn't see her again.

"It looks bad this time, Frank," Miller was saying to me. We had been joined by his partner, Arthur Stevens.

"We know all about the extortion scheme," Stevens said.

"You want to come clean now?" Miller picked up the routine. "If we've been given the wrong information and the girl is not part of it, you need to tell us before she's processed. You know what's going to happen to her, don't you?"

"I want a lawyer," I said. "I cannot afford a lawyer. I'm asking that a lawyer be appointed to represent me. Do you understand me?"

"We'll send for an attorney right now," Miller said. "But if you don't tell us something soon to clear the girl there won't be anything we can do to stop her being stripped, searched, and put in the lockup. You remember how the lockup was for you, don't you? It's worse for women, especially women who are not used to that kind of thing."

"If you're trying to torture me," I said, "you're doing a damn good job. I think that's against the law. You want to arrest yourselves?"

"I'm just trying to say that if you have information to clear the girl, give it to us. I'm trying to help her, Frank," Miller said.

"I'm not going to say anything until I can talk with an attorney and have an attorney present. If I were to talk now, as upset as I am, you might trick me into saying something I don't mean and would regret. For instance, you might make me say something like, 'I'm going to kill whoever did this to Johnny Mae and me,' even though I wouldn't mean it. And then I would have to explain why I said it if I didn't mean it. You see what I mean?"

"You think you're better and smarter than everyone else, don't you?" Stevens sneered. "You and those damn black bitches living like some kind of hippy commune. You need to be locked away from decent people. You don't care where you put your dick, do you?"

"The condition I'm in, I might even start hallucinating," I said to Stevens. "I might think you're someone else and I might say, 'Man, you are the dumbest, ugliest son of a bitch I ever met. You look like a pig. Why didn't your mother flush you down the toilet?'"

Detective Stevens moved faster than I thought a man his size could. His fist caught me right under the left cheek bone. The blow knocked me backwards out of my chair and onto my back on the floor. He was over me with those big meat hook hands of his before I stopped skidding but Miller caught him by the arm and backed him away from me before he could do me any real damage.

Miller was laughing to himself. Stevens wasn't laughing. His face was red, his neck was bulging, and he was breathing so hard he was almost wheezing.

"He beat you at your own game, Arthur. Give the man his due," Miller said.

Detective Stevens grabbed the door knob, jerked the door open, and slammed it behind him as he left the interrogation room.

"Not a good idea, Frank. You don't want to tease a bulldog."

"Well, hell, if he's rabid, shoot him. You shouldn't have let him hit me." I was being a wiseass but Stevens had knocked me cross-eyed.

"I'm sorry about that, Frank. I told you before, I can't always control him."

"Get me a lawyer before I get mad and hurt somebody.

I've got one side of my face I haven't even used yet."

"I said I'm sorry."

"Sorry doesn't get it. Sorry doesn't even begin to get it. I want a lawyer. I'm going to hold my breath and turn blue until I get one. I've already got a good start."

They threw me in lockup. It didn't smell any better than the first time I was there. I didn't know how long I could stand it before I gagged. I've heard that people who live next to chicken houses or hog farms get used to the smell after a while and don't even know it's there. I wondered if jail is the same way. I didn't want to be there long enough to find out.

It was like homecoming at the old high school. I knew at least two of the guys from the last time. Plus, Tiny, Skeeter and Leroy were all there. Tiny looked like he owned the place and Leroy was right at home but Skeeter hadn't faired much better than Johnny Mae. He was quiet and still except for a slight swaying motion and a barely audible whimper.

Tiny looked up at me. "Heard they got you too. Who did that to you?" he said, looking at my face. I could tell from the feel of it that it was swelling and was probably turning blue.

"Detective Arthur Stevens," I said. "I insulted his mother."

I sat down on the floor next to Tiny and spoke softly.

"They got Johnny Mae too, Tiny."

"Johnny Mae locked up? Shit. Ain't no need fo' that. She ain't got nuthin' to do with the goin's on here."

The look I saw in Tiny's eyes scared me and I was pretty sure he didn't hold me responsible. I knew he was capable of violence. It showed all over him like little beads of nitroglycerine sweat coming out of his pores. I didn't know how much more bad news he could take without an explosion.

"I'm sorry," I said. "I would have done anything to keep her out of it."

"I ain't sayin' it was your fault."

"She was at my place. They arrested both of us. I called her roommate in Atlanta. Help should be on the way for her. What in the hell is going on?"

"Near as I can tell, we all in deep shit."

I couldn't help it. I laughed. He laughed. My face hurt.

"What Johnny Mae doin' at your place, Frank?"

Well, gee, Tiny. I've been sleeping with your only daughter, the one you asked me to look after. I hoped he was going to be a tolerant father.

"Johnny Mae and I have been seeing each other," I said.

"Seeing each other? You mean . . . you and Johnny Mae?"

He was smiling. That was good.

"I be damned." He shook his head and laughed to himself. "I be damned. I knowed you was the right man for her. You don't treat her bad, Frank. You do, you and me gon' have some words."

"I would never treat her wrong, Tiny. But right now I'm not able to do her any good. I called for some help to come and take care of her. She has friends with money in Atlanta."

"You mean Anthony Boudreau?" Tiny said. The way he said it didn't seem to indicate approval or disapproval.

"Yes. He and her roommate Reggie will get her a lawyer and bail if she needs it."

"Umm," was all he said. "You got a lawyer?"

"I've asked for one."

"Public defender?" he said.

I nodded. He laughed again.

"What are you laughing at?"

"You gon' end up in the 'lectric chair."

"That bad?"

"Some of 'em. Maybe you get lucky."

"Do you know what kind of evidence they have?"

Tiny shook his head.

"Listen to me, Frank. No tellin' how long you might be inside this time. This is a dangerous place. They some mean people and some crazy people in here. Everbody here need somebody to look after 'em. You lucky. You got me. I'll take care of you but you got to learn how things is done inside. You do just 'xactly what I tell you to do. You understan'? I won't tell you wrong."

"You get me out of here alive," I said, "and I promise this time we will definitely be partners in a barbecue business."

"You gon' get out alive. An' I'll try to keep you from bein' chewed up too bad." He slapped me on the leg.

Oh, not dead, only maimed and scarred. I kept thinking about Johnny Mae.

"How is it on the women's side?"

"Johnny Mae don't need to be here," he said.

"Who do you think is behind all this?"

"Stafford Willingham. You find out who killed Willingham an' you find out who's throwin' dirt on us. Who you think it is?" he asked.

"I think it's probably someone who was in business with him. Whoever put the $25,000 in my bank account had access to Willingham's account and didn't mind giving away a big chunk of money to pin the blame on me. There had to be something really big at stake for them to do that."

"What about his wife?" Tiny asked.

"She gets his money anyway. She didn't need to kill him."

I stopped myself. The last time Detective Miller had me in custody he said Willingham had made out a new will leaving Johnny Mae a large inheritance. Maybe Shirley was being cut out of his will. Maybe Shirley was behind it after all. Wait a minute. Miller said Willingham had already changed his will before his death. Killing him after the will change wouldn't help Shirley, would it? I didn't know. I didn't know any of the specifics of the will or how much Willingham was worth. He might have left Johnny Mae, Shirley, his other wife and children enough to make them all rich.

"Maybe when we find out the evidence fo' why they locked us up, we know somethin' more," Tiny said. "If they planted evidence maybe they left some footprints."

"How're we going to get out of here?" I said. "I've got no money for bail. Do you?"

He shook his head.

"Do they even allow bail in murder cases?"

"Sometimes," Tiny said.

"What?" I said. "Like if it's your first murder?"

Tiny laughed.

"Why don't the two of you shut up? You been talkin' ever since you got here."

Two white toughs stood side by side looking at Tiny and me in a way that had meanness all over it. The biggest one of them walked toward me. I got to my feet. He stopped about a foot and a half from me, leaning toward me.

"Why're you talkin' to this old darkie anyway?"

"He's my fiancé's father," I said.

That remark had the natural effect of making him madder.

"You marryin' a colored whore?"

He hardly got the words out of his mouth. I don't know who hit him first. The same time my fist flattened his nose, Tiny knocked his legs out from under him. Tiny caught hold of his arm before he even hit the floor and in one powerful quick motion twisted the guy's hand and pulled his arm back against Tiny's knee, breaking his elbow. The guy let out a horrible scream.

The second white guy made a move toward us as soon as I hit the first one but Leroy caught him under the throat with an elbow smash and the guy dropped to his knees struggling to breathe. Before he could recover and get to his feet, Leroy chopped him across the top of his right shoulder, breaking his collarbone. He moaned and held his right arm with his good left hand. He didn't get up. No one else in the cell moved. The whole fight didn't last ten seconds.

The first guy was yelling, crying and cursing. Three jailers came in a hurry, night sticks ready to break heads. We all moved away from the bars, leaving the two injured men lying on the floor moaning and writhing. The big guy's bleeding nose was leaving a big mess on the cell floor.

"Aw'right, who in the hell did this?" One of the jailers demanded. He was a heavyset man with reddish blond hair and freckles.

Nobody said anything.

"Shit," he said. "Get back against the wall, all of you. Face the wall!"

We all stood facing the wall while the jailers opened the cell door and dragged the two men out.

"Any more of this and we'll give all of you a round with the cattle prod," he said.

The cell was quiet after that. Tiny sat back down and I sat down beside him.

"Pretty good punch, Frank." He grinned at me.

"It was the only one I had." I felt good about winning the fight. I was pumped up on adrenaline.

"You done all right," he said, "for an angel of mercy."

Before the afternoon was over a jailer came and called my

name. I was taken to an interview room and left in the presence of a young woman in glasses who was dressed in what might pass for a woman's version of a pin striped suit, tie and all.

"Mr. Glover? I'm Melissa Gresham." She offered me her hand in a very good attempt at a firm handshake. "I've been assigned by the Public Defender's office to represent you."

I knew at that point that my case was lost.

Chapter 22

Melissa Gresham

"It's Hayes," I said, "Frank Hayes."

"I beg your pardon?"

"I'm Frank Hayes, not Tiny Glover."

"Oh." A sudden red flush washed over her face. She looked nervously inside the case folder on the table and turned to me with a look of confusion. "Please excuse me just a moment." She turned sharply and left the room.

She was back in ten minutes or so, a file folder in her hands. She gave no indication she had made an error.

"I'm sorry, there was a mixup about which case I was assigned to. You're Frank Hayes, right?"

"Yes, and you, I assume, are still Miss Gresham. May I ask, Miss Gresham, have you had a lot of experience defending clients accused of murder?"

She stiffened and snapped her head up to look at me. Her nose was pointed just a little too high to suit me.

"I'm fully qualified under Georgia legal practices to defend you, Mr. Hayes."

"Are you a real attorney?" I said.

"I'm a third-year law student at Mercer University. I've worked in the Legal Defense Clinic for the past two years and I've assisted the Public Defender's office on many court cases. I will be supervised on your case by the law firm of Green and Green. This is my first murder trial but I assure you that you will get an adequate defense."

"Adequate for what? To satisfy the letter of the law?"

She ignored my sarcasm.

"If at any time you are dissatisfied with my professional performance you may ask for a new attorney. But I don't think you'll feel the need to do that. When did that happen?" she asked, indicating the bruises and swelling of my face.

"I was assaulted during questioning this morning by Detective Arthur Stevens."

"Detective Stevens did that?" Her face said she was not convinced of my veracity. "Let me see your hands."

I held out my hands to her. She turned them over. The knuckles of my right hand were swollen and bruised.

"How did you do that? Defending yourself against Detective Stevens?"

"In the lockup this morning. There was a little rumble in the cell. A local desperado insulted my fiance and my future father-in-law."

"So you're the one who broke the prisoner's nose and arm?" she asked.

I was sinking fast in her estimation.

"I broke his nose. Someone else broke his arm."

There was a pause accompanied by brief contemplation.

"Oh," she said. "Well, that's too bad."

"What's too bad? That I broke the guy's nose or that I didn't break his arm?"

"No, it's too bad you were involved in a fight this morning. You see, if Detective Stevens struck you during interrogation after booking . . . it was after you were booked, I presume?"

"Yes. I was arrested, brought to the station, booked, and interrogated by detectives Miller and Stevens. It was during the interrogation that Detective Stevens assaulted me."

"Hmm."

"Hmm, what?"

"When you were booked on charges you were photographed. I assume you had no bruises or swelling on your face at that time?"

"That's right. I wasn't hit until after I was photographed."

"Well, then, it's too bad you were involved in the fight in the lockup because we could have photographed you now to document charges of assault and brutality against the interrogating officer. There were witnesses to the fight?"

"Yes, several."

"So Detective Stevens will say you received your bruises as a result of the altercation in the lockup rather than as a result of any assault by him. And he has witnesses who can testify as to the fight in the lockup. Too bad. We might have used the assault to your advantage. I'll have you photographed and we'll file the complaint against Stevens anyway, but our complaint is weakened because of the incident in the lockup, you see?"

I was beginning to have a little more respect for Miss Gresham. She had a head on her shoulders and she wasn't afraid to use it.

"We'll ask for bail," she said. "Do you have any money to make bail if it's granted?"

"I had $200 in my pocket when I was arrested. I get paid tomorrow by the city. My take-home pay is $454."

"Per week?"

"No, not per week. Per month. But it'll be my last paycheck because I've been fired. I also have $27,000 in my checking account but $25,000 of it doesn't belong to me, and my checking account is frozen anyway."

"I read in the police report about the $25,000. Where did the money come from?"

"I don't know. The police told me it came from the

account of Shirley and Stafford Willingham. I assume it came from whoever is framing me for Willingham's murder."

"Tell me about the extortion note."

"What extortion note? I don't know anything about any note. Extortion for what?"

"The police found an extortion note in Mr. Willingham's effects instructing him to deposit $25,000 into your bank account at First Citizens Bank of Macon. The note contains your account name and number."

"Anyone could have used my bank account number to frame me."

"Who would have your account number?"

"Anyone I ever wrote a check to."

"The note was written on the typewriter in your office."

I was dumbfounded. I tried to think.

"Anyone could walk into my office and use my typewriter most any time, day or night. Now that I think about it, anyone at City Hall could get into my personnel record and find the information on my checking account. I have the office deposit my check to my account. The office secretary does that. She knows my account number. Which reminds me, you better get to her and stop her from depositing my check. If you don't, it'll be deposited to my frozen account and we may not have access to it. But back to the extortion note. What information was I supposed to be using to extort money from Stafford Willingham? Was I supposed to be threatening to reveal that he was a son of a bitch? I think everyone already knew that."

"The note threatens to reveal Mr. Willingham's affair with the black girl, Johnny Mae Glover, if $25,000 is not deposited to your bank account."

That hit me like a baseball bat. Someone knew about Johnny Mae. But what did they know about her? They had it all wrong.

"Johnny Mae Glover was not Willingham's mistress," I said. "What did the note say exactly?"

"I don't have a copy of it yet. I just found reference to it in the police file. So you did know about the relationship between Willingham and the Glover girl?"

"I didn't know anything. I suspected something. But she wasn't his mistress."

"But you did know some information incriminating to Mr. Willingham?"

"Everything I tell you is confidential? Between you and me only, right?" I asked.

"Between you and your attorney. Technically, your attorney consists of me and the firm of Green and Green. Neither I nor the firm can reveal privileged information received in the course of preparing your defense."

I told Melissa Gresham the whole story about Johnny Mae and me and of my suspicions that Willingham was Johnny Mae's father.

"If that's true," she said, "the D.A. would argue that it gives you a much stronger weapon for extortion, don't you see? An illegitimate black child by a leading white businessman is potent stuff. It could wreck marriages and careers. Of course your knowledge of it puts you right back in the middle of it."

"What about the change in his will?" I said.

She flipped through the papers in the file she was holding.

"What change in his will? I don't see anything in the police report about a change in his will."

"Detective Miller told me Willingham made a change in his will the day he died, leaving something substantial to Johnny Mae."

"It may have been just an interrogation ploy to get you to

talk. I'll track that down. I assume Mrs. Willingham would have known about any change in his will?"

"I don't know if she knew about it before his death. She should know about it now."

"What about Mrs. Willingham?" she asked.

"What about her?"

"Could she be behind her husband's murder?"

"Good question. I don't know."

"According to the police report, you admitted to being sexually involved with Mrs. Willingham."

She squirmed a little when she said 'sexually involved' and she looked at her papers rather than me.

"Does this embarrass you?" I asked.

She snapped her attention back to me again. Her movements were very fast. I'm sort of a laid back kind of person when it comes to movement and gestures. She was quick as lightning.

"Embarrassed? No, I'm not embarrassed. I'm an adult. I know what sex is. I do it too."

I smiled at her but she didn't return the smile. She waited for me to answer her question.

"I had a one-time-only encounter with Shirley Willingham at their lake house where she took me."

"How did that come about?"

"It just happened. I went there at her request to have lunch. It was the same morning we inspected Mr. and Mrs. Glovers' house regarding the building inspector's report."

"Did you initiate the sex or did she?"

Now I was feeling embarrassed.

"I think perhaps it occurred to both of us at the same time."

"Spontaneous?"

"Yes . . . spontaneous."

"Do you often get spontaneously sexually involved with women?"

"No, I don't."

"What about Miss Glover? You met her and became sexually involved with her the same week you became involved with Mrs. Willingham?"

"Johnny Mae is something very different."

"It's a line of questioning you certainly need to give some thought to. If this goes to trial you can be sure the D.A. will grill you about it. Your credibility is vulnerable in this area."

My credibility is vulnerable? That sounded like legalese for *I look like a liar*. I felt the need to move off the topic.

"Last week the police suspected Shirley Willingham of hiring me to kill her husband. What happened to that theory?"

"That's still a possible argument the D.A. could use."

"But it doesn't fit with the extortion note if the $25,000 was payment from her to me to kill her husband."

"No, it doesn't. But let's assume another scenario for a moment. Let's consider the possibility that Mrs. Willingham is behind the murder of her husband and she planned all along to frame you for it. She could have taken you to her lake house for the purpose of seducing you so your fingerprints and other evidence would be there to incriminate you. She could have arranged for the extortion note. The $25,000 came from the joint account of Mr. and Mrs. Willingham. She could have gotten your checking account information from any number of places, including your checkbook when you were with her. She certainly had the resources to arrange for her husband's murder."

"Yes, all that's true." I had to admit. "But if his will had already been changed, what would she have to gain? Her motive couldn't have been to prevent him from changing the will."

"I don't know, but we don't know that she was aware of the change in his will. We have to continue to regard Mrs. Willingham as a possibility."

"She may be involved but I don't see it."

"Why not?"

I shrugged. "Male intuition, I guess."

"There is no such thing. I'll file a request under discovery to see all the bank records of your account and the Willingham account. We'll find out how the money got there. You are telling me the whole truth about the money and about your involvement with Mrs. Willingham, aren't you?"

"Absolutely. I have no idea where the money came from. I had one sexual encounter with Shirley Willingham on the Tuesday before her husband was killed on Friday and that's all." Well, that's all *before* the murder anyway. But afterwards didn't count, did it?

"Did anyone else know or suspect about Mr. Willingham's true relationship to Miss Glover?"

"I would bet that Tiny Glover has probably known about it for twenty-five years."

I told Miss Gresham about Tiny's relationship to Johnny Mae, about his manslaughter conviction and prison time for the death of Johnny Mae's mother. She sat with her jaw slack, shaking her head.

"My God. Another complication. So Tiny Glover had every reason to hate Stafford Willingham and want him dead?"

"Yes, he had every reason, but it's nothing new to him. Why would he suddenly decide he had to kill Willingham after all these many long years?"

"Didn't you recently become acquainted with Tiny?"

"Yes."

"The D.A. could argue that you or someone else revealed something to Tiny that rekindled his rage, don't you see?"

"Perhaps they could make the argument but I can't think of anything I did or said that would have increased his anger at Willingham."

I thought of Tiny's dark brooding after he saw Johnny Mae and Stafford Willingham together the afternoon Willingham came to the Glovers' house. If he were mad enough he might have gone over and strangled Willingham on the spot. But after the heat of the moment had passed I couldn't see Tiny planning a cold blooded murder. At least I didn't want to see it.

"I don't think Tiny could have done it," I said.

"Why not?"

"Because I think Tiny is a redeemed man."

"You certainly have generous feelings towards the other possible suspects in Mr. Willingham's murder. Do you think maybe your opinion of them is colored by your closeness to them?"

"I don't know. What I do think is that the police are following incriminating evidence planted by Willingham's killer. They're not looking in the right direction for his real killer."

"Who do you think the real killer is?" she asked.

"A business associate of Willingham."

"Which business associate do you have in mind?"

"I don't know. I think it has something to do with the east Macon golf course and country club development."

"But you don't have knowledge of anything more specific?"

"No," I said. "Now that I think about it, there must be

more than one person."

"How do you figure that?"

"What are the chances one person would know all the things and could do all the things that were done to set me up? They had to know something about me and Johnny Mae, Shirley Willingham, Stafford Willingham, Tiny Glover, the lake house, the bank accounts, my shotgun . . . and they had access to $25,000 they could turn loose. There has to be more than one person. Somebody with money is behind it."

"The police and the D.A. also think there was more than one person involved . . . you, Johnny Mae, Tiny, Andrew, and Leroy."

"I swear to you I'm not involved in any way with Willingham's murder and I don't know who is. I'm guilty of being rude to Willingham in front of witnesses and of being indiscreet with his wife. I'm also guilty of being in love with Johnny Mae Glover. But that's all. I know nothing whatsoever about any extortion or murder plot."

"OK, if I were the D.A., this is the case I would be building against you. You and Miss Glover were lovers. The two of you conspired to blackmail Willingham with the threat of exposure of his past. The police know Mr. Willingham paid a visit to the home of Miss Glover's grandparents two days before his death. While he was there he had a private conversation with Miss Glover. Two days later $25,000 is transferred from his account to yours. Something went wrong after you got the money and you had to get rid of Willingham. Andrew and Leroy had access to your shotgun but the police seem to think Tiny Glover actually set the trap."

"What evidence do they have against Johnny Mae, Tiny, and the others?"

"I don't know that yet."

"We're all easy targets. Someone is covering their own

guilt."

She stood to leave and offered her hand. "I'll ask for a bail hearing and get started filing motions. Please let me know if you think of anything that might help."

"Yes, I will. Try not to get too discouraged."

She looked at me quizzically. "About what?"

"About my case. I'm not guilty. Somebody out there is and they must have left a trail."

"Oh, I'm not discouraged. If I win this one, my reputation will be made."

"My chances must be pretty bleak then."

"Just kidding," she said. "I'm hoping we'll find a way to break their case."

"Do you know what's happening to Johnny Mae?"

"She has legal representation. That's all I know."

Chapter 23

Lightning Bolt

Bail was not granted. It didn't make any difference. I couldn't have paid it. I couldn't have paid even the ten percent a bail bondsman would have charged.

I hated jail. I looked at the days crossed out on the calendar on my wall. This was the last day of the sixth week I had been locked up. I couldn't smell it most of the time now. That was depressing. It meant I was a real prisoner. I had been put in a cell with a forger named Charlie Preston. It was educational. Charlie told me a hundred ways to forge checks, bonds, contracts, and all manner of items without getting caught. Somewhere along the way he had slipped up. He assured me it wasn't his fault.

Tiny, Skeeter and Leroy were still locked up but they were moved to the county farm and I had no contact with them. The cases against Skeeter and Leroy were mostly circumstantial. They had been seen associating with me, the two of them were in possession of my car, and according to my own statements, the shotgun had been in the trunk of my car. And of course Leroy had a record. Tiny's case was a little more perplexing. A search of his house had turned up $1,000 and a wrist watch belonging to Stafford Willingham hidden under a floorboard. I didn't know what to make of that.

I didn't know what had happened to Johnny Mae. My heart was broken over her. The worst part about everything that had happened was I was separated from her and didn't know if she was all right or if she was suffering and needed help. There was no reply to letters I sent through my attorney to Reggie to give to Johnny Mae. I had no communication from anyone outside, including Shirley Willingham. I couldn't blame anyone for not wanting to be involved with me. I had to rely on Miss Melissa Gresham.

I decided I liked Melissa. She could hold her own. I didn't like her supervisors at Green and Green nearly as much. To them I was a bother, a drain on their time, another loser they were forced by the bar to represent pro bono. To Melissa Gresham I was her first murder case and she wanted to win it.

Things were moving much too slow to suit me. The D.A.'s office blocked every move Melissa tried to make on my behalf. I knew she was working hard for me but I wondered how much support she was getting from Green and Green. She had made a number of discoveries. The extortion note did threaten to reveal a sexual affair between Willingham and Johnny Mae. Whoever wrote the note didn't know the truth about them. In my mind that seemed to eliminate Shirley Willingham. She had seen the photographs of Johnny Mae as a child in Stafford Willingham's files and she suspected that Stafford was Johnny Mae's father.

We were still at a loss as to who might be the author of the note. Melissa cautioned me that it could have been written as false evidence to divert suspicion from someone just like Shirley Willingham. That left me even more confused.

If there was a change in Willingham's will, the change never got recorded. All of his personal estate was divided between Shirley and his first wife and children. Shirley got half and his first wife and each of their children got equal shares of the other half. There was no mention of Johnny Mae in the will.

The bottom line was I didn't know any more about what was really going on than when I was first arrested. But when things finally started to move with my case, they moved more quickly than any of us had anticipated and they moved in a most unexpected direction. It began with what started as a routine visit from Melissa.

"I've been trying to track down the source of the $25,000," she said. "The bank confirms the money came from the account of Stafford and Shirley Willingham but they don't have a copy of the original transfer order. They say it came in by telephone."

"Telephone?" I said. "They take $25,000 transfer requests by telephone?"

"Apparently they do it routinely with certain customers and follow up with a written confirmation. In the case of this transaction, the written confirmation never arrived."

"No written evidence," I said. "Whoever did it left no trail."

"I went to the personnel department at City Hall to ask if they remembered anyone making requests in regard to your personnel or payroll records prior to Willingham's murder. Neither the personnel or the payroll department was aware of any inquiry. No one asking about you. Nothing that anyone could remember, or would say."

She threw up her hands. "I'm at a loss where else to look for evidence of tampering with your bank account."

She took a letter from her briefcase and handed it to me. "I did go by your old office, and a Miss . . . your office secretary?"

"Sue Watson," I said.

"Yes. Sue Watson gave me this certified letter for you that she's been holding along with your other personal items. She seems like a nice girl. She was very concerned about you."

"She's a good kid."

The return address was Barnes and Ingram, Attorneys at Law, Atlanta. It was addressed to me at City Hall and marked

Personal and Confidential. The first thing I thought of was Johnny Mae. I looked at the postmark date.

"Look at this." I showed it to Melissa. It was postmarked two weeks after Willingham's death.

"Miss Watson said it was marked personal and confidential and she thought she was supposed to give it to no one but you. She said she had been holding it until you came for your things."

I ran my finger under the edge of the sealed flap and removed a letter and a document from inside. My life would never be the same from that moment on. I read it in disbelief. I handed the letter to Melissa. As she read it tears formed in her eyes and ran down her cheeks. She began to laugh and she stood up, came to me and put her arms around me.

"I knew you didn't do it," she said through teary eyes.

"Yeah, I did too, but you could take everyone who believed in my innocence, put them in this room together and still have room for a pool table."

I looked at the letter again, making sure I had not read it backwards or something.

September 18, 1970

Mr. Frank Hayes
City Hall
Macon, Georgia

Dear Mr. Hayes,

Or perhaps I may be permitted to call you Frank. At our last meeting in the mayor's office you accused me of being guilty of neglect of my responsibilities. I was angry at you for having said it to my face, but I have come to realize that my anger was raised by the truth of it, not at the injustice to me of it having been said. I find myself owing you a great debt. It is because of your actions on behalf of John and Sara Mae Glover that I was brought back into contact with a daughter I have never really known.

I will not try to excuse myself. I will only say that in 1944 the times were very different from today and I was a young man who made some tragic errors in judgment. You need to understand, Esther, Johnny Mae's mother, never told me the child was mine. After she married Walter Glover, I gave up any effort to see her again. I never forgot about Esther, but I tried to forget about the past.

Johnny Mae was twelve years old when I saw her for the first time. She was with her grandparents at the city park but I would have recognized her anywhere because she was the image of her mother except for the green eyes and the color of her hair. Looking at her then I knew in my heart she was my daughter.

She was an extremely capable girl. Everything that she is, she is because of her talents and abilities. It is to my shame that I cannot take any rightful credit for her successes as any father might. But I did take it upon myself, perhaps to alleviate my own feelings of guilt, to see to it that nothing stood in the way of her abilities.

When the plight of John and Sara Mae came to my attention recently I was outraged, as much at myself for having let them fall from my sight as at those who were instrumental in their problems. I have now set about, in the anonymity that has become my curse, to help them in ways that I am able.

I don't pretend to know what there is within you that gives you the passion for justice you obviously possess. But I can see you care about the Glovers and about Johnny Mae. I can also see you are a man of integrity and bravery. It is because you are the man you are that I am offering you a burden of responsibility.

I have arranged a trust into perpetuity for the benefit of Johnny Mae, her immediate family, and her descendants. I am asking you to serve as executor of that trust. Neither Johnny Mae nor any of her family are to be told of the nature and origin of the trust until after my death, and then only upon your best judgment. You will be forwarded a document describing the mechanism of the trust's operation. I am depositing $25,000 into your personal checking account at the First Citizens Bank of Macon to be used at your discretion, pursuant to your new responsibilities. Additional funds are available to you as you may need them through the firm of Barnes and Ingram. I would hope that you can find some unobtrusive way to assist John and Sara Mae Glover to secure a stable, wholesome, and happy environment for their remaining years.

You are not required to communicate with me

in any way unless you desire it, but I would be pleased to know of Johnny Mae's wellbeing. If the time ever comes when you tell her of this arrangement, please ask her to try to forgive me. I lacked the good judgment and courage to do what I should have done so many years ago.

I hope you will not, but should you choose to decline this responsibility, return the money to Barnes and Ingram and an executor will be chosen by them.

You are an honorable man. You have my trust and my thanks. May God protect and strengthen you.

Stafford Willingham

"I thought the guy hated me," I said. "Why would he choose me?"

"It's clear enough in the letter. He chose you because you love his daughter," Melissa said, tears flowing from her eyes. "And because you're a person he trusted to do the right thing." She took a tissue from her purse, dabbed at her eyes, and shook her head like a cat shaking off a sneeze. "I've got to stop acting this way. We have a lot of work to do. I'll get this to the judge and a copy to the D.A. right away. We should be able to get a dismissal hearing by tomorrow."

"Dismissal?" I said. Somehow I couldn't believe the sound of the word.

"Yes. The backbone of the prosecution's case is broken. They may argue about it but they'll have no choice. Their entire prosecution rested on the use of the $25,000 as payment to you either as a result of extortion or for a murder-for-hire."

"Then let Tiny, Skeeter and Leroy know as soon as possible."

"I'll notify their attorneys. I feel confident about the results of the hearing but I can't absolutely predict the outcome, you understand? Life is sometimes unpredictable." She gathered her things in preparation to go. "You're going to need a different kind of lawyer. You need to be thinking about what you're going to do."

"I won't be thinking of anything else until I get out of here."

"I wish I had been able to do something to prove your innocence. I did believe in you."

"Melissa, you've been the only ray of hope in my life for the past six weeks. If it hadn't been for you I'd have hung myself with my shoelaces."

She smiled. "No, you wouldn't. But thank you. Be ready for a hearing sometime tomorrow. I'll let you know if there's any delay."

I was taken back to my cell where I lay on my cot and daydreamed. My dreams were full of happy things for the first time in almost two months. They say it takes three weeks to become adjusted to a total change of environment. I had been in jail for six weeks and hadn't become adjusted but I realized now how much I had changed and adapted. Much of the change had been to my detriment. I had become angry, depressed, and filled with pessimism. My head had been filled with thoughts of retribution. Now I wanted to get out so I could let it go, purge myself of it and never lose my happiness again. The letter from Stafford Willingham made that a possibility, almost a certainty.

Chapter 24

Over In A Flash

It didn't happen the next day. The D.A.'s office insisted that the authenticity of the letter from Willingham and the trust agreement be verified. On mid-afternoon of the second day my very pleased attorney and I appeared before the judge, along with the prosecutor from the D.A.'s office and Mr. Frederick Carter, the trust manager from the firm of Barnes and Ingram. Attorneys for Johnny Mae, Tiny, Skeeter and Leroy were also present.

In response to questioning by Melissa, Mr. Frederick Carter responded.

"Yes, the firm of Barnes and Ingram has conducted various business arrangements for Mr. Willingham over many years. I am the manager of the Willingham accounts. There is no doubt it was Mr. Stafford Willingham who called me on Friday morning, the day of his death. We discussed several matters of which only Mr. Willingham had personal knowledge. During that conversation he dictated to me the specifics of the trust he wished to have established. He indicated he would be mailing me a piece of personal correspondence to be forwarded to Mr. Frank Hayes when the trust was prepared. I immediately began work on preparation of the trust, and written correspondence arrived from Mr. Willingham the following week authorizing the establishment of the trust according to the terms we had discussed."

"Was there any indication that Mr. Willingham was not making those requests to you of his own free will?" Melissa asked.

"None whatsoever. I would not have followed his instructions had I thought otherwise. Mr. Willingham was quite coherent, even tempered, and his usual self as I had come to know him."

Melissa handed Carter the letter. "Is this the letter you received from Mr. Willingham?"

Carter glanced at the letter. "Yes, it is. I did not read the letter because it was personal, but I placed my initials and the date on the back of the pages for purposes of authentication." He indicated a small notation on the upper right corner on the back of each of the pages.

"Is that a normal practice?" Melissa asked.

"In agreements of this magnitude it is customary to provide means of authentication."

"Can you verify the handwriting in the letter to be that of Stafford Willingham?"

Carter examined the letter. "Yes, this is the handwriting of Stafford Willingham."

"And is this the trust agreement you prepared for Mr. Willingham?" She asked, giving him the document.

He looked it over for several moments. "Yes, this is the copy of the trust document I mailed to Mr. Frank Hayes according to Mr. Willingham's instructions."

"Your Honor," Melissa said to the judge, "these documents effectively destroy the prosecution's case and I move for a dismissal of all charges against my client and the other defendants charged in this case."

The judge turned to the prosecutor. "Mr. Washington?"

James Washington looked like a wayward boy who was being forced to give back candy he had taken from his little sister. He lifted his head, took a deep breath and said, "In view of this new evidence, Your Honor, the prosecution concurs in the recommendation that charges against defendants Frank

Hayes, Johnny Mae Glover, Andrew Jackson and Leroy Jackson in this case be dismissed. But due to the nature of the evidence presented against Mr. Walter Glover, we ask that charges against Mr. Walter Glover be allowed to stand."

It was over more quickly than I could absorb.

"Defense's motion for dismissal is granted, with the exception requested by the District Attorney's office. The bailiff is directed to release from custody with the apologies of this court those defendants so named."

"Your honor," Melissa raised her voice. "In view of the nature of the evidence just introduced, the defense requests that any and all disclosure of it be prohibited."

"Your Honor," Washington interjected, "the prosecution objects."

"The prosecution's objection is noted and overruled. The defense's motion is granted and it is ordered by this court that records of these proceedings be sealed. There being no further business before us, this court is adjourned."

I wanted to kiss Melissa I was so happy and grateful to her. But somehow, kissing my lawyer didn't have the right sound to it. But I did hug her.

"Thank you," I said. She smiled and nodded to me and had her attention pulled immediately to a discussion with other attorneys standing around us.

I looked across the room toward the man I thought must be Johnny Mae's attorney. He was the best dressed, the best groomed, and the only black man in the room. I needed to talk with him to find out about Johnny Mae. I thought I probably should discuss the trust with him. I approached him and offered my hand. He was a very statuesque man with the kind of bearing you might expect from someone accustomed to associating with people of dignity. I felt like his inferior.

"I'm Frank Hayes," I said, unnecessarily. Who else would

I be? "You are Johnny Mae's attorney?" I asked.

He declined my handshake. I couldn't blame him. I would, too.

"Yes, I am Mrs. Boudreau's attorney."

I wasn't sure what he had said. "No, I asked if you are Johnny Mae Glover's attorney."

"Yes, I am. She is Mrs. Anthony Boudreau now. She is no longer Johnny Mae Glover."

I tried to smile but I didn't think I wanted to smile. I knew what he had said. "What do you mean?" I knew what he meant. I just couldn't accept what he had said. I wanted him to answer the question again a different way. I wanted him to say, "Yes, I'm Johnny Mae Glover's attorney and she's waiting for you in the corridor." That's not what he said. He looked away from me as if I were too far beneath him for him to address me. It must have been the same way my ancestors refused to speak to his ancestors and it stung now just as it must have stung them.

"What do you mean?" I said again.

There was a hand on my arm. I looked in the direction from which it had come. It was Melissa's hand. She was looking at me in a very strange way. She was saying something.

"Sit down, Frank." She had me by one arm and someone else had me by the other arm. They sat me in one of the wooden courtroom chairs. She put a hand on the back of my neck and gently pressed me forward. "Put your head between your knees, Frank. You're going to pass out."

I don't know exactly how long I was sick. It may have been ten minutes but it was the worst ten minutes of my life. Every time I thought I was going to feel better the reality of what he had said came rushing back to me and made me sick all over again. I tried desperately to think of a way for him to take back what he had said but it was like a house of mirrors. Each time I looked I saw a distorted vision of reality. After a while my nausea subsided and my head quit spinning. By that time everyone but Melissa and I had left the courtroom. She got me on my feet and walked with me into the hallway.

"Come sit down a minute," she said and led me to a row of chairs lining the hallway outside the courtroom. She sat beside me and put her hand on mine.

"Frank," she said in a gentle voice, "I'm sorry."

"Did you know about Johnny Mae?" I couldn't believe Melissa would have kept it from me. I had trusted her with everything.

She looked down for a moment, bit her lip, and looked up at me.

"Yes, I knew, but I couldn't tell you while you were in jail."

So it was true. I felt cheated and betrayed.

"What if I hadn't gotten out?"

"Then I would have told you. But I knew what it could do to you."

No more than it was doing to me now. "How long has she been married?"

"Two weeks."

"Two weeks? Two weeks? Couldn't she have waited?"

"She had no way of knowing how long you would be in jail, Frank. I know this is hard for you."

"You have no idea."

"Perhaps not. I won't argue that, but you have to respect her decision."

"What do you think I'm going to do? Kill her new husband?"

"No, I don't think that. I just don't want you to suffer over it. He's been very supportive of her."

"He was there and I wasn't. Is that it?"

"That's part of it. I understand that they have a long history together. It must have been a hard choice for her. This has been a terrible experience for her too, you know."

"Yes, I know it must have been. Did you talk with her?"

"I talked with Reggie. She's very concerned about you too. Nobody wants you to be hurt, Frank. You have to believe that."

Well, I was hurting. This was too final, too permanent. This changed everything. The Glovers wouldn't need my help now, not with Anthony's money. And what about the trust? How could I be the executor of the trust for her when I couldn't bear the pain of seeing her? Why hadn't Stafford Willingham picked someone else? Why had he gotten us all in this mess?

"I don't think I'm ready to handle all this," I said.

"No, you're probably not. Give yourself some time. Go to the beach or somewhere for a month. Everything else can wait. Things will look better to you when . . ."

When my heart had healed? Was that what she was trying to say? I might go away but not for a month. I might go away and not come back.

Melissa stood up and gently pulled at my arm.

"Come on, Frank. You're a free man."

I thought about what Mr. Glover had said about his father when he was told he was a free man. Like him, I wasn't sure what freedom meant to me. I hadn't been released from the chains of slavery, I had been torn from a bond of the heart that I couldn't bear to let go. I suddenly faced a world that was all confusion and had nothing in it I could have that I wanted. I couldn't help feeling that if Johnny Mae hadn't been black and I hadn't been white, I might not have lost her. Was I paying for the sins of our fathers . . . or the sins of Stafford

Willingham? Mainly, I was wallowing in self pity. It finally hit me that Tiny was still in jail.

"I want to make bail for Tiny," I said. "When can I get at the money in my checking account?"

She looked at her watch. "The bank's closed now. It will be tomorrow before I can get an order from the court. Probably by tomorrow afternoon you should be able to use the account."

"How much is his bail?"

"I'll find out from the clerk's office."

We walked down to the property room to pick up my personal items. The property clerk gave me my wrist watch and an envelope containing the money I had come in with. I looked up and saw the little old man who had been in lockup with me my first time was being processed in again. I walked down the hallway to where he was standing alongside one of the jailers.

"Hey, Pop," I said.

"Hello, Mr. Hayes," he said.

"You remember my name?" I was surprised.

"Sure. Everybody down here knows your name now."

I couldn't exactly consider that an honor. In fact, it actually horrified me. I was definitely going to have to start keeping better company.

"What are you in for?" I asked.

He didn't answer.

"Public drunkenness and trespassing," the jailer said.

"I just set down to rest and fell asleep," the old man said.

"You got a lawyer?"

He shook his head and lowered his eyes.

Melissa was standing in front of the property room watching me. I walked back to her. I took the envelope from my pocket and counted the money inside. Two hundred and ten dollars. I took out $100 and handed it to Melissa.

"What's that for?" she said, not taking the money from me.

"See that old man down there?"

She looked over my shoulder in his direction and nodded. I hadn't noticed before how pretty she was when she wasn't my lawyer.

"He needs an attorney. This is your retainer."

She pushed the money away from her.

"Keep your money. I'll represent him without charge."

"Is he eligible for bail?" I said.

"He probably just needs to pay a fine."

"Will $100 do it?"

"Probably," she said.

I held out the money to her again. "Then use the money to pay his fine and keep him out of jail. If it's any more than that, send me a bill."

"You'll go broke bailing all the little old men out of jail."

"Not all of them. Just him."

"Why him?"

"Something he did for me."

"What?" She said, looking in his direction again. "He doesn't look like he could do anything for anyone."

"He asked me for help when I needed it."

"Frank, I think you're just upset," she said, taking my hand.

I tucked the money in her coat pocket. "I am upset, but I'm sure about this. You know how things stick with you sometimes? Well, he sought my protection when I was low and feeling scared and sorry for myself. When I was at my lowest he still looked up to me. Somebody helped me and now it's my turn to help him. It's an obligation I have, something I have to do in order to keep the universe in balance. He's a helpless old man. He shouldn't be in here."

She looked at me a long moment thinking about what I had said. "You're a funny man, Frank."

"I don't feel so funny right now."

Melissa went to the clerk's office and paid the old man's fine. She brought me $50 change back. She told me Tiny's bail was set at $10,000.

"It looks as though you have to make your first decision as executor of Johnny Mae's trust," she said, "unless you have some other money I don't know about."

"That's an easy one. My decision as executor is that I should bail her father out of jail. Besides, it'll be just a short-term use of the money. He won't skip out. I'll get all the money back when he makes his appearance in court. Can I hire you to represent him?"

"I can't do it without the permission of Green and Green."

"See if they'll agree to it. Tiny needs you working on his case."

"I'll find out tomorrow morning. You need a ride?"

"It seems as though I always need a ride. I have a car and a motorcycle and I'm always looking for a ride."

"You want a bite of supper?" she asked.

"You want to be seen with a jailbird?"

"We'll go to some dark out-of-the-way place where no one will recognize me," she said.

Her offer sounded good to me and I was about to say yes, but as we came down the steps of the courthouse I saw Mr. Frederick Carter walking toward his parked car. He would be going back to Atlanta and that's where I wanted to go.

"Can I take a raincheck, Melissa? There's something I

need to take care of."

I was looking in Carter's direction. Melissa saw him and turned to me.

"Do you think that's a good idea, Frank?"

"What?"

She reached out and put her hand on my arm. "I know where you're going. I'm speaking to you as a friend, not as a lawyer. I don't want to see you get hurt any more."

I was touched by her concern. I really was. She had worked hard for me and been very supportive and I probably should have listened to her. I squeezed her arm and kissed her cheek. She didn't pull away. I probably should have gone to dinner with her.

"I'm sorry," I said. "It's something I have to do."

I trotted to catch up with Carter before he got to his car.

Chapter 25

Don't Cry, Reggie

Mr. Frederick Carter was somewhat put off by my request for a ride with him to Atlanta but he was gracious about it. I didn't really feel like talking and Carter didn't have a lot to say, so it was a pretty quiet ride. That was fine. I had a lot to think about. I did ask him how I would go about resigning if I decided I didn't want to be the executor of Johnny Mae's trust. He said all I had to do was send him a letter and return any unspent portion of my compensation. But Willingham had anticipated that too. The trust required a six-month waiting period before any request for change of the executor would go into effect. "A period of contemplation before final action is taken," as Carter described it.

I had him drop me in front of Johnny Mae's apartment. Only it wasn't her apartment anymore. The last thing Carter said to me before I got out of the car was, "Mr. Willingham was afraid of someone or something, Mr. Hayes. In view of what has happened, I think it would be prudent for you to exercise caution."

There was no doubt about it, I would definitely be looking over my shoulder and around corners. I was relieved to see my motorcycle still sitting in the parking space, chained to the lamppost. Someone had thrown a tarp over it.

I was actually shaking with nervousness as I raised my hand to knock on Reggie's door. I hoped she still lived there. The door opened and when she saw who it was she put her arms around me and hugged me.

"Come on in, Frank."

Reggie still looked the same but she wasn't the happy-go-lucky, good-time girl she had been the last time I saw her. She sat facing me on the sofa. She had tears in her eyes.

"Don't cry, Reggie," I said. "Because if you cry, I'm going to cry, and I don't want to cry now. I want you to tell me what happened. Where is Johnny Mae?"

"I can't tell you that, Frank. Even if I knew I couldn't tell you because she made me swear not to, but I don't know where she is. She and Anthony went off somewhere together after the wedding."

"Why did she marry him? If she loved me why did she marry him?"

"She was in love with you, Frank. I've never seen a person more in love than she was with you. When we brought her back from Macon she worried herself sick about you and tried to find out what was happening to you. But her lawyer wouldn't let her see you or call you or write to you. For days she stayed in her room and cried. She was aching for you. Anthony was here every day. He didn't know what was wrong with her. When your letters came she read them and cried some more. Then one day about three weeks ago a calm just came over her. She quit crying. She cleaned herself up, got her hair done and called Anthony."

"What did she say to him?"

"She told him that his kindness during this really bad time made her realize what a fool she was not to have married him the first time he asked her and if he was willing, she was willing."

"Just like that?" I said.

"I think she just reached the point she couldn't stand any more hurt. She was in pain, Frank. She was in terrible shape when we got her out of jail. You wouldn't even have known her. She had never been in any kind of trouble. She had never been near a jail. She was always such a good girl. It just killed her. Anthony and his family offered her a safe and loving place to go. They flew to the Boudreaus' condominium in the Bahamas and were married there."

"How long was she in jail?" I thought about my own experience and it hurt me to think about Johnny Mae going through what I did.

"It was almost a week. At first her attorney couldn't get a hearing. Then the D.A. didn't want her to have bail. Anthony's father finally was able to arrange a call from the U.S. Attorney General's office and that's what got things moving."

"The U.S. Attorney General's office?" I asked, unable to comprehend what it took to arrange that.

"You've got to know what it was like for her, Frank. I mean, she left a dirt poor black neighborhood in Macon, Georgia . . . you saw it . . . and went to Fisk University. Do you know what kind of folks attend Fisk? They're colored folks like you never see in Macon, Georgia. They come from families that have money. And I mean real money. The kind of money that very few white people in Georgia have. They know people with influence. And their families have education and culture. They don't mix with the bigots and white trash that black folks in Macon, Georgia have to live with. It was a life Johnny Mae never dreamed existed before she saw it. That's the world Anthony was offering her."

I sat thinking about what she was saying, realizing I wouldn't have been able to do what Anthony and his family had done for her. It didn't make it any easier for me, just more hopeless.

"When we met at Fisk, Johnny Mae and I hit it off right away. I was from Chicago and she was from Macon, Georgia. The only thing we had in common was that neither of us was rich. From the time we met, we were best friends. We did everything together. Anthony was a medical student at Mahary. His family didn't like Johnny Mae much at first. They thought she was after Anthony because of their money. But it wasn't Johnny Mae after Anthony. It was Anthony after Johnny Mae. He chased her and chased her. Oh, Anthony's a good boy. He always treated Johnny Mae the way she ought to be treated. And Johnny Mae liked Anthony OK. It's just that she never was crazy in love with him, like . . ."

"Like she was with me?" I hoped that's what she was going to say. "Couldn't she have waited?"

"Waited for how long? The case against you looked so tight, like they were going to lock you away for a lifetime. That's what her lawyer said. It's what everybody was saying. It was a balancing act, Frank. She loved you but she was afraid every day that Anthony was going to find out the truth about the two of you and she would lose him too. She had to make a choice. She couldn't keep on the way she was. I'm sorry, Frank. I wish it was some other way. I still want to be your friend, and always will. I know you loved Johnny Mae and she loved you regardless of everything else, but it's over for the two of you now."

Somehow I had hoped Reggie would tell me something different, something that would give me hope that Johnny Mae wasn't really gone from my life. But I had just been dreaming. I stood looking at my motorcycle, wondering where I should go. The first place would be back home to Macon. I had to see about Tiny. After that . . . I didn't know.

Chapter 26

A Pile of Debris

There was something reassuring about the sound and feel of the Harley Sportster. Lovers and emotions might be unpredictable but the effect of the bike on me was a constant. A good long ride on the machine did wonders to recharge me and bring my perspective back to ground. At times it was as if the throb of the deep throated exhaust was my heartbeat. Sometimes it was as if the machine was a wild animal trying to show me that it was faster and stronger than I was. Sometimes it just wanted to show me a wild time. And sometimes it soothed and calmed me. It had all the virtues of a good woman.

I pulled off Interstate 75 at the Forsyth exit and parked the Harley in front of the Waffle House. I'd left my billfold there the night of my first arrest. By some miracle it might still be there and I had to say thanks to Doris for making the call to Johnny Mae for me.

It turned out Doris didn't work there anymore and nobody knew anything about my billfold. I had a bowl of chili, a cup of coffee and a piece of apple pie and headed south again toward Macon. I was disappointed I hadn't been able to tell Doris my appreciation.

I had left Atlanta late and it was past nine in the evening before I pulled into my driveway. I hadn't been in the apartment in a month and a half and I didn't know what I expected to find. What I found was that my lock had been changed. Well this was a hell of a note. I had the clothes on my back, my motorcycle, and no place to stay. The real estate company that managed my apartment was closed and there was nothing I could do about getting into my apartment until tomorrow.

My options weren't very great. Ron had let me sleep on his sofa one night when I first got to town and my car had died. That didn't sound very appealing. I rode down Riverside Drive thinking that a nice clean room in the Hyatt might be a good change. But ten minutes later I found myself turning into Northwoods on the street where Shirley Willingham lived. I had never been in her house but I had driven past it and I knew where it was.

I had really mixed emotions about what I was doing as I approached her driveway. My libido was suddenly put in check when I got within sight of her house. Shirley was standing in her open doorway with a man. His back was to the street. The outside of the house was dark and they were backlit from the lights shining from inside the house. I was too far away to see who he was. I flipped off my lights, turned off my ignition, and coasted the motorcycle to a stop under the cover of a tree. I still couldn't see who was with her but I could see that she knew him well and he was much more than just a friend.

I couldn't say I was angry. It was more disappointment. Don't ask me why. The woman was free to do what she wanted. You get right down to it, I was probably no more than an occasional amusement to her anyway. I guess one of the reasons I was on my way to see her was that I needed to find out how things were with her and why I hadn't heard a word from her since I was arrested. I mean, there could be lots of good reasons. I just wanted to see if she had one. OK, I was also thinking of sex. So kill me. I had been in jail for six weeks. I was twenty-five years old. Blame it on the motorcycle. It wasn't as if I was being unfaithful or anything, was I?

Something caught my eye besides the heavy petting going

on at Shirley's front door. A small red glow brightened and then faded in the dark across the street. Someone was parked on the side street watching Shirley's house. Jesus, I have to tell you, a chill ran down my spine, I mean, for real. It could be nothing. It could be the police . . . maybe Shirley was still a suspect in Stafford's death. But it could also be the same person who killed Stafford. Whoever it was must have seen me when I rode up.

"This the way you spend your evenings now, Frank?"

The low voice came out of the dark right behind me. I almost fell off my bike.

"Jesus, Miller, you scared the shit out of me."

"Keep your voice down," Detective Miller said. "You're interfering in something here. Keep yourself out of sight until everything is quiet, then roll your motorcycle out of here and don't let anyone see you. You better come by my office tomorrow."

"Tell Stevens not to smoke when he's on stakeout." I nodded in the direction I had seen the glow. "You can see him in the dark a mile away. Who are you watching, Shirley or her friend?"

There was no answer. Miller was gone. I pushed my bike further behind the shrubbery and waited. Luckily the wait was short. The guy got in his car and drove around the circular driveway into the street and turned back in my direction. As he passed under the street light I recognized him. It was Craig Linder, the building inspector. What the shit? Right after he passed, an unmarked car containing Detectives Miller and Stevens pulled out from the darkness across the street and followed Linder's car. All things considered, I thought this was not a good time to be paying Shirley Willingham a visit.

I got a room at the Hyatt, got a toothbrush and razor from the hospitality desk, took a long hot shower, and tried to make sense out of what had happened to me that day. I put all my clothes in a laundry bag and hung them on the door with instructions that they be returned to me by 8:00 next morning. My thoughts wandered to my lawyer, Melissa Gresham. It's not what you think. Well, that too, but what got me to thinking about her was wondering if she could tell me what I would have to do to get a private detective's license. I don't know why I thought I needed one . . . perhaps my dissatisfaction with the police investigation and the recurring thought that I could do a better job of it.

Despite my laundry instructions, I planned to sleep late the next morning. But doors slamming and the sound of showers running woke me at 7:00 a.m. I took another shower. That's something six weeks in jail had left me with . . . a craving for frequent hot showers. I found my clothes laundered, pressed, and hanging in a bag on the doorknob outside my room. I don't know how many people have their blue jeans, denim shirts and underwear laundered and pressed but I thought it was pretty cool. Breakfast at the Hyatt was great too. I could appreciate staying in a good hotel. My appreciation was dulled somewhat when I had to pay the bill.

I had to post Tiny's bail and several overdue bills needed to be paid but I couldn't get money from the bank until Melissa got the account unfrozen. I took the opportunity to go to the county farm to visit Tiny.

The county farm was the forced labor division of the county jail. They used prisoners at the farm to grow vegetables and meat for county operations like the jail. That's also where they kept the prisoners who did county road repair. I was a little surprised they had housed Tiny there, because of the seriousness of the charges against him. Sometimes they put troublemakers and dangerous prisoners there so they could use the hard work to keep them tired and docile.

Tiny was showing the effects of being back in jail. He was

harder and more serious. He had lost the little smile that used to play in his eyes and on the corners of his mouth when he was happy. I wanted to see that back again.

"The public defender tells me I ain't gettin' out, Frank."

"I should have bail posted for you by this afternoon."

His face showed a little optimism. "Sho' 'nuff? Where did you get money fo' bail? You couldn't even get bail fo' yo' self."

"I've suddenly got someone looking after me" I said.

"Who is it? It's that Willingham woman, ain't it?"

I shook my head. "No. It doesn't matter. I've got to ask you about the wrist watch, Tiny. Where did it come from?"

"I think it come off o' Willingham's dead body."

"That's what the police think too. How did you get it?"

"A local boy bought it on the street."

"Which one of the boys was it?"

Tiny looked away from me. He seemed to be staring at something across the room. I didn't know if he was going to trust me with the information, but he said, "It was Skeeter that brought it to me. He say his cousin Marcel bought it from somebody on the job where he worked."

"Do you believe him?"

He looked back at me. "Yeh, I believe Skeeter. Skeeter don't lie to me 'bout nothin' big. He get in a little trouble sometime but when he get scared 'bout somethin' he come to me. He come to me with the watch when he seen Willingham's name engraved on the back of it."

"What were you going to do with it?"

"I was gon' give it to you," Tiny said, looking up at me. "Skeeter brought it to me after I seen you last time, befo' the police come to arrest me."

"Who does Skeeter's cousin Marcel work for?"

"I mention to you once befo', Marcel do shit work fo'

Scott Taylor."

"Scott Taylor," I said. "His name keeps showing up. Marcel bought the watch from somebody on Scott Taylor's job?"

"Tha's what Skeeter say Marcel tol' him."

"Did he say who it was?"

Tiny shook his head. "He don't like to name names if somethin' looks like trouble."

"I need to ask you one more thing, Tiny."

He looked up at me through squinted eyes. The way he looked at me I felt like a traitor even asking him.

"The police are saying the money they found with the watch was payoff to you for killing Willingham."

"You want to know where the money come from, Frank?"

"I just want to know if there is any way we can use it to help clear you of the charge. I mean, for instance if you sold something for $1,000."

"You know what I do for a livin', Frank. I buy and sell old stuff, odds and ends, whatever I can find that somebody want t' give away or sell me cheap an' I think I can make a dollar or two off it. I barely make enough to live on. But ever' time I sell somethin', I try to put back fifty cents or a dollar into a little kitty I been keepin'. When I get enough put back, I been plannin' to get out of the junk business and into the barbecue business. That thousand dollars is what I been able to save."

"How are we going to get the police to believe the truth?" I said.

Tiny shook his head. "I don' know, Frank. I been hopin' you can think of somethin'. You s'pose to be lookin' after me."

He grinned at me and I saw a little bit of that old devilish smile back in his eyes.

"You keep your fingers crossed and if things go right I

should have the money to make your bail before the day is over."

"I trust you, Frank."

I headed to Detective Miller's office. He had somebody with him when I arrived. From where I was waiting I could only see the back of the guy's head. I went to a pay phone in the hallway and called Melissa's number. The voice that answered was a young woman's. It wasn't Melissa but it sounded vaguely familiar. California accent maybe. It had to be her roommate.

"Is Melissa in?" I asked.

"For sure, but she's in the shower right now I think. Wait a minute, I'll check." There were sounds of the phone being clunked on a hard surface and movement in the distance, voices, footsteps. "She wants to know, like, who's calling?" she said.

"Frank Hayes."

"Just a minute." More sounds in the background. "Frank Hayes," her voice repeated from across the room.

More sounds. Wait, then more sounds, then Melissa's voice. "Frank?"

"Yeah, it's me."

"What's going on?"

"I need to talk with you. Have you got a few minutes this morning?"

"How about lunch?" she said. "But I'll have to be back on campus by 2:00."

"OK. Could you check on my bank account?"

"Sure. Meet me at the courthouse at noon."

"Do you mind a motorcycle ride?"

"No, I'd love it."

A woman after my own heart. When I looked in Miller's

office again he was alone. I tapped on his door. He looked up and motioned to me.

"Come in and sit down, Frank." He was matter-of-fact. Not hostile, but not particularly warm either.

I sat down and he closed the door. He walked back around and sat down in his chair. He picked up a fishing reel lying on his desk.

"What do you know about Willingham's death?" He twirled the handle of the reel.

"Are you going to advise me of my rights?"

"You're not a suspect." He twirled the handle again. "What were you doing watching Shirley Willingham's house last night?"

"It's a little threesome we have. They do it with the lights on and I watch from the bushes outside the window. Then Linder comes out and I go inside and he watches. What were you doing there?"

"Who do you think set the trap for Willingham and set you up, Frank?" He twirled the handle.

"You know whose name keeps popping up every time I turn around?" I said.

Miller seemed more interested in seeing how long he could make the handle of his reel twirl. "Who?" he said.

"Scott Taylor."

Miller looked at me with a level stare. He stopped the handle from twirling. "You think he's the one?"

"He's in the middle of it some way. I've got a reliable source who tells me Willingham's wrist watch surfaced on one of Scott Taylor's jobs after Willingham's death."

"Who told you that?" Miller asked.

I shook my head. I wasn't willing to divulge that identity. I told Miller about my run-in with Taylor at the riverfront fill site.

"His truck was in Ron's garage for repair alongside my car. Taylor had the opportunity to take the shotgun. People who know such things tell me he has a reputation for being dangerous."

"Anything else?" he said.

"Yeah, a couple of things. Two of Scott Taylor's carpenters showed up at Mr. John Glover's house to do some repairs. They weren't happy about being there. Said they were following orders from Taylor."

"What does that have to do with anything?" Miller asked.

"I'm just giving you the pieces. You have to put them together. There is something else you're not going to like after you think about it."

"What's that?" He was spinning the handle of the reel again.

"The bogus extortion note. It implied that Johnny Mae is a prostitute and that she was involved in a scheme to blackmail Willingham."

Miller shrugged. "So what's your point?"

"Think back in your memory. The first night you arrested me. It seems to me that someone told me a story about how another fellow's cousin, a white boy, got involved with a colored prostitute who got him in over his head, got him involved in the blackmail and extortion business."

Miller stopped spinning the reel handle and was holding it in a death grip. "What're you saying?" His complexion turned red.

"I'm just giving you the pieces. You put them together. The picture may not be pretty. Personally I don't believe it was a coincidence that my setup looked just like the story you told me."

He caught himself, put the reel down, picked up a pencil

and started playing with it. "Who do you think wrote the blackmail note?"

"Who had access to my typewriter?"

"Lots of people." He threw the pencil down on his desk.

"Craig Linder was one of them. Why don't you tell me why you were watching him last night?"

"Forget about last night." He got up from his desk. His demeanor told me our meeting was over. "Why don't you come back to see me when you have something concrete to tell me?"

"When I have something concrete I'll be telling it to the D.A.," I said. "I'm giving you the chance to help me."

He smirked and shook his head, clearly in disbelief that I was so full of myself.

I found Melissa at the courthouse. She was wearing jeans, sandals, a white blouse, and a blue denim vest. Her blonde hair was tied back with a red bandana. She looked like your above average cute college coed.

"Your bank account should be unrestricted by now." She smiled at me. "If you want to make Tiny's bail we can take my car to pick him up, as long as we get me back to campus by 2:00. I have an appointment with my advisor at 2:30 and I have to change out of these clothes."

"What's wrong with those clothes? You look great."

"You're sweet, but campus dress code requires that all 'young ladies' wear dresses or skirts and blouses at all times on campus."

I laughed. "It sounds like the dark ages."

"*In loco parentis*," she said.

"I don't know Latin. That was something about loco parents, wasn't it?"

"Close."

She drove me to my bank where I had a very businesslike transaction with my old friend Vice President Wallis who still didn't look as if he wanted to let me have access to my account. But we left the bank with a cashier's check in the amount of $10,000, plus some pocket money for me. A quick stop at the courthouse where Melissa posted bail for Tiny, and we drove to the county farm and picked up Tiny who was waiting for us outside the gate. He was smiling again.

Melissa's car was a VW Beetle. I'm a little over six-three and Tiny was big all over. The three of us in her car reminded me of one of those tiny little cars in the Shriners' parade with about ten guys inside. Tiny was so glad to get out of jail and I was so glad to have him out, we wouldn't have cared if we had been riding in the back of Tiny's beat-up old pickup. It was a great day.

At Tiny's suggestion we went to the Pig and Whistle for a lunch of barbecue and beer. He and I must have thoroughly embarrassed Melissa with the amount of food and drink we consumed and with our somewhat loud and raucous behavior. If we did, she hid it well. I knew she had been worried for weeks about the outcome of my case. Her body language now said she was relieved and relaxed. Without that stuffy pinstriped suit she wore to court I could see she had a great little body to be talking with. Maybe she had been worried about me too.

Some of the other customers reacted uneasily during our telling of various jail stories. Looking at us from their point of view we must have seemed a little scary. I wondered what they thought about the pretty and prim Melissa consorting with a couple of loud and obnoxious jailbirds. Nobody actually got up and left or moved to another table but they were unusually quiet and some of them gave us quick, furtive glances.

Melissa started glancing at her watch and I knew we had to get Tiny home and her back to campus. We loaded back into her VW and headed across the river to east Macon. To people in traffic around us we must have looked like escapees from the state mental hospital. We were laughing entirely too much.

Melissa saw it first when we turned onto Flewellyn Drive, probably because she was driving and watching the road ahead. She reached over and touched my arm and gave me a quick glance. I looked in the direction she was looking and saw it but Tiny must have already seen it because something between a moan and a growl was coming from the back seat.

"Stop the car! Stop the car!" he was shouting even before we got to Mr. Glover's driveway.

"Easy, Tiny. Easy, Tiny," I was saying, and Melissa had started to whimper.

There was a crowd of neighbors gathered on the street in front of Mr. and Mrs. Glover's lot. A county sheriff's car sat in the street and I could see a uniformed officer moving toward it. A large tractor-trailer, the kind that carries construction equipment, was parked in the empty lot next to the Glovers' front yard. There was a bulldozer sitting just to the rear of where the Glovers' house should have been. The house was gone. It had been razed. There was nothing recognizable left of it, only fragments and pieces of wood, glass, and roofing metal . . . just a pile of debris.

The dozer operator and the truck driver were standing looking back in the direction of the street where a small group of people gathered around a figure lying prone on the ground.

Tiny was in a rage and was yelling as he pushed out of the back seat. "Get away from him! Get away from my daddy!"

Chapter 27

Dangerous Fury

John Glover lay on his back on the bare sandy soil of what used to be his front yard. Mrs. Glover stood next to him holding a handkerchief to her mouth, reaching anxiously down toward him, crying and tugging at the sleeve of Reverend Jerome Brown who stood with an arm around her. One of the women of the neighborhood was bent over Mr. Glover fanning his face and talking to him. Mr. Glover did not move.

Before I could get three steps from the car, Tiny was on his knees at his father's side demanding to know what had happened to him. I dropped down beside him and could see Mr. Glover's chest rising and falling in a jerky pattern. His eyes were half closed and glazed. He had spittle and white foam on his lips.

"What is it?" Tiny was asking. "What happened to him?"

"It's a heart attack or a stroke," 'Rome said, placing a hand on Tiny's shoulder. "We've called for an ambulance."

"How long he been like this?" Tiny said. He was rocking back and forth on his knees, shaking his head and rubbing his hands on his legs.

"Not long," 'Rome said, "just a few minutes."

Melissa was on her knees on the other side of Mr. Glover wiping his face with a handkerchief.

"Somebody bring some cool water, please," she said.

One of the neighborhood men walked to the tractor trailer, took a cooler of ice water from it and brought it back.

Melissa poured some of the cold water on her hands and on the handkerchief and patted it gently onto Mr. Glover's face and neck. His eyes were unresponsive to her efforts.

Tiny got to his feet, looking around him, explosive in a fit of grief and rage. On the front corner of the Glovers' yard next to the street was a large pile of their furniture and personal belongings, obviously cast there without care or regard to their value.

"Who done this to they house?" he growled.

'Rome handed Tiny a document. Tiny took one look at it and threw it to the ground.

"Who done it?" Tiny said, turning in the direction of the two men standing next to the idling bulldozer. He started in their direction. I caught up with him and stepped in front of him.

"Take care of your father, Tiny," I said. "These men only work for somebody else. I'll find out who's behind it."

He didn't even look at my face. He just pushed me aside. "I'm gon' kill 'em both." His voice was a ferocious thing to hear. I knew that he could.

I caught 'Rome's eye and pointed to Tiny's mother. The two construction workers climbed up on the bulldozer trying to get to high ground. I put a hand on Tiny's shoulder to stop him. I knew pretty well what he would do.

He whirled around with a clenched fist that would have knocked me cold if I hadn't known it was coming and stepped out of its range. Then I did something I hated to do but I knew I had to. As Tiny's fist swung past me I stepped into him, threw my arm around his neck and pulled him backwards off-balance across my leg and to the ground on his back. I held onto him as tight as I could and talked into his ear.

"Don't hurt me, Tiny. I can't let you fight those men. The police are here and they'll put you back in jail. You've got to take care of your mother and your daddy. I promise you I'll get whoever is behind this."

He was furious, thrashing like an angry snake. His hands grasped for a hold anywhere on me. "I can't let 'em get away." He growled at me, twisted and kicked, trying to get loose from my grip.

"I promise you I'll get them," I said.

He was all rage and fight for a few seconds, then I felt him relax. He lay still for a while, breathing heavily.

"Let me up." His voice had grown soft.

'Rome and Tiny's mother were standing next to us. I released my hold on Tiny's neck. He rolled over on his knees and stayed there for a minute as if he were deciding whether to fight or give in. I was on my knees in the sand in front of him, breathing hard. He looked me in the eyes. I hoped I didn't look like a frightened lamb at the sight of his fury. I waited.

He put out his hand to me. "Help me up," he said.

Mrs. Glover fell against his chest as soon as he was on his feet. If she hadn't been there I don't know what the outcome might have been. Tiny put an arm around her. We started back toward where Mr. Glover lay. Tiny stopped and turned toward the men on the bulldozer. He raised his arm and pointed at them.

"You best get away from here," he said, turned and walked back to his father.

The crowd had grown larger and their emotions were stirred by what had just happened. There was a lot of murmuring and a few loud voices yelling their indignation. I could see the sheriff's deputy in his patrol car, ending a radio call. As I walked toward him he got out and came around the front of it in my direction.

"You'd better get those two men away from here," I said

to him, pointing toward the two white construction workers.

The deputy was clearly shaken. I was worried he might not be able to control the situation. An ambulance and three more police cars were coming down Shurling Drive, their sirens screaming and their lights flashing.

"Move your car down the street and put them in it," I said to the deputy.

He put his hand on his night stick and looked at me as if he might have in mind putting my unconscious body in his car. He glanced at the two men and then back at the restless mob of people. He got back into his car, started it, turned on his flashing lights, drove slowly down the street and stopped opposite the bulldozer. He got out, walked to the dozer and motioned for the two men to come with him.

The ambulance and the other police cars came careening down the narrow street amidst a cloud of dust and a shower of gravel as the drivers slid their vehicles to a stop. Doors flew open and uniformed personnel of the police department and the emergency medical team formed a flurry of movement around Mr. Glover. Thank God the police used good judgment in dealing with the angry neighbors. There was shouting and angry voices but nobody threw anything or hit anybody and the level of tension eased up.

The EMTs worked quickly and methodically and had Mr. Glover receiving an I.V. drip and oxygen in less than three minutes. They loaded him on the stretcher into the ambulance as worried family, friends, and neighbors looked on. Tiny wanted to ride with his dad but he looked after his mother instead and they followed the ambulance in Reverend Brown's car. Some of the neighbors were picking up the Glovers' belongings and carrying them to Tiny's garage. The crowd began to disperse. Melissa and I were left standing looking at each other. She came over and put her arms around my waist and cried. I held her in my arms. I felt like crying myself.

I called Reggie as soon as I got a chance at the hospital. She didn't know how long it might take to notify Johnny Mae or how long it might take Johnny Mae to get to Macon. I didn't know how I was going to handle seeing Johnny Mae when she did arrive.

When I left the hospital Mr. Glover was in intensive care. Tiny was comforting his mother as best he could, considering the emotional state he was in. Reverend Jerome Brown tried to minister to all of them. 'Rome was a good man. If there truly was an angel among us it was 'Rome.

Melissa had been a trouper. She hadn't met the Glovers before that day so she had enough emotional distance between herself and the situation to stay calm and keep a cool head. That was good, because someone needed to. She had been alert enough to pick up the document Tiny had thrown on the ground at his father's house. Outside the hospital she showed it to me.

"What is this?" I asked.

"A demolition permit," she said, "from the city building inspector's office."

"What?"

Melissa stayed with the Glovers. I borrowed her VW and went to City Hall.

Chapter 28

Over Troubled Waters

"It was a mistake." Craig Linder's voice was almost pleading.

"A mistake?" I asked, not believing that he expected me to believe it.

"A stupid mistake. It was all the changes around here. I tried to tell Tommy Lee I couldn't find experienced inspectors but he insisted I replace them. You heard him."

"You're trying to blame this on inexperienced inspectors? Who's running this place, The Three Stooges?"

"I've had four turnovers since you were here last. Somehow the Glover house never got taken out of the system. It was left on the unresolved citation list by mistake. The deadline for repairs passed, then 30 days more, and the paperwork was automatically forwarded to the sheriff's office ordering demolition."

"The form has your signature on it, Craig," I said.

"I signed a blank form. I always keep blanks signed in case I'm out of town, so that legal deadlines can be met."

"You signed a blank form, some idiot failed to take the Glover house off the citation list, another fool failed to recognize it as the mayor's pet project and sent the order for demolition?"

"That's basically what happened," Linder said.

"I don't believe it. Who was supposed to take the house off the unresolved citation list?"

Linder tried to avoid looking at me.

"Who was it, Craig?"

He threw a stack of papers onto the desk. "It was when Curly Jenkins and Ellis Moore were the field inspectors."

Curly and Moe. I should have guessed.

"Who's the inspector that ordered the demolition?"

"A fellow named Tillery who's been on the job only a month. Emmet Tillery."

"Tillery?" I asked. Craig nodded his head. Why did that name sound familiar to me? Then I remembered. The guy whose nose I broke in jail was named Tillery. But surely Craig wouldn't hire someone with a jail record to work in the inspector's office. No, his name hadn't been Emmet. It was Buddy or something like that.

"Who's going to pay for the *mistake*?" I asked.

Linder sighed, closed his eyes and shook his head slowly. "I don't know. The city may be liable."

"*May* be?" I said, not believing his lack of grasp of the situation. "Not only was their home destroyed, Mr. Glover is lying in the hospital unconscious as a result of the *mistake*."

"I'm sorry," Linder whined. "Look, it was not intentional. It wasn't really anyone's fault. It just fell through the cracks with all the coming and going of people around here."

"You're still here," I said, "and George Dolly is still here. What were the two of you doing?"

"Look, Frank, I know you're upset."

"Upset?" I laughed. "Everything that's happened to me, to my friends, and to people I love, and you think I'm upset? I'm not upset. I'm ready to kill someone."

"I didn't hear you say that, Frank."

"You better open up your ears and open up your eyes, Craig. Something more than building inspection is going on around here."

"What do you mean by that?"

"You think about it and get back to me," I walked out of his office.

He was crazy if he thought I was going to buy that story. Down the hall George Dolly was in his office. I had some unfinished business with him that was connected somehow to this mess.

"Hello, Frank." He got up from his desk and shook my hand. He hadn't changed an ounce since the last time I saw him two months ago. I nodded to him.

"Did you ever find out who was behind the dump-and-fill operation in the greenway flood plain?" I asked.

George looked at me as if he hadn't decided if he were going to discuss official business with me.

"Just wondering," I said.

"The property belonged to Willingham Realty," George said, as if that explained everything. He blinked and looked away from me. "You'll have to excuse me. I've got a pile of things backed up on me. You may have heard, we're short of personnel around here. Craig can't seem to keep building inspectors on the payroll. I'm having to do everyone's work."

"I don't guess you know anything about the demolition order on Mr. Glover's house, do you?"

George immediately grew defensive and I could see the end of this conversation coming.

"I don't know anything about it. You'll have to excuse me. I have to get ready for a meeting of the planning and zoning board."

My head was ringing with the sound of my adrenaline pumping as I walked out of City Hall. A mistake, my ass. I didn't believe that for a second. The big question was, what reason was compelling enough for someone to resort to physical destruction of the Glovers' house? And who was behind it? It was clear that someone connected with the building inspector's office was involved in it. I thought of the police following Craig Linder the night before. Was Linder the one? And I couldn't get the two idiots, Curly Jenkins and Ellis Moore, out of my mind. Maybe they weren't as stupid as they seemed. But what interest could they have in seeing the Glovers' house destroyed? And the dump-and-fill operation on land owned by Stafford Willingham? That meant Scott Taylor was working for Stafford Willingham. How did that fit into the puzzle? And there was still the unanswered question of Shirley Willingham and Craig Linder. I still had lots of questions and no answers.

From City Hall I had to run by my apartment manager's office to pay my back rent. The manager was a jerk. He treated me like some kind of criminal. But I exchanged three month's rent for a key that would open the new lock on my door and vowed to find a new place to live. I had hoped I would be looking for a place to share with Johnny Mae, but that was all gone now. I knew what I was doing when I told Reggie to get Anthony's help for Johnny Mae. But the fact that I had made the choice didn't make it hurt any less.

When I arrived back at the hospital there was little change. The doctors said Mr. Glover had suffered a severe stroke. He was still unconscious. They were not making encouraging sounds about the prospects for his recovery. I didn't have a lot of experience around people of his age or stroke victims so I was not much of a judge of his appearance, but to me he looked bad. I'm not one to wish for anyone near death to hold on just for the sake of holding on, but in this case I wanted Mr. Glover to hold on. If not for his sake then for Tiny's because I knew Tiny was likely to go off like a bomb when his father died. And I didn't want Mr. Glover to die before Johnny Mae could get there. There might be something she needed to say to him before he was gone. I knew there was something I needed to say to him.

Even though they were letting only family members attend Mr. Glover for brief periods, and I certainly didn't look like a family member, I managed to get into his room alone with him. I sat next to his bed and took his hand in mine. I doubt he heard anything I said but I told him I was sorry I had let him down and I felt that a lot of what had happened to him was because of me . . . because of what I had done, or hadn't done. I told him I loved Johnny Mae, that it hadn't worked out for us but she was in good hands. I told him I would look after his wife and would try to be a friend to Tiny. I told him I would do my best to see justice done and if he needed to go, he could go without worry for those he was leaving behind. His hand moved ever so little and I wanted to imagine he was trying to tell me he forgave me and it wasn't really my fault what had happened. But the movement was probably only an involuntary contraction of his muscles.

I found Melissa asleep on one of the square cushioned sofas in a corner of the visitor waiting area. She looked exhausted and she didn't look comfortable. I sat down beside her and lifted her up against me and put an arm around her. She wrapped an arm across my waist and snuggled against me but she never woke up. I wondered if in her sleep she thought I was her teddy bear. She smiled and murmured something. Whatever she thought I was, she liked it. I found myself nodding off after sitting still for a few minutes.

I awoke to the sounds of urgent voices. On the other side of the room two people coming in were met by 'Rome Brown and Mrs. Glover. It was Johnny Mae with a tall and handsome light-skinned black man who had to be her husband, Anthony Boudreau. I suddenly hoped she wouldn't see me, that she would go on by without knowing I was there. I didn't know what I would say to her and I certainly didn't want my presence to cause her any pain at this point in her own grief. I wasn't certain but I thought, just as she headed toward Mr. Glover's room, her eye may have stopped on me for a fleeting moment. But I couldn't tell if she had recognized that it was me.

I left Melissa sleeping and I walked to the nurses' station where they told me there had been no change in Mr. Glover's condition. Down the hallway Anthony Boudreau stood just outside Mr. Glover's hospital room door waiting, looking into the room. He must have been watching Johnny Mae with her grandmother and grandfather. He was about six feet, well built, well groomed and well dressed in casual clothes. His skin color was a little lighter than Johnny Mae's and his hair was dark brown, very curly, and trimmed short. Even though I didn't know him I couldn't picture him with an Afro cut. He looked like what he was—a well-educated upperclass professional. From the attention he paid to Johnny Mae and her family and the consideration he showed them, he appeared to be a kind and sensitive man. He probably didn't deserve the hatred I felt in my heart for him at that moment. If anything, he probably deserved my thanks for taking care of Johnny Mae. But at that moment I could have easily pushed him off the Ocmulgee River bridge and waved as he floated away.

All right, I know it wasn't fair to him. I knew in my heart of hearts he was probably a good man, but the kind of emotional turmoil I was feeling didn't lend itself to considerations of fairness. I wanted the hurting in me to stop and it seemed reasonable to me at the time that having Mr. Anthony Boudreau out of the picture would remove a source of my hurt.

I had to face the fact that Johnny Mae had made her choice and Anthony Boudreau was it. The only sensible thing for me to do at the moment was to be somewhere else. I walked back to where Melissa lay.

"Hey, Sport," I said, patting her shoulder. She opened her eyes. "You look all tired out. Why don't I take you home?"

She was still only half awake. She managed to say, "OK." I helped her to her feet and walked her down the hallway and out into the night air.

"How long was I asleep?" She stretched and rubbed her eyes.

"About an hour."

"I was dreaming. Did anything happen while I was asleep?"

"No. Everything is the same," I said. "What were you dreaming about?"

She smiled and giggled, "It was a crazy dream I have about school. I was dreaming I had forgotten I signed up for a class. It was the day of final exams and I had never been to class."

"I have that dream sometimes too," I said. "I wonder if every student has it? Were you naked?"

She laughed and turned her head away from me. She looked back at me and was blushing. "Yes, I was. How did you know that?"

"I told you, I have the same dream."

"I was. I was completely naked. And I was in the classroom and the instructor was giving the exam and I was the only one who was naked but nobody seemed to notice. And I had to go to the dean's office because I wasn't prepared to take the exam and I was still naked. Then everything changed and I was in court with your case and I was standing completely naked before the judge."

"Maybe that's why we won."

She laughed and looked at her watch.

"I'm starved," she said. "You want something to eat?"

I realized I was hungry too. She drove me to a little all-night grill, the kind of place I used to hang out when I was a student. The jukebox was playing Jimmy Hendrix and the place was full of the sounds of people having a good time. We ordered the special of the house: a pitcher of beer, hamburger steak smothered with grilled onions, a baked potato and a salad. Two mugs of the cold beer and my head was spinning, but between the beer and the food I was feeling better.

Simon and Garfunkel's *Bridge Over Troubled Waters* was playing on the jukebox. I looked across at Melissa and she was smiling at me again.

"That's you, Frank."

"What's me?"

"You're a bridge over troubled waters."

I smiled and shook my head. "No, I'm more like the elephant that broke the bridge and caused everyone to fall into troubled waters."

Her face grew more serious. The smile faded from her lips. She looked into my eyes.

"Was that Johnny Mae who came into the hospital?"

"I thought you were asleep."

"The voices woke me up. She's a very beautiful woman."

I didn't want to be having whatever conversation we were having but I owed Melissa a large debt.

"Yes," I said, "she is."

"Don't you want to talk with her?"

"Yeah, sure I want to talk with her. But I think that time has passed. I don't know what I could say to her. She has a husband now and her own life. I would only be indulging my own needs and it would cause her problems."

I was finding the conversation increasingly difficult. I squirmed in my seat and changed the subject.

"Tiny loves that old man lying in the hospital. If Mr. Glover dies I don't know what Tiny is likely to do. He's boiling inside. He's going to want to see some justice and I need to find some answers. I feel like I'm sitting on a ticking time bomb."

"I think you're taking too much responsibility on your own shoulders."

"A lot of what's happened is my fault."

"Oh, Frank, you can't say that . . ."

"Yes, I can. I did some stupid things and I stumbled blindly into things that were already going on. I've been the trigger for a lot of what's happened. Right now I feel like I'm in way over my head and need some help."

"The main thing you're going to need help with is staying out of trouble," she said and winked at me.

Melissa was smart and she was pretty. She was growing on me in a way that felt good. Call it rebound or whatever you want but what I wanted to do more than anything right then was curl up somewhere with her and forget all the troubles in my life. She seemed to be giving me cues saying she was having the same feelings. But what did I know? I had been in jail for six weeks and the woman I loved had just married another man. I was in a delicate condition. Maybe I was seeing what I wanted to see. To tell you the truth, I didn't know what I wanted.

It was late. Melissa dropped me at the courthouse where my motorcycle was parked and I did what became a regular habit for me when I was troubled. I got on my Harley and rode alone through the dark streets of Macon at midnight. The streets had no depth at night. It was like riding through a tube of darkness broken by spots and bands of light. Riding the bike kept my body occupied but let my mind examine the things it needed to think about. You see things differently at night. And this night all I saw was trouble. Not finding any answers, I headed my bike toward home.

It felt strange to be back in my apartment. Unless you've been through it you don't think of the little inconveniences being in jail can cause, the kinds of things you take for granted that are disrupted by a prolonged absence. Little things like your electricity. My electricity was turned off. Thank goodness the gas was still on so I had hot water, and I had candles for light. Candlelight isn't so bad once your eyes adjust to it. A lot of wonderful things have happened by candlelight.

One of the biggest shocks was in the kitchen. The ghostly remains of the last meal Johnny Mae and I had were still on the table and on the stove. Everything had long since dried up until it looked like mummy food or had been eaten by mold. It was like walking into an ancient tomb where life had once existed. I was undecided whether I should wash the pots and pans and dishes that were caked with dried food that clung like barnacles or whether I should dump the whole lot in the garbage and start new. Then it occurred to me that I didn't have any garbage pickup. My garbage fee hadn't been paid in two months. I would wash and clean tomorrow in the daylight after I got my electricity back. The thought of washing dishes by candlelight didn't hold any appeal for me. I didn't go near the refrigerator. I knew there had to be something awful growing in it.

I hoped the smell of Johnny Mae somehow would still cling to my pillow but she was gone. Everything just smelled musty. I changed the bed clothes and forced my window open so fresh night air would come into the room.

I hadn't expected it to be so quiet. After six weeks in jail where sound never stopped, my apartment was almost frighteningly quiet as I lay in the dark trying to go to sleep. I had longed for quiet for weeks but now it was as if my mind kept waiting for the sounds that I listened for in jail, the sounds that said danger was near, or trouble was rising, or it was safe to sleep. Oddly, now it seemed the night was too quiet. There were only sirens in the distance and the occasional sound of a dog barking. I would have to learn again how to live normally.

I awoke at 4:30 in the morning shaking with fear and with my heart pounding. It took me several moments to figure out what was wrong with me. It was the sirens. The sound of sirens was coming through my open window and I realized I had been half aware of them in my sleep. I got out of bed and looked out the window. I couldn't see anything. I slipped on my jeans and walked out into the parking lot. There was an orange glow on the horizon in the direction of east Macon.

Chapter 29

Fireballs From Hell

When I turned my Harley onto Shurling Drive flames rose above housetops in three directions and the glow of fires lit the sky in half a dozen more places ahead of me. Ash was falling so thick in the air I had to shield my eyes from the particles as I rode toward Flewellyn. About halfway up, the street was blocked by a fire truck and a police cruiser in front of an old row house style wooden apartment building. The fire was too far along to save the building, not that it was worth saving. I remembered seeing the empty apartments on past trips through the area. For Rent signs were still sticking in the ground in the front yards of some of them.

I took one of the narrow dirt side streets and wound my way in the direction I knew the Saint James A.M.E. Church lay. I caught glimpses of people running but I couldn't tell if they were running toward the fires or away. I could see police sitting and watching in their cruisers and police on foot in riot gear near where firemen were battling blazes. I saw people watching but I didn't see rioting, fighting, or looting.

The streets were blocked off completely near Saint James A.M.E. Church. I turned my bike down a dirt drive and across vacant lots until I came out on the street that ran beside the church. 'Rome Brown and a line of neighborhood residents were passing buckets of water from a fire hydrant and spraying water from garden hoses onto the side of the church. A fire truck with its ladder extended was parked in front of the church and a fireman high on the ladder sprayed water onto the church roof. A charred scar blackened the side of the church leading up to the roof but I didn't see any flames. I parked my bike in the ditch next to the street and ran to where 'Rome was standing.

He looked too exhausted to lift the buckets of water being handed along the line. I stepped into his place to relieve him.

"How bad is the damage?" I yelled to him.

He shook his head and raised his hands saying he didn't know.

"Is there anything inside that needs to be saved?" I yelled.

'Rome didn't answer. He just dipped a handkerchief into a bucket of water as it passed and washed the soot and ash dust from his eyes.

I looked past the church. The pile of rubble that had been the Glovers' house was a red-hot bed of coals. Sparks streaked into the sky from it and yellow flames licked the air first one place then another. In the yard next to the burning ruin the tractor trailer was burned almost beyond recognition. The tires were melted from it, the glass was cracked and melted from the windows, and the metal was burned a misshapen charcoal gray. What was left of the bulldozer was like a surreal sculpture of a bulldozer in torment.

The heat radiating from the fires and the red-hot coals sapped the energy from my body as we worked into the early morning hours trying to hold back the fire that rose up from the nearby buildings and dry vegetation. At times it was like a living creature against the sky. My skin felt like a bad sunburn. My mouth was dry and my lips were parched. My clothes were hot against my skin. I could smell singed hair and I hoped it wasn't mine.

In the midst of the smoke and dust and haze I saw Shirley Willingham open the door of her big black Lincoln and come hurrying across the sandy ground toward the church. Her hair was tied up under a cap and she was dressed in denim and boots and was carrying a flashlight. She went straight to where 'Rome was standing. She spoke to him and motioned animatedly. She headed toward the front door of the church. I ran to intercept her.

"Come with me, Frank," she yelled. "We need to find out if there is fire inside the church."

"What if there is?" I yelled back.

"Then we'll put it out."

Sounded like a good plan to me. I stopped her just as she reached for the door handle. I splashed water on the metal handle. It didn't sizzle. I wet my hand and touched a finger lightly to it. It was hot but not burning hot. I opened the door just a crack. I was afraid we might be met by a fire monster waiting just inside the door that would pounce on us and eat us for a late night snack.

It was dark and smokey inside but there was no sign of flame or hot coals. Her little flashlight was of almost no use in the dark interior but from what we could see there was more water damage than anything else. We stepped back out onto the church steps and were met by a shower of sparks and ashes. The heat of the fires was causing winds to blow through the streets and alleys, whipping up smoldering fires and spraying cinders, ash and sparks in all directions. The heat was blistering.

"We need more water here," she yelled, and trotted off across the yard in the direction of the fire boss.

She talked to him and gestured in the direction of the church. The fireman gestured in return and shook his head. I thought she was wasting her breath but it wasn't ten minutes until another fire truck pulled up to the rear of the church and began a second spray of water onto the ancient structure.

By the time daylight arrived, most of the burned buildings looked like last night's campfire. They were ruins of black charcoal posts and beams, a few remnants of blackened boards here and there, and lots of gray ash and white smoke. But the old church was standing. It was smudged and blackened in places but it was standing.

I looked at Shirley and she looked at me and we began laughing at each other. Neither of us had color or features that were recognizable through the layers of gray and black that covered us.

"Do you have a camera with you?" I asked. "We need to get a picture of the way we look. No one will ever believe it."

She laughed and shook her head. We both looked up to see two people approaching whose only recognizable human features were white eyes and white teeth showing from behind crooked smiles. It was 'Rome and Tiny. They were carrying a pitcher of Kool Aid and paper cups someone had brought. We sat on the steps of the church in near exhaustion and savored the cool, sweet liquid.

"What happened?" I asked 'Rome.

"Nobody seems to know. It all started when most everybody was asleep or inside their houses. It was as if, all of a sudden, fireballs from hell descended all over the neighborhood."

"Somethin' mighty wrong about it," Tiny said. "I'm not sayin' lots of folks wouldn't 'a liked to see some things burn." He was looking in the direction of the burned-out tractor trailer and bulldozer. "But nobody seen nothin' and everbody say that nobody done nothin'."

"You're saying the fires weren't started by people in the neighborhood?" Shirley asked.

"The police gon' say they was. But I'm sayin' it don't look right to me. I didn't see nobody burnin'. I saw lots of folks watchin' and lots of folks helpin' fight the fire but I didn't see nobody start a fire or even try to keep a fire burnin'."

"You're saying someone set the fires to make it look like a neighborhood riot?"

"Mm hmm. That's what I'm sayin'."

"For what reason?" she asked.

Tiny shrugged. "Lots of people got reasons."

"What burned last night?" I asked him.

"Mos' all low rent empty rundown stuff."

"If specific property was targeted then somebody had a reason," I said.

"Mm hmm. Sho' did."

"You know what it was?"

Tiny shrugged. "You have to find that out, Frank. I'm just sayin' don' believe the police when they say it was neighborhood brothers and sisters."

"I'm certainly grateful to the Good Lord above," 'Rome said, "that we were able to save the church."

"Amen," Tiny added.

"And I'm grateful to you, Mrs. Willingham," 'Rome said, "not only for your courage last night but for your help in our efforts to have our church building placed on the National Register of Historic Places."

Even covered in ash and suffering from complete exhaustion, Shirley still had poise. "I'm sure what little I did last night made little difference to the fire," she said. "I'm just happy we were able to save the church."

Our conversation was overshadowed by the arrival of a TV news van on Bertha Street. A WXIA reporter and cameraman came toward us. Shirley stood up to meet them and before anyone could duck for cover the camera was rolling and interviews were underway. Once Shirley identified herself she quickly became the interviewee of primary interest. Tiny led me to one side.

"I want to show you somethin'."

We walked around behind the church and stopped in the yard outside the entrance to 'Rome's office.

"'Rome been sleepin' in the church lately to keep an eye on things. This come sailin' through a church window las' night 'bout midnight."

Tiny took his foot and scraped aside the sandy soil, uncovering a beer bottle containing liquid. The neck of the bottle was stuffed with a rag.

"Cracker don' know how to make no cocktail," he said. "He only know how to drink Bud." He looked at me with a frighteningly serious look from behind the comically colored face of gray ash. "It didn' break. 'Rome heard it and found it befo' it done its job."

"Someone tried to burn the church," I said.

"Mm hmm."

"Leave it there. If we're lucky the police might get some fingerprints off of it."

I rubbed the sooty coating off the face of my watch.

"Somebody gon' pay for this, Frank."

"Tiny, I swear to you I won't stop 'til I find out who's behind it."

"Then what?"

"Then one way or another we'll be sure they get what's coming to them. But we've got to be careful. You have to stay out of trouble. I can't run a barbecue business by myself."

"Don't you be worryin' about me, Frank Hayes."

"I'm worrying about me, Tiny."

"You better be. You get yo' white ass in jail ag'in, I might not be there to help you. But you know, right now the way you look, you might pass for colored."

I was heading back to my motorcycle when Shirley caught

up with me.

"Can I give you a ride, Frank?"

"No, thanks." I pointed to my motorcycle, now the uniform color of gray ash. "It doesn't look like much at the moment but I have my bike."

"We need to talk soon," she said. "My lawyers tell me the court released the hold on your bank account. We need to have Stafford's money transferred back into my account."

So that was it. She was no longer interested in my manly attributes. She wanted her money back. I didn't know exactly how to handle what I had to tell her. But I gave it my best try.

"Shirley, your husband hired me to do a job for him. That's what the money was for."

"What kind of job?"

"I can't tell you that but if you want to confirm the truth of it you can contact Mr. Frederick Carter at the firm of Barnes and Ingram in Atlanta. They're the ones who handled the deal for Stafford."

"What would Stafford pay you $25,000 for? And why didn't you know anything about it before?"

"I only found out about it while I was in jail. The job he hired me to do is confidential. I can't tell you what it is. I'm sorry, but it's true."

"Stafford is dead now. The money came from our account and it belongs to me now."

"I've agreed to do the job, Shirley. I know it's probably asking more than you're willing to do, but you have to trust that I'm telling you the truth."

I didn't think I had the ability to stop Shirley Willingham in her tracks but I did. She clearly didn't like my answer but she had no retort. I was sorry to have to refuse her, for more reasons than one, but I couldn't tell her about the trust.

"I need to talk to you too," I said, "about Craig Linder."

This time she was not only speechless, I'm sure that under all that ash and soot she went pale.

"It's not what you think," she said.

"I don't know what I think, except that he may be mixed up in Stafford's death."

"Craig?" she asked. The thought seemed completely foreign to her.

"I'll call you later today or tomorrow," I said. "We'll talk about it. Right now I've got to get caught up with some pressing matters."

The most pressing matter I had at the moment was to get my bike to a car wash. It was bad enough for me to look like a child of the ashes but I had to wash my bike. It looked too much like the mummified food in the dirty dishes in my apartment. It gave me a strange sense of comfort to see the shine and polish return as I sprayed the pressure wash over the Harley. The only signs of its ordeal by fire were a couple of small scorch marks on the seat from sparks that had fallen on it. Just a couple of small scars to give it character. Very much like me.

Chapter 30

Just Little Guys Here

I wanted more than anything to get some sleep. I had slept only three hours or so last night and the firefighting had drained all the energy out of me. But I didn't have time to sleep. I had some things to be taken care of. In addition to my electricity being turned off and my garbage not picked up, I had seen in my pile of back mail that AHGF, American Home Guardian Finance, was sending me late notices for payment on the loan for my motorcycle. If I didn't get down there and settle up, they would be coming to repossess my family jewels. And I didn't know where my car was but it was a good bet Ron had repossessed it and was holding it in his lockup pending payment of the $200 repair bill.

I took a cold shower at my apartment and grabbed a breakfast big enough for three people at a little place on Riverside Drive. The TV in the restaurant played and replayed video tape of the fires from the night before, along with live and continuous coverage of the aftermath. There were interviews with the police chief and the fire chief, with neighborhood residents, with people passing in their cars, with Shirley Willingham talking about the community's brave efforts to save the church, and with the mayor.

The mayor was in full battle mode. Video of him from the night before showed him in his underground command center beneath the parking deck at City Hall talking on the phone and in various serious poses and postures. There were shots of the mayor's tank rumbling haltingly through the dark streets of Macon turning first one way then backing up then turning another way. There was video of the police standing on the street in full riot gear and of firefighters spraying water on burning buildings. The sequence ended with the mayor's statement in front of City Hall just one hour ago declaring the streets of Macon safe and assuring viewers that business will go on today as usual. Thanks to quick action and a show of strength by the brave men and women of Macon's well-trained and well-armed police riot force, he said, the urban rioting had been contained within a small area inside the east Macon community, the fires were now mostly extinguished and all that was left was cleanup. The mayor said he personally had been in contact with community leaders and had their full cooperation in putting an end to the lawlessness of a few lawless people. There had been twenty arrests. The mayor assured his public, "We're here to defend the peace and provide for public safety and we will protect the property of our good law-abiding citizens. And I have a message for all would-be rioters and looters who may be out there. The Macon police have standing orders to shoot looters on sight. If you want to start trouble in Macon, Georgia, we'll show you what trouble is." Didn't I hear those lines in a movie somewhere once?

My breakfast would have digested better if the TV had been turned off. A couple of customers in the restaurant advised that they were carrying guns in their cars, just in case anything happened. Leave it to the mayor and the news media to instill panic in the citizenry. I drove by Georgia Power to settle my electricity issue and headed downtown.

I've notice there are at least two kinds of people in the world. When things get really bad and it looks like you're going to become the next meal for some indescribably evil creature, one kind of person crawls into bed under the covers, assumes the fetal position, thumb in mouth, closes his eyes and whimpers. The other kind of person turns for counsel, rebirth and resurrection to the one constant source of strength in the universe, the motorcycle.

As everything else around me went to hell I felt a growing attachment to my motorcycle and I needed reassurance that it would remain *my* motorcycle. If I didn't get to Bob Felton, my personal financial manager at American Home Guardian Finance, and pay my overdue notes, he might repossess my dream machine and reduce me to whimpering under the covers.

I found Bob Felton in his office admiring himself in a small mirror he kept in his desk. He was very magnanimous and understanding about my recent circumstances but he couldn't miss the opportunity to give me a lecture on the virtue of a good credit rating. I was so taken with Bob's treatise on virtue that I took the opportunity to tell a few lies.

"Bob, I believe Mr. John Glover is one of your customers."

"Good old Mr. Glover," he said, straightening his tie. "We've been doing business together for many years. I knew him before I came to AHG when I was with Macon Finance Company. John is a fine fellow. I just wrote him a debt consolidation loan a couple of months ago to try and help him get back on his feet."

"That's what his son told me," I said. "I don't know if you've heard, but Mr. Glover's house was destroyed in the fires in east Macon last night."

A varnished look of sincere concern came over Bob's face. "No, I didn't have any idea. Did he lose everything?"

"Most of his personal items were saved but his house was destroyed. Mr. Glover was injured trying to save the house and he's in the hospital in critical condition. Things don't look very good for him. He's had a stroke and his family has asked me to take care of his business affairs for him."

"I'm so sorry to hear that. Such a fine old gentleman." Bob put his hand over his heart and shook his head slowly. "They don't make 'em like John Glover anymore."

"You probably know, Mr. Glover is a very private man. He doesn't tell anyone his business, including his family, which makes it difficult for them now that he's not able to take care of his business or tell anyone what needs to be done. I wonder if you could tell me if Mr. Glover's account is up to date? His family authorized me to pay up any back amounts."

Bob was picking some speck I couldn't see from his coat. He looked at me in a strange way. "I don't believe Mr. Glover has an account with us anymore."

"He doesn't? I think this would be the new account you were just telling me about."

"Let me check his file," he said, and walked into the adjoining office.

He was gone hardly more than a minute and returned carrying a thin file folder. He laid the file open on the desk for me to see.

"Just as I thought, Mr. Glover's loan was acquired by another institution just a week after he opened it with us."

"You mean someone bought the loan from you?" I asked.

"It's a common business practice. Financial institutions buy and sell finance papers routinely."

"Who bought it?"

Bob shrugged. He ran a hand over his oiled hair. "I don't guess it's violating any confidence to tell you. You'll be dealing with them sooner or later anyway if you're taking care of Mr. Glover's accounts. It was a local company by the name of Investment Adventures. The transaction was handled by their attorneys in the firm of Green and Green."

Green and Green? I wanted to tell him there must be some mistake. It couldn't be Green and Green. That's the law firm Melissa worked for. I tried to keep my composure.

"How did they know you were holding a loan against Mr. Glover's property?"

"I can't remember for certain in this particular case. We've had a lot of transactions lately. They may not have even known whose loan it was. We have standing orders from some companies. If anything in a certain category comes in, we automatically put a tag on it for them. Different companies like different kinds of investments. We've got one guy in Atlanta comes through town once a month looking for any papers holding guns as collateral. The guy collects all kinds of guns. He buys up the paperwork and sometimes he ends up with something he wants. You know, somebody forfeits and he acquires the collateral. I can tell you from personal knowledge, he's got some mighty rare and expensive items through loan foreclosures."

Bob took a ring of keys from his desk drawer and walked to a metal door in one wall of the office. He inserted a key, twisted it in the lock, and pulled the handle.

"Come here, let me show you something."

Inside the walk-in safe was a wild assortment of items, from jewelry to paintings, to shotguns and small appliances. He slid open a drawer and motioned for me to look inside. He must have had three dozen pistols in every make, size, model and color. He lifted out a wooden box and opened the lid.

"I'm especially fond of this one."

A shiny new chrome-plated Smith and Wesson .38 revolver with a six inch barrel and pearl handles sparkled up at me.

"I'm thinking of keeping this one for myself," he said. "See anything you want?"

I told him no, thanks.

"You change your mind, you let me know. I can give you a

good price."

"How often do you have to foreclose on a loan?" I asked.

"It depends on the customer. It's like life insurance, it's all a question of probabilities. You look at a customer's credit history and you decide whether or not to take a chance. Sometimes the customer pays on time and in full, sometimes the loan goes bad and we take the collateral. You gotta' use your brain and know what you're doing. You gotta' know your customers. But that's why some people make it in this business and some people don't."

"Anybody collecting paper on east Macon property?"

Bob laughed as he closed the safe door. "Everybody in town. That country club goes in, east Macon property will be good as gold. A lot of people are looking to make a lot of money."

"Has Investment Adventures bought any other papers from you on east Macon property?"

"Everything we had." Bob sat back down and was inspecting his teeth in his little mirror.

"Who are they?"

"Who?"

"Investment Adventures. Who owns the company?"

"I don't know all of them. Funny thing about that. I do know that Stafford Willingham was one of the owners. Now there was a great man. He was a real businessman."

"How do you know Willingham was connected with the company?"

"His name was on some of the papers that came through here. I was saying, funny thing about that. Stafford Willingham himself was in here the week he died, asking about east Macon properties."

"What did he want to know?"

"Wanted to know what we had. I told him Investment Adventures had already picked up all the papers we had on east Macon. That's the only time I ever met Mr. Willingham. I was surprised he would involve himself personally in a small deal like ours, but I guess it just goes to show how important some people think the east Macon development potential is."

"Why doesn't your company just hold onto the debts instead of selling them?"

Bob grinned at me like the cat that had eaten the canary. "We've all got our place in the business. We're just little guys here. Our main business is interest income. The big boys with the big bucks pay us good money for the paper. We do our job, they do theirs. Besides," he admired his manicure, "I have a few investments myself."

The self-important little shrimp Bob Felton filled me with disgust. An industry that fed on its clients' inability to pay filled me with disgust. I would never look at a finance company the same again. I stopped at the cashier's window and wrote out a check for the balance of my motorcycle loan. I didn't care if I had to wait tables to pay my rent, I wasn't going to pay American Home Guardian another nickel in interest or let their hooks stay in me another minute. As I walked out the door I looked back. Bob was wiping a spot of dust from the toe of his shoe. I left American Home Guardian Finance feeling the overwhelming need to wash my hands and wash out my mouth.

I had to call Melissa. The Green and Green connection with the Glovers bothered me. I knew that some company was behind the Glovers' troubles but I didn't want Melissa to be anywhere near it. I couldn't believe she knew anything about her employer's involvement. I arranged for her to meet me for lunch. I picked up some carryouts from the deli on Cherry Street and rode to the Rose Hill Cemetery off of Riverside Drive.

The cemetery is a quiet and beautiful spot where people often go to eat their lunch or to meditate during the day. It's a hundred and fifty years old, give or take a century. A wooded section contains the graves of slaves from before the Civil War. Some of the markers are so old the lettering is weathered off or there is no marker at all. Crypts and mausoleums of the old and wealthy families of Macon are dotted and clustered about the cemetery and along the bluff overlooking the river, many of the families now gone and the owners forgotten. Ancient magnolia trees, cedars and oaks grow along the paved drive that winds in a gliding and twisted path among the family plots. There are marble markers of angels, doves, six-foot urns, and of the likenesses of children.

The back side of the cemetery borders on the Ocmulgee River and you can sit on benches or on the grave stones or on the thick leaves in the shade beneath the magnolia trees and look down on the quiet river below. It's here you can sometimes see lovers in intimate conversation sitting with their arms around each other, their heads resting on each other's shoulders. That's where Melissa found me waiting for her.

We had lunch and chatted for a while. I didn't bring it up at first. I didn't know how she was going to react to knowing that her bosses were involved with the Glovers' troubles. But eventually I had to get to it.

"I found out this morning that Green and Green handle the accounts for a company named Investment Adventures."

If she showed any reaction I didn't see it.

"Investment Adventures?" she said. "That sounds like stocks or bonds or real estate speculation."

"You never heard of it?"

She did a funny little thing with her lips.

"I don't think so. Green and Green is a big firm. They

have hundreds of accounts."

"How long have you worked for them?"

"I don't work *for* them. I interned with them for a year and now they supervise my court cases. I worked a little in the finance and investment side when I first started my internship but I've always been more interested in criminal law. What's the deal about Investment Adventures?"

"I think they may be behind the destruction of the Glovers' home and other problems in east Macon."

"What makes you think that?" She had turned very serious.

"They've been buying up debts that hold east Macon property as collateral, including Mr. Glover's loan from American Home Guardian Finance. Green and Green handle their contracts and manage their legal actions."

"You're telling me Green and Green are the attorneys who filed the papers to take possession of the Glovers' home?"

"That's what the manager at American Home Guardian told me. He's the one who sold the Glovers' loan to Investment Adventures, and Green and Green handled the transaction."

Melissa had grown rigid. Her eyes were fixed and unfocused, like her thoughts were turned inward.

"There's more bad news," I said. "Stafford Willingham apparently was a major investor in Investment Adventures."

The woman who looked out at me was suddenly a lot harder and meaner than the girl I had been talking with a minute earlier.

"Those sons of bitches knew when I was handling your case that another of their clients had a competing interest," she said. "This stinks. They had access to my case file and my notes. They read everything I had for your defense. Those sons of bitches."

"So what's the big deal?" I asked. "We won, didn't we?"

"We won because of the unexpected appearance of Stafford Willingham's letter. Without that letter or some other magic bullet we didn't really have a snowball's chance in hell."

"You mean we would have lost?" I asked. "But it was all just a frame up."

"Yes, it was, wasn't it? And a damn good one too. Jesus H. Christ. Green and Green were representing the interests of both Stafford Willingham and his accused killer."

"And perhaps his real killer."

"They had to know. It couldn't have been an oversight. The firm is big but it's not that big. They keep master lists of clients just for the purpose of avoiding conflicts of interest."

"Do they?" I asked. "And just how difficult would it be to get a copy of their master client list?"

Suddenly Melissa was snapped back to her more proper senses.

"Frank, do you know what you're asking me to do?"

"Investigate the company that framed me for murder? Had me locked in the Bibb County jail for six weeks?" I could have added, caused the destruction of my relationship with the woman I loved, but I didn't.

"If I were to get caught it would ruin my career as an attorney."

"Yes, you're right. Well then, what are the chances you could get copies of all the files on Investment Adventures?"

"Frank!" She stopped and thought a moment. "I suppose there's no other way they'll ever be exposed. But if I'm caught and get kicked out of law school," she pointed her finger at me, "you have to promise to marry me to keep me out of poverty."

I didn't say anything. We looked at each other for a long moment that grew uncomfortable. The moment passed but it didn't pass before we both realized we had entered into a new relationship that formed a serious bond between us. If she made the commitment to put herself in this kind of dangerous situation for me, then I owed her a big personal commitment in return.

Chapter 31

A Legal Cloud

I didn't want to put Melissa in danger. But she wouldn't have it any other way. She was convinced, and I think she was right, the only way to get to the bottom of the Investment Adventures connection was to have a look inside Green and Green's files. She was ready to go down to their offices and have it out with them but we both knew that wouldn't get us what we needed. We would have to devise a plan to get to the records. I made her promise she wouldn't do anything foolish without me. Well, you know what I mean.

There were some other records I needed to have a look at that didn't involve corporate espionage. When we first met, Mr. Glover had come to my office carrying a manila envelope that I now realized might have contained important papers and documents. Because of the mayor's intervention in the situation and what had looked like a settlement of Mr. Glover's problems, I had put aside all thoughts of the envelope. Now I needed to take a close look inside it because now I had some idea what I might be looking for. I hoped the envelope had not been burned and was among the Glovers' possessions stored in Tiny's garage.

When I arrived back at the hospital Mr. Glover had been moved to a room on the fifth floor. I felt better about him as I rode the elevator up. It was a good sign that he was out of intensive care. The elevator stopped, the doors opened, and I was standing face-to-face with Johnny Mae.

There was no one on the elevator with me and there was no one standing waiting with her. I saw the sudden look of a frightened rabbit in her eyes and her lips parted just a fraction as she took in a sharp, shallow breath. I couldn't let her get away without at least a word. I reached out and took her coat sleeve and gently guided her into the elevator with me. She pressed the button for the first floor. The doors closed and the elevator started down. I put my hands on her shoulders to pull her to me but she put her hands against my chest and stopped me.

"Don't, Frank. I can't. I'm sorry. I can't have any complication."

I tried gently again to pull her to me. She stepped back from me.

"Isn't there some way . . ." I said.

She closed her eyes for a moment and shook her head in rapid little jerks.

"I didn't want it this way," she said. Her eyes had grown misty.

I looked up at the red number display. We were already passing the third floor on the way down. Johnny Mae looked up at the number then back at me. There was desperation in her eyes. She threw herself into my arms and my lips found hers. It was just like I had remembered her, only sweeter. She kissed me the way I remembered. I held her in the embrace and didn't want to let go. Just as the elevator bumped to a stop at the first floor she pushed away from me and pulled back within herself.

"Goodbye, Frank. Thank you for everything. I'll never forget you."

The elevator door opened. She turned, stepped out into the lobby and walked away.

I thought it was all settled in me. I thought I had accepted that it was over between us. Now I was reeling again. I could see she loved me and that made it harder to take. If she had changed her mind, decided she really found me distasteful and didn't want to have anything further to do with me, it would have been easier. But this was something I was going to have to struggle with. It wasn't as if it was dead and over. It was still alive but she was now the wife of another man.

The doors closed and I stood inside the still elevator, not moving, leaning with my back against the wall. I could smell her and taste her and I wanted to burn the sensation into my nerves so it would never leave me.

I don't know how long I stood there. The elevator chimed, the doors opened and a very meek looking couple started in, saw me, and stopped, wondering I'm sure what I was doing standing in a closed elevator. I looked up at the number display, shrugged and said, "Oh, I thought I was going up."

I don't think they were completely convinced of my innocence but they rode up with me. I got off on the fifth floor and located Mr. Glover's room. Mrs. Glover was in with him and Tiny was sitting in a waiting area down the hall. I stepped into the room and gave Mrs. Glover a hug. She patted my hand. The only change I could see in Mr. Glover was that his eyes half opened and closed a couple of times while I was standing there. He still had wires and tubes connected to him and monitors showing his pulse and blood pressure.

I walked to where Tiny was and sat down beside him. I put my head in my hands.

"You see Johnny Mae?" he asked.

I nodded.

"Skeeter tol' you."

I looked up at him. "What?"

"He tol' you she'd rip out yo' heart and stomp all over it. A woman like her can break a man's heart."

I couldn't say anything.

"You done good by her, Frank. You took all that anger

and hate she had and turned it into somethin' else. I tol' you, you was the one."

"You didn't tell me what it would do to me."

"I know about hurt, Frank," he said.

I suddenly felt myself humbled. Here I was with my heart bleeding all over the floor, feeling pitiful and sorry for myself, and I was sitting beside a man who had lived for twenty-five years with a tragedy and loss that made me look like a lovesick teenager. He had watched Johnny Mae's mother, the woman he loved, die in his arms because of his hand.

"I'm sorry, Tiny. I didn't mean . . ." What? To open an old wound that had never healed.

"The Lord got some plan for you, Frank. You got to trust that everthing gon' work out. It got to, 'cause you and me has still got some things to do. We still got to ketch the devil."

"I think I may be on to something," I said. I told him I needed to look at Mr. Glover's old documents that I hoped were stored in Tiny's garage. We left his mother sitting with his dad and headed to his house in his old pickup.

"Where is your mamma staying?" I asked.

"She stayin' with me," he said.

I thought to myself, that's probably the first time in twenty-five years the two of them had stayed under the same roof. It had to be good for both of them.

"She don' like the way I keep house." He chuckled.

As we passed over the Ocmulgee River bridge and turned in the direction of Tiny's neighborhood we drove past the mayor's Sherman tank sitting in the ditch on the side of the road. One of the tank's tracks had broken and fallen off and the big steel rollers and gears that powered the tank's travel sat partly buried in the dirt by the weight of the huge machine.

"Damned old piece of junk." Tiny laughed.

"Good thing he didn't buy a good one," I said. We both had a good laugh. I hated to think what might have happened if the tank had made it to its destination. The news media might be telling a different story that day.

Tiny's neighborhood looked like some war-torn village of Europe or third-world country. Blackened walls, gutted shells of buildings, burned out cars and trucks marked the alien landscape. A gray smokey haze drifted just above the rooftops. The air smelled of things burned and those still smoldering . . . pine lumber, asphalt shingles, upholstered furniture, plastic, rubber tires, clothes. Some of the smells were pleasant like a winter's wood fire in the fireplace. Others were acrid and pungent, burned the eyes and offended the nostrils.

Here and there neighborhood residents alongside firemen were shoveling sand onto smoldering debris while the remains of other structures were left abandoned to burn themselves until nothing remained but gray ash and those things that wouldn't burn. Cleaners and carpenters were at work on the St. James A.M.E. Church. 'Rome Brown was among them. He looked up and began walking toward us as Tiny pulled his pickup to a stop in the front yard of his house. I waved and spoke to 'Rome as he stopped Tiny to ask about the latest report on Mr. Glover.

I opened the weathered wooden doors to Tiny's garage to let in the light so I could begin searching through the piles of the Glovers' belongings for the old envelope I hoped would be there. I wondered for the hundredth time if any of this would have happened if I hadn't blundered into the Glovers' lives. I knew the reality of it was that something had already been in motion before I ever met John Glover. That's why he had come to my office looking for help in the first place. Still, I couldn't get the thought out of my head. If I had been smarter or shown more discretion maybe this all would have turned out some other way. Well, I could feel guilty the rest of my life but that wasn't going to do the Glovers any good. If I was to help them in any way, I had to use my brains for a change.

"Lord, Lord, what is Yo' plan?" I heard Tiny's voice behind me. "Is this all that's left of they lives?"

In the spot where Tiny was standing a beam of sunlight shining through the window of the garage illuminated his black face, making it appear to float in the air. The light rays through the smokey haze formed a gray halo around his head. An angel from hell, I thought to myself . . . a converted angel from hell.

"No, Tiny. All they were is still inside them and in you and Johnny Mae. These items just mark points along their path through life."

Tiny stared at me as if I had just spoken words from On High.

"I need you to remind me ever once in a while," he said.

We sorted and searched through the jumble of personal possessions, trying to straighten and restore items to their proper condition as we went. I was about to give up hope when Tiny said, "I think maybe I found somethin'."

He had found a wooden box something like a half-size military foot locker with a small lock on it.

"Mamma told me about this box. She said the old man keeps what he call his important stuff in it and hid it under the bed." Tiny chuckled.

"There's no way we'll ever find the key to the lock," I said.

"Ain't much of a lock," Tiny said. He walked over to a workbench at the end of his garage and came back with coffee can full of keys.

"In the junk business you don't never throw away a key," he said.

He dumped the keys out into a pile and sorted through them. He looked at the keyhole in the lock and tried several of the old keys until he found one that would fit inside the lock. The first one didn't work, or the second. But the third key went into the keyhole and with a little jiggling and gentle twisting it turned and the little lock sprang open.

"You just got to have faith, Frank. They's only so many kinds of locks. One like this ain't no real trouble."

He opened the lid on the wooden box and inside lay the manila envelope along with what looked like dozens of other letters and documents.

"The old man can't read," Tiny said, "so he keeps everthing. Makes my mamma mad. She say he would keep the wrappers off o' candy if she didn' throw 'em out." He laughed gently to himself, a smile on his face.

I sat on Tiny's front porch and took the envelope and some of the other papers from the box. I could see I was going to need Melissa's help. There were letters, contracts, and agreements going back decades. If they held any meaning for present events, Melissa might be able to decipher it. I called her and asked her to join me for supper.

Tiny dropped me off in front of Melissa's apartment with the box and I loaded it in the trunk of her car. There were several students coming and going from her apartment so I waited outside for her. We drove in her car to a Mexican place in a new upscale business area north of town just off the Interstate toward Atlanta. It was noisy inside so we ate on the patio. A warm breeze was blowing just enough to be pleasant. As far from east Macon as we were, the air still held the faint smell of smoke.

We had steaks with salads and flan for desert. The waitress cleared the table and we sat drinking margaritas, watching the clouds passing over a full moon and talking about the things that had happened until sprinkles of rain began to fall.

"I guess that's a signal to us that it's time to look in Mr. Glover's box," Melissa said. "We could go back to my place, but my roommate has friends over and it'll be noisy there."

We went to my apartment. I apologized in advance for the state of the kitchen. I put the dirty dishes in hot soapy water to soak and we sat at the kitchen table. I emptied the assortment of envelopes and papers out of the wooden box onto the table and Melissa arranged them in order by date. Then she grouped them into four separate piles and went through the items one by one.

As I watched her I thought of the three women who had sat at that table with me. Shirley had been an accident, a very pleasant and sensuous accident. She was the kind of woman whose picture men like to keep on the wall in some private place. She had lots of beautiful parts. She was also an enigma. She had brains, she showed loyalty and compassion, and she might be a scheming, husband-killing murderess. Whatever else she was, she had been good to me in a very personal way. She might also have framed me for murder.

Johnny Mae had sat in the same chair at the same table. I didn't know if I could ever get over Johnny Mae. She was beautiful and passionate. She had gotten inside me in a place only one woman in a lifetime could get. I loved being with her, talking with her, watching her. I dreamed of her. If I closed my eyes and breathed deeply I could smell the aroma of her still. The taste of her was still on my tongue. I could hear the sound of her voice and feel the touch of her against me. My vision of heaven would be Johnny Mae in my arms and at my side for the rest of my life. All I really wanted from life was to be with her and to make her happy. It was not to be. I had to stop thinking of her so much if I was ever going to find happiness again. I didn't know if I could stop thinking about her.

I looked at Melissa. Such a normal, optimistic, idealistic kid. She was what I should be. She was pretty and sweet and innocent. She was smart. She had worked hard to save my ass. I knew she was falling for me. I wouldn't try to stop her. She already had my admiration and my gratitude and I thought we could have a lot more together. I was certainly attracted to her.

"He's a pack rat," she said, "which is good, because along with a lot of worthless paper he saved some interesting things."

She indicated the first of several piles. "This pile contains legal documents and papers relating to his home and property. These," she said, placing her hand on the second pile, "are loan and finance papers and related correspondence for household items, such as appliances and furniture." She touched a third pile. "These are various legal notices. And this fourth pile is miscellaneous papers, some of which are generally interesting but don't appear to have relevance to the Glovers' current problems.

"And these," she indicated some remaining papers, "I'm not sure what they are." She unfolded an ancient looking faded document that was splitting at some of the creases and had corners falling from it. "Look at this," she said.

"What is it?"

She studied it for a moment. "It's a letter from The United States Department of War, The Bureau of Refugees, Freedmen, and Abandoned Lands. Oh, my gosh, that's the Freedman's Bureau. It's dated 1870 and it's addressed to all former slaves, explaining their new rights to work under labor contract and to own property."

Something flashed into my mind. "The idiot building inspectors asked me once if Mr. Glover had shown me his letter. This must be what they were talking about. They must have thought the document wasn't genuine and that the old man was crazy."

She unfolded another tattered document, studied it for a minute and pointed to it as she talked. "This is a copy of the last will and testament of Henry H. Stevens leaving forty acres of land and a house to Josiah Glover, dated 1884." Melissa's eyes were full of sparkle. She was like a child at Christmas time.

"Must be John Glover's father," I said.

She unfolded two more documents on the table.

"This one is a surveyor's description of the forty acres signed by the surveyor and by Henry H. Stevens. And here is a declaration from Josiah Glover deeding one acre of that land for the founding of New Hope Church in 1888."

"Where is it located?" I said.

"It would have to be verified by comparison with other records at the county courthouse, but it appears to be the current site of the St. James A.M.E. Church."

"Jerome Brown and Shirley Willingham would know if it's the same church. They just did the application to establish historic preservation status for the St. James Church. If it is the same, then the Glovers' house sitting next to the church is on property that was part of the original land deeded to Josiah Glover."

Melissa nodded her head. "So," she said, her eyes wide, "where's the rest of the forty acres?"

"God Almighty. Are you saying Mr. John Glover owns forty acres of east Macon?"

"Thirty-nine acres to be more precise, subtracting out the church property."

"Can you tell about where in current-day Macon the property lines would be located?"

"Do you have a map of east Macon?"

I searched among files I had brought home from the office related to the beautification program and the scenic waterfront greenway. I had full topographic and street maps of the entire city and parts of the county. I spread them on the table. Melissa read the property description and checked points on the maps.

"It'll take a surveyor to find the markers on the ground, but assuming St. James A.M.E. Church is on the site of the original New Hope Church, then my best guess would be that the forty acres of land originally belonging to Josiah Glover run approximately here." Melissa indicated a rough rectangle on the map.

"Right through the middle of the proposed golf course," I said, "including the site of the clubhouse."

"A million dollars worth of property," Melissa said.

"So, does John Glover still own it?"

"That's going to take a damn good real estate attorney to figure out. My guess would be yes. You know why?"

"Because Mr. Glover's packrat archives don't contain anything to the contrary?" I asked.

"That's certainly consistent with it. But no, it's something else. And it makes it all fit together."

"OK, Sherlock," I said, "you're five steps ahead of me. What makes it all fit together?"

"Think about east Macon. Give me a one sentence description of the real estate there."

"What do you mean?"

"Upscale, would you say?" She smiled.

"Low value, low rent, dilapidated, spotty development."

"And why is that?" She asked. "Anything particularly wrong with the area? Chemical waste? Impenetrable swamp?"

"Nothing wrong with it. Just underdeveloped urban blight, as the developers would say."

"If we're right, if the land was never legally and clearly

transferred from the Glovers' ownership, then existing property titles in the area all have clouds over them. No one has been willing to put development money into the area because no one can get clear title to the property."

"OK. So what's going on now that makes the land any more desirable? What would make it worth killing for?"

"One way to remove a cloud from a title," she said, "is through inclusion of the property in a federal urban development project."

"Operation Breakthrough," I said. "Those clever bastards."

Melissa nodded. "Once the property is declared to be part of the project, a challenge period is established after which clear title is granted to current property owners or to successful challengers if there are any."

"So, if Investment Adventures is the current owner at the time the project is declared, they get clear title because John Glover wouldn't know how or be able to mount a challenge. But why wouldn't documents showing clear ownership by Mr. Glover or somebody else already be on file in the county records or somewhere?" I asked.

"Many reasons. One of the most common is that courthouse records are burned or destroyed over time. Sometimes, as might have happened in this case, original deeds were never filed at the courthouse."

"How would that happen?"

"State law doesn't specify that deeds *must* be filed at the courthouse, only that the courthouse is the official depository of such records. Mr. Glover could keep his deed in a shoe box and it would be a perfectly legal deed. He would only be required to produce it in order to sell the property or settle some dispute, or if he wished to make it a part of the public record. That all assumes that Mr. Glover knows that he has the deed, that he understands the process and the need to file at the courthouse, or that he is aware that there has been any challenge to his ownership."

"In this case the old man probably didn't understand any of that. He told me that when his father found out he was no longer a slave, the plantation owner made a deal to deed part of the plantation land to Mr. Glover's father if his father would stay on at the plantation. I think John Glover understood the land had been deeded to his father and that he had inherited the right to the land. He may not have known much more than that. But someone knew about Mr. Glover's legal claim to the property."

"Or they may have just known that no clear title could be acquired for the land," Melissa said. "The important point is, the clouds on the titles have prevented any major development in the area. Someone devised a scheme to give clear titles to the property and make a fortune in the process."

"Investment Adventures?"

"Investment Adventures is one of the players but it looks like lots of people are involved. The mayor and council had to apply for the urban development grant from the federal government. Someone who knew about the uncertain line of ownership of the east Macon property went to great lengths to acquire the property, including the use of the building inspector's office. And we don't know how the death of Stafford Willingham fits into all this, assuming our scenario is even close to what's been going on."

"We know Willingham was involved with Operation Breakthrough, and with Investment Adventures," I said. "I think it's time we found out all we can about the mysterious company. I think it's time for a midnight visit to Green and Green."

Chapter 32

The Midnight Shift

"It's no problem for me to be in the office after hours," Melissa said. "I have Tiny's court appearance coming up to prepare for and I've been there many times working on cases in the wee hours of the morning."

"How do we explain me if someone sees us?" I asked.

"It's not at all unusual for women working at night to have a friend along for company. I'll just tell them you're my boyfriend and hope they don't recognize your face from the wanted posters."

"I could wear a false mustache."

"Just wear a baseball cap pulled down over your eyes and slouch a lot. That's the way most of the boyfriends look that I see in the offices at night."

Melissa parked on an unlit street two blocks from the Bankers Trust building. She said we should wait twenty minutes until the janitorial service began their nighttime cleaning of the building at about 11:30. Janitorial services are one of the many businesses with almost invisible employees who come and go in the night. All the big office buildings downtown had to be serviced after regular business hours. Floors had to be swept, mopped and waxed. Rugs had to be vacuumed, trash cans emptied, furniture dusted. The presence of the cleaning crew coming and going from the offices would reduce the chance anyone working late at Green and Green would notice us there.

It was quiet on the street. An occasional car or garbage truck passed along one of the connecting streets.

"I'm scared, Frank," Melissa said. "I've never been involved with criminals on this end of things."

I laughed. "This isn't crime, Melissa. At worst this is impersonating a boyfriend."

Melissa laughed and clung to my arm. "No, at worst this is criminal trespass and grand larceny. I really am scared."

I looked into her eyes and I could see she really was scared. She was holding tight to me. I leaned over and kissed her lips. I don't know why I thought that might make her less afraid but it did seem to have a calming effect on her. It had some kind of effect on her anyway. I kissed her several more times. I needed calming too.

"I want you to know, Frank," she said, "in case we get caught. I wouldn't do this for anyone else."

I wondered what I was doing there, about to drag a nice innocent girl like Melissa into a criminal act.

"Maybe this is the wrong thing to do, Melissa. I've made some bad mistakes in the past. Maybe this is another one. If you want out of it we can turn back now. Maybe we can find some other way."

"It's too late to turn back, Frank. We're in it together for better or worse. If it turns out right we'll be heroes. If it goes bad, well, at least I'm a lawyer." She giggled. "We'll have our own legal representation."

I giggled along with her. We were having a bad case of the nerves.

"Why was Willingham killed?" I asked, thinking out loud, more than anything else.

"Million of dollars," Melissa said. "That's what the east Macon property will mean to developers. My guess is someone was fighting with Willingham over the property."

"Yeah, that has to be it."

"What are the big reasons for murder? Money, love,

revenge, property, reputation, power, threat of discovery? Of course it could be something much more personal than real estate. Maybe it involves his wife. She had an affair with you. Maybe he discovered she was involved with someone else and there was an argument or the threat of exposure."

"Yeah, listen, I'm sorry about that. I was a fool to get involved with her."

"Why are you apologizing to me? You didn't even know me then."

"I'm sorry anyway. I don't want you to think that I . . . well . . ."

"That you're a woman chaser? I've seen Shirley Willingham. I don't think she was blameless. I can see how, in a weak moment you might . . ."

"Shirley is a beautiful woman," I said.

"What about Johnny Mae?"

"I was in love with Johnny Mae."

"You *were* in love or you *are* in love?"

"Johnny Mae is gone. I don't deny I'm feeling a lot of pain but I know it's over. There were too many differences that separated us."

I turned to her in the dim light from the street.

"You know I'm an emotional mess."

"You're not so bad. I'm amazed you're in as good shape as you are."

"What about you?" I said.

"What about me?"

"Are you in love with anyone?"

"Anyone besides you, you mean?"

I was surprised at how easily she said it. It felt good.

"No. My past has been very innocent compared to yours. I've just had the usual college sweethearts. Nothing to get really excited about. Oh I've had a number of lawyers try to seduce me, and a judge, but they didn't interest me. I've never been involved with a criminal before."

That set off another round of giggles.

"You think when this is over we might go back to my place and make love?" I asked.

"Sure," she said.

I kissed her for a long time.

"You think it's possible to have sex in the front seat of a Volkswagen?" I asked.

"Probably not with someone as tall as you." More giggles.

I didn't really want to go on with our espionage right then but it was time to put up or shut up. Melissa drove her car the two blocks to the Bankers Trust Building. I could see members of the janitorial crew moving about inside the first floor as we drove past the front of the building. She parked her car in the reserved spaces in the basement parking garage. There were two other cars parked in the Green and Green spaces. One was a late model Mercedes and the other was a new Chrysler.

"Looks like a couple of people are in the offices," I said, "and it doesn't look like the hired help unless Green and Green pays a really good salary."

"The Mercedes belongs to one of the partners. I don't know who the other car belongs to."

"What if we came back later, like at three or four in the morning?" I said.

"Then we would be noticeable. If anyone saw us we'd stick out like a neon sign," she said. "Look, why don't I go up alone. If anyone sees me they won't think anything of it. If you're there you'll just attract attention."

"You sure you want to do this alone?"

"I think it's best. Let me see what I find. If we need to

come back we can come back. I may not even be able to get to the records. You stay here. I'll go up."

This wasn't the plan and not what I had prepared myself for but it made sense. I walked her to the entrance.

"How long do you think it will take?" I asked.

She shrugged. "Don't know. I'll have to locate the files. I may have to wait for that, depending on whether anyone is in the file room. I'll have to examine the files for anything relevant. I'll have to make copies. It could be an hour, maybe more, maybe less."

"Don't take any chances. I'll be here waiting." I gave her a quick kiss. She used her key to open the outside door and disappeared into the building.

Late at night the parking garage was spooky. The lighting produced long shadows and dark recesses. Strange sounds echoed through the hollow structure. The most unsettling thing was that I could feel the floor vibrate underneath my feet. Why would the concrete floor of a parking garage underneath a twelve story building be vibrating? I wrote it off to the fact that I knew nothing whatsoever about the engineering of tall buildings.

Waiting can be nerve wracking. Where should I wait? In the car? I would be very visible there. In the shadows? If a security guard or someone saw me there I would look really suspicious. I opted for the shadows. I had the contingency plan that if someone came along I could stroll over to the car and get in. Or I could walk over to the entrance and look at my watch as if I were waiting to meet someone.

Thirty minutes passed and nothing happened. Then the contingency I had overlooked happened . . . What if someone came who knew me? A cream colored Cadillac pulled down the ramp and I immediately recognized Mayor Tyler sitting on the passenger side. I had to stay hidden. I stepped around the corner behind the entrance doorway. I could hear the voices of the mayor and another man as they walked from the parking spaces past me.

"Hell, Tommy Lee," the first voice said, "there's nothing to worry over. Everything is still on track. You just need to relax and enjoy it. Everyone has a lot at stake and no one is going to let it be spoiled by a few complications."

"A few complications?" the strained, hushed voice of the mayor said. "Murder is not a few complications. Murder is a disaster for this project. I can't be connected in any way with murder."

"Well none of us can," the other voice said. "The police have their man. By the time Glover comes to trial the evidence against him will be airtight. Once he's convicted, interest in the Willingham murder will be no more than tea party gossip."

"I don't know why I ever agreed to become involved in this," the mayor said.

"It's for the good of the city, Tommy Lee. Just think what it will do. Listen, you're tired out. You've had a hard forty-eight hours. Everything will be clearer and more optimistic after you've had some rest. These people have been looking forward to meeting you. It'll just take a minute. Then we'll have another drink and I'll take you home so you can get some sleep."

It took only one glimpse of them as they stepped through the entranceway for me to recognize the man in the company of the mayor. It was Jeffrey Green. He was right, you couldn't forget the bright green blazer and tie.

My mind was turning over what I had overheard as I waited for Melissa. The death of Stafford Willingham was somehow connected to whatever deal Jeffrey Green and his friends were putting together. Green was a member of the planning and zoning board and I had been present when he paid a visit to Craig Linder's office on some kind of business. Could it have been the east Macon development?

I looked at my watch. An hour and fifteen minutes had passed since Melissa went inside. Finally the door opened and she came walking quickly out. Her briefcase was bulging. I caught up with her after a couple of steps.

"How did it go?" I asked.

"Let's get out of here." She continued walking toward the car.

Melissa was in the car and had the motor running by the time I got her briefcase stowed in the back seat and my door closed. As she was backing the VW out of the parking place I motioned toward the Cadillac. I told her the conversation I had overheard between the mayor and Jeffrey Green.

"I heard them when they came in the offices upstairs. There's some kind of big deal going on. There were people in and out the whole time I was there. Every time I tried to use the copy machine I was interrupted. I ended up bringing the whole Investment Adventures file with me. We'll have to make copies and I'll take it back tomorrow."

"Were you able to find out anything?"

"Yeah, a lot," she said, "but not exactly what we expected."

I looked at her and raised an eyebrow. "What?"

"Investment Adventures has bought at least fifty parcels of land in east Macon amounting to a total of about thirty-five acres. Most of them were loan foreclosures. They paid anywhere from $500 to $7,500 each for them. Their total investment appears to be about $75,000. Most of the parcels will be prime real estate if the golf course and country club development go through. One estimate I saw of the total developed value was between 7.5 and 10 million dollars. Of course that would be after housing has been built on those parcels outside the golf course."

"Whew," I whistled. "So Willingham may have been killed over ten million dollars."

"The Glovers' house and lot are among the fifty parcels."

"What attorney's name is on the documents?"

"Jeffrey Green," she said.

"Things look like they might be fitting together. What is it you didn't expect?" I asked.

"The Ownership of Investment Adventures," Melissa said. "The prime investor and major stockholder is not Stafford Willingham. It's Shirley Willingham."

"Shirley Willingham?" All the pieces of the puzzle were suddenly trying desperately to rearrange themselves inside my head. "Shirley Willingham is behind the seizure and destruction of Mr. and Mrs. Glovers' home?"

"I never did trust Shirley Willingham," Melissa said. "I tried to give her the benefit of the doubt because I thought my judgment was tainted after what she did to you. But there's no doubt. It's her name and signature all over the documents and correspondence in those files. Shirley Willingham has been a key player in what's happened in east Macon and what happened to you."

"You think Shirley is behind the death of her husband?"

"With what I've just seen, it looks like it."

As we drove through the dark streets toward my apartment with the incriminating evidence in the back seat of the car I had this unreasonable fear that we were going to be pulled over by a night duty patrolman for being out too late or something and be found out. But it didn't happen. Thirty minutes later we found ourselves in my apartment in my bed in each other's arms. We fell asleep still embraced, just as the first light of day brightened the night sky.

Chapter 33

The Game Is Afoot

"I swear to God I don't know anything about it." Shirley Willingham's face was filled with tension and her voice was firm and insistent. "I never formed a business with these people. I don't even know who they are except for Jeffrey Green, and I've never had any dealings with him. I never signed any of these documents. These are not my signatures. You have to believe me, Frank. I would never be involved in something like this."

"You're saying someone is using your name to operate a business you know nothing about?" Melissa asked.

"That's exactly what I'm saying."

"Why would someone pick you?" Melissa insisted.

"I don't know. Stafford was involved in the management of a lot of different companies. He put my name as an officer or a member of the board of directors more than once. It's a common practice in business. It allowed him to keep things under his control. Maybe that's what happened here."

"You think Stafford signed your name to these documents without telling you?" I asked.

"I don't know. It wouldn't be like him. But I do know that these are forgeries. Get a handwriting expert. These are not my signatures."

"Would you come with us?" I asked. "I know someone who can verify whether the signatures are authentic."

My old cellmate Charlie Preston was still locked up in the county jail serving time for forgery. He was glad to have visitors. I took him a carton of cigarettes. That was high pay for what I was asking him to do. I laid on the table the Investment Adventures documents and samples of Shirley's signature we had watched her write just a few minutes before. He glanced at the documents for perhaps ten seconds.

"Forgeries," he said.

I gave him samples of Stafford Willingham's writing on canceled checks Shirley had supplied.

"Is this the person who forged her signature?" I asked.

He compared the signatures for a few moments.

"Nope," he said, "definitely not," but he continued to look at the documents. "The other signatures on the articles of incorporation are also forgeries."

I was taken aback and I was beginning to wonder if Charlie had been a good choice.

"How can you tell that, without something to compare them with?" I asked. "Were you the one who forged them?"

Charlie smiled indulgently at me. "No, it wasn't me." He pointed to two separate pairs of signatures on the articles of incorporation. "These two signatures were made by the same person and the other two signatures were made by a second person."

"You can tell that from nothing but the signatures?" Melissa asked.

Charlie looked at Melissa and a corner of his mouth curled into a smile.

"You got a blank piece of paper?" he asked. Melissa tore a sheet of paper from her legal pad. Charlie got up from his chair and faced the wall, his back to us.

"There are four names on the articles of incorporation. Two of you each write the signatures of two people. Write with your left hand, upside down, or anyway you want, to make the signatures look different from your own."

Melissa copied the signatures of two of the names on the document. I copied the third with my left hand. Just as an extra trick I indicated to Shirley for her to copy the fourth signature. When we were finished we placed the document on the table.

"OK," I said.

Charlie turned around and sat down at the table. He studied the signatures for perhaps thirty seconds. He looked up and smiled at us.

"This is too easy," he said, "and you didn't follow my instructions." He pointed to the signature I had copied. "You did this one, Frank. I shared a cell with you for six weeks. You couldn't disguise your handwriting from me if your life depended on it."

He pointed to the signature Shirley had written. "Mrs. Willingham, you did this one, probably with your left hand. And Miss Gresham, the last two are yours. I've never seen your signature but they were done by the same person and I know the signatures of Frank and Mrs. Willingham so they must be yours."

I looked at Melissa and Shirley. They were convinced.

"What can you tell us about the forgers?" I asked.

"Do you have any other samples of their writing?"

Melissa took a pile of documents from her briefcase. The largest sample of writing was on a bank account information document that had been completed by hand. Charlie studied the samples for several minutes, switching back and forth among them.

"I'm only working with what I have here, you understand. If I had a better sample I could be more precise. There are two people's handwriting here plus that of Mr. Jeffrey Green. Both male, probably middle aged. One is more intelligent and intellectual. He's very compulsive. He probably works in a job as a clerk or a bureaucrat where he handles legal or financial documents. He could be a manager. He's the one who filled out the bank account information. The other one is more prone to volatile emotions, outbursts of temper. He's the most openly and immediately dangerous."

"Is either one of them a murderer?" I asked.

"Either one of them could be," Charlie said, looking at me. "If you catch up with them, either one of them could be, if they're cornered."

"You can tell all that from their handwriting?" Shirley asked.

"I can tell you more than that. Would you like to know about their sexual appetites or preferences?"

"Is it relevant?" I asked.

Charlie smiled and shrugged. "Have you discovered any sexual aspect to the case?"

I shrugged in return.

"Is Jeffrey Green one of the forgers?" Melissa asked.

Charlie shook his head. "But he is a dangerous man. He'll do anything to get what he wants."

"Is he a murderer?" she asked.

"He probably wouldn't do it himself, but only because it would be smarter for him to get someone to do it for him."

I gave Charlie the carton of cigarettes and thanked him.

"Come back and see me sometime, Frank. And bring your lady friends with you. I appreciate the company."

When we were back in the car Melissa said, "That guy gave me the creeps. You can't tell how much he really knows and how much he's making up."

"He convinced me about the signatures," I said. "I believe Shirley is telling the truth."

"I do too," Melissa conceded.

"Well thank goodness," Shirley said. "But what do we do now?"

"I've been thinking about that," I said. "I have a plan."

We had dinner in a private dining room at the Hyatt to reduce the chance someone who knew us would see us together or overhear us. I outlined my plan to them.

"OK. Someone used Shirley's name as the majority stockholder and director of a fraudulent company that amassed fifty parcels of land, right? Mr. Glover's documents show the land was deeded to his father, and it was inherited by him. If the land is declared a part of the east Macon urban development project, Mr. Glover has a good chance of filing a successful challenge to regain ownership of the property."

"That's all very iffy," Melissa said, "but I'll grant you the argument."

"What if we jump ahead of that whole process and take the property out of the hands of Investment Adventures."

I looked at Shirley. "I believe that you're not a conspirator in any of what's happened, Shirley. What if I were to ask you to exercise control of the company that claims you as its owner? Sign back over to Mr. Glover all the parcels of land they're holding. Put it in a family trust, whatever would make it secure."

Shirley raised her eyebrows and her eyes widened. I could see her thinking. I turned to Melissa.

"Do you have enough information in the Green and Green files to draw up the papers for the property transfers?"

"We would need to file the deeds at the courthouse." She was quiet for a moment, deep in thought. "Yes, we could do it."

"Isn't this going to be dangerous?" Shirley asked.

I looked at her and at Melissa. "It could be. I now think that may be what happened to Stafford. After the public ceremony at City Hall, Stafford met Mr. and Mrs. Glover again after all those many years. You said there was a change in him, Shirley. I believe Stafford began his own investigation into who was causing the problems Mr. and Mrs. Glover were having. He may have checked the property records and found out American Home Guardian Finance made a loan to Mr. John Glover and was holding the Glover house as collateral. Bob Felton, the manager at American Home Guardian, told me Stafford paid a visit to American Home Guardian the week he was killed. I think Stafford went there to buy the loan Home Guardian was holding against the Glovers' home, probably with the intention of returning the property to Mr. and Mrs. Glover free and clear. Bob Felton told me he told Stafford that Investment Adventures had already bought the Glover loan along with all the other Home Guardian loans with east Macon property as collateral. I think Stafford then began an investigation into Investment Adventures and that investigation carried him to his death."

Shirley had grown pale and began to cry. "He found my name on the documents and he thought I had undermined him." She was shaking her head and crying. "He died thinking I was going behind his back."

"I don't think so," I said. I don't know whether I really believed it or just wanted to give Shirley some comfort. "I think Stafford found out what was really going on. I think he probably started measures to counter Investment Adventures and they killed him to protect their investments and their identities."

"Someone put a lot of planning into this scheme," Melissa said.

"And a lot of money." I said. "What was the total you calculated from the records, Melissa?"

"About $75,000 for the land purchases."

"Not much if several investors are involved," Shirley said. "For seven investors, for example, it would be only a little over $10,000 apiece."

"And they're looking to make over a million dollars apiece," I said. "That's the motive."

"I still don't understand why they used Shirley's name," Melissa said.

"I just remembered something someone said to me not long ago," I said. "He said you have to be one of the big boys to get in on the country club development, or have someone on the inside. I think they were using Shirley's name to give the impression that Stafford was really behind Investment Adventures. That would make it look just that much more enticing. If Stafford Willingham was involved, it had to be a good thing."

"It would be a very risky proposition," Shirley said. "Macon isn't that big a town. As soon as the country club deal is completed, Stafford would have found out about the scam."

"By then they would have transferred everything out of Investment Adventures into some other company, very much like what we're about to do. With the help of Green and Green their identities would be buried under a trail of paper. How long before these documents are discovered missing, Melissa?"

"Soon. May have been already. It's an active project."

"Why don't we copy everything from the files that's important. Keep any originals we need and replace them with copies and return the files to Green and Green's file room? If they discover the files missing it will alert them that something is going on. If the files are there, that will give us a little time. Do you think you can get the files back in place without someone noticing you?"

"Yes, I think so," Melissa said.

I turned back to Shirley. "How about it, Shirley? Are you willing to do it?"

"Yes, I am. I'm willing to do anything if it will help catch Stafford's killer and stop them from making money off of it."

We drove to the offices of Willingham Realty and spent a couple of hours copying the Investment Adventures files. We then drove to the Bankers Trust Building. Shirley and I waited in the car while Melissa went up to the offices of Green and Green to leave the copies in place of the originals. She was in and out in ten minutes.

"The place is buzzing with activity. I don't think anyone noticed me. I put the files back in the same spot in the file room. It's a big company. If anyone was looking for the files today they'll probably just think someone in the firm had them at their desk."

"What kind of support do you need in order to do this?" I asked Melissa.

"I need a law office. But I can't use Green and Green. With fifty parcels of land there will be over a hundred documents. I need deeds and legal forms. I'll need a notary."

"You can use my attorney and his staff," Shirley said. "I can call him tonight."

Melissa looked up at me then turned to Shirley and smiled. "I appreciate the offer but I think it may be a good idea to keep this completely away from the local community of attorneys. There are many ears and eyes and people talk with their friends. We can't let any wind of this get out until it's done."

I thought Melissa was right but I think another of her reasons was that she didn't completely trust Shirley or Shirley's attorney. Neither did I.

"How do you want to do it?" I asked.

"I think the best place to do it is at the law school clinic on campus. I can get plenty of student help and it's not unusual for the clinic to have students in and out of the courthouse working on projects. Students don't mind working long, odd hours. We can do most of it at night when no one is around to notice."

"Sounds like a plan to me," I said. "Shirley, we'll keep in close touch and let you know when the documents are ready for your signature. Afterward we can all have a glass of champagne."

"I'll be glad to help at the clinic or any way I can," Shirley said.

We agreed to touch bases the next day in case anything new developed. As we drove back to where we had left Melissa's car I asked Shirley about the watch that was found in Tiny's possession.

"The police showed me the watch to verify that it was Stafford's," Shirley said. "It was his, all right. It was given to him by the Realtors Association for thirty years' membership. It had an inscription and his name engraved on the back. But it was a watch he never wore. The last time I saw it was at the lake house in a drawer, and that was a year ago or more."

"So anyone could have gotten the watch at any time," I said.

"We've had hundreds of people at the lake house for parties and meetings during the past year. Stafford never said anything about the watch being missing but I don't think either of us would have noticed. After the police asked me, I looked and the empty box the watch came in was still in the drawer."

"And lots of people would have known Stafford owned the watch with his name inscribed on it," Melissa said, "because it was probably given to him in a ceremony."

"Yes, that's right," Shirley said. "And there was an article about the award in the newsletter of the Realtors Association. How did Tiny get it?"

I looked at Melissa and she nodded.

"One of the neighborhood boys brought it to Tiny. He says it was bought from one of the men who works for Scott Taylor."

"Scott Taylor?" Shirley's face showed disapproval.

"Have you had dealings with Scott Taylor?" I asked.

"Not I," she said. "But I know that Stafford had some difficulty with him from time to time."

"What kind of difficulty?"

"Stafford said Taylor is a bit of a ruffian and a loose cannon. He can't be depended on to honor an agreement. He substitutes inferior materials and takes shortcuts. Several times he's taken payment for a job and then not paid his subcontractors or his creditors."

"Sounds like your typical construction business hooligan," I said.

"Why do people do business with him?" Melissa asked.

"You can't really get away from it in the real estate development and construction business. It's something you learn to deal with. It's part of doing business. You just make sure to never get yourself in a position where someone like Taylor owes you money. And when they do a job for you, you pay them in steps as the work is done." Shirley paused for a moment. She pressed her lips. "The seamy side of the business is one of the reasons Stafford wanted me out of it."

"It doesn't sound like a business I would like to work in," Melissa said.

Shirley laughed. "And what did you say your profession is, my dear? Defending murderers, rapists, child molesters, assorted perverts and other social misfits?"

"That's true," Melissa said, "but that's where I met you and Frank."

We all had a laugh at that.

"You want to be careful about Scott Taylor," Shirley said. "He has a certain reputation for violence and his judgment is pretty bad at times."

Shirley parked next to Melissa's car. I asked Melissa to give me just a minute alone to talk with Shirley. The look Melissa gave me would have melted steel but she waited in her car for me. I sat inside Shirley's car but didn't close the door, mostly so Melissa could see there was nothing physical going on.

"What about Craig Linder?" I asked Shirley.

"I met Craig years ago before Stafford and I were involved when I was still in business for myself. We went out a few times. After Stafford and I were married we continued to have professional contact with Craig because of his position with the Planning and Zoning Office. One day last week Craig called me up and asked me out to dinner. I went. He wanted to begin seeing me again. I told him no. That's all."

"Has Craig been in your lake house during the past year?"

She looked at me. "Yes. With groups of friends and business associates. Not alone with me, if that's what you're asking."

"That's not what I was asking." That was partly the truth. "Craig would probably have known that Stafford received the watch. He had quite a bit of contact with Stafford and may well have known that Stafford didn't wear the watch. I was wondering, could Craig have had an opportunity to take the watch from the lake house?"

"I suppose he could. As much as any of the guests at our house could."

"Thank you," I said. "Thanks for all you've done and what

you're doing."

I got out of her car and started to close the door.

"You and Melissa be careful, Frank. Stafford's killer is out there somewhere and someone is not going to be happy with what we're about to do."

"You be careful yourself," I said. "Right now you're the key to unraveling this whole puzzle. If certain people find out what we're up to, you could be in danger."

"You could come stay at my place to look after me." Her smile said she was teasing, but I wasn't sure.

When I got back in the VW, Melissa was peeved.

"So, what was that about that I couldn't hear?"

"She invited me to be her personal bodyguard."

Melissa slapped me but it didn't have any sting to it. I related the conversation I had with Shirley.

"Do you think Craig Linder is involved?" Melissa asked.

"What, with Shirley or with Stafford's murder?" This time she pinched my ear until I said uncle. "I believe what Shirley told me."

I was awakened in the early hours of that same morning by a phone call.

"Frank, this is Detective Miller. This is a courtesy call. I just thought you ought to know before you hear it somewhere else."

I thought he was going to tell me John Glover had died.

"Shirley Willingham is in the hospital in critical condition. Her car went off the road near the river. There was a fire. They don't expect her to live."

Chapter 34

Evil Strikes Hard

I asked Detective Miller to meet me at the hospital. There were things I needed to tell him. I called Melissa. I think she took the news harder than I did.

"Oh, no, no," she cried, "not her, not like that. I'm so sorry for all the horrible things I thought about her. She was so beautiful. Oh, no."

"It wasn't your fault or mine," I said. I wanted to believe it. I'll always wonder if my actions caused Shirley's attacker to do something he wouldn't have done otherwise. "I'm on my way to get you. Bring the files on Investment Adventures."

I was at Melissa's door in fifteen minutes and we were at the hospital in another ten. Detective Melvin Miller was waiting for us outside the intensive care unit.

"She's still alive," he said. He put a hand on my shoulder. "It's not something you want to see, Frank."

"No, I don't want to see it. But I owe it to Shirley not to desert her now."

The hospital staff wouldn't let anyone in her room for fear of giving her an infection. I was allowed only as close as an observation window. When I did see her I wished I hadn't. The image of her will be with me forever. There are things I want to remember always but I have prayed to no avail to be able to forget what Shirley looked like that night.

Most of her that wasn't under cover was wrapped in sterile bandages but where I could see her skin it was red, blistered and mottled. Her hair was gone and most of her exposed flesh was covered in some kind of protective jelly. Half of her face was bandaged. I could see one eye. It was closed. The eyebrow was singed away. The skin on her face that I could see was swollen, puffy and discolored. I would never have known who she was if I hadn't been told. She had tubes and wires running in and out of her. She didn't move except for shallow breathing. She didn't know we were there. I prayed that she didn't know anything. I wanted to speak to her to comfort her but there was nothing I could do.

I practically stumbled back out to the waiting room.

"I'm sorry." Miller said. "I hope you understand, I have to ask some questions. The faster we move, the more likely we can find out what happened to her."

"I think I know what happened to her," I said. "I just don't know who did it."

I had made up my mind to tell Miller everything. I had discussed it with Melissa on the way to the hospital and she agreed. But first I had to have a little time to myself and have a good cry. I would never wish for anyone to be burned and disfigured but I kept thinking what a tragedy it was that it happened to Shirley, of all people. The images I had in my mind of that beautiful body, those blue eyes and those sweet lips were forever replaced by the images I had just seen of her. Two people in my life I had grown to care about over the past months now lay in the hospital hovering between life and death. For their own good I wished for a quick and painless death for both of them and I hoped for an eternity in hell for the persons responsible.

When I got myself together enough to go back inside the hospital Melissa had briefed Miller on most of what we knew or suspected. I told him Shirley had agreed to help us flush out the real investors in Investment Adventures and I had overheard a conversation the previous night between Jeffrey

Green and the mayor in which the mayor was having cold feet in connection with some big deal which we assumed to be the east Macon development.

"I guess you haven't heard about the mayor?" Miller said.

"No, what about him?"

"It'll be in all the papers tomorrow. Tommy Lee was arrested tonight for public drunkenness and indecency."

About all I could say was, "So what else is new? Everyone knows Tommy Lee is a drinker."

"Everyone on the inside knows it," Miller said, "but there's never been public knowledge or direct proof. He was found a little after midnight running naked down a street in his neighborhood. He was so high he didn't even know where he was. He was accompanied by a lady whose services he apparently had purchased."

"I guess his political career is over," I said. Then it occurred to me. "It was a setup, wasn't it?"

Miller could only shrug. "At a time like this and with this many connections, I don't believe in coincidences. It is not beyond possibility that yes, he was set up. The problem with a man like Tommy Lee and a situation like this is there are lots of people for lots of reasons who would like to see him take a fall. It could be connected with what you've told me or it could be something else entirely."

I told Miller how most of the fires in east Macon had been on property acquired by Investment Adventures and I told him about the Molotov cocktail thrown through the window of the St. James A.M.E. Church.

"We'll check the bottle for prints," he said. "We might get lucky. Why would Investment Adventures or anyone else want to burn the church?"

"Shirley Willingham was working with Rev. Jerome Brown to have the church put on the National Register of

Historic Places. If that happens, the church could not be moved or torn down or altered in any significant way. It would make the neighborhood undesirable as a golf community development. Investment Adventures' holdings would be worth no more than what they paid for them."

"The only way to get the church out of the picture was to destroy it," Miller said. "OK, I'll accept that as a plausible argument. So where does all this leave us now?"

While I was outside crying my eyes out I kept thinking how the attack on Shirley had killed our only chance to take control of the scheme that was wrecking our lives. With Shirley gone there was no way to seize control of the fraudulent company. No way to flush out Stafford Willingham's killer. But somewhere amid my anguish and my tears my mind showed me the way to carry our plan to completion.

"Green and Green are neck deep in all of this. Jeffrey Green knows he's been supporting a direct conflict of legal interest. And he knows Investment Adventures is using Shirley's name illegally. In the copies of the Green and Green files we made there's enough proof of wrongdoing and collusion to destroy Green and Green and perhaps to implicate Jeffrey Green in the attempted murder of Shirley Willingham. Jeffrey Green is now the weak point in the whole scheme. I say bring him in, give him the third degree and sweat the names of his co-conspirators out of him."

"Your portrayal of police methods is a little colorful, Frank, but I take your point," Miller said.

"You might have Arthur Stevens hit him a few times."

It was 3:30 a.m. when Detective Melvin Miller got Jeffrey Green out of his bed and dragged him to the police station for questioning. At Miller's request Melissa and I observed the interview.

"Do you want an attorney present?" Miller asked.

"I am an attorney," Green said, his nose well out of joint. "What am I being charged with?"

"At the moment we're not filing charges, but the charges we're considering include conspiracy to commit murder, criminal fraud and racketeering, plus conflict of interest, and criminal conspiracy in the Stafford Willingham murder that I'm sure the judge and the bar association will have a special interest in."

"Ridiculous." Green sneered.

"I'll get right to it." Miller laid the file folder on the table. "Do you want me to go through the items in this folder one by one or do you want to begin cooperating now?"

"What is that?" Green looked down at the folder.

"A complete set of documents detailing your involvement with a company called Investment Adventures."

Green wavered. "What about it?"

"A fraudulent company composed of fraudulent identities and fraudulent signatures. There's enough incriminating evidence in this folder to have you disbarred and locked up until you're an old man."

Green shot a hot look at the oneway mirror we were sitting behind but didn't say anything.

"Shirley Willingham's name was used fraudulently and without her knowledge in a land speculation scheme. Mrs. Willingham discovered that scheme today and now lies in the Macon General Hospital near death, a victim of attempted murder. If she dies, which is a very real prospect, it will be murder. Green and Green and you in particular, Mr. Green, are at the top of our list of suspects."

Jeffrey Green was clearly shaken. It didn't look as if he was aware of the attempt on Shirley's life, or he could have been a good actor. He was after all an attorney.

"That's ridiculous," Green said. "I know nothing about it."

"You know nothing about what, Mr. Green? The fraud or the attempt on Mrs. Willingham's life?"

"Neither. I was with friends all evening. I was home by midnight."

"Did I say the attempt on her life occurred before midnight?" Miller shot back. "Why do you think the attack on her occurred before midnight?" Miller didn't wait for him to answer. "And what about the mayor?"

"What about him?" Green asked.

"We know the mayor was involved with you in the land speculation scheme. We know Tommy Lee had cold feet about it. But I guess you're not involved with what happened to the mayor either? It looks right now like Tommy Lee was set up to take a fall. But you overlooked something you couldn't have known about."

The specter of something overlooked seemed to shake Green again. Miller should have been a poker player. He had a good bluff.

"I'm not involved in any deal with the mayor."

"You were overheard yesterday evening discussing it with him. I have witnesses of strong moral character who will testify that the mayor was upset and you were trying to calm him down."

"The only discussion I had with the mayor concerned his own fears about his political future."

"Bullshit. You were drinking with him last night into the early hours. He had cold feet and you were worried he was going to do something stupid that could cost you millions of dollars and your reputation, not to mention your law practice."

Green didn't say anything.

Miller spread out on the table half a dozen Investment

Adventures documents containing Jeffrey Green's signature.

"Those came from my company files," Green protested.

"No shit, Sherlock."

"How did you get those? You have no legal right to them."

"We obtained them legally but you didn't. We know the other signatures on these documents are forgeries," Miller said. "You signed these documents as legal counsel and witness and submitted them to the Secretary of State, to the Bibb County Commissioners, and to a number of your professional associates. You never met with Shirley Willingham or the other people whose names appear as members of this company. These articles of incorporation to the State of Georgia are forgeries perpetrated by you. These property deeds are forgeries submitted by you. All these legal notices and actions are fraudulent forgeries submitted by you. We have you cold on the forgery and conspiracy charges. As soon as we learn the true identities of the owners and directors of Investment Adventures and tie them to the death of Stafford Willingham and the attempted murder of Shirley Willingham, we're going to charge you with accessory to murder and attempted murder. I'll have to tell you too, we have a Molotov cocktail with fingerprints from the arson of the St. James A.M.E. Church. As soon as we link the owner of those prints to the Investment Adventures scheme, you will be charged with accessory to arson. You better tell us the identities of the persons behind Investment Adventures. This is your last and only chance to cooperate."

Green knew that some of what Miller said was bluff. He also knew some of it was not.

"I was never part of any conspiracy. I handled the paperwork in good faith. All contact with the corporation was through an intermediary."

"Who?"

"I dealt only with Scott Taylor."

Chapter 35

A Plan Takes Shape

I had been on the business end of Detective Miller's interrogation techniques and didn't like it. Watching him grill Jeffrey Green gave me pure pleasure. Miller charged Green with criminal fraud over the forgeries and had him sent to the county lockup. It would have done my heart good if I could have been there to see it but I had far more important matters that needed my attention. Detective Miller sat down with Melissa and me.

"The good news is we have the first real identity connected with the Investment Adventures fraud." Miller took a sip of coffee, leaned back and closed his eyes. "The bad news is, Scott Taylor is out of town and has been all week. We've had him under investigation since the Willingham death. He couldn't have been directly involved in the attack on Mrs. Willingham."

"He didn't have to be here to have someone do it for him," I said.

"Do you know for certain she was attacked and it wasn't just an accident?" Melissa asked.

"Yes, ma'am, there's no doubt. There were two sets of skid marks and evidence of a side impact to her automobile. We found traces of white paint on the left front panel of the car, indicating she was forced off the road. And I'm sorry to have to tell you this but there's evidence the fire to her car was caused by arson and not by the accident."

"Arson?" I asked, not wanting to believe the implication. "You mean someone tried to burn her alive?"

"Yes, sir, I'm afraid that's exactly what happened."

Melissa got up and left the room. I went after her to make sure she was all right. I found her getting a drink of water at the fountain in the hallway. She stumbled just as I got to her and I caught her as her knees buckled. I wrapped my arm under hers and helped her to a nearby chair. All the color had drained from her face. I made her bend over and put her head between her knees. A lot of that going around lately. I held her there for three or four minutes until she sat up by herself.

"I'm better now," she said, but she didn't look much better.

I sat beside her and put my arm around her shoulder. She leaned her head against me.

"I'm sorry, Frank. I should be used to it. I've heard lots of horrible stories before. But I've never known the victim personally. And this seems so close to us. We were just talking to her. We were riding in her car just before it happened. Whoever did it must have been following her the whole time. It's almost as if they did it right in front of us."

Melissa tried to stand up.

"Frank, I'm going to be sick."

The women's restroom was just down the hallway. I half carried her down the hall and through the door. A woman washing her hands at one of the sinks looked up at us and let out a little scream.

"She's ill," I said. I helped Melissa to one of the stalls and held her as she vomited into the toilet. I thought I was being real strong but when I smelled the vomit the feelings I had been holding inside erupted and I knew I was going to be sick too. I left Melissa propped against the side of the stall and I went to the sink and stood there several minutes splashing my face with cold water until the nausea passed. I wet a handful of paper towels and took them to Melissa. I put some of them on the back of her neck and I patted her face with the others. After a while she straightened up and turned to face me.

For the first time I was embarrassed, suddenly finding myself inside a stall in the ladies' room with her.

"Is this what it's like being married?" she asked.

I just laughed. Melissa washed her face at the sink and we looked up to find three women standing inside the doorway looking at us. I took Melissa by the arm and walked past them.

"She was ill," I said, putting on my most innocent face.

"I was ill," Melissa said. "He is helping me."

The women didn't say anything. Detective Miller was waiting in the hallway.

"Do you two feel better?" He asked. He sounded as if he meant it.

"Yeah, we're better," I said. "Sorry. It just hit close to home."

"I know," he said. "It's not like reading about it in the paper, is it?"

"We're going home," I said. "We'll talk with you tomorrow."

Miller looked at his watch. "How about later today? Say, after lunch when you wake up? Come by my office."

I drove Melissa in her car to her place. She packed a light bag and went home to my apartment with me. We showered together and went to sleep that night in each other's arms.

We didn't go to Detective Miller's office that afternoon. When we finally woke up and got enough coffee into us to get our brains working I told Melissa the plan that had come to me last night at the hospital. After talking about it for a few minutes she agreed we should do it.

"What the hell," she said. "They can kick me out of the profession only once."

She drove to the campus law clinic where she began rounding up a crew of students to help her and I rode my Harley to the hospital. I went first to the intensive care unit. Shirley was not in the room where we had left her. I went to the nurses' station to ask where she had been moved.

"Are you a member of the family?" the nurse on duty asked.

"Just a friend." Actually I was much more than that.

"Mrs. Willingham died early this morning," she said. "I'm sorry."

I hadn't been ready for that. When I saw her the night before I knew in my heart she must be dying. I had hoped she could die rather than go through the agony that consciousness would bring her. But standing face to face with the fact was different from the hypothetical.

"Are you all right?" the nurse asked. "Would you like to sit down?"

I couldn't answer right then. I walked to the waiting area, sat down and closed my eyes. If I could have turned back the clock at that moment and done anything to make things turn out differently, I would have. But I knew as I sat there I had to keep moving forward. I knew what Shirley had intended to do and I was going to see that it was done, even in her death.

When I regained control of myself I rode the elevator to the fifth floor hoping I wouldn't hear the same message again, this time about John Glover. Tiny and his mother were in Mr. Glover's room. If Mr. Glover had changed for the better I couldn't really tell it but he didn't look any worse. I spoke to Mrs. Glover. We talked for a minute and I motioned for Tiny to follow me outside. We stood in the parking lot in the late afternoon light. I told Tiny the story I wanted him to hear.

"You tellin' me my old man's a millionaire?" Tiny was incredulous.

"The land he owns could be worth several million dollars."

"How come he never told nobody?"

"He did tell someone. He told lots of people. I'm sure at one time or another he told lawyers, bankers, and city officials. But nobody believed him."

"Just a crazy ol' man, they thought." Tiny shook his head. "I thought it too."

I continued the version of the story for Tiny's ears. "He had the original documents to prove the land belonged to him but nobody believed they were authentic. The land was deeded to your grandfather by the owner of the Stevens Plantation in 1884 and then inherited by your father. It got broken up and sold off over the years but Stafford Willingham bought up the pieces one by one and put the property back together again. From the time Stafford was a very young man he knew your father and he had fond memories of him and your mother. He had intended to give the property back to your father in an estate trust to protect it. I think whoever killed Stafford Willingham killed him because of it. Somebody wanted to get their hands on the property because they knew it will be worth a fortune when the golf course development is approved."

"I be damned," Tiny said. "I had hard feelin's for Mr. Willingham. I was wrong 'bout what he was up to."

"We were all wrong," I said. "Whoever killed Stafford Willingham killed his wife too and for the same reason. They did it to stop her from signing the property over to the Glover trust."

"The Glover trust," Tiny repeated. "Sho' does have a nice sound to it."

"After they killed Stafford they thought they had control of the property again and could go ahead with the development. The church was in their way because it could stop the development of a golf community subdivision where the neighborhood is now. So they tried to burn it."

"I know'd they was tryin' to burn the church an' I thought all along it was because of the country club. I was right about that. I just didn' know 'xactly how all the pieces fit together."

"I still don't know all the pieces."

"You know who's doin' it?" Tiny asked.

"Give me just a little while longer on that. I could be wrong and I don't want you going out and killing the wrong person." I smiled at him and he grinned and shook his head at me but we both knew I was close to the truth of the matter. I didn't know what Tiny would do if he had a name and I'm not sure Tiny knew either.

"Awright, Frank. I trust you on this. You done all right so far. Can I tell my mamma about the property?"

"Give me two more days. It should be recorded at the courthouse by then and there will be nothing anyone can do to change it."

I had hoped the promise of something really good in their future would cool Tiny's rage over his father's condition. It seemed to have the effect I was looking for because he was laughing and talking to himself under his breath as he went back into the hospital. It wouldn't bring Mr. Glover's health back but maybe it would keep Tiny under control until the guilty parties, whoever they were, were locked up in the county jail. The one small flaw in my plan was that I didn't know who the guilty parties were and I didn't know how I was going to catch them.

I had one name to start with. Scott Taylor. I hoped the transfer of property held by Investment Adventures into a trust in Mr. Glover's name would flush the rest of the roaches out of the woodwork. But I had known as soon as I saw Shirley's condition that she might never be able to personally sign the legal documents. I had worked out a plan for that too.

Melissa and her student compatriots worked around the clock for two more days to finish the paperwork. Every deed had to be prepared with an exact description of the size, location and boundary markings of its parcel of property. The trust had to be drawn up along with all the contracts of transfer between Investment Adventures and the Glover trust. Fifty parcels of land, fifty deeds, fifty contracts transferring the parcels to the trust. The trust document was dated the afternoon before Shirley Willingham's death, the afternoon we had met in a private dining room at the Hyatt where hotel restaurant staff could testify they had seen us together for several hours going over deeds and legal documents.

"You haven't told anyone what we're doing, have you?" I asked Melissa when I picked her and the documents up at the law school clinic.

She looked at me in disbelief. "Do I look like an idiot?"

"Do you have the trust document?"

"Yes, I have the trust document," she said, still feigning disbelief. "And no, no one else has seen it."

"Then let's go do it."

We took the trust document and as many examples of Shirley Willingham's signature as we could get our hands on and paid a visit to Charlie Preston in the county jail.

Chapter 36

Mont Blanc

"You want me to what?"

"I want you to show me how good you are, Charlie," I laid the trust document and the samples of Shirley Willingham's signature on the table in front of him. "I want this signature so perfect that the best handwriting expert in the world couldn't tell it's a forgery."

Charlie Preston leaned back in his chair, grinned at me and nodded his head. "Suppose I can do what you ask. What kind of payment could you arrange?"

"I can give you the very best legal counsel you can get, free of charge."

"For how long?"

"For all current charges against you."

"Appeals too, if I need them?" Charlie asked.

"Appeals too. But not for new charges on new offenses after you get out."

Charlie looked hurt. "Frank, how could you think I would ever face new charges?"

"Only through some miscarriage of justice, I'm sure," I said. "I can also offer you an honest job if you want one."

Charlie smiled and winked at me. "Give me plenty of scratch paper," he said. "And I'll need a good bright light and a big magnifier." He indicated with his hands. "And bring me the pen she liked to use or one just like it if she had one. And a bottle of Pelikan royal blue water proof ink. It looks like that's what she was using."

I knew Shirley had a pen she liked. It was a Carte Blanc or whatever the name is. Black with gold inlay. Very impressive. I had seen her take it from her purse. I went by the police station and asked Detective Miller if anyone had claimed Shirley's personal effects after the car wreck. He took me to the property room and we located a box with what remained of her purse in it. Just as I thought, the pen was there. It was a Mont Blanc and it was badly damaged. I asked Miller if I could borrow the pen.

"You're up to something, Frank. But I'm not going to ask what and I don't want to know."

Miller turned his back and I put the pen in my coat pocket. I went to Friedman's jewelers downtown and found a duplicate of Shirley's pen. The price was about what my car was worth but I was using Willingham's money anyway so I bought two, one in medium point and one in fine . . . and a bottle of Mont Blanc royal blue ink. The jeweler insisted I should use no other brand of ink. The jewelry shop was also using several of the type of magnifier Charlie had requested. After a little haggling I talked the manager into selling one of them to me. At an office supply store I picked up a bright spotlight type desk lamp. It took some fast talk from Melissa to get the lot of stuff into the attorneys' consultation room at the county jail.

"Damn good job, Frank." Charlie admired the pens and the other items. "The woman had expensive taste in pens. These are real quality. Can I have these when we're finished?"

"I'll have them waiting for you when you get out," I said.

Melissa had brought a stack of the same kind of paper the trust document was typed on.

"Give me a couple of hours," he said.

We left Charlie in the consultation room and went to get a cup of coffee. We sat outside the room and waited.

"You have any second thoughts about this?" I asked.

Melissa took my hand in hers. "Sure. Legally I'm an accessory to fraud. It goes against all my beliefs and training. But I know it's the right thing to do. If we take Green and Green to court on this it might not be settled in the Glovers' lifetime. You put this before a jury, there's no way to predict if the jurors would be able to make the right choice. I know in my heart what the outcome should be and I feel an obligation to make it happen. Mr. Glover has been taken from and taken from. It's time the law gave back what's rightfully his."

"How does this make you feel about the practice of law?"

Melissa shook her head. "I've got to think that one over. All I know is, people like the Glovers need someone to represent them."

"No argument there."

After an hour and forty-five minutes Charlie knocked on the door.

"I defy the devil himself to tell me Shirley Willingham didn't sign that document," he said, admiring his work under the magnifier.

Melissa and I took turns comparing Shirley's signature with his copy. We couldn't tell which was which, and we knew.

"It's some of my best work," he said.

"Charlie Preston," I said, "may I introduce you to your attorney?"

"Miss Gresham," he said, shaking her hand, "I've seen and admired your work too."

As Melissa and I were leaving, Charlie pulled me aside.

"There's talk about a scam involving the building inspector's office," he said.

"What have you heard?"

"From what I hear, the way it works is this. The building

inspectors start showing up for some trumped up reason and become a nuisance. All of a sudden the property owner needs to have repairs made. The building inspector recommends a contractor. A few thousand dollars later the repairs are made and the building inspector passes the job. You can't afford a few thousand dollars, the building inspector can give you the name of a finance company."

"American Home Guardian Finance?" I asked.

"You know the scam?" Charlie asked.

"Just a lucky guess."

"They're not the only one. There are others. Everybody is putting money in everybody else's pocket. If the homeowner doesn't make his payments on time, somebody ends up with the property."

"What have you heard about Willingham?"

"Which one?" Charlie asked.

"Either one."

"Stafford Willingham, for reasons no one knows, comes around asking questions hitting right at the center of the scam. The next thing you know, Stafford is dead."

"What about Shirley Willingham?"

"Nobody knows why that happened, except maybe you."

"Any word on who did it?"

Charlie shook his head.

"Any word on who actually pulled the trigger on Stafford Willingham?"

"No one seems to know, but scuttlebutt says some of Scott Taylor's men have been running their mouths."

"Have you heard anything about who set the fires in east Macon?"

"Taylor has some men working for him who have problems with the black race. You might say they have a" prejudicial eye. Two of them probably did it but it wasn't their idea. They're not exactly idea people."

"You got names?"

Charlie shook his head.

"Thanks, Charlie. You hear anything else, you ask to see your attorney. She'll get word to me." I gave him one of the Mont Blanc pens. He looked at it and smiled.

"You watch out for yourself and Miss Gresham, Frank. You're tangling with some dangerous people. Anybody who would do what was done to a classy lady like Mrs. Willingham wouldn't think twice about killing you."

On the way to the courthouse I told Melissa what Charlie had told me.

"Any surprises there?" she asked.

"No. He just confirmed for me what we've been finding out."

"Are we any closer?"

"I don't know."

Our transactions in the property records office at the courthouse caused quite a commotion. I had no problem getting the notary to notarize my signature on the fifty deeds and the fifty title transfers but the county clerk had to consult with a judge before she would accept my filing of the trust document containing Shirley Willingham's signature. The clerk showed Melissa and me into Judge Barrow's office. Luckily, Melissa had appeared before Judge Barrow on several occasions and he knew her professionally.

"You prepared this trust document?" Judge Barrow asked.

"Yes, your honor. I drew it up to carry out the wishes of Mrs. Willingham. She wanted to return certain parcels of property from the company of which she was director and majority stockholder to the estate of Mr. John Glover who was the original owner of the property. She wanted to be sure the property was protected so I recommended that it be put in a trust for the lifetime of the Glovers."

"And this is Mrs. Willingham's signature?" he asked.

Melissa nodded. "I witnessed the endorsement myself."

"And you are Mr. Frank Hayes," he asked. "The person designated as the executor of the trust?"

"Yes, I am, your honor. I administer two separate trusts for the Willingham estate."

"And you're transferring the designated parcels of property in accordance with the wishes of Mrs. Willingham?"

"Yes, Your Honor, I am."

Judge Barrow looked over the trust document again, signed it, and handed it back to the clerk of the court.

"Will you be setting up your own practice in Macon, Miss Gresham?" he asked.

"I haven't decided."

"The profession can use more dedicated young people like you. I hope you decide to stay with us."

We took our copies of all the documents we had filed with the clerk and said hardly a word until we were back in Melissa's car and driving toward her apartment.

"I can't believe we actually did it and got away with it," Melissa said. "What do we do now?"

"Nothing. Word will spread from the courthouse to everyone who has an interest in east Macon. Let's wait and see who starts squealing."

My plan may have been a good if risky one. But like so many good plans, there were unforeseen events on the horizon that interjected themselves. We went back by Melissa's apartment so she could pick up a few more of her things. I went inside with her. It was the first time I had been in her apartment but not, I discovered, the first time I had seen her roommate. All of a sudden I connected the California accent.

"Don't I know you?" I asked her.

"Jennifer, this is Frank. Frank, Jennifer."

But Jennifer had already recognized me and had in turn put on a rigid body posture that shouted denial.

"You were with the other girl at the bar at the Dew Drop that time."

"No, I'm sure you're, like, mistaken," the California accent said.

"No, I remember you clearly. A car payment, wasn't it? You needed $200 for a car payment. You had spent the money your daddy sent you on a bikini or something?"

"Jennifer?" Melissa was asking.

Jennifer wasn't any better liar now than she had been that night.

"I don't know anything about what happened to the mayor," she blurted out.

"Really?" I said.

"Jennifer?" Melissa said again.

"Oh, Melissa, I'm sorry. I wanted to tell you but you were involved with Frank and I, like, couldn't tell you."

"Tell me what, Jennifer? You and the mayor?"

"No, not him. Get real. He's a creep."

"Craig Linder?" I asked.

"He's nice to me," Jennifer said. "He's sweet and he loves me."

"Craig Linder?" Melissa said. "How did I miss all this? How long has this been going on?"

"I met him the night I ran into Frank at the Dew Drop. I went there with some friends to hear Del Shannon. He was playing at the lounge. Craig and the mayor, like, just happened to sit down with Frank at the table next to us. We were just talking, like, and one thing led to another. Craig asked for my phone number and he called me a couple of days later. I've been seeing him ever since."

"For three months?" Melissa asked.

"Well, you've been busy with your court cases and all, and you haven't been around. I would have told you about Craig for sure but . . .like, it just got awkward."

"My God, Jennifer," Melissa said, "he's old enough to be your father."

"He's not so old. I like him a lot. I told you, he's very good to me."

"Not nearly as good as you are to him, I'll bet," Melissa said.

"It's not like that," she protested.

"I need to know about four nights ago," I said, "the night the mayor was arrested. Were you with Craig that night?"

"Yes, for sure, we were together."

"Was the mayor with you that evening?"

"Part of the time. Craig and I had dinner in Atlanta. The place we ate was really cool. We came back to Macon around 11:00 and stopped at the Dew Drop for a couple of drinks, you know. No big deal. The mayor was there with some people. He was, like, really drunk."

"Who were the people he was with?"

"I don't know, just people. Anyway, it was like Craig was worried the mayor was too drunk to drive. Craig is always worrying about the mayor. So he talked the mayor into coming with us. He dropped me here and he left to take the mayor home. That's the last I saw of them. The next thing I hear, the mayor was, like, arrested. What a bummer."

"What did Craig have to say about it?" I asked.

"Why don't you ask me yourself?" The voice of Craig Linder said from the doorway behind me.

Chapter 37

They Make Deals

You could have frozen ice cubes on the chill that went up my spine at the sound of Linder's voice. I was less than calm as I turned to see him standing in the doorway. He looked past me and crossed the room to where Jennifer was standing. He put an arm around her, kissed her temple and said something to her that made her smile. She put an arm around him and leaned against him. I took it as a good sign that he was more interested in comforting her than in bashing me.

"I don't know anything about what happened to Tommy Lee," Linder said. "I left him on his doorstep around midnight. He was almost too drunk to stand on his feet so I never thought he would do anything but go inside and pass out."

"You didn't see anyone in the neighborhood or on the street when you dropped him off?" I asked.

"I don't recall anyone but I don't know that I would have noticed unless it was something unusual."

"Such as a prostitute in his neighborhood? The mayor lives in a pretty exclusive area. Something like that should have stuck out," I said.

"You would think so," Linder said. "But I didn't see anything that I remember."

"Where did you go after you dropped the mayor off?"

"I went home. As I said, it was after midnight. I had to be at work the next morning."

"Do you hold any interest in a company named Investment Adventures?" I asked.

The turn of conversation took Linder aback. He hesitated before he answered.

"Yes, I have a little money invested in them, why?"

"Who are the major stockholders in the company?"

"Shirley Willingham was the majority stockholder. That's one reason I invested my money with them. It was my thinking that with her as a key player it must be a legit operation."

"When was the last time you saw Shirley?"

"A few days ago." He was beginning to get nervous. "What are you getting at?"

"Did you know the police have been following you for quite some time?"

He looked at me skeptically. "Following me? Why?"

I raised my eyebrows in a question. I didn't answer. He was shaken by the news.

"Why would they be following me? Surely not . . . They wouldn't think I was involved in Stafford or Shirley's death?"

"You tell me," I said. "Do they have any reason to suspect you?" He only looked puzzled. "They followed you to Shirley Willingham's house one night recently."

That hit a spot he didn't want pressed. He looked at Jennifer in some anticipation and then at me with agitation. "That was on personal business."

My laugh wasn't what he wanted to hear. "I was there, Craig. All I saw was monkey business. But it *was* very personal."

"Craig?" Jennifer said, and pushed him at arm's length.

"Don't listen to his insinuations, Jen," Linder said. "He doesn't know what he's talking about. He's trying to find someone to blame his troubles on."

"Insinuations?" I said. "Those kisses you were planting on

Shirley Willingham weren't insinuations."

Linder lunged at me with a fist that might have been more effective if he had been holding a club in it, but he wasn't. I dodged the blow, caught his arm and had it twisted behind him before he could recover himself.

"You son of a bitch," he growled at me.

Jennifer screamed and rushed to his side in an effort to protect him that was more symbolic than real. Nevertheless, her affection for him had an effect on me. I was about ready to give him a few of my best punches but I held off.

"I may be a son of a bitch," I said, "but I'm not a killer. And it's a killer I'm looking for. Someone with their money in Investment Adventures killed Shirley Willingham and her husband to protect their investment."

"What?" Linder said. "Why kill them? Shirley had invested more money than anyone in the company."

"Check your investments now. Shirley signed all the property holdings over to a land trust in the name of John Glover. Someone with money in the company knew what she was going to do and killed her in an effort to stop her. But they were too late."

"What?" Linder asked, not wanting to believe me. He went limp. "She wouldn't have. Jesus, I had $10,000 invested in those properties. You mean she just signed it over? She didn't sell it?"

"Signed it over free and clear," I said.

"Well I didn't know anything about it. Jesus. I can't believe it. But I certainly wouldn't have killed her for any amount of money, even if I had known. Shirley and I were friends for years. Before she married Stafford, Shirley and I were a couple. I've always been fond of her. I would never do her harm. The people I deal with don't kill people. They make deals. They make money. Sometimes they lose money. But they don't kill anyone over it. They just make more money."

"Let him go," Jennifer insisted, pushing at my arm.

I thought Linder's flash of anger was over so I released the hold on his arm. He sat down on the edge of one of the beds. Jennifer sat close to him.

"Who are the other investors in the company?" I wanted to know.

"I don't know the other investors. Jeff Green told me about the company. He swore me to secrecy. There's lots of competition to invest in the country club development. You know that. All he told me was that Shirley was the majority stockholder and the director of the company. Jeff said it was going to be a big moneymaker. I've known Jeffrey Green for years. He's a member of the planning and zoning commission. I trusted him."

"How well do you know Scott Taylor?" I asked.

"Taylor? I don't have any personal acquaintance with him. He's not the kind of person I associate with."

"What about professional dealings with him?"

"Taylor is in the construction and development business. He has a plan or a subdivision plat, a zoning waiver, or one sort of business or another before the commission on a regular basis."

"Any problems with him?"

"Yes. Compliance problems, procedural problems. Taylor is an independent sort. Likes to do what he wants to do."

"Regardless of the law?" I added.

"Sometimes," Linder said. "I've had complaints. Several times I've had George Dolly follow up and check Taylor out. Taylor has always come up clean in the end. He does what he can get away with but we don't let him get away with much."

"Do you know that someone in your office is running a

scam in cahoots with local contractors and finance companies?"

"In my office? What kind of scam?"

I explained the workings of the scam involving falsified inspections, unneeded repairs, and finance referrals. Linder's face grew red.

"Why wouldn't I have heard about this before now?" he asked.

"You tell me."

His eyes were gazing into the distance, unfocused, as he examined his own thoughts.

"It must have been Curly Jenkins and Ellis Moore," he said.

"Yeah, I'm sure they were involved in it. They filed the false inspection report on John Glover's house. But neither of them has the brains to run a scam. They only got away with their part in it because they're known to be stupid and no one would suspect them of deliberate falsification. Who else would handle the inspection reports, the appeals, and the condemnation orders?"

"There's no one else but myself and George Dolly."

As soon as he said the words I knew it.

"George Dolly," I repeated. "Good old dependable George Dolly. The man who's been around City Hall forever. The man who knows everything, who offends no one. The man who fades into the woodwork. The man who cleared Scott Taylor."

"I can't believe George would be involved in anything illegal. Certainly not murder," Linder said.

"Well it's sort of come down to George or you," I told him.

"It's not me," Linder said.

"It's not him," Jennifer said. "You don't know him. He wouldn't, like, kill anyone."

I looked at the two of them. "I hope you're right. Because if he is capable of murdering a woman he was once fond of and who he claims to still be fond of, then you're not safe either, my dear."

If the thought bothered her she didn't show it. She was obviously in love with Linder and would believe him capable of no evil.

Melissa and I left Craig and Jennifer in the apartment and headed to my place in Melissa's car.

"Do you believe him?" Melissa asked.

"Right now I'm not willing to believe anything on face value."

I had Melissa stop within sight of her apartment building at the first pay phone we came to. I reached Detective Miller at the police station.

"I'm not telling you how to do your job," I said, "but I would follow Craig Linder very closely right now. He had $10,000 in Investment Adventures and he just found out he lost all his money. It'll be very interesting to see who he talks with next about it."

"We're already on him," Miller said.

"According to information I just got from Linder, I think George Dolly at City Hall may be involved with Scott Taylor in the scam, along with two former building inspectors named Curly Jenkins and Ellis Moore."

"Interesting," Miller said. "I'll check into it. Where are you going now?"

"I'm going to have something to eat and go to my apartment. I'm bushed."

"Is Miss Gresham with you?"

"Yes, she is. Why do you ask?"

"Keep her close to you. By tomorrow everyone involved

with Jeffrey Green will know that you and she worked with Shirley Willingham to turn the tables on them. It won't be safe for either of you in this town until the murderers are caught."

I saw the accuracy of Miller's words when we arrived back at my apartment. Someone had taken a not-so-subtle tour through it. Not in a way that said they were looking for anything. It looked more like they were leaving little signs to threaten or frighten me. A picture cracked in the living room. A glass broken on the kitchen floor. My bathroom mirror broken.

"What were they looking for?" Melissa asked.

"Us, probably," I said.

I had an idea that would allow me to take care of some legal matters and maybe keep us out of harm's way.

"I think maybe it's time we got the hell out of Dodge for a while. How about a road trip?"

Melissa immediately perked up.

"Sure," she said. "Where to?"

"Someplace nice in Atlanta."

"Now?"

"Sure. Why not?"

We packed a small duffle bag with a change of clothes and some overnight things and tied it across the front of the motorcycle. The sun was low in the late afternoon sky when we headed north on Interstate 75. It felt great to be back on the road on the bike with Melissa's arms wrapped around my waist. The breeze was just warm enough to keep off the chill as the orange sun set behind the trees.

Halfway to Atlanta we pulled off for a break at Forsyth. I stopped in front of the Waffle House.

"Is this one of the nicer places in Atlanta you were talking about?" Melissa asked.

I kissed her and tickled her ribs. "Nothing but the best for you, baby."

I was pleasantly surprised to find Doris waiting tables again. Melissa and I sat down next to each other in one of the booths. Doris brought two cups and a pot of fresh perked coffee. She recognized me at once and was all smiles.

"Is this the one you're so in love with?" she asked.

Melissa looked down self-consciously, knowing that Doris probably was asking about someone else.

"Yes, it is," I said.

Melissa leaned over and kissed me on the neck.

"Well, she's a pretty little thing," Doris said. "Honey, you got quite a man here."

"Yes, I do, don't I?" Melissa said.

"You better take good care of him. You turn him loose, I might want him for myself."

"Sorry, Doris," I said, "I'm nobody's but hers."

"What're you love birds having today?"

We had my Waffle House standard snack . . . apple pie and coffee. As we walked out the door I told Melissa I forgot to leave Doris a tip. I went back inside and put $50 under the dessert plate.

"You and Doris old friends?" Melissa asked as we sat at the traffic light.

"I've stopped here a few times. She took a liking to me."

I took us to a very picturesque bed and breakfast inn I had passed on previous trips through Dunwoody. Lucky for us they had a vacancy. It was quiet, comfortable, and private. There was an inviting looking restaurant a couple of blocks away. We had a pleasant, relaxed dinner, took a warm shower and spent a quiet evening in bed.

"Can we sell the property we just stole and live quietly

here in this bed and breakfast?" Melissa said. It was a nice thought.

I told Melissa what I had in mind to do and asked her advice. The next morning we got up late and had the breakfast portion of our bed and breakfast. I made reservations for us there for the rest of the week and we headed downtown to see Mr. Frederick Carter at the legal firm of Barnes and Ingram.

"You've done quite well for the Glover family in a short period of time," Carter said. "Mr. Willingham obviously made a good choice in naming you executor, as did his wife."

"Mr. and Mrs. Willingham were dedicated to righting a very old wrong," I said. "I take my responsibilities seriously."

I told Carter the way I wanted the property and the money to be handled.

"Do you think he's the man for the job?" Carter asked.

"He's the very best man for the job. He's dedicated to his family, he has high moral character, judgment and discipline. He's not an educated man but he has experience and character that not many men have. I would certainly trust him with my life and fortune. I want you to understand, I never want him to know where the money is really coming from."

"Just as you wish, Mr. Hayes. The documents will be prepared and complete instructions will be filed here with the trusts so that whoever should succeed me will continue the arrangements according to your wishes."

Melissa and I spent that night at the bed and breakfast and I would have been content to stay there the rest of the year. I called Tiny to check on things and found out that Shirley Willingham's funeral was scheduled for the next afternoon.

"I know you feel as though you ought to go," Melissa said, "but do we have to? I'm afraid to go back."

"There's nothing to worry about," I told her. But the

God's truth is I didn't know what to expect. I had my own fears as we headed out of Atlanta in the direction of Macon the next morning. Somebody out there was liable to be mad enough to kill.

Chapter 38

Outrun The Devil

Shirley Willingham's funeral was made more sad by the absence of Stafford's side of the family. Shirley's parents and her younger sister had driven in from out of state. The only thing her parents knew about me was that I was the man who had been charged with Stafford's murder and later released. I could be of no comfort to them.

There was a good showing of Shirley's friends from the beautification commission, the historical society, the League of Women Voters, the realtors' association, and from among those she worked with at the Department of Family and Children's Services. Craig Linder was there and Detective Miller. At the graveside service I stood off to one side with Mrs. Glover, Tiny, and 'Rome Brown. I'm sure some of Shirley's society friends had to wonder about our presence.

Shirley's little sister Denise came over and spoke with us. There was a strong family resemblance. She had the same beauty as Shirley but was very shy and demure compared with the way Shirley had been. I don't know if Shirley had told Denise about me or if Denise just sensed something. But I got the feeling she was aware there had been something between Shirley and me and she seemed to take comfort in the things I said about her big sister. If Denise or her parents knew anything about any history between the Glovers and the Willinghams they gave no indication of it.

Melissa didn't want to go to the funeral and I can't say I blamed her. I rode to the cemetery with Tiny and Mrs. Glover. As we made our way back to Tiny's truck after the graveside service I touched his arm and nodded my head in the direction of the red super duty pickup parked a hundred yards away on the street outside the graveyard. There were two men in the truck but at that distance I couldn't tell who they were.

"I see that," Tiny said. "They here to pay they respects, you think?"

"Not the respectful kind, I would imagine."

"Maybe they waitin' to talk to you, or me," Tiny said.

"Let 'em wait," I said.

We drove from the cemetery to the hospital without incident. Mr. Glover was no better. It didn't look good for him. Mrs. Glover was trying to be strong about his condition but I could see it was taking its toll on her. I had called Melissa to pick me up, and Tiny and I walked out into the parking lot together while I waited.

"I'm here ever' day and ever' evenin'," Tiny said. "I been hopin' the old man knows I'm here, but I can't tell if he does."

"He'll hear your voice," I said, "even if he can't let you know it."

"Wish I hadn't waited so long."

"You can tell him and your mamma about the property. It's all filed at the courthouse. You should be getting a letter in a few days from the Atlanta law firm that's handling the trust, explaining the whole thing. At least he's lived long enough to see his property returned to his family name."

"It's a great thing, Frank. I know you had somethin' to do with it, and I know you ain't tol' me everthing."

"I just did what Stafford and Shirley Willingham asked me to do. I can't take credit for it."

"You lyin' to me, Frank. But that's all right. The reason I know you lyin' is 'cause you done stirred up a hornet's nest."

Tiny was leading us in the direction of his truck while we

were talking.

"Skeeter said Marcel told him Scott Taylor has got it in for you. He say Taylor's dozer man been braggin' 'bout how Taylor's gon' kill yo' ass."

Tiny opened the door to his truck and reached behind the seat. He pulled out a cloth bag and stuck it inside my leather jacket. I knew by the feel of it that it was a pistol, a large pistol.

"You don't go nowhere without that on you or close by you," he said.

I didn't ask Tiny where the gun came from. I thought about refusing it but I also thought about me or me and Melissa having to face Scott Taylor without some way to defend ourselves. Taylor or one of his associates had killed two people already. I pushed the pistol under my belt.

I didn't tell Melissa about the gun. She had spent most of the day visiting people she knew who might have heard any rumblings coming from the courthouse or from the legal community. She had friends among the clerks at Green and Green and they told her bedlam had broken out when the partners found out the details of Jeffrey Green's involvement with Investment Adventures. And more bedlam when they discovered that original documents were missing from the file room. The clerks had been told to give highest priority to locating those missing Investment Adventures documents.

At the courthouse there had been a string of visitors to inspect copies of numerous deeds to east Macon properties. There were reports of a number of flared tempers. Among the visitors were Mr. Henry Wallis, vice president of my bank, two members of the planning and zoning commission, Craig Linder and the mayor, and my very own personal financial manager, Bob Felton from American Home Guardian Finance.

"Warms the heart, doesn't it?" I asked Melissa.

"A lot of people are very upset," she said. "In your words,

don't you think it's time we got the hell out of Dodge?"

"I'm looking forward to getting back to the bed and breakfast for an early turn-in, how about you?" I was trying to change the topic away from the subject of her fears.

"Do you think maybe we should drive my car instead of the motorcycle?" she asked.

I had already anticipated this choice. I didn't really think the underpowered VW would offer us any safety advantage. I had gone by Ron's garage earlier in the day to get my car out of hock so we could drive it to Atlanta but Ron's garage was closed and I couldn't see any sign of him or my car anywhere. If we got into trouble the Harley was capable of 120 miles per hour. That was faster than most any vehicle on the road and if necessary it could go places the beetle could only dream of in its wildest fantasies.

"I think we should take the bike. We can drive the beetle when we're old and gray and the weather gets cold."

I don't know if she was persuaded by my reasoning but she agreed. We traded the VW for the Harley at my place. We hadn't known how long we might be in Macon so we had packed the duffle bag and brought it along. While Melissa was inside my apartment I took the pistol from inside my jacket and stuffed it into the duffle bag.

We stayed off the Interstate. I went up the slower more pleasant Highway 23. It was late in the day. We stopped in Juliette at the Whistle Stop Café for supper and it was already dark when we got back on the road.

I saw the headlights in my rearview mirror and thought nothing of it because we had seen light traffic on the road. But as they drew nearer I could see they were the headlights of a super duty pickup truck. In this part of the country there are lots of super duty pickup trucks. Most every family owns at least one somewhere on the family tree. Some have one on every branch. But this particular truck was coming up fast. I increased my own speed to put some distance between us and the truck.

The truck kept coming. I glanced down to see my speedometer registering 80 miles per hour. Eighty on that two lane road was OK on the straight stretches but Highway 23 has lots of curves, some of them sharp. When I slowed for the curves the truck closed in on us from behind. Melissa had grown uncomfortable with the speed we were going and yelled in my ear to ask if we could slow down. But before I could answer she looked back and saw the truck coming up fast.

I would have been able to outrun him if it weren't for the traffic. We were running up fast on a string of slow-moving cars and a sudden flow of headlights in the oncoming lane. Ditches and drop-offs fell off to either side of the road and there was no place for me to go. I braked hard and ran right up to the bumper of the car in front of us. The truck pulled within ten feet of my rear wheel. I could see the woman in the car in front of us looking in her rearview mirror and glancing back to see who was following her so closely.

I heard a loud pop, felt something hit me hard in the back about midway down on the left side and Melissa cried out. She squeezed her fingers into the flesh of my stomach and I knew she had been shot. My back was throbbing and I was having trouble getting my breath. There was another pop and I saw a bullet hole appear in the trunk lid of the car in front of us. Melissa was still holding tight to me. I could hear her moaning. There was only one thing I could do.

I leaned the bike just to the left and accelerated hard. We past the car in front of us and drove straight down the center line of the two-lane road between the lines of passing vehicles. Seeing my headlight, the oncoming drivers veered away from me to the outside of their lane to try and avoid me. As I passed cars and trucks on my own side of the road some of them swerved to the right and braked, putting further distance between me and the pickup which got trapped behind the column of traffic. Horns were blowing at me from all sides. Melissa had slumped against me but she was still holding to me.

By some miracle or the hand of God I passed between the two columns of traffic without a collision. I accelerated away from the head of the column and looked in my mirror and caught a glimpse of headlights turning and bobbing as some of the vehicles came to a full stop. I felt something wet through the back of my pants and I knew one of us was bleeding.

I couldn't stop for fear the pickup would catch up with us again but I had to find out how badly Melissa was hit. She hadn't said anything after the first shot other than the cry and the low moaning. There were no headlights or taillights visible in either direction now. Ahead was a long narrow two-lane bridge across a creek. I knew that at the far end of the bridge there was a side dirt road fishermen used to get to the creek below. I slammed on the foot brake and the handbrake as hard as I could without causing the bike to skid as I passed over the bridge. I turned the bike onto the dirt access road moving as fast as I could, turned onto a footpath and drove underneath the bridge. I needed to turn off the headlight so we wouldn't be discovered but I needed the light so I could have a look at Melissa.

I turned off the ignition and kicked the stand down to hold the bike upright. I pulled my right leg up over the gas tank and swiveled around to catch Melissa in my arms. My turning broke her grip on me and she slumped toward the ground. I caught her and carried and half dragged her into the beam from the headlight. Her eyes were rolled back. She was unconscious. Blood covered the front of her coat, and her blouse was soaked on her left front. The bullet had gone through her. That's what hit me in the back. I was hurting like hell but I couldn't tell how bad I was hit. I couldn't feel any of my own blood. I knew I would be dead now if she hadn't taken the bullet meant for me.

She was breathing but I could hear a gurgling sound. I ripped open her blouse so I could see the wound. Blood was running from a round bullet hole the diameter of a pencil in her chest and air bubbled out of it when she breathed. The location of the wound was dangerously close to where I thought her heart should be. I rolled her over to look at her back. There was no blood there. I didn't know why but that looked like a good thing to me. I took off my belt, laid it across her back and rolled her over again facing me. I put my handkerchief over the chest wound and buckled my belt over the outside of her jacket to hold the compress in place. I kept talking to her, trying to reassure her. She had not spoken or opened her eyes since I got her off the bike. I had to get her to a doctor or a hospital within minutes or I was sure she would die.

The closest hospital was back the way we had come to an intersection three or four miles back and then across ten miles to Forsyth. The big unknown was whether the pickup was still in pursuit or if it had turned back toward Macon.

I turned off the motorcycle's lights and tried to calm the sound of my own breathing so I could listen to Melissa's breathing and her heartbeat and listen for the sounds of traffic. Her breathing and her heartbeat were both frightening. I tried to think. My back was throbbing with sharp pain and it hurt to breathe. Then I heard it . . . the high pitched screaming sound of a straining engine. They were looking for us, trying to catch up with us. I was afraid to turn the headlight back on. I felt in the dark for the duffel bag. The revolver was inside. I had tied the closure strings with a double bow knot but in the dark in my haste to untie it I managed to pull it into a knot I couldn't get loose in the dark. I could hear the truck drawing closer.

We had one hope . . . that the truck would keep up its speed and not check any of the side roads. There was no sign the truck was slowing. If I had been using my best judgment I probably would have let the truck go on past with the hope that it would keep going and I could get a head start back toward a hospital. But I listened to Melissa's labored breathing in the dark and realized I didn't even know if I could manage to get her back on the bike with me or if the ride would kill her.

I had seen in my headlight that the drainage ditch leading to the creek from the highway was lined with chunks of granite. I ran through the dark to the embankment and felt among the granite rocks until I found one about the size of a grapefruit and pulled it loose from its spot. It weighed a good five pounds. The sound of the truck engine was growing louder. It increased in pitch and intensity as the truck raced down the slope of the long incline of the highway approaching the bridge.

I scrambled up the embankment until I reached the edge of the bridge. I knelt there in the darkness in the bushes just out of the beam of the approaching headlights. I looked around the end of the bridge just barely enough to verify that it was indeed the super duty pickup that was screaming down on me.

As the truck reached the far end of the bridge I estimated it was traveling at near one hundred miles per hour. I stood up and in one quick movement took one step into the roadway and hurled the heavy granite stone directly at the driver's side of the windshield. The truck was coming so fast that the stone hardly had time to leave my hand before the truck was upon me. I dove back over the bank at the very instant the truck reached the spot I had been standing and the five pound missile the size of a cannonball crashed through the windshield.

The driver had seen me in the road and tried to veer away but the narrow bridge confined him. The truck hit the side of the bridge, glanced back into the center of the road and because of a reflexive jerk of the steering wheel by the driver, flipped on its side and began a series of rolls that carried it down the middle of the highway and over the embankment onto the granite boulders below.

After so much deafening sound and thrashing, crashing movement, there was suddenly silence and darkness. I ran back to the motorcycle under the bridge, turned on the headlight and aimed it in the direction of the wreck. I saw no movement in the truck.

I ran to the pickup. It was resting on its top, bent and mangled almost beyond recognition, but the words Taylor Construction were still legible on the door. All the windows were broken and the top was crushed in. The driver was Scott Taylor. His crushed face was unrecognizable but his name was stenciled on his shirt. He was dead. There was one passenger in the truck. As I tried to see through the light who it was I heard the approach of oncoming traffic. The passenger moved. He was alive. I was suddenly aware of the smell of gasoline. The gas tank had ruptured during the wreck and gas was running down the side of the truck cab and pooling on the ground underneath. The glint of silver metal caught my eye. On the ground beside my foot was the gun that had fired the bullet that hit Melissa. I picked up the gun and looked at it. I had seen it before. A pearl-handled, chrome-plated Smith and Wesson .38 revolver. From inside the truck I heard the voice of the man who owned the gun, "Frank Hayes, you bastard, get me out of here."

I could see headlights in the distance coming down the long slope toward the bridge. Help would be here in a moment but they would never see us from the highway. I had to attract their attention. I heard movement from inside the truck. I heard Melissa cry from under the bridge. I looked at the gun again. My hand was stained with the blood from Melissa's wound. I thought of the way Shirley Willingham had died, and Stafford Willingham, and I thought of John Glover lying unconscious in the hospital because of them. I aimed the pistol at the pool of gasoline and fired.

Chapter 39

Race Against Time

The raw gasoline erupted with a roar into a fireball as large as the truck itself and lit up the surrounding ditch and trees as if floodlights had been turned on the landscape. The first cars to cross the bridge slowed and stopped and within seconds men were running down the embankment toward the wreck.

"You all right, son? You hurt? Anybody else in the truck?" were the first words out of their mouths.

"I'm not hurt bad," I said. "Under the bridge. Help her. She's bleeding and needs to get to a hospital."

Three men carried Melissa up to the highway. A woman came striding toward us.

"I'm a registered nurse," she said. "Let me have a look at her." She motioned for them to lay Melissa where the headlights would shine on her. "What happened to her?" she asked, looking at me as she checked Melissa's breathing and felt her arms and legs for breaks.

"She's been shot in the back . . . by the men in the truck. The bullet came out through her chest. It's bleeding and bubbling air."

"Her lung is collapsed," the woman said. "It looks as if she's lost quite a bit of blood. You did the right thing by trying to stop the bleeding. We need to keep her alive until we can get her to the Forsyth hospital. That's the closest place."

"Put her in my station wagon," one of the men said. "I'll take her."

"Would you go with us, please?" I asked the nurse.

She looked at me and gave me a quick smile. "Sure, I will."

They laid Melissa in the back seat of the station wagon. I crawled in with her and held her in my arms. The nurse sat on the other side of her.

"How long has she been unconscious?" The nurse asked as we accelerated south toward the Forsyth intersection.

"I don't know for sure. Maybe ten minutes before you got here."

"Has she said anything?"

"She cried out for me once just before you arrived. That's all."

The nurse had a hand on Melissa's neck checking her pulse.

"How is she?" I asked.

"Try not to worry. Just keep talking to her." She turned to the driver. "Drive as fast as you safely can."

In some ways it was the longest fifteen miles I've ever traveled. But in some ways it's all a blur in my memory. All I can really remember is holding onto Melissa, telling her I loved her and praying to God that he would let her live.

When we pulled in sight of the emergency room entrance to the Forsyth hospital the driver began blowing his horn and flashing his lights. By the time he had the station wagon stopped, ER staff had already scrambled to meet us at the curbside. Someone had called the hospital and told them we were on the way. They lifted Melissa onto a gurney and rolled her into the emergency room.

An ER doctor asked if I was hurt. I told him I was and he led me to a treatment room. He asked what happened to me as he and a nurse removed my coat and shirt. I told him everything I thought was relevant.

After examining me from head to foot and finding a large inflamed bruised area on my back, he sent me to have x-rays made. Perhaps half an hour later he returned to the treatment room with the results.

"You have a cracked rib," he said. "Something gave you quite a hit. It must have hurt."

He picked up my leather jacket and inspected the back of it. He stuck his finger through a tear made by the bullet. Then he felt along the bottom edge between the leather and the lining with his fingers until he found something. He turned the jacket inside out and made a small slit in the lining. He reached inside with his fingers and lifted out an almost perfect lead bullet.

"There's the little devil," he said. "The bullet passed through Miss Gresham, piercing and collapsing her lung. When it hit you it still had enough impact to punch a hole in the leather of your coat and crack your rib but it stopped there and didn't penetrate your back. You're a very lucky man. You can see from the x-ray," he said, holding up the negative film that made almost no sense to me, "the rib the bullet cracked lies directly over your heart. That young woman saved your life."

"What about her?" I asked for the tenth time.

"We're sending her to Grady Hospital in Atlanta. They have a surgical team that specializes in gunshot wounds."

"How bad is she hurt?"

"She wasn't as lucky as you. She could use your support."

The ride to Grady Hospital by ambulance was another thirty-five minutes. I rode in the back with Melissa. They had her sedated and she was breathing oxygen and receiving an I.V. drip. She didn't open her eyes or move during the entire trip. I talked to her as calmly as I could manage, to let her know I was with her.

They took her immediately into surgery after our arrival. I sat alone in the waiting room for three hours with no word. When a doctor I had never met came out to talk to me I expected the worst.

"Are you the husband or relative of Miss Gresham?" he asked.

"I'm her fiancé," I said, hoping he would accept that as close enough. "She has no family here. I was with her when she was shot."

"She's in recovery now and should be moved to a private room within the hour. She's breathing normally and her vital signs look good. She had tissue and artery damage and considerable blood loss, but nothing critical. The bullet missed her heart by less than an inch. It was that close," he said, indicating the last joint of his little finger. "Her condition is guarded at the moment. She'll need some time but her prospects are hopeful."

As I sat next to her bed in her hospital room I realized how relieved I was. I said another prayer and thanked God for saving her. I was awakened from my chair sometime later by Detective Miller. He had been called to the scene by the adjoining county sheriff's office and had followed us to the hospital. We went to a nearby break room, got some vending machine coffee and sat down at a table.

"We're pretty sure the driver was Scott Taylor," Miller told me. "Both bodies were burned beyond recognition. The fire was so intense it changed sand on the ground into a layer of glass but we found Taylor's billfold near the wreck. And it was Taylor's truck. We don't know the identity of the passenger. We should be able to determine that within a day or two when someone turns up missing."

"I can give you a short list to check out," I said, "but you probably already have the names on your own list."

He nodded. "We'll check those first. Witnesses verified the pickup was in pursuit of your motorcycle. You want to tell me what happened there at the bridge?"

"Taylor got blocked in behind traffic and I managed to get out ahead of him. I found a place to pull off the road under the bridge out of sight to see how bad Melissa was hurt. She had managed to hold onto me but she was unconscious by then and bleeding bad and I knew I had to have help for her. I saw car lights coming and I went up to the road to try to flag somebody down. But it was Taylor. He came barreling across the bridge like a bat out of hell. He saw me and tried to run me down but he was going too fast and he flipped the truck. It went crashing down off the side of the road and caught on fire. Some good people saw the flames and stopped to help us."

"The bullet that lodged in your jacket is in good enough shape we can match it to the gun found in the truck. As far as I'm concerned they got what was coming to them. It should have happened before they killed the Willinghams."

I knew the identity of the passenger in Taylor's pickup. The gun that had fallen to the ground was the same pearl-handled, chrome-plated Smith and Wesson .38 revolver Bob Felton showed me in his office at American Home Guardian Finance. But I couldn't tell Miller. I wasn't supposed to have seen the pistol at the scene of the wreck. It was burned up inside the truck. Pass judgment on me if you will but I would kill those bastards twice over for what they did to Shirley and Melissa. Final judgment on that is going to have to be between God and me. If I'm lucky, Melissa will be there to handle my case.

"I found your duffel bag and brought it along. Thought you might need it. I had your bike taken to the Macon impound. It'll be there when you're ready for it."

He indicated the bag sitting on the floor beside his chair.

I had seen it but hadn't said anything about it. I didn't want to have to explain the gun inside it.

"You can pick up the gun at the police property room," he said, reading my mind. "It hadn't been fired. I don't think there will be any problem with it. It's some kind of antique. You need to get yourself a new gun."

"I hope I never need one again," I said.

"Oh, by the way," he said as he was leaving, "we found the car that matched the white paint on the fender of Shirley Willingham's car. It was a city vehicle signed out to the mayor."

"Tommy Lee didn't do it," I said. "He was too drunk to drive himself to the toilet that night. Talk to Craig Linder. He'll verify he was with Tommy Lee at about the time Shirley was killed."

I went back to Melissa's hospital room and must have fallen asleep again because when I opened my eyes Melissa's parents were there from Birmingham. At first they were glad to find out I was a friend of Melissa. But when they learned more about exactly who I was it was clear they wanted nothing to do with me and they didn't want me anywhere near Melissa. They were upset and confused. I could understand it but it hurt.

I checked into a motel down the street from the hospital, took a shower and lay down on the bed. I pulled Melissa's things out of the duffel bag, holding her clothes to my face, trying to find the smell of her in them.

By visiting hours the next morning Melissa was conscious and had asked to see me. Her parents were reluctant to leave us alone in the room but they did. Melissa was pale and looked like a sick child but she was beautiful to me.

"I've been worried about you," she said, raising one arm for me.

"Worried about me?" I smiled and kissed her lightly on the lips. "You took the bullet for me. I'm the one who's been worried."

"Nobody told me what happened."

"It was Scott Taylor. He wrecked his truck trying to catch us last night and was killed along with his accomplice whom the police think was Bob Felton. They hadn't identified the body last I heard. Don't you worry about any of that. It's all over. You just rest and get well."

"My parents want to take me home to Birmingham. I don't want to go."

"It's probably the best thing until you get your strength back. You were hurt pretty bad. I'll come over there as soon as all the details are cleaned up here. It shouldn't be more than a few days, a week at the most."

"I love you, Frank."

"I love you, Melissa. But don't let your parents hear it. I don't think they like you associating with me."

"They'll learn to love you," she said.

I left Melissa's room to find familiar visitors sitting in the waiting area.

Chapter 40

Sweeping Up

It was Craig Linder. Jennifer was with him. She rushed in to see Melissa as soon as I came out.

"Frank," Craig said. He smiled warmly, reached out and slapped me on the shoulder with his right hand. I flinched.

"Oh, sorry," he said. "I didn't know you were hurt."

"Cracked rib."

"You're a lucky son of a bitch," he said. "I talked with Detective Miller."

"It wasn't luck, Craig. It was all skill and daring. You and I need to talk."

"Yes, we do. Why don't you ride back to Macon with Jennifer and me? I have some things to tell you."

Whatever else was going on, I wasn't afraid of Craig Linder. I didn't believe he was a killer. I told Melissa I had to get back to Macon but would see her in just a few days. I left the hospital with Craig and Jennifer before noon and we headed back home.

What Craig had to tell me was that he had been doing some examination of his office records. He had pulled all the cases over the past five years involving citations of building violations filed by his inspectors. He had personally made a dozen phone calls to homeowners and businesses named in the records. Almost all the property owners said they had been pressured to use certain contractors and most had used a contractor named by the building inspector. Based on his findings, Craig had gone to the District Attorney and asked that a grand jury be convened to investigate potential corruption, payoffs, and other wrongdoing between employees of his office and local contractors.

I went that afternoon to the office of my old boss, George Dolly. George was uncharacteristically nervous when he saw me.

"You got your life insurance paid up, George?" I asked.

"Don't threaten me, Frank Hayes. I'll have you locked up again."

"I'm not threatening you, George. I'm giving you some advice. A grand jury is being convened even as we speak to investigate this office. We both know what they're going to find."

I thought George was going to faint.

"What made you get into the scam? Was it the money?"

George was beyond denial. He was struggling for plausible defense. "I have a family, Frank."

"We all have someone. All the more reason to live righteous lives. We have people depending on us. None of us can afford to be involved with criminals like Scott Taylor."

"It's the way business is done, Frank. You must know that."

"It's the way business *has* been done, but you and your associates are not going to do it anymore. You've hurt a lot of people."

"I never wanted any part of that. It was strictly business with me. I recommend a contractor, they pay me a small fee. That's all."

"It's more than that, George. What about the false inspection reports?"

"Most of those buildings needed some kind of repair," he insisted. "Ownership carries certain responsibilities with it.

Those people weren't looking after their property."

"George, you caused people to lose their homes, their savings. You were behind the demolition of Mr. Glover's house. There was nothing wrong with that house. You caused him to have a stroke and end up barely hanging on to life."

"It was a shack. He was a sick old man already, Frank. I didn't cause that."

"All the more reason not to take advantage. He couldn't defend himself. He was a helpless old man. And what about his wife? She's almost an invalid herself."

George made a big mistake then. He smiled and said, "Get off your high horse, Frank. It's not the old man you care about. It's that good-looking granddaughter. You've been getting some of that black pussy."

I grabbed him by the coat lapels and pulled him out of his chair. I hit him as hard as my cracked rib would permit, which was hard enough to knock him through the wood and glass partition that separated his office from the main hallway. He landed on his back amid splintered wood, shattered glass and tangled Venetian blinds. Employees from other offices ran into the hallway to see what the commotion was. Their faces showed shock and disbelief. Craig Linder came walking down the hall from his office. He picked Dolly up from the floor.

"Did you fall and hurt yourself, George? I've been saying for years, we need to get rid of these glass walls. I've almost stumbled and fallen into mine on several occasions. You better go get yourself cleaned up."

Dolly shot bullets at me with his eyes but he didn't say anything. He held his hand to his jaw and disappeared into the men's room. Craig looked at me over a suppressed smile.

"Good shot for an injured man. Why don't you go somewhere and cool off? Dolly will be taken care of."

"I just had to have a little satisfaction," I said. "That

punch was the one John Glover will never be able to give him. Better me than Tiny Glover. Tiny would have killed him."

I think I re-cracked my rib. I walked in pain from the second floor of City Hall down to the city vehicle lot on the next block. Curly Jenkins was in the office.

"Mind if I take a look at the vehicle log book?" I asked.

Jenkins gave me his usual smirk. "Help yourself." He pulled a thick black notebook from the shelf and dropped it onto the desktop.

I turned the pages to the date of Shirley Willingham's wreck. The log showed that the evening before at about 6:00 p.m. a city car had been signed out to the mayor.

"Now, that's really funny," I said.

"What?" Jenkins' lip curled in a very unflattering manner.

"This log says the mayor checked out a car at 6:00 p.m. the night of Shirley Willingham's wreck."

"Yeah, what about it?"

"I just happen to know the mayor was in a dinner meeting with some very prominent businessmen from about 5:00 p.m. until about 8:00 that evening. How could he have signed this log?" I was bluffing but I was betting Jenkins didn't know it.

"Well, it might not have been 6:00." He looked at the log, took a pen and retraced the number 6, changing it to a 5. "No, you see, it was a 5. It just looked kinda' like a 6." He was still sneering.

"You know, the police are taking fingerprints from that car. I'll be willing to bet they won't find the mayor's prints anywhere on it. You know why?"

"No, why?" Jenkins said.

"I talked to Bob Felton last night before he died in that wreck."

Jenkins' sneer was gone, replaced by a nervous twitch of his jaw muscle.

"He was dying. He begged me to help him. He told me all about your little building inspection scam. It was a deathbed statement. You know what that means?"

"I know what a deathbed statement is," he said, "but you're lying. I saw that truck. Nobody was alive in that truck."

"He was alive before it burned. Taylor was dead. His head was knocked just about clean off. But Felton was alive. He knew he was going to die if I didn't get him out of that truck. He told me you were driving the city car that ran Shirley Willingham off the road that night. He said you're the one who set fire to her car."

"The son of a bitch was lying." Jenkins' hand was shaking. "I wasn't there. I ain't involved in no murder. I just checked out the car. That's all."

"Who did you check it out to? Felton said you drove the car."

"No, I didn't. I left the car parked on the street where Felton told me to. Him and Rufus Nalley did it. There's this whore the mayor sometimes hangs out with, the one that was with him that night. Taylor give her some speed or some bennies or something to put in the mayor's whisky. They told me the mayor was suppose to be in the car. But he somehow got away from 'em."

Craig Linder, I thought to myself. Unknown to him, when he found the mayor at the Dew Drop that night and gave him a ride home he rescued the mayor from the setup for Shirley's murder. Craig and Jennifer would be able to identify the men with the mayor that night at the Dew Drop. I picked up Jenkins' phone and called Detective Miller's office.

"You need to get over to the city vehicle yard right away," I said. "Curly Jenkins can tell you who killed Shirley

Willingham."

While we waited for Miller I told Jenkins, "You better come clean with Miller if you want to keep your ass out of the electric chair."

"I didn't do no murder," he repeated. "All I did was check out the car. Did Felton really tell you what you said?"

"Yes, he did. I'm ready to testify to that and take a lie detector test." I lied to convince him I was telling him the truth, to keep him from having second thoughts about talking to Miller.

"That son of a bitch," he said.

My thoughts exactly.

Detective Miller arrested Curly Jenkins and based on information obtained from him arrested Rufus Nalley, the bulldozer operator who worked for Scott Taylor. Nalley was not as easy to break. Miller arrested three other members of Scott Taylor's crew on suspicion of arson in connection with the east Macon fires. During each of their interrogations he showed them the unexploded Molotov cocktail recovered from St. James A.M.E. Church and told them it had their fingerprints on it. There were no useable fingerprints on the bottle and the bluff didn't work on three of the four. But the fourth, a local piece of trash named Peanut Vining confessed to driving the car but said Rufus Nalley had actually set the fires.

Rufus Nalley was the man who had sold Stafford Willingham's watch to Marcel. He was also the dozer operator who redesigned my car. When the forensics people ran a check of the evidence against Nalley's fingerprints they made a match with a single fingerprint found on the inside of the drawer where Stafford Willingham's watch had been kept at the lake house. That was enough to implicate him in Stafford Willingham's murder.

When faced with the incriminating testimony and evidence against them, Vining and Nalley did the honorable thing. They blamed it on a dead man, Scott Taylor. They described a series of crimes Taylor had been involved in, including the murder of Shirley Willingham, for which he had purchased their limited skills. Vining and Nalley were convicted on the evidence of their own confessions and sentenced to life terms in the Georgia State Prison system. Neither of them would live out their sentences.

The grand jury investigation initiated by Craig Linder implicated three employees of the city building inspector's office, twelve businesses in the Macon area including the firms of Green and Green, American Home Guardian Finance, and Taylor Construction. Before the grand jury indictments came in, George Dolly committed suicide. American Home Guardian Finance was bought out and still operates under another name in Macon, Georgia and other cities.

Jeffrey Green resigned from the firm of Green and Green and started his own practice in Johnson City, Tennessee. He was eventually convicted there of converting his clients' alimony payments to his own use and was disbarred and imprisoned by the State of Tennessee.

Charlie Preston pled guilty to charges and was sentenced to time served. He moved to California and opened a consultation service performing handwriting analysis and authentication.

It took longer than two weeks to clean up the details in the murder investigation. As soon as I could get away I made what was planned as a weekend trip to Birmingham to see Melissa. She was wrong, her parents weren't going to grow to love me. They made it plain they couldn't stand the thought of me alone with their daughter. We had an uncomfortable visit and I returned to Macon the same day.

After six weeks Melissa was mostly recovered physically. She had been forced to drop her law school classes due to her injury and her resulting absence from campus. She got permission to take the classes again the following year but the impact on her law school career hit home hard with her. She had already interviewed for jobs and was looking at some good prospects. That was all washed up now because she wasn't going to finish on schedule. Her "affair" with me, as her mother referred to it, had cost her a year of law school and her first real job.

And like so many relationships that are spawned in adversity, ours began to look less and less desirable to Melissa the farther away from it she got. To be fair, she had experienced a near-death trauma because of me. I can see how the little voice inside her would be warning her to stay away from what had caused so much hurt. She transferred to the University of Alabama where she finished her law degree and went on to a successful career as a public defender. She married a fine man and has children of her own.

Chapter 41

An End And A Beginning

My one most terrible failing in the whole affair in Macon was that I didn't pick up on the real problem with John Glover's property before Stafford Willingham got involved and unearthed the dirty business involving the building inspectors. If I had listened to Mr. Glover that first day, if I had looked carefully at the old tattered documents in the envelope he handed to me, everything might have taken a different course. His life might have ended happily. He might have been able to see some justice before his death. He might have reconciled with his son Tiny.

As it happened, Mr. John Glover died one month to the day following the stroke brought on by the destruction of his house. He regained consciousness, was able to sit up in his hospital bed and could be fed a little by mouth. But no one knew for sure if he ever knew who or where he was. Tiny said he did. Tiny said the old man looked him in the eye and recognized him. He said he was sure he saw just the smallest smile and a tear in Mr. Glover's eye. Tiny believed they were reconciled before Mr. Glover's death. I don't know. I don't begrudge Tiny his belief. I truly hope he was right. I could certainly feel a lot better about things. But I just don't know.

Following Mr. Glover's death the plan I had laid out with Mr. Frederick Carter of Barnes and Ingram went into effect. Tiny was named executor of the Glover trust to manage as his best judgment dictated. He was provided with a monthly check in the amount of $2,000 purportedly from an old life insurance policy paid out by his father and left in Tiny's name many years before for the care of Mrs. Glover. The money actually came from the compensation that would have been paid to me as executor of Stafford Willingham's trust.

Mrs. Glover expressed the desire to have her house rebuilt as it had been on the spot where it had stood. Tiny oversaw the construction. Mrs. Glover lived in the rebuilt house another ten years and died of natural causes at the age of eighty-five. The Glover house still stands today next to the St. James A.M.E. Church which is now listed on the National Register of Historic Places. There's a brass plaque on the church dedicated to the memory of Stafford and Shirley Willingham.

Tiny sold twenty-three acres of the Glover property to the development of the Macon-Bibb County golf course and country club. In return he received the sum of $230,000 and the exclusive license to supply freshly cooked barbecue to events at the country club. With part of the money he established a restaurant he named Tiny's Bighouse Barbecue that he operated until his death thirty years later.

I came back to Macon for Tiny's funeral. He and I had kept in touch and I had passed through Macon a couple of times to see him. I had not seen Johnny Mae in those intervening years. She was at Tiny's funeral.

When I stood at Tiny's graveside and looked at Johnny Mae I could still see the beautiful young woman I had been so in love with. She was as beautiful in middle age as she had been at twenty-five. She was smoother and softer, with a gray streak in her hair. She was no longer angry at anyone or anything. She seemed very happy and at peace. She was accompanied by two of her children . . . a beautiful dark haired girl of about twenty named Michelle, and a good-looking son of twenty-six named Tony, after her husband. Tony's wife and his three children were with him.

"Grandchildren?" I asked, looking into Johnny Mae's beautiful green eyes. I thought I saw a sparkle in them as she looked at me. "It can't have been that long."

"It's been longer than that, Frank. Another lifetime. You're as handsome as ever. You look as if life has treated you well." She reached out and took my hand.

It was wonderful to touch her hand again. But it wasn't the same. It was as if she were the same person but at the same time she was someone else. There was an affection in her touch, a kind of urgency. More than the hand of a friend.

"You're as beautiful as ever," I said. "I've thought of you a million times. Wondered how you were doing. Hoped you were happy and well."

"I've had a good life, Frank. Probably not as adventurous as it might have been with you, but a good life. Anthony and I have been very happy."

"Is he well?"

She nodded. "And the children are a joy."

Quite unexpectedly her eyes were filled with tears and she turned her back to me.

"Are you all right?" I asked.

Before she could answer, her daughter Michelle saw that something was wrong and came to her mother's side.

"You all right, Mom?" she asked. "You want to sit down?"

Johnny Mae sat down in one of the chairs under the awning at the graveside. I sat in a chair next to her. She turned and smiled at her daughter through teary eyes.

"I'm fine," she said, "just the emotions of the moment. You go on with your brother to the car. I'll be along in a minute. I'd like to talk with Mr. Hayes a moment."

Michelle looked at me uncertainly, smiled, shrugged, and said, "OK, we'll wait for you."

Johnny Mae took some tissues from her purse and dabbed at her eyes. She took a few seconds to regain her composure.

"We reach a certain age, Frank, when we don't need to keep secrets anymore," she said, looking at Tiny's grave. "Barnes and Ingram informed me about the trust."

"Do you know who Tiny was?" I asked.

She nodded her head. "Yes, Mamma told me before she died. I never told him I knew. I didn't know how. But I had grown to love him even before I knew, because of the way he took care of Mamma. Whatever happened between him and my mother, he had tried to atone for it. He was a good man."

"He repented and paid for his sins every day of his life," I said. "Not everyone deserves to be forgiven their sins but Tiny is one of those who did deserve it. He told me how much he loved your mother and how much he loved you." I could see she was about to come apart at the seams.

"I only wish things could have been different," she said. "I wish I had known him sooner for who he was. There are so many things I wish I had known."

"We've all made our mistakes."

She opened her purse again and took out an envelope. She held it for a minute while she closed her eyes.

"That's why there's something I need to tell you."

She handed me the envelope.

"Forgive me, Frank. I had so much at stake then. The times were different. I had so much to lose. You were gone from me. I thought I was doing the right thing. I see now I was wrong. I'm sorry."

I opened the envelope and took out a picture from inside it. At first I was delighted, then confused. I thought it was a picture of Johnny Mae when she was young. She had the same green eyes, the same smooth skin, the same sharp features, the smile, the reddish blonde hair. But there was something out of synch. It was her, but it wasn't her, the same feeling I had when I took her hand a few minutes before. And the photograph wasn't old. The clothes she was wearing weren't the fashion of the seventies. She was wearing a tennis outfit with a Nike shirt. I looked up at Johnny Mae. She was trying to smile, trying not to cry.

"She's my oldest child, Frank. She's twenty-nine. Her name is Frankie. She's your daughter. I think you need to get to know her."

Chapter 42

What Was Old Is New

The address Johnny Mae gave me was in Sedona, Arizona where she said Frankie was a partner in an Internet services company.

"She's very independent, Frank. She's adventurous and she has a very strong sense of justice," Johnny Mae said. "She gets that from you."

"Does she know who I am?"

Johnny Mae nodded. "I told her you're coming."

On the plane ride out and the drive up from Phoenix I kept wondering what I was going to say to her. She was almost thirty years old. I had never known her. As far as I knew she hadn't known I existed until a couple of weeks ago. She would probably just think I was a middle-aged reject her mother had mistakenly become involved with thirty years ago. I almost turned back more than once. But every time I looked at the picture of her I knew I had to make the effort.

I was sounding the way I had when I first met her mother. I desperately wanted her to accept me and I had to give it my best shot. A desperate middle-aged father. That would be a turnoff for any daughter. I didn't feel middle-aged. I felt young.

When I got my first glimpse of the painted cliffs around Sedona I could see how it got its reputation as a mystical place. It stands like brightly hued sculpture in the middle of scrub desert. The floor of the valley is covered in waves of rolling rubble from cliffs that once encircled the valley but now remain after millions of years of erosion as etched and pitted pillars, domes and spires against the blue sky and white clouds. The prevalent color of the soil is a reddish mineral something like burnt sienna, of a little more pink hue than terra cotta, and is spotted over with pale green desert scrub bush and varieties of weeds, flowers, and lichens. There are no hardwood trees, tall pines or the thick ground cover I'm accustomed to seeing grow so lushly and abundantly back home. Here where there's dead wood it's been dried, stripped and gnarled by the dry winds and extreme temperatures.

There's nothing to break the view all the way to the horizon except the huge multicolored eroded cliff formations that resemble a castle here, a fortress there, the dome of some forgotten capital building on one side, the Greek Parthenon on another, and a few ancient flying saucers scattered about the valley floor and turned to weathered stone and rubble.

The overall effect of the place was to give me a feeling of history beyond time, older than mankind, larger than human architecture, unspoiled by the litter of civilization. But if I looked carefully I could see just the glimpse of a roof or the corner of a house hidden among the small valleys and slopes.

A narrow winding road took me to a spread-out town that was a cross between the wild frontier and a window into the next dimension of the universe. Along the outskirts there were varieties of wood buildings, wagons, horned steer skulls, and other artifacts reminiscent of the old west. Scattered here and there were geodesic domes and other evidence of retro-hippies. American Indian motifs popped up most everywhere, as well as an occasional Indian teepee. There were touristy areas with strips of gift shops and cafes, signs advertising Jeep and horseback tours, and a red earth colored McDonald's in adobe style with turquoise arches. There were subdivisions of adobe style ranch houses and others of cedar and glass with swimming pools filled with blue water. In places the architecture was designed to meld into the rugged surroundings. In other places it looked like a space ship that had just set down. The place was very weird. I liked it.

I went to the address Johnny Mae had given me. The house was an interesting mixture of upper middle class and cave dweller. It was built into the side of a stone covered hill. Parts of the house were modern concrete and glass and parts of it were natural stone, minerals, and desert wood. There was a nice pool of blue water to one side. A note on her door said simply, 'I'm atop Vortex 5.'

I had no idea what Vortex 5 was so I stopped in the visitor center and asked. I was given a map of the area and a strange but nice lady wearing lots of turquoise and silver jewelry drew a circle on it indicating the spot.

"Vortex 5 is one of the very strongest vortexes," she told me.

Ten minutes later I was walking up the side of an incline of red rock and scrub bush. Beside the path a teenaged Zuni Indian girl was selling from a blanket covered in necklaces with trinkets in the designs of various Indian charms. I paid her seven dollars for a necklace with a silver chain and a dancing silver Kokopelli which the girl said was a spirit to bring all-around good luck. She didn't have one for father-daughter reunions. I asked her if she could point me in the direction of Vortex 5. She pointed straight up the side of the dome-shaped hill next to us.

The stones in the pathway up the side of the hill were worn slick from the passage of many feet. As I climbed higher I noticed the warm wind was blowing upward on all sides from the canyon floor toward the top of the dome and increased in intensity the higher I climbed. The colors produced by the late afternoon sun on the cliffs surrounding the valley were bands of bright shades of red, yellow, white, blue, and gray, interspersed with splotches of green.

As I neared the top of the dome I became dizzy, almost disoriented, not from the climb but from the combination of the visual and physical sounds, shapes, colors and movement. The dome, not more than fifty feet across at its top, stood high above the valley floor that stretched into the distance until it encountered the stone cliffs rising in formations on all sides. The cliffs were composed of many strata of rocks and minerals that had weathered at different rates, resulting in horizontal ledges and shadows that made the cliff walls look as if they were spinning past in a blur. In some ways, standing atop the dome was very much like standing atop a tower but with changing images in the cliffs spinning around you in bright colors, and strong upward winds lifting your clothes and hair as if at any minute you might be lifted into the heavens.

When I first saw Frankie she was sitting at the highest point of the dome with her back to me looking toward the sunset. I watched her profile turn before me as I followed the spiraling path up to her. She was as beautiful as her mother had been at her age. I could see Johnny Mae in her but it sent little waves of electricity through me when I saw myself in her too. She watched me as I approached. I stopped a dozen feet away, not knowing what to say or do.

"I've been waiting for you," she said, "wondering what I would feel, what I would say to you."

She stood up and came closer to me, looking at my face and into my eyes. She was taller than her mother. Her hair was lighter, containing more blonde than Johnny Mae's.

"I've wondered what it was about you that made my mother so desperately in love with you."

"You need only look at yourself," I said.

She thought about that for a moment.

"You look just like you do in your picture. Even the same clothes," she said.

I looked at my leather jacket, my jeans and boots. "You've seen a picture of me?"

"I found one a long time ago in Mother's things."

"Did you know who I was?"

"I didn't know your name. I knew you were something. An old boyfriend, maybe."

"I've worn this style clothes since the time I met your mother. I bought matching coats and boots for us in Atlanta the first day we . . . when we first met."

"I have her coat still. She gave it to me."

We just looked at each other for some time. I don't think either of us could quite comprehend the implications for our lives.

"I find my mind rethinking all of my life," she said. "Little conversations and things that happened long ago suddenly have a new meaning. Everything I knew I don't know anymore. All my thoughts and emotions are in a whirl."

"The same thing's been happening to me. Every event in my life that's happened I think back now and wonder where you were, what you were doing, what you looked like."

"Yeah," she said. "It's funny. I see why she did it now."

"Did what?"

"Mom's always been compulsive about photographing and recording everything. I have albums full of photographs of my entire life. They're all labeled and dated. I have old home movies, report cards. She kept all my old toys, even my old clothes. She knew that someday this was going to happen. Now I know that every time she recorded one of the events in my life she was thinking of you. She must have loved you very much."

"She was thinking of all of us," I said.

I stood looking at my daughter and had the strangest

sensation. I was taken back in time thirty years to the moment at City Hall in Macon, Georgia when Stafford Willingham had stood talking to his daughter Johnny Mae for the first time in twenty-five years. I could remember my feelings of disgust for him at the thought that he had abandoned Johnny Mae and her mother, had left them behind and led a prosperous life of his own without them.

Now everything was turned upside down. The times were different, the circumstances were different, but I was standing at the same spot in my life. I had led a life of my own, sometimes happy, sometimes not. Like him I was now aware of a life I had never had with a daughter I never knew.

We all paid the price, some of us more than others, for a cycle of events that drove and overwhelmed so many lives and resulted in the deaths of so many people. My feeling of loss for not having known and raised my child was exceeded only by my joy in finding her.

"You and I have been given a new chance," I said. "A link was broken in our lives and we have the chance to put it back together. I want to try but I won't do anything that will make you unhappy."

She was looking into my eyes, watching my face, searching my soul, the same way her mother had those many years ago, looking to see if I was a person to be trusted, if my motives were pure. I could feel my heart in the grasp of her fingers.

"I can tell you about the past that separated us before you were born if you want to hear it. It's your past as well as mine and your mother's and you have the right to know. I'll honor your wishes, whatever you decide, but there is one thing you have to know."

She was still looking into my eyes. I hoped that she saw the truth.

"I loved your mother as much as one person can love another. I never stopped loving her. And I've loved you since before you were born even though I didn't know you existed. Can you understand that?"

"Yes," she said, "I can. I've seen it in Mother when she's looked at me. She's carried that love all these years but I never really understood what it was until now. There's a lot I need to know about."

"There's a lot I need to tell you and a lot I need to learn from you."

"This is going to take some getting used to. I don't know what to call you. I already have a dad."

"You can call me Frank if you like."

"Can you stay a while?" she asked.

"Until you get tired of me and run me off."

We sat and watched the sunset until it slid behind the canyon wall.

"What kind of business is it exactly that you're in?" I asked.

"I create things, find new ideas. Sometimes I find things that have been lost."

"Hmm," I said. "That's kind of what I do. I'm a private investigator."

"Interesting," she said.

"There's one thing."

"What's that?"

"Can you explain to me what a vortex is?"

"That's what we're in," she said. She put her arm through mine and laid her head on my shoulder.

About the Authors

Charles Connor

I grew up in suburban and rural Alabama during the 1940s, 50s and 60s in and around the little communities of Caffee Junction, Green Pond, and McCalla, just outside Birmingham. All around me were the ruins of ore mines, coal mines, lakes and railroads from another time. The population was almost entirely white with little pocket communities of blacks, mostly older residents who had not been part of the heavy black migration north and into the cities. It was the end of an era.

There were no computers, Internet or cell phones. We walked or rode bicycles as kids and built hotrods as teens. The whole world to us was what we saw right around us. Then I went off to college at the University of Alabama and everything changed for me. Everything I knew—all my models of reality— were wrong. I knew nothing. I had to relearn everything. I ended up with the brother of Vice President Mondale as my major professor in American Studies and the world of ideas opened up for me. The university world and friends became my life.

I received B.A. and Masters degrees from the University of Alabama, attended graduate school at Vanderbilt and received a doctorate from the University of Georgia. I taught at several state universities in the southeast and met Beverly, my wife of forty-three years, at ETSU. We settled at the University of Georgia where Beverly received four degrees and became a highly successful author of mystery and suspense novels. I joined the faculty there and founded the Harriette Austin

Writing Program and the HAWC writing conference and directed them for twelve years before my retirement.

We now live in Oak Ridge, Tennessee (The Secret City, home of the atomic bomb and the world's fastest computer) where I reflect on life, write, do some modest cooking, and support Beverly in her writing. Murder In Macon is my first novel.

Beverly Connor

Beverly Connor is the author of the Diane Fallon Forensic Investigation series and the Lindsay Chamberlain archaeology mystery series. She holds undergraduate and graduate degrees in archaeology, anthropology, sociology, and geology. Before she began her writing career Beverly worked as an archaeologist in the southeastern United States, specializing in bone identification and analysis of stone tool debitage. Originally from Oak Ridge, Tennessee, she weaves her professional experiences from archaeology and her knowledge of the South into interlinked stories of the past and present. Beverly's books have been translated into German, Dutch, and Czech, are available in standard and large print in the UK, and in ebook format worldwide. Murder In Macon is her first noir mystery.

More information about Beverly Connor and her work can be found on her web site. Please visit her at beverlyconnor.net. (You can visit Charles there, too.)

Introduction to Murder In Macon:
http://beverlyconnor.net/Author_Beverly_Connor/IntrotoMIM.html

Murder In Macon Summary:
http://beverlyconnor.net/Author_Beverly_Connor/Murder_in_Macon.html

Links

Here are some recommended links to people, locales and the time period that provided inspiration for the writing of Murder In Macon.

Macon, Georgia: http://www.maconga.org. Important people in Macon's history, music, politics, etc.: http://en.wikipedia.org/wiki/List_of_people_from_Macon,_ Georgia, and http://en.wikipedia.org/wiki/Ronnie_Thompson_(Georgia_p olitician).

The Allman Brothers, of course, at: http://en.wikipedia.org/wiki/The_Allman_Brothers_Band.

See, especially, this wonderful article on Little Richard: http://en.wikipedia.org/wiki/Little_Richard, and this article on Charles Connor (no relation to the author), the original drummer for Little Richard who created the backbeat rhythm that became the backbone of rock and roll: http://en.wikipedia.org/wiki/Charles_Connor.

Macon's Rose Hill Cemetery where Frank and Melissa talked: https://rose hill cemetery macon ga

The Ocmulgee National Monument: http://www.nps.gov/ocmu

Otis Redding: http://otisredding.com

The Harriett Tubman Museum: https://www.tubmanmuseum.com